PRAISE FOR

THE IRON DRUID CHRONICLES

"Outrageously fun."

—*The Plain Dealer*

"[Kevin] Hearne is a terrific storyteller with a great snarky wit. . . . Neil Gaiman's *American Gods* meets Jim Butcher's Harry Dresden."

—*SFF World*

"Superb . . . plenty of quips and zap-pow-bang fighting."

—*Publishers Weekly* (starred review)

"[Atticus is] a strong modern hero with a long history and the wit to survive in the twenty-first century. . . . A snappy narrative voice . . . a savvy urban fantasy adventure."

—*Library Journal*

"[The Iron Druid books] are clever, fast-paced and a good escape."

—*Boing Boing*

"An exciting mix of comedy, action, and mythology . . . [Atticus] is one of the best main characters currently present in the urban fantasy genre."

—*Fantasy Book Critic*, on *Tricked*

"Funny, razor-sharp . . . plenty of action, humor, and mythology."

—*Booklist* (starred review), on *Shattered*

HEXED

HEXED

BOOK TWO OF THE IRON DRUID CHRONICLES

KEVIN HEARNE

NEW YORK

2022 Del Rey Trade Paperback Edition

Published in the United States by Del Rey, an imprint of Random House, a division of Penguin Random House LLC, New York.

Del Rey is a registered trademark and the Circle colophon is a trademark of Penguin Random House LLC.

Originally published in mass market in the United States by Del Rey, an imprint of Random House, a division of Penguin Random House LLC, in 2011. "The Grimoire of the Lamb" was originally published in a digital edition by Del Rey, an imprint of Random House LLC, in 2013.

ISBN 978-0-593-35964-8
Ebook ISBN 978-0-345-52255-9

Printed in the United States of America on acid-free paper

randomhousebooks.com

3rd Printing

Book design by Caroline Cunningham

For my father,
who never saw these books in print,
but at least left us knowing
his son had achieved his dream

PRONUNCIATION GUIDE

Just as with the Irish words in *Hounded*, I wouldn't want anyone to see the Polish, Russian, German, and Irish in *Hexed* and think to themselves, Do I really have to read that stuff properly? You don't. I want you to enjoy yourself, and if you prefer saying words any old way you like, then I'm on your side. But if you're the sort who'd like to hear precisely how things should sound coming out of the mouths of these characters, then I've provided the guide below to help you do that.

NAMES OF THE POLISH COVEN

Written Polish has a few letters that aren't pronounced the way they are in English. Rather than try to explain them all, please take my very informal phonetic pronunciations here and trust me—unless you'd rather not.

Berta = Berta (this one's just like it looks; I promise things will get interesting soon)

Bogumila = BO goo ME wah (However, her American nickname, *Mila*, would be pronounced ME lah, because otherwise Americans would constantly question why she pronounced her *l* like a *w*)

Kazimiera = KAH zhee ME rah

Klaudia = Klaudia (just like it looks)

Malina Sokolowski = Ma LEE nah SO ko WOV ski (that's right, no *l* sound in her last name)

Radomila = RAH doe ME wah

Roksana = Roke SAH nah

Waclawa = Va SWAH va

Irish Phrases

Bean sidhe = BAN shee

Dóigh = doy (means *burn*)

Dún = doon (means *close* or *shut*)

Freagróidh tú = frag ROY too (means *you will answer*)

Múchaim = MOO hem (means *extinguish*)

Irish Doodads

Fragarach = FRAG ah rah (named sword: The Answerer)

Moralltach = MOR al tah (named sword: Great Fury)

The remaining phrases in Polish, Russian, and German can all be listened to online as sound files on my website, kevinhearne.com, if you feel like clicking on over there—see the Goodies page.

Irish God

Goibhniu = GUV new (member of the Tuatha Dé Danann; master smith and brewer of fine ales)

HEXED

CHAPTER 1

Turns out that when you kill a god, people want to talk to you. Paranormal insurance salesmen with special "godslayer" term life policies. Charlatans with "godproof" armor and extraplanar safe houses for rent. But, most notably, other gods, who want to first congratulate you on your achievement, second warn you not to try such shenanigans on them, and finally suggest that you try to slay one of their rivals—purely as a shenanigan, of course.

Ever since word got around to the various pantheons that I had snuffed not one but two of the Tuatha Dé Danann—and sent the more powerful of the two to the Christian hell—I had been visited by various potentates, heralds, and ambassadors from most of the world's belief systems. All of them wanted me to leave them alone but pick a fight with someone else, and if I successfully lanced the immortal boil that vexed them, I'd be rewarded beyond my wildest dreams, blah blah barf yak.

That reward business was a giant load of shite, as they'd say in the U.K. Brighid, Celtic goddess of poetry, fire, and the forge, had promised to reward me if I killed Aenghus Óg, but I hadn't heard a word from her in the three weeks since Death carried him off to hell. I'd heard plenty from the rest of the world's gods, but from my own? Nothing but the chirping of crickets.

The Japanese wanted me to mess with the Chinese, and vice versa. The old Russian gods wanted me to stick it to the Hungarians. The Greeks wanted me to knock off their Roman copycats in a bizarre manifestation of self-loathing and internecine jealousy. The weirdest by far were those Easter Island guys, who wanted me to mess around with some rotting totem poles in the Seattle area. But everyone—at least, it sure seemed like everyone—wanted me to slay Thor as soon as I had a free moment. The whole world was tired of his shenanigans, I guess.

Foremost among these was my own attorney, Leif Helgarson. He was an old Icelandic vampire who had presumably worshiped Thor at some point in ancient history, but he'd never told me why he now harbored such hatred for him. Leif did some legal work for me, sparred with me regularly to keep my sword arm sharp, and occasionally drank a goblet full of my blood by way of payment.

I found him waiting for me on my porch the night after Samhain. It was a cool evening in Tempe, and I was in a good mood after having much to give thanks for. While the American children had busied themselves the night before by trick-or-treating on Halloween, I had paid plenty of attention to the Morrigan and Brighid in my own private ceremonies, and I was thrilled to have an apprentice to teach and to share the night with. Granuaile had returned from North Carolina in time for Samhain, and though the two of us were not much of a Druid's grove, it was still a better holy night than I had enjoyed in centuries. I was the only real Druid left, and the idea of starting a new grove after such a long time of going it alone had filled me with hope. So when Leif greeted me formally from my front porch as I came home from work, I was perhaps more exuberant in my response than I should have been.

"Leif, you spooky bastard, how the hell are ya?" I grinned widely as I braked my bike to a stop. He raised his eyebrows and peered at me down his long Nordic nose, and I realized that he was probably unused to such cavalier address.

"I am not a bastard," he replied archly. "Spooky I will grant you. And while I am well"—a corner of his mouth quirked upward a fraction—"I confess not so jocund as yourself."

"Jocund?" I raised my brows. Leif had asked me in the past to call him on behaviors that broadcast how much older he was than he looked.

Apparently he didn't want to be corrected right then. He exhaled noisily to express his exasperation. I thought it amusing that he employed that, since he had no need to breathe. "Fine," he said. "Not so jovial, then."

"No one uses those words anymore, Leif, except for old farts like us." I leaned my bike against the porch rails and mounted the three steps to take a seat next to him. "You really should spend some decent time learning how to blend in. Make it a project. Popular culture is mutating at a much faster rate these days. It's not like the Middle Ages, when you had the Church and the aristocracy keeping everything nice and stagnant."

"Very well, since you are the verbal acrobat who walks the tightrope of the zeitgeist, educate me. How should I have responded?"

"First, get rid of 'well.' Nobody uses that anymore either. Now they always say, 'I'm good.'"

Leif frowned. "But that is grammatically improper."

"These people don't care about proper. You can tell them they're trying to use an adjective as an adverb and they'll just stare at you like you're a toad."

"Their educational system has suffered serious setbacks, I see."

"Tell me about it. So what you should have said was, 'I'm not stoked like you, Atticus, but I'm chill.'"

"I'm 'chill'? That means I am well—or good, as you say?"

"Correct. At least it does at this particular moment. In a few months or a year it will change to something else, and change again."

"But that's nonsense!" Leif protested.

"It's modern vernacular." I shrugged. "Date yourself if you want, but if you keep using nineteenth-century diction, people will start to think you're a spooky bastard."

"They already think that."

"You mean because you only come out at night and you suck their blood?" I said in a tiny, innocent voice.

"Precisely," Leif said, unaffected by my teasing.

"No, Leif." I shook my head in all seriousness. "They don't figure that out until much later, if they ever figure it out at all. These people think you're spooky because of the way you talk and the way you behave. They can tell you don't belong. Believe me, it's not that you have skin like two-percent milk. Lots of people are scared of skin cancer out here in the Valley of the Sun. It's once you start talking that people get creeped out. They know you're old then."

"But I *am* old, Atticus!"

"And I've got at least a thousand years on you, or have you forgotten?"

He sighed, the weary ancient vampire who had no need for respiration. "No, I have not forgotten."

"Fine. Don't complain to me about being old. I hang out with these college kids and they have no clue that I'm not one of them. They think my money comes from an inheritance or a trust fund, and they want to have a drink with me."

"I find the college children delightful. I would like to have a drink with them too."

"No, Leif, you want to drink *of* them, and they can sense that subconsciously because you radiate this predatory aura."

His affectation of a henpecked husband sloughed away and he looked at me sharply. "You told me they can't sense my aura as you do."

"No, they can't consciously sense it. But they pick up on your *otherness*, mostly because you don't respond like you should or act like a man of your cosmetic age."

"How old do I look?"

"Ehh," I appraised him, looking for wrinkles. "You look like you're in your late thirties."

"I look that old? I was turned in my late twenties."

"Times were tougher back then." I shrugged again.

"I suppose. I have come to talk to you about those times, if you are free for the span of an hour or so."

"Right," I replied, rolling my eyes. "Just let me go get my hourglass and my freakin' smoking jacket. Listen to yourself, Leif! Do you want to blend in or not? The span of an hour? Who says shit like that anymore?"

"What's wrong with that?"

"No one is so formal! You could just say 'if you're free' and end it there, though it would have been better to say 'if you ain't doin' nothing.'"

"But I enjoyed the anapestic meter of 'for the span of an hour' followed by the iamb—"

"Gods Below, you compose your sentences in blank verse? No wonder you can't carry on a half hour's conversation with a sorority girl! They're used to talking with frat boys, not Shakespearean scholars!"

<Atticus? You're home?> It was my Irish wolfhound, Oberon, speaking directly to my mind through the connection we share. He was probably on the other side of the door, listening to us talk. I told Leif to hold on a second as I spoke with him.

Yes, Oberon, I'm home. Leif's out here on the front porch, acting his age.

<I know, I smelled him earlier. It's like Eau de Death or something. I didn't bark, though, like you said.>

You're a good hound. Want to come hang out with us?

<Sure!>

I have to warn you, it might be boring. He wants to talk about something for a while, and he's looking particularly grim and Nordic. It might be epic.

<That's okay. You can rub my belly the whole time. I promise to be still.>

Thanks, buddy. I promise we'll go for a run when he leaves. I opened the front door and Oberon came bounding out, oblivious to the fact that his wagging tail was delivering steady blows to Leif's upper arm.

<Let's go down to Town Lake after the dead guy says good-bye. And then Rúla Búla.> He named our favorite Irish pub, from which I'd recently been banned.

The management of Rúla Búla is still mad at me for stealing Granuaile away from them. She was their best bartender.

<Still? But that was ages ago.>

It's been only three weeks, I reminded him. Dogs aren't all that great with time. *I'll let you run around the golf course and you can keep any rabbits you catch. Flop down for your belly rub. I have to talk to Leif now.* Oberon promptly obeyed, rattling the timbers of the porch as he thudded heavily onto his back between my seat and Leif's.

<This is the best! There's nothing better than belly rubs. Except maybe for French poodles. Remember Fifi? Good times, good times.>

"All right, Leif, he's a happy hound now," I said as I scratched Oberon's ribs. "What did you want to talk about?"

"It is fairly simple," he began, "but as with all simple things, vastly complicated."

"Wait. You sound too accomplished with adverbs. Use *really* and *very* for everything," I advised him.

"I would rather not, if you will forgive me. Since I am not trying to disguise my true nature with you, may I speak as I wish?"

"Of course," I said, biting back the observation that he should use contractions more often. "I'm sorry, Leif, I'm just trying to help, you know."

"Yes, and I appreciate it. But this is going to be difficult enough without running my words through a filter of illiteracy." He took a deep, unnecessary breath and closed his eyes as he slowly exhaled. He looked like he was trying to center himself and find a chakra point. "There are many reasons why I require your aid, and many reasons why you should agree to help me, but those can wait a few moments. Here is the short version," he said, opening his eyes and turning to look at me. "I want you to help me kill Thor."

<Ha! Tell him to get in line!> Oberon said. He chuffed as he always did when he found something particularly funny. Thankfully, Leif did not recognize that my dog was laughing at him.

"Hmm," I said. "Thor certainly tends to inspire murderous thoughts. You're not the first person to suggest that to me these past couple of weeks."

Leif pounced. "One of the many reasons you should agree to help. You would have ample allies to secure whatever aid you needed and plenty of grateful admirers should you succeed."

"And plenty of mourners should I fail? If he's so universally hated, why hasn't someone else done the deed?"

"Because of Ragnarok," Leif replied, obviously anticipating the question. "That prophecy has everyone afraid of him, and it has made him insufferably arrogant. Their line of reasoning says that if he is going to be around for the end of the world, then obviously nothing can be done about him now. But that is poppycock."

I smiled. "Did you just say Ragnarok is poppycock?" Oberon chuffed some more.

Leif ignored me and plowed on. "Not all of the prophesied apocalypses can come true, just as only one of the creations can possibly be true, if any of them are. We cannot be tied down by some ancient tale dreamed up in the frozen brains of my ancestors. We can change it right now."

"Look, Leif, I know you have a saga full of reasons why I should do this, but I really can't internalize any of it. I simply don't think it's my duty to do this. Aenghus Óg and Bres both came to me and picked a fight, and all I did was finish it. And, you know, it could have easily gone the other way. You weren't there: I nearly didn't make it. You've seen this, I imagine?" I pointed to my disfigured right ear. A demon that looked like the Iron Maiden mascot had chewed it off, and I hadn't been able to regenerate anything except a mangled mass of cartilage. (I'd already caught myself singing, "Don't spend your time always searching for those wasted ears.")

"Of course I've seen it," Leif replied.

"I'm lucky I got away with so little damage. Even though I haven't paid a huge price for killing Aenghus, I've had several unpleasant visits from other gods as a result. And that's only because I'm still small potatoes. Can you imagine what the rest of the gods would do if I managed to knock off someone big like Thor? They'd all take me out collectively just to remove the threat. Besides, I don't think it's possible to kill him."

"Oh, but it *is* possible," Leif said, raising a finger and shaking it at me. "The Norse gods are like your Tuatha Dé Danann. They have eternal youth, but they can be killed."

"Originally, yeah," I agreed. "I've read the old stuff, and I know that you're after Thor version 1.0. But you know, there's more than one version of Thor out there now, just like there are multiple Coyotes and various versions of Jesus and Buddha and Elvis. We can invade Asgard, kill Thor 1.0, and then, if we manage to avoid getting creamed by the rest of the Norse, we could come back here to Midgard only to have the comic book Thor smite the hell out of us like the naughty varlets we are. Did you think about that?"

Leif looked utterly bewildered. "Thor has a comic book?"

"Yeah, how did you miss this? There's a movie about him based on the comic too. He's a heroic kind of guy here in the States, not nearly so much of a dick as the original one eventually became. He'll ignore you unless you draw attention to yourself, and storming Asgard will probably get his attention pretty fast."

"Hmm. Say that I can put together a coalition of beings willing to participate in the physical assault on Asgard and accompany us back to Midgard. Could I count on your aid in such a scenario?"

I slowly shook my head. "No, Leif, I'm sorry. One reason I'm still alive is that I've never gone toe-to-toe with a thunder god. It's a good survival strategy, and I'm going to stick with it. But if you're going to do something like that, I recommend avoiding Loki. He'll pretend to be on your side, but he'll spill his guts to Odin first chance he gets, and then you'll have that entire pantheon coming after you with a wooden stake."

"That might be preferable to me, at this point, than continuing to coexist with him. I want revenge."

"Revenge for what, exactly?" Normally I don't pry into vampiric psychology, because it's so predictable: The only things they tend to get exercised about are power and territory. They enjoy being asked questions, though, so that they can ignore you and appear mysterious when they don't answer.

Leif never got the chance to answer me, though he looked ready enough to do so for a half second. As he opened his mouth to speak, his eyes flicked down to the base of my throat where my cold iron amulet rested, just as I began to feel the space between my clavicles heat up—even burn.

"Um," Leif said in perhaps his most inarticulate moment ever, "why is your amulet glowing?"

I felt the heat surge like mercury on an August morning, sweat popped out on my scalp, and the sickening sound of sizzling in my ears was a little piece of me frying like bacon. And even though I instinctively wanted to peel off the necklace and chuck it onto the lawn, I fought back the urge, because the smoldering lump of cold iron—the antithesis of magic—was the only thing keeping me alive.

"I'm under magical attack!" I hissed through clenched teeth as I clutched the chair arms, white-knuckled and concentrating on blocking the pain. I wasn't working on that only to silence my screaming nerves; if I let the pain get to me, I was finished. Pain is the fastest way to stir up the reptilian brain, and once awakened, it tends to shut off the higher functions of the cerebral cortex, leaving one witless and unable to function beyond the instinctive fight-or-flight level—and that would have left me unable to communicate coherently and connect the dots for Leif, in case he was missing out on the salient point: "Someone's trying to kill me!"

CHAPTER 2

Leif's fangs popped out and he launched himself from his chair to the edge of my front lawn, scanning the darkness for assailants with all his senses. Oberon likewise leapt to his feet and growled at the night, threatening whoever was out there with all the menace he could muster.

I knew already that they would find nothing. Someone was doing this from afar.

"Witches!" I spat as my amulet continued to cook my upper chest. The spell itself had ceased and the red glow was beginning to fade, but the smell of grilled me was still wafting up to my nose. The effort of shutting down the pain and trying to restore my melted skin was quickly draining my reserves, so I struggled to my feet and hobbled gingerly down the steps to the lawn, where I could kick off my sandals and draw power from the earth. I bent over and rested my hands on my knees, intending to let the amulet dangle from my neck away from my skin, but it remained where it was—fused to my flesh. Not good.

"I would agree that you are a victim of witchcraft, but I sense no one nearby but the usual residents," Leif said as he continued to search for trouble. "However, now that you have delicately broached the subject—"

"Is that what I just did?" I said, tension straining my voice. "Delicately broach the subject of witches? Because I thought I was doing something else entirely, like getting my ass flame-broiled by witches."

"I beg your pardon. I was flailing about for a segue and utterly failed to find a facile one. My professional reason for visiting you tonight was to tell you that Malina Sokolowski has agreed to your latest terms without revisions or amendments. She's ready to sign the nonaggression treaty as soon as you are."

"Yes, well." I winced as I pulled on the amulet's silver chain, peeling it off my chest and taking some blackened skin with it. "This kind of puts her nonaggression to the lie, doesn't it?"

"No." Leif shook his head. "She would not do this so close to settling a peace between you."

"Maybe it's the perfect time to take a shot at me. We haven't signed anything yet, so that puts her high on my list of suspects." Malina was the new leader of a coven of Polish witches who called themselves the Sisters of the Three Auroras, and they had claimed the East Valley— the local sobriquet for the cities of Tempe, Mesa, Scottsdale, Chandler, and Gilbert—as their territory since the eighties, long before I arrived. When I rolled into town in the late nineties, they pretty much ignored me; I was only one guy, after all, and I displayed zero aggression and not much in the way of power beyond a talent for herbal remedies. We'd been content to live and let live until our interests diverged: They were interested in helping out a god who wanted to kill me (in exchange for what I originally thought was passage through Tír na nÓg, but turned out to be an estate in Mag Mell), and I was interested in staying alive. That was the point where they discovered they had epically underestimated me. There used to be thirteen of them, but six of them died while trying to kill me, and despite all Malina's noises about doves and olive branches, I still believed she would take any chance she got to avenge them.

"I do hope you will not suggest that I pay her a visit," Leif said in a stuffy voice.

"No, no, I'll call on her myself."

"You relieve me excessively. Your inquisitive neighbor, by the way, is taking an interest in us."

"You mean Mr. Semerdjian?"

"That's the one." I cast my eyes sideways across the street, moving my head only a smidge. I could see one pair of blinds in the house opposite mine parted fractionally wider than the rest, and in the dark space between them no doubt lurked the darker eyes of my poisonous neighbor.

"You don't, uh, smell anything different about him, do you?" I asked Leif.

"Different in what way?" my attorney asked.

"No whiff of the Fae about him? No whiff of demons?"

Leif chuckled wryly and shook his head. "The world will never plumb the depths of your paranoia."

"I hope not, because then it might catch me unprepared for something. What does he smell like?"

Leif wrinkled his nose in disgust. "Like a chili dog with mustard and cheap light beer. His blood courses with grease and alcohol."

<Wow. I didn't think he would smell that good,> Oberon said.

"All this sniffing of blood reminds me that I have yet to drink tonight," Leif said, "so I think I will leave you to your healing and your own personal witch hunt, now that my duty is done. But, ere I go, will you at least consider joining me and others in an alliance against Thor? Dwell on its benefits for a time, as a personal favor to me."

"All right, as a favor to you," I said, "I will consider it. But, honestly, Leif, I do not wish to give you any false hope here. Killing Thor is an honor I dream not of."

Icy glares from vampires are far icier than icy glares from people. And when the vampire giving you an icy glare is originally *from Iceland*, you are confronted with the archetypal origin of the term, and you shouldn't be surprised if your core body temperature drops a few degrees. Leif threw one such glare at me for a few seconds, then said quietly, "Are you mocking me? When you quote Shakespeare, it is often to mock someone or to point out their folly."

<Whoa, he's got you there, Atticus,> Oberon said.

"No, Leif, I'm just under a bit of stress here," I said, gesturing at my sweating face and the still-steaming amulet dangling from my neck.

"I think you are lying."

"Come on, Leif—"

"Forgive me, but our association has allowed me some small knowledge about the way you think. You quoted Juliet just now. Are you suggesting I am something like Romeo here, Fortune's fool, perhaps, driven to a rash and ill-considered confrontation with Tybalt out of revenge for Mercutio's death? And you think perhaps I will end tragically, like Romeo, if I pursue this course of action against Thor?"

"That is not what I meant at all. That is not it, at all," I said, "but if that were my intent, I would have chosen to speak as Benvolio rather than Juliet: 'Part, fools! You know not what you do.'"

Leif stared at me, utterly still, the way only vampires and pet rocks can manage. "I've always preferred *Hamlet*," he finally said. "'Now could I drink hot blood, and do such bitter business as the day would quake to look on.'" He spun on his heel and moved quickly—perhaps a bit too quickly for a normal human—to the door of his sleek black Jaguar XK convertible parked in the street, where he muttered a sulky "Fare thee well" before leaping in, gunning the engine, and screeching off in an undead hissy fit.

<Dude. If that was a Shakespearean quote duel, he just kicked your ass.>

I know. But I slipped in some T. S. Eliot and he didn't catch it. Hopefully next time I won't be recovering from an assassination attempt, and then I'll do better. I was still hunched over awkwardly, trying to prevent the amulet from falling back to my chest, and I needed to do something about it—but I didn't want to do anything in front of Mr. Semerdjian, who was doubtless still watching me.

Oberon, I want you to go across the street and park yourself on the edge of his lawn, sort of off to one side, and stare at him.

<That's it? Just sit? Because I don't want to do anything else while he's watching.>

That's it. I need you to distract him, is all. Ever since you left him a present that one time, he's been terrified you'll do it again. It's the gift that keeps on giving.

It was a shame that Mr. Semerdjian and I didn't get along. A slightly pudgy gentleman on the wrong side of sixty, he tended to get excited quickly and loudly and would probably have been great fun to watch a baseball game with. We might have gotten along famously if he hadn't been such a jerk from the moment I moved in—which is kind of like saying the drowning victim might have lived if only he had been able to breathe water.

<All right, but I'd better get a sausage out of this.>

Deal. We're still going for that run too.

<Wait. He doesn't remember any of that business in Papago Park, does he?> Oberon was referring to an unfortunate incident during which a park ranger had died and Mr. Semerdjian had tried to lay the blame at our door.

Nope. Leif took care of all that with his patented vampiric mindwipe. That thought led me to reflect that having a vampire around was pretty handy sometimes; I hoped Leif wouldn't remain angry with me for long.

<Okay, I suppose this will be kind of fun.> Oberon trotted across the street, and the space between the blinds abruptly widened as Mr. Semerdjian abandoned all attempts at subterfuge. <I can see his eyes now.>

While the two of them were engaged in an ocular tête-à-tête, I drew power from the earth and summoned a thick but very localized fog. Arizona is legendary for its dry air, but in the first week of November with a storm rolling in, it's not that hard to find some water vapor to bind. While that took time to condense, I shifted my concentration to healing my burned skin and made better progress now that the amulet wasn't cooking it faster than I could heal.

Since the amulet was still far too hot, I walked hunched over to my garden hose and turned it on, checking to see if the fog had rolled in properly before continuing. I could still see Oberon, who was sitting underneath a streetlight, but not the windows of Mr. Semerdjian's house, so that was good enough. I held one hand up in front of my face to protect it from steam, then turned the hose on the amulet.

It hissed and spat and the expected steam geysered up, but after a few seconds it noticeably began to cool.

<Hey, I think he's coming outside,> Oberon called.

That's fine. Just stay still and stare at him. Wag your tail if you can manage.

<I can't. I really don't like him.>

I heard Mr. Semerdjian explode out of the house in high dudgeon. "Get out of here, you filthy mutt! Shoo! Go away!"

<Did he just call me a mutt? That was rude. Hey, he has a rolled-up newspaper in his hand.>

If he comes at you with it, growl at him.

<Cool. Here he comes.> I heard Oberon growl menacingly, and Mr. Semerdjian's peremptory commands abruptly changed to shrill pleas a couple of octaves higher.

"Ahhh! Nice doggie! Stay! Good dog!"

<He must think I'm daft. He comes at me with a newspaper, intending to slap me upside the head, and then he says "good dog" and expects me to forget all that? I think he deserves a couple of barks.>

Go for it. The amulet was cooling down rapidly now; a few more seconds would allow it to rest on my chest again without doing further damage. Oberon barked viciously, and Mr. Semerdjian's panicked voice immediately leapt to Mariah Carey territory.

"O'Sullivan! Call off your dog, damn you! O'Sullivan! Get over here! Where did this fucking fog come from?"

Satisfied, I turned off the hose and stood up, letting the amulet fall back against my chest. It wasn't fully healed, but it was getting better and I had the pain firmly under control. I walked leisurely across the street to where Oberon was still sitting.

"Here now," I said calmly as I coalesced out of the mist into a wan column of light next to my hound. "What's all the fuss, Mr. Semerdjian? My dog is simply sitting here, offering you no violence whatsoever."

"He's off his leash!" he spluttered.

"So are you," I observed. "If you hadn't advanced upon him in a threatening manner, he never would have growled at you, much less barked."

"Never mind that!" Semerdjian spat. "He's not supposed to be running around loose! And he definitely shouldn't be on my property! I should call the police!"

"I believe the last time you called the police on me, you got cited for falsely calling 911, did you not?"

Semerdjian's face purpled and he shouted, "Just get off my property! Both of you!"

Step backward into the street with me until we disappear from his view, I told Oberon. *Now.* We retreated, keeping our eyes on Mr. Semerdjian as we let the mist envelop us, and I imagined what it must look like to my neighbor: He watched a man and his dog walk backward in tandem without the man giving the dog any audible command, until they vanished like spectres into vapor.

That should creep him out pretty good, I told Oberon. Sure enough, Mr. Semerdjian called after us as we turned up the street.

"You're a spooky bastard, O'Sullivan!" he yelled, and I stifled a laugh at the irony of his insult. "You and your dog had better stay away from me!"

<That was fairly amusing,> Oberon chuffed. <What's that word for when you play a joke on someone?>

A prank, I said, beginning to jog as Oberon trotted beside me. I released the binding on the water vapor, letting the fog disperse. *We are like the Merry Pranksters of 1964, giving Mr. Semerdjian his own customized Acid Test without the benefit of any acid.*

<What's an Acid Test?>

Well, I'll tell you all about it when we get home. Since you are apparently a filthy mutt—

<Hey!>

—you need a bath, and while you're in the bath I'll tell you all about the Merry Pranksters and the Electric Kool-Aid Acid Test. But now let's run to the market and get you your promised sausage.

<Okay! I want one of those succulent chicken–apple ones.>

You mind if I make a call? I need to call Malina and let her know her spell didn't work. I pulled out my cell phone and began to look up Malina's number.

<Sure. But before I forget, I think you should know that Leif was probably lying to you just now.>

How so? I frowned.

<Well, you remember how I got a nose full of demon four days ago when you rescued me in the Superstition Mountains?>

That was three weeks ago, not four days, but yes, I remember.

<Well, Leif told you Mr. Semerdjian didn't smell like demon, but he kind of did. He still does, actually. Shape-shift into a hound if you don't believe me; that lame human nose isn't doing you any favors.>

Wait. Hold up, I said, stopping in the middle of the street. Oberon pulled up after a few steps and looked back at me, tongue lolling out. We were still on 11th Street, just over a block away from my house; streetlamps periodically cast cones of light like yellow party hats in the darkness. *You still smell demon even though we're all the way down the street?*

<Yeah. And it's getting worse.>

Oh, no, that's not good, Oberon, I said, putting my cell phone back in my pocket. *We need to go back to the house. I need to get my sword.* A block ahead of us, something shifted in the shadows. It moved unnaturally above the ground, the size of a small Volkswagen, and then I discerned what was moving it: grotesquely long insectile legs, supporting a bulk that vaguely resembled a grasshopper. Insect size is supposed to be restricted to six inches or so, due to the limits of their tracheal systems, but apparently this demon didn't get the memo.

Run home, Oberon! Now! I pivoted and sprinted at top speed for my front yard and immediately heard the demon leap into pursuit, its legs drumming out a chitinous clacking on the black asphalt. We weren't leaving it behind; if anything, it was gaining on us. There would be no time for me to get my sword.

CHAPTER 3

Demons smell like ass—nasty ass that slithers down your throat, finds your gag reflex, and sits on it with authority. I got an overdose when Aenghus Óg unleashed a horde of them on this plane with the command to kill me, and now I finally caught a whiff of this one. It wasn't a fragrance that Gold Canyon candles would be offering anytime soon.

Some of the demons had been strong enough to resist Aenghus Óg's binding at first and run for the hills to work their own mischief. Though Flidais—the Celtic goddess of the hunt—had tracked most of them down, I knew a few must still be out there and they'd eventually come looking for me. Despite Aenghus's demise, his binding was the sole reason they were on this plane, and until they obeyed its commands they'd never be truly free; the binding would just keep tugging at them until they lost the will to resist. I had killed most of the horde with Cold Fire, but this one must have gotten out of range pretty fast, and only now had it tracked me down in obeisance to the binding.

Run around to the back, Oberon, I said. My friend was already ahead of me. *There's no way you can fight this thing.*

<I'm not going to argue,> he said. <I wouldn't want to take a bite of something that smells that bad, anyway.>

I was coming up hard on my lawn, with the demon close behind; I could hear the whistling of its spiracles in addition to the skittering of its six legs. Once I hit the earth, I could draw power and slap the thing with Cold Fire, but there were drawbacks to that plan: One, Cold Fire took some time to work, and, two, using it weakened me so much that I'd be completely vulnerable after casting it.

With no sword to penetrate its chitin and no safety cushion for Cold Fire, I'd have to depend on my magical wards to take care of the demon before it took care of me. That, too, would take some time, but perhaps I could dodge behind my mesquite tree and stay out of the range of its serrated front legs long enough for my Druidic juju to do its work.

The earth is all too willing to help out with getting rid of demons: They don't belong on the earth, are in fact anathema to it, and thus it takes very little coaxing to set up a demonic ward around one's house. Teach the earth to detect a demon's presence upon it and encourage it to tidy up the soiled area, and you're done—sort of.

The problem is that the earth isn't renowned for its reaction times. Every ten years I like to meditate for a week and commune with its spirit, which people like to call Gaia nowadays, and she chats fondly about the Cretaceous period as if it were something that happened just last month. A security-conscious Druid cannot afford to take the long view on intruders, however, so I set up my mesquite tree as a first line of defense and as an alarm bell for the elemental of the Sonoran Desert. The elemental would get the earth's attention much quicker than I could—and perhaps make an appearance as Gaia's champion. The truth was I didn't exactly know what would happen when a demon awoke the earth's wrath; I was simply betting the earth would win.

When my foot touched the grass of my front yard, I practically cried out in relief, drawing power immediately to replenish my spent muscles and hyperoxygenate my blood. It gave me a burst of speed and allowed me to narrowly miss a plunging stab from the demon. Its clawed foreleg whistled past my calf and sank convincingly into the sod, and it reminded me of a trick I had used on some Fir Bolgs when they'd attacked me at home.

"Coinnigh!" I yelled, pointing a finger back at the insect's claw as I ran, commanding the earth to close tightly around it and prevent it from escaping. It slowed the demon down but failed to immobilize it; the chitin was too slick for the earth to grab on to, and, after a couple of mighty yanks, the horror was able to free itself. Still, it accomplished two things: It gave me time enough to duck behind the mesquite tree, and it definitely tripped my wards.

Thorny vines of bougainvillea shot out from my porch posts, attempting to snare the demon, which I now noticed was not grasshopperish at all, but rather a monstrous black wheel bug, complete with a ridged, coglike wheel of dorsal armor and a menacing beak it used to plunge into its victims and drain all their juices. The vines weren't strong enough for that much hell; they shriveled almost upon contact. The lawn began to ripple and quake underneath the creature, and the roots of my mesquite tree shot up from underneath it and wrapped themselves around the beast's back four legs. That definitely got its attention. It keened its frustration at the upper range of human hearing as it thrashed about, but like the vines, my poor tree's roots could not stand the demon's touch for long. They were strong enough to hold it for perhaps ten seconds only, and had I known they would do such yeoman service, I would have used Cold Fire and ended it.

"O'Sullivan! What the *fuck* is that thing?"

Gods Below, Mr. Semerdjian was still outside! And with the fog dispersed and the streetlights doing their job, he had a clear view of something mortal eyes should never see. I didn't know how to begin explaining this. "Uh, little busy!" I said.

"You're going to need a damn big can of bug spray!" he called. "Or maybe a rocket-propelled grenade. I have one in the garage, you want it?"

"What? No, Mr. Semerdjian, don't! It won't help! Just stay where you are!"

I had to shut him out. If I allowed him to distract me, I'd be demon chow. The black wheel bug tore free of my tree's roots and advanced on me once again, across a lawn that was still heaving violently. It sliced at me with its tubelike beak, stabbing past the trunk of the tree almost too fast to track, and it grazed my shoulder and opened up a burning cut. My tree was having none of that. The canopy of branches began to whip against the demon's head and thorax, not doing much damage but successfully blinding it with a curtain of feathery green leaves. The wheel bug reared back and flailed away at the branches, severing many of them with each sweep of its sharply bladed fore-claws, and it appeared this additional delay would last only a few more seconds before its attention refocused on me. There wasn't enough time to get inside and retrieve my sword, but perhaps there would be enough time for Cold Fire to work. I pointed at the demon and had the trigger word for the spell formed on my lips, but then I saw that the cavalry was coming.

Behind the wheel bug, a huge saguaro cactus was growing from the churned sod of my lawn at a ridiculous rate. Not content merely to cram a century's worth of growth into the space of a few seconds, it showed signs of sentience and the ability to move—singular abili-ties for a saguaro. It could be nothing but the Sonoran Desert ele-mental my mesquite tree had called, Gaia's champion sent to fight the spawn of hell. It loomed out of the night and smashed a heavy spined arm across the back of the demon's abdomen, just behind the cogs of its wheel.

The demon's carapace cracked a bit and it screeched in that bone-shuddering register, whipping around to hack at the saguaro's trunk and arms. It lopped off an arm and even took off the top of the cac-tus, but this wasn't a creature that fell over from decapitation; there was no head to decapitate. When such accidents occur in nature, sa-guaros just seal themselves internally and grow new arms, no prob-lem. The elemental wasn't even slowed down. Another arm whacked at the demon's head, crushing one of its globular black eyes and spraying jets of ichor across my lawn.

The demon knew it was in a fight for its life now. This wasn't a puny human it had to eat before it could do whatever it wanted on this plane; this was a champion of the earth itself, the corporeal manifestation of an entire ecosystem, and a particularly deadly one at that. The black wheel bug directed a flurry of scissoring blows at the saguaro, trying to cut off all its arms so it could then deal with the trunk, but the arms grew back even faster than it could sever them. It wasn't ten seconds before a long one on the far side of the trunk twisted around and crashed through the demon's skull. The arm kept going all the way down the elongated body, splitting the creature in two and dumping its flanks to the ground, where the legs spent some time twitching a spastic dance of death.

Immensely appreciative for the aid and trying to ignore the unholy stench, I sent my thanks through my tattoos down into the earth, communicating with the elemental in a sort of emotional shorthand, since human languages meant nothing to it.

//Druid grateful / Aid welcome// I said. The elemental was flush with victory and pleased with itself. It offered to repair the damage to my lawn, my tree, and my vines, wanting to leave no trace of hell in its territory, and I accepted graciously. It didn't quite know what to do with the demon mess; the head and thorax were little more than black tar at this point, but the abdomen and legs were still fairly intact and clearly not of this earth. It didn't want to absorb the demon into the ground, but it seemed to realize I couldn't stuff a giant wheel bug down the garbage disposal either. I offered a suggestion: Encase it all in rock, condense and crush every bit of it down into liquid, and then leave me with a stone keg crafted with a plug near the bottom. I'd give it to some ghouls I knew (actually, Leif knew them, he had them on speed dial), they'd have a party with it because demon juice was like Jägermeister to them, and then they'd return the keg cleaned out and ready to be reabsorbed into the earth. The elemental was pleased with this solution and began to work on it right away.

"O'Sullivan?" an uncertain voice pulled my consciousness back aboveground. It was Mr. Semerdjian.

"Yes, sir, how may I help you?" Everything was back to normal—that is, the vines looked great and so did my mesquite tree. The saguaro cactus using its many arms to mold stone as if it were clay and making loud bug-crunching noises was admittedly worth comment.

My neighbor raised a shaking index finger to point at the saguaro. "That moving cactus . . . and the big bug . . . and you, you spooky bastard. What are you?"

I stuffed my hands in my pockets and grinned winningly at him. "Why, I'm the Antichrist, of course."

Mr. Semerdjian responded by fainting, which seriously surprised me. I'd expected a vulgar expression of disbelief, like a middle finger or a clutching of the crotch, because the man had seen a giant demon and casually offered to blow it up like a tough guy. Why would saying the name of the boogeyman from Christianity make him lose his mind?

Actually, his collapse was a blessing. When he woke up, everything would be swell and I'd deny that any of it ever happened. If he tried to get anyone else to believe him, well, they wouldn't. The cut on my shoulder was already healing over.

The elemental finished its work and left the stone keg full of distilled demon on my empty driveway, where I could easily camouflage it and the ghouls could load it into their refrigerated truck. Sonora said its farewells and then the saguaro sank back into my lawn, cleaning up as it disappeared, leaving no sign that anything supernatural had occurred. My lawn even looked like it had been freshly fertilized.

<Is it safe now?> Oberon asked from the backyard.

Yeah, come on out. I have a couple calls to make. First I called 911 for Mr. Semerdjian, establishing an official record of my concern for his welfare. If he woke up calling me the Antichrist, he'd get a strong dose of sedatives and maybe one of those snug little straitjackets to play around in. Next I called my daytime lawyer, Hal Hauk, to get the number for the ghouls. I didn't think Leif would want to talk to me right now, and besides, he was probably having an ASU student for breakfast.

After I rang the ghouls, the ambulance arrived for Mr. Semerdjian, and I waited for them to take him away before making my last call, to Malina Sokolowski.

"Hello, Malina," I said with relish when she answered the phone. "I'm still around. Your little spell didn't work."

"You were attacked too? Those *bitches!*" she spat. "Damn them!" She was clearly upset; she'd never used anything but the politest, formal language with me. "It makes me wonder who else got hit tonight and who else is dead now."

That wasn't the response I expected at all. "Wait. What bitches? Who's dead? Malina, who's dead?"

"You'd better get over here," she said, and hung up on me.

CHAPTER 4

<D id I just hear you say something about bitches?> Oberon asked hopefully.

"Yeah, but not the kind you're thinking about, unfortunately," I said aloud. "Are you willing to try going for that run again, buddy? We need to pay Malina Sokolowski a visit."

<She's the witch who doesn't like dogs, right?>

"Well, I don't know many witches who do like dogs, so she's hardly exceptional in that regard. Witches tend to be cat people."

<Can I get my sausage before we go to her house, then?>

"Of course," I laughed. "And thank you for reminding me. Just let me go inside and get my sword. I want to be prepared this time. Stand sentinel out here?"

<Sure.> I ducked inside to get Fragarach, the old Irish sword that cut through armor as though it were crepe paper, and slung the scabbard across my back so that the hilt protruded above my right shoulder. As I stopped at the fridge to take a couple chugs of Naked berry juice, Oberon called to me from the porch.

<Atticus, there's a man out here on foot who doesn't smell like a man.>

I shoved the juice back in the fridge and hurried for the front door. *Does he smell like a demon?* I asked.

<No. He smells kind of like a dog, but not quite.>

I hauled open the door and beheld a slim Native American man in the street. Straight black hair spilled past his shoulders from underneath a cowboy hat, and he was dressed in a white sleeveless undershirt, blue jeans, and scuffed brown boots. He held a grease-stained brown paper bag in his left hand, and he had a smirk on his face.

He waved leisurely with his right hand and said in a slow, friendly voice, "Evenin', Mr. Druid. I reckon you know who I am?"

I relaxed and fell into the unhurried rhythms of his speech. By speaking like him, I would make him relax as well, and he'd be more likely to trust me. It was the first rule of fitting in: Talk like a native. As soon as people hear a foreign accent, it's like ringing the doorbell of xenophobia. They immediately classify you as the other instead of as a brother, and it was this fundamental aspect of human nature that Leif had seemingly forgotten. It applies to dialects and regional accents as well, which is why I'm obsessed with mimicking those properly whenever I can. Ask any Boston Yankee what happens when they get pulled over by police in the Deep South, and they'll tell you that accent matters. So I took my time with my reply, as if I had all day to get to the end of a sentence, because that's the way my visitor spoke. "I surely do, Coyote. Only question is which tribe you're callin' from this time."

"I'm callin' from the Diné," he said, using the proper name for the tribe the United States called Navajo. "Mind if I come up and sit a spell?"

"Not a'tall," I said. "But you catch me poorly equipped for comp'ny. Ain't got any tobacco in the house, 'shamed to say."

"Aw, that's all right. I'll take a beer if you got one."

"That I can handle. Come set on the porch here and I'll be right back." I dashed inside and snaked a couple of craft brews from the fridge, while Coyote walked up to the porch. I had the tops popped off and was back outside as he was settling into his chair. I held a bottle out to him and he smiled.

"Mmm, fancy beer," he said, taking it from my hand and examining the label. "Thanks, Mr. Druid."

"Welcome." We both took a swig, sighed appreciatively like men are supposed to do, and then he held up the bag in his left hand.

"Got some sausages here for your hound. Mind if I give 'em to 'im?"

<Sausages!> Oberon's tail began to wag madly. <I thought I smelled something yummy!>

"What kind o' sausages?" I asked.

Coyote chuckled. "Old paranoid Druid. You never change. Normal sausages, perfectly safe. Chicken–apple flavor. I didn't want your hound to go hungry while we talk."

"That was right nice o' ya, Coyote. My hound and I both thank ya for it." If he knew Oberon wanted chicken–apple sausages tonight, that meant he was close by when we first ran into that demon—close enough to help, but he clearly chose not to. It also meant he could hear Oberon's thoughts. I took the bag from him and opened it up to find eight perfect chicken–apple sausages the size of bratwurst, still warm and smelling delicious. I tore open the bag and laid it down on the porch in front of Oberon so he could get at them easily. He wasted no time inhaling them.

<These are awesome! Tell him I said so!>

"Good." Coyote nodded, taking another swig of beer. He seemed unaware that he had replied before I had repeated Oberon's words. "So, seen any demons 'round here?"

Oberon stopped chewing and raised his head, ears perked, and I studied Coyote carefully for any signs of suddenly sprouting horns or the stench of brimstone. He threw his head back and laughed at us. His canine teeth shone in the pale yellow light of the streetlamps.

"Hoo-ee, you oughtta see your faces! I bet ya seen a demon, all right! Lemme guess, a big black bug?"

"Yeah. But I reckon ya didn't have to guess, didja?" I asked.

"Naw, I saw him comin' this way afore I got here. But he ain't the only one out there, ya know."

"Yeah, I figured," I said.

"I 'spect you did, Mr. Druid. And you're the reason they're runnin' 'round here, eatin' people."

"What do you care if a demon makes mischief in town?" I asked.

"What do I care? If a demon went 'round eatin' white men like you, you're right, I wouldn't care. But I said they're eatin' *people*, an' by that I mean they're eatin' my people, Mr. Druid. My people are feedin' a demon that's here because of you. So we have somethin' to talk about, you an' I."

"I see." I nodded, and Oberon took this as a signal that it was okay for him to finish off his repast. "Where and when did your people die?"

"A maiden at Skyline High School was eaten yesterday, when all t'other kids were eatin' lunch inside."

"What, at the school? Where ever'one could see?"

"Nobody seen it happen but me. She was by herself, eatin' flat-bread outside. An', besides, humans can't see this one. You coulda seen it, though. An' I seen it for sure."

"What did it look like?"

"Huge black thing with wings." Oberon belched and I felt a bit of indigestion as well. I knew what the demon Coyote meant. It was one of the first creatures out of hell when Aenghus Óg opened the portal and the first demon to disregard the binding. It was very strong, and since it flew, there was no way I could kill it with Cold Fire, which required the demon to be in contact with the earth. "So what're ya gonna do?" Coyote asked.

"I'm gonna wait," I said. "Eventually it'll come after me here, and when it does, I'll be ready."

"Lemme suggest a different plan," Coyote said, his half smile still playing about his face. He pointed the mouth of his beer bottle at me. "You'll go out to that school tomorrow an' kill that demon afore it kills again. There are more of my people at that school, an' I don't wanna lose another one 'cause you wanna wait."

"Why don't you just kill it, Coyote?"

"'Cause I ain't responsible for it bein' here, paleface. You are. An' it's a demon from the white man's religion, anyways, so my medicine won't be as strong against it as yours. But I'll help ya if I can."

"Well, my medicine might not be any stronger. I may be a white man, but this thing don't figure into my religion neither. Besides, I'm awful busy with problems of my own."

Coyote's perpetual smirk vanished, and he glared at me from underneath his hat brim. "This *is* your problem, Mr. Druid. Or didn't I make that clear? You'll fix this situation or you'll answer to me. An' to Pima Coyote. An' Tohono O'odham Coyote, an' Apache Coyote too. An' while ever' single one of us might die in the first fight, an' maybe the second an' third fights too, you know we'll keep comin' back. How many times can you come back from the dead, Mr. Druid? Me an' my brothers can come back all we want, but I reckon we only have to kill you oncc."

<Atticus?> My hound flattened his ears and showed his teeth, but didn't quite growl at our guest.

It's okay, Oberon. He can hear you, so don't give anything away. I'll let you know if I need you. He subsided but kept watching Coyote warily.

I nodded for Coyote's benefit. I didn't tell him I was awfully tough to kill, since the Morrigan had promised never to take me. Still, Coyote could do a lot of damage I might never recover from, as my mangled right ear testified. I just wanted to know how serious he was about this, and now I had my answer.

"Think ya can give me a ride out there?" I asked. "I ain't got a car." Skyline High School was on the east side of Mesa, near the borderline with Apache Junction—which, of course, was the city right outside the Superstition Mountains where the demon had escaped from hell. It would be a twenty-mile bike ride for me one way, which would be less than comfortable.

"I ain't got a car neither." Coyote grinned as he took another slug of beer, threats forgotten. "But that shouldn't stop me from gettin' one by tomorrow."

"All right, pick me up here at ten in the mornin'," I said. "And bring a bow. We're gonna shoot us a demon out o' the sky."

"With regular ol' arrows?" Coyote's eyebrows rose so high they got lost underneath his hat.

"No, we'll get ourselves some special arrows," I said. "I think I know where we can get us some holy ones, some demon-slayin' arrows."

"You do? I ain't never seen any for sale in any of those Cath'lick churches," Coyote said.

"When were *you* ever in a Cath'lick church?" I asked incredulously, and Coyote started to laugh. It was infectious laughter, the kind that hooked a smile out of your own face. "I mean, how would you know, right? They could be passin' out holy arrows with their Jesus crackers and you'd never know any different."

Coyote hooted and hollered and howled his laughter, and it wasn't long before I was doing the same. He doubled over; he slapped his thighs; he laughed silently for a while because he was out of breath; he laughed until he had tears streaming from his eyes. "I bet it was just like that, Mr. Druid!" Coyote finally managed to gasp. "Them priests would come on up to the soldiers and say, 'In the name of the Father and the Son, here's a cracker, now go kill some fuckin' Indians!'" And abruptly the laughter died in our throats, and our smiles fell quietly like death shrouds on the fallen. It was simply too close to the truth to be funny. We spent some small while staring down at the flower bed in front of my porch. I cannot speak for what Coyote was thinking, but personally I was haunted by the ghosts of those who had trespassed against me; I was the only survivor of the Holy Roman Church's war against Druidry.

Coyote eventually wiped at his cheeks, drained his bottle, and said, "Thanks for the beer an' the laugh, Mr. Druid." He stood up and put the empty on my porch rail, then held out his hand to shake, a huge grin on his face again. "You'd be a good guy if ya wasn't so damn white."

I shook his hand firmly, grinned back, and said, "An' you'd be a good guy if ya wasn't a damn dog." That set Coyote off to laughing again, but this time it seemed not entirely human. He let go of my hand and then I saw what was happening. He fell to all fours, and in another heartbeat he was bounding off my porch in his animal form, yipping his amusement into the cool November night.

He didn't even leave any clothes behind; they just sort of melted away somehow. Oberon noticed too. <Bitchin',> he said. <You should learn how to do that.>

"Right." I looked down at Oberon and clapped my hands together as Coyote disappeared from view. "*Now* we can go see the Polish witches."

<I think Coyote's messed with your head,> Oberon observed. <You just said that like it's some sort of treat.>

CHAPTER 5

Detecting some ambivalence, I asked Oberon if he'd rather stay home than visit the witches.

<Actually, a run doesn't sound all that great right now,> he admitted. <I just had all those sausages. I think a nap would be nice. Maybe you can pop in a Clint Eastwood movie for me.>

"Sure. Besides, you don't like witches, right?"

<Well, no. But neither do you. Except now you're ready to trot over to Malina's gingerbread house because she said so—and right after someone tried to off you, I might add. Have you thought that maybe you're making her day here? Do you feel lucky?>

"I guess I know which kind of Eastwood movie you'd like to watch." I got Oberon set up in the living room with a Dirty Harry flick and then took off on my bike, sword strapped to my back in plain sight, heading for Malina's condo near Town Lake.

Ever since I'd started to carry Fragarach around regularly—just in the last few weeks—I had noticed an interesting phenomenon: Hardly anyone thought it was real. Most people took a look at the guy on a bike with a sword and assumed I was still living with my mom and harboring an unhealthy obsession for anime. Or they supposed the sword was a prop for a role-playing game or some other fantasy, because the idea of carrying a sword for personal defense in an age of firearms caused them too much cognitive dissonance. While I paused at the stoplight on Mill and University, one citizen even inquired if I was on my way to the comics shop.

Malina lived in the Bridgeview condos, a twelve-story tower of glass and steel built just after the turn of the century in Tempe's rush to develop the Town Lake district. She and the rest of her coven owned the entire ninth floor—though now there were six vacancies. Granuaile, my apprentice, lived on the eighth floor, directly underneath the condo of Radomila, the coven's erstwhile leader. I thought it would be wise to check on her before knocking on Malina's door, so I rang her bell.

"Who is it?" her voice called through the door. "Oh, it's just you."

She answered the door in something scanty, and I experienced a moment of panic as prurient thoughts pushed aside the innocent inquiry I'd been planning to make about her safety. Granuaile was not plain; she was a tall, lithe redhead with green eyes, a mouth that looked delicious, and an extremely sharp mind. The latter was most important, for otherwise she would not be my apprentice. It was difficult to dwell on her mind, however, when so much of her athletic build was on display—more than I had seen to date, in fact. She usually dressed very modestly and I appreciated it, because it kept my thoughts of her (mostly) innocent. But now that she was dressed in a low-cut pale-green nightie, all slinky and clinging to her shape—

Baseball! Must think of baseball. Not the curve of her . . . *curveball!* Randy Johnson has a wicked slider too. Oh, how I would love to slide—

"Atticus? What's wrong?"

"Huh? Oh. Um. Hi." I'd been reduced to monosyllables by a nightie.

"Why are you looking up? Is there something above my door?" She took a step closer to me and leaned over to see what I was looking at and, oh, my—

"There's some tit, uh, titillating wallpaper up there! Yes! Fantastic interior decorating here, I just noticed."

"You've seen it before. What's going on?"

Just the facts, Atticus. "Someone attacked me tonight and I wanted to make sure you were okay," I said, trying to remember who held the record for stealing second base.

"Oh, well, yes, I'm fine. Who attacked you?"

"Still trying to find out. It was a magical attack, not a physical one. Actually, there was a physical one too, but that was a demon, and an elemental killed it for me so that's all right, the ghouls are on their way, but I'm not sure my neighbor's ever going to be the same, though you don't have to worry about Oberon, he's fine." Sweet honey of Dagda, now I was babbling.

"What?" Granuaile said.

"Look, there's no time to discuss it; just lock yourself inside and close all your windows. I'm going to put a ward on your door to keep you safe tonight while I go deal with this."

"You think someone's going to attack me?"

"No, no, it's a precaution only. Now get inside and close the door— shoo. But open up the shop for me tomorrow; I won't be in 'til after lunch."

"All right," she said uncertainly. She turned, and I looked at the ceiling so that my peripheral vision would not drag my focus downward. "I guess I'll see you tomorrow, then."

"Sleep well," I said as the door closed, shutting that body away from my eyes, and I sighed in relief. "Damn, I need a cigarette after that. And I don't even smoke."

Druid's Log, November 1: Buy attractive apprentice some shapeless, ugly clothes as soon as possible; maybe convince her to shave her head as well. Tell her all the cool Druid initiates are doing it.

I didn't need to put a ward on Granuaile's door, since I had placed one there a week ago without telling her, right after she returned from North Carolina and confirmed she still wanted to be an initiate.

After taking a couple of deep breaths to regain my composure and focus on my purpose, I used the stairwell to head up to the witches' floor. I had no illusions that I would catch them unawares; they probably knew the moment I'd entered the building, much less ascended the stairs to their floor. I took a moment to mutter a binding on all my hair and skin, to make sure none of it escaped to fall into the hands of a witch. I had to be careful with my magic usage here; nine floors up from the earth, I had a limited supply of energy upon which to draw, just what was stored in my bear charm. I can't really sling magic around the way witches can, in any case. In a situation like this, my sword would serve me better. Fragarach (the Answerer in Irish) wasn't simply a sharpened piece of steel: The Tuatha Dé Danann had given it a couple of bonus utilities when they forged it ages ago, and I intended to employ one of them now.

I drew it from its scabbard, thereby breaking a state law or two about deadly weapons, and opened the door to the ninth floor. The hallway was clear and uncomfortably silent, the lights dimmer somehow, and the air close and quiet like the dark, stuffy space underneath a blanket. On the other floors, where trust-fund college kids and young professionals lived, you could hear muted music and laughing and *The Daily Show*'s mockery through the doors. The witches were having none of that.

"It's Atticus," I called as I rapped my knuckles on Malina's door. The percussive sound seemed to offend the hallway's sense of decorum, and the quiet chastised me as it dropped into my ears like cotton balls. I stood presenting my left side to the fish-eye peephole, so that my sword arm was hidden from view.

While I waited for her to answer, I thought of how reckless I was being right then. Oberon's words rang in my ears, along with the shrill voice of paranoia in my head. Meeting the witches on their own turf without a nonaggression treaty and without support of any kind was really asking for it. I still didn't know quite what they were capable of; if Malina was to be believed, they had held this territory against all comers for nearly thirty years. The threshold could be booby-trapped or enchanted. I could be walking into a cage fight with a demon. Hell, she could open the door with a Glock 9 in her hand and put a bullet in my ear, or throw a cat at me, or call me a damn hippie.

She did none of those things. I heard the locks tumbling open—regular, everyday locks—and then she stood before me with red-rimmed, puffy eyes and said, "Waclawa's dead."

It took me a moment to process that she'd said someone's name. I know forty-two languages—many of them extinct now—but Polish isn't one of them, and in general I'm not that great with the Slavic tongues. Waclawa, I recalled, was one of the names on the list of Malina's coven members.

"I'm sorry," I said. "How did she die?"

"The police will probably call it spontaneous combustion," she ground out bitterly, "but there was nothing spontaneous about it." Malina wore a diaphanous purple tunic over a white camisole. She had on a black skirt that fell to her knees and hugged her hips; her legs were sheathed in black tights, and she wore pointy high-heeled ankle boots of jet suede. Her lips were painted a soft pink, and now they were pressed together in regret. I marveled again at her hair—gentle waves of blond silk that one simply never sees except on silver screens, framing her face and spilling down past her collarbone. Normally her skin was white and smooth as marble, inviting caress, but now it was flushed and blotchy because she was upset. She opened the door farther and gestured. "Come on in."

I didn't move. "Forgive me, but I need two questions answered first." I moved my sword into view but did not raise it or threaten her with it. "Will you answer?"

Malina's eyes flicked down. "If I answer incorrectly, then I get the sword?"

"No, the sword makes sure you answer correctly. It's kind of special that way."

Malina narrowed her eyes. "What sort of questions?"

"Nothing about your coven's secrets, nothing personal. They regard my immediate safety only."

"Do I get a quid pro quo?"

I sighed. Everything with this witch was a negotiation. "I freely tell you I have no intention of attacking you without being attacked first."

"I already knew that. I want to know about your magic."

"No, that is not a quid pro quo." I shook my head. "The value is not the same."

Malina raised her eyebrows. "You are suggesting that innocent questions about your magical abilities are more important than questions of your immediate safety?"

"Of course, for the answer to the latter will do me no good past this evening, and the former will inform you forever."

"I am too upset to enjoy fencing with you about this. Ask your questions about personal safety."

I raised Fragarach slowly, deliberately, and pointed it at Malina's throat. "*Freagróidh tú,*" I said in Irish, and Fragarach turned cold in my hand, its blade gleaming blue and enveloping Malina's head in a soft cloud of cyan light. The witch blinked.

"The sword can cast a spell?" she said. "Most unusual. Was this the reason Aenghus Óg wanted the sword so much?" I was sure it was one of the reasons, but the true answer had more to do with Fae politics and a personal vendetta against me. I had not come to discuss my sword's magical capabilities.

"I'll ask the questions," I replied. "Did you have anything to do with the attempt on my life tonight, or do you have any knowledge of who might have been involved?"

"I personally had nothing to do with it, nor did any from my coven, but I do have knowledge of who might have been involved."

The temptation to ask "Who?" was nearly overwhelming, but I bit it back; it could wait, and I only had one question left. I carefully composed it, then asked, "Do you, or any other person, creature, or spirit within your home, intend to cast any spell on me while in the building, or are there enchantments that I may unknowingly trigger during my visit?"

"Neither I nor any other person, creature, or spirit in my home intends to cast a spell on you. I do not wish to tell you about our enchantments, for I feel that intrudes uncomfortably into the area of coven secrets, which you promised not to explore. . . ." Malina frowned for a moment and then continued, her eyes widening as she realized she could not stop herself. "But of course you tripped an enchantment the moment you walked into the building, as all nonresidents do—a simple low-level alert. And another that identified you as carrying a magical item. And then another in the hallway that—*Zorya Vechernyaya, zamknij mi usta!*"

I really needed to pick up some Polish if I was going to continue dealing with Malina, though I did catch that she invoked one of the Zoryas, the star goddesses from whom her coven derived its power. "Whatever you're trying, it won't work," I said. "You must answer the question fully before you are released. You were speaking of an enchantment in the hallway."

Malina decided to try a physical response: She attempted to slam the door in my face, or at least made an abortive movement as if she wanted to do so; that was when she discovered Fragarach wouldn't let her move more than a couple of inches. Since the sword's enchantment had been originally intended to interrogate highly hostile enemies, it was a defensive measure more than anything else—can't have people stabbing you when you're pumping them for information. I smiled gently and said nothing. The only way she could be free now was to answer the question, and the spell would compel her to speak soon enough if she insisted on being silent.

She insisted.

Fifteen seconds later—a decent holdout—she was telling me everything about the hallway and glowering at me for it as her volubility waxed.

"The hallway has an enchantment that removes a few hairs from your head if you do not live on this floor. Crossing the threshold of my door will do the same thing. There is a knife in my kitchen that will slice into your fingers if you try to use it, thereby producing blood we may seize upon. And if you use our bathroom, your waste will be stored for later use."

"Eww, gross," I said. First impression of a valley girl, ever. I swear.

"That is all. Release me from this spell now," Malina said.

"I have promised to ask you only two questions regarding my safety, and that is what I have done. The fact that you did not want to answer the second question demonstrates I had good cause to be worried. And, of course, you did not want to answer because you know that possession of my hair, blood, or any fragment of my cells for magical purposes is expressly forbidden in the nonaggression treaty we have yet to sign."

Malina seethed quietly, and I continued, "I am going to release you shortly. Before I do, I want you to know I hold you and your coven blameless in the recent attempt on my life. I'm not going to ask you any more questions now, for that would violate my promise, but I would appreciate it very much if, once you are released, you would share what you know about who tried to kill me. If the party responsible for attacking me is the same party that killed Waclawa, then I offer my aid in avenging her."

The witch's expression softened minutely, and after a brief hesitation she gave me a curt nod. "That is reasonable. I will return any hair taken from you immediately and dispel the enchantment on my threshold so that you may enter safely. But you will never use this sword's power on me again, nor on any member of my coven."

I didn't nod or give any other sign that I agreed to that but instead released her and said, "Let us proceed, then." I was curious to see whether the silent hallway had succeeded in taking my hair when I had put a binding on it specifically to prevent that from happening.

"Who attacked me?" I asked.

"Just a moment," she said. She spoke a few words of Polish, and the door frame flared with white light for a brief second. "It's safe for you to come in now."

"Thank you," I said, and stepped into her condo. It was decorated in purples, ranging from intense violet to soft lavenders, and anchored by black leather furnishings and steel appliances. The wall above the obligatory big-screen TV boasted a large painting of a triple goddess figure, presumably the Zoryas. Pale wax candles dotted the room with fingers of light, emitting a scent of orange peel and cardamom.

"I think custom demands that I offer you refreshment," Malina said as she moved to the kitchen, "but you won't take any, will you?"

"No, but I thank you for the thought. It is a meaningful gesture in itself."

"Will you be seated?" She gestured toward the inviting leather couch in the center of the living area. The black coffee table had several magazines scattered about on it—*Organic Living* and *Rolling Stone*, I noted with some surprise. Then I wondered at myself: What did I expect, *Ritual Animal Slaughters Quarterly*? I almost accepted her offer, because the couch did look comfy, but then a tense whisper of caution suggested that she could say something in Polish and make it eat me.

"I prefer to stand, thank you. And with my sword drawn, though I will keep it pointed at the ground. I do not wish to take much of your time, only what is necessary to establish who attacked me and to retrieve anything of mine your enchantments may have removed."

Malina was not used to being so flagrantly mistrusted, and I think she was close to taking offense. But, let's face it, most people outside her coven didn't know she was a witch; they thought her nothing more than an alluring, successful, cosmopolitan woman with glamorous hair and a penchant for wearing sexy boots.

"Fine," she said shortly, pulling a cork out of an already open bottle of Rosemount Estate Shiraz that waited on her granite countertop. She started to pull a glass out of her cupboard, but then thought better of it and tossed the cork carelessly over her shoulder, deciding to drink straight out of the bottle since I wouldn't be partaking. "Let's get to it, shall we?" She took a gulp or two for courage before continuing. "Waclawa is nothing more than a collection of cinders now on the lake shore, thanks to a certain hex I haven't seen since my younger days in Europe. It's not something my coven can do, I assure you, nor would we want to. This hex cannot be cast without the aid of dark powers, and it takes three witches in tandem to cast it. That," she said, aiming her bottle at me meaningfully, "should give you an idea of what we're confronted with."

"If I was targeted at the same time as the rest of your coven, it means we're dealing with two dozen witches plus eight demons."

"Correct—well, the demons may not still be around. But I'm sure they left something of themselves behind." Her eyes grew round significantly, and I began to wonder how much wine she had already consumed.

"Oh, no. Let me guess. Eight of those witches are eating for two now."

"Very good, Mr. O'Sullivan. That's generally how these things work. In nine months, eight demon babies will be born—and more soon after, if the witches care to try again. There's only one coven large enough and soulless enough to try this, and we have run into them before: They call themselves *die Töchter des dritten Hauses.*"

"The Daughters of the Third House?"

"Yes. They are the bitches I was referring to on the phone." Her face twisted and she looked as if she was going to scream a curse or five, but she mastered her temper in time and instead observed calmly, "I see you speak German."

"*Ja,* several versions of it. Why did you survive when Waclawa did not?"

Malina shrugged. "She was outside when it happened; the rest of us were at home. Here on our floor we are very well protected, as I am sure you are protected somehow. Had we all been outside at the time of the attack, we'd all be dead."

"If that's so, then you would think that they would have timed the attack better, to ensure more of you were vulnerable."

"You are assuming they're aware of our defenses. They have no conception of the wards the Zoryas provide us. Their magic is as different from ours as it is from yours. To their way of thinking, they have cast a hex no one can survive. They will be surprised to learn otherwise."

"Why was I targeted? Why were you targeted, for that matter?"

"They targeted *us* partially to settle an old score," she replied, tapping her chest with the bottle and then remembering it held a rather tasty vintage. She took another drink before continuing, and moved into the living area. "But mostly, we—and I include you in that *we*—are all that's left protecting the East Valley territory, whether you realize it or not."

"I didn't sign up for that."

"It's not the sort of thing one signs up for." She put her fist up to her mouth briefly to mask a delicate belch. "They perceive you to be a guardian of this area, therefore you are. Perception is reality, Mr. O'Sullivan."

"Why not go after the werewolves? Or Leif?"

"They represent entirely different spheres of influence. The were-wolves care only about other lycanthropes; since magic doesn't touch them, they couldn't care less who rules the territory. The vampires care only about other undead. We, on the other hand, must worry about all magic-casters."

"Must we?"

"Look at places with high crime. The West Valley as opposed to the East Valley, for example. The west-side cities, including Phoenix, have higher rates of crime, poverty, and auto accidents than the east. Why do you suppose that is?"

"Socioeconomic status and poor civil engineering."

"No, it's because the West Valley is not under our aegis like the East is."

"You are suggesting that your coven is solely responsible for the East Valley's relative peace and prosperity?"

"Not solely responsible, just largely responsible. The Zoryas are protective goddesses, not the vengeful sort that wants blood and sacrifice."

"That's fascinating," I said, "but hardly germane to the point, which is where can I find this German coven and how do I kill them?"

"Kill them the way you killed my sisters," Malina said coldly. She didn't know I hadn't really killed any of them—five had been werewolf snacks, and the sixth had fallen prey to another witch, one who was on my side. "As for where they are, I imagine they are in town somewhere. I cannot give you a precise location, because I do not know myself. We will attempt to divine their location after midnight."

"Excellent. I will try to divine their location also. Would you say this coven is more powerful than yours?"

"Certainly they are at the moment, outnumbered as we are. They left us alone while we were at full strength. But now they know we are depleted, the East Valley is a lovely place to live besides being a rich place to exploit, and they think they can win."

"Can they?"

"In a sense they already have. We cannot leave this floor of the building until the threat of that hex is removed, because we cannot protect ourselves individually from it. At the same time, we are unlikely to defeat them solely by magic with only six of us. So it is up to you, Mr. Sullivan, to go out and thwart them if you can."

"I think you're confusing me with a superhero. Heroes go around thwarting dastardly villains. They give the evildoers to the police, and the bad guys always say they would have gotten away with it if it weren't for those meddling kids." A groove appeared between Malina's eyes as she tried to attach my words to something that made sense to her, and I could see she failed. Not a big fan of Saturday morning cartoons, I guess. "Druids, on the other hand, take revenge on people who try to cook them."

"Well, that I can understand."

"Good. Tell me why the East Valley is so desirable."

"Why do people fight over it, you mean?" Malina gave up pacing the living room and plopped herself on the comfy leather couch, tilting her bottle of Shiraz yet again.

"Yes. Explain it to me as if I were a child, because in truth I have never understood the territorial urge. Why do groups of magical beings fight over pieces of real estate when we could easily spread ourselves thin over the surface of the earth?"

"I thought it would be obvious, Mr. O'Sullivan. In a densely populated industrial society, the citizens are predisposed to think of magic as ridiculous. Therefore it is easier to blend in, easier to prey on them if we were so inclined, and far easier to profit from them. As a single individual, you can go where you wish with relative ease; but a larger group needs a larger herd to hide in and a larger economic engine to afford us the life we'd prefer to live. Urban centers are therefore both our protection and livelihood, and it is natural that we compete for the choicest places to live."

"You can't share?"

"To some extent we can, yes. We share this territory with the Tempe Pack, for example. We share it with you. But when too many magic users populate a given area, the risk of exposure increases, as does the risk of overtaxing the economics."

"I beg your pardon. How exactly do you overtax the economics? I run a bookstore and apothecary shop. All members of the Tempe Pack have legitimate jobs. Don't you do the same?"

Malina laughed. "Why, no, Mr. O'Sullivan, I don't. People give me everything I want. The same goes for my sisters."

"You mean people just give you money?"

"Yes, that's right." She twirled a lock of her hair around a finger and smiled brightly at me.

"Of their own free will?"

"Well, that's how they remember it." She shrugged a shoulder and raised a hand, palm up. "So it must be true, mustn't it?" She smirked wryly.

"And you have no moral problem with that?"

"None whatsoever. Actually," she leaned forward and lowered her voice, as if sharing a confidence in a public place, "we are on the payrolls of two dozen different companies as consultants, but we do absolutely nothing for our paychecks, just like normal consultants." She leaned back and continued at normal volume, "We do, however, provide a service to the people of the East Valley."

"Dare I ask what that may be?"

"Why, we keep it free of truly nasty witches, of course, as well as some other unsavory individuals. This could easily become a hellish place to live without our protection. And that's what will happen if *die Töchter des dritten Hauses* take over this territory. Not to mention the damage that the Bacchants can do once they get here."

"What? Bacchants are on their way here? Now?"

"Even as we speak. You know, the ones from Las Vegas. I mentioned them to you before, didn't I?"

"Yes, I believe so." I struggled to appear nonchalant, but I was dangerously close to needing a new pair of underwear. Back when I was an initiate—this was decades before Jesus—Bacchants were the scariest creatures in the world, according to the archdruid. Anything that could scare the archdruid damn well gave me nightmares; I nearly shat kine whenever Bacchus was mentioned even obliquely for my first few centuries.

Kids today don't know much about the Bacchants, except perhaps for the story about Orpheus told in Ovid's *Metamorphoses*. I had an ASU student looking for it in my shop last week, and he defined the Bacchants for me as "those drunk chicks who killed that one dude because he wouldn't have sex with them." His professors must be so proud. I asked him if he knew what maenads were, and instead of correctly answering that it was just another name for Bacchants, he bizarrely thought I was referring to my own testicles—as in, "'Ere now, mate, don't swing that bat around me nads." The conversation deteriorated quickly after that.

Now that I'm much older and hopefully wiser, I know that the archdruid's fear was partially his own chauvinist terror of women who did whatever they wanted, but I also know that it was partially well founded.

Bacchants carry around thyrsi, which are staves wrapped in ivy leaves that give them the power to throw an instant party: Slap the ground with them, and wine bubbles forth. They dance and drink themselves into a frenzy, and then they acquire tremendous strength, sufficient to rip apart a bull (or a man) with their bare hands. As a corollary, their frenzy tends to have a ripple effect on people around them, turning fairly civilized parties into orgies of debauchery. It isn't the sort of magic that specifically targets anyone, and I suspected much of it had to do with simply stimulating human pheromones, so I feared my amulet wouldn't protect me from it. In addition to this, Bacchants are not burned by fire, and they cannot be harmed by iron weapons. The former didn't really apply to me, because Druids don't go around chucking fireballs at their enemies, but the latter presented me with a huge problem, since I basically used my sword whenever I wanted to do unto others before they did unto me. Bacchants were therefore well protected against the talents of Druids, while I feared myself defenseless against their magic.

"We have driven them back twice in years past," Malina said, "but now they not only outnumber us, they can also fulminate a fine frenzy without fear of us showing up, because we're stuck here until the German *hexen* are destroyed. I wouldn't be surprised to discover that the two groups are working together to take over the territory."

"This," I said with a sardonic smile and waggling my left index finger at her, "is starting to sound suspicious to me."

Malina's eyes widened in mock surprise. "Only now it's starting?"

"Yes," I said, ignoring her sarcasm, "it sounds to me like you want me to run around and take care of your problems while you just hang out at home and watch movies or something." I changed my voice to her pitch and tried to affect a Polish accent. "Go slay the German *hexen* for me, Druid, and while you're at it, take care of those bothersome Bacchants and win one for Orpheus."

Malina glared at me. "Was that supposed to be an imitation of my accent? It sounded like a Russian trying to imitate Bela Lugosi and failing miserably. My accent is far more sophisticated and dignified."

"My imitation of your accent is not the issue."

"Well, I'm making it one. And, besides, you offered to help avenge Waclawa."

"And so I will. But what does your coven plan to do to fight the *hexen*?" I asked. Malina deflated, considered her bottle, then thought better of drinking any more and sighed heavily, throwing her head back on the couch. The movement flung her hair about her head like a yellow whorl of silk, coming to rest on the black leather cushion like a halo. She had the power to enchant her hair so that it made men give her whatever she asked for, but I was beginning to think she hardly needed to use magic on it. The white column of her neck beckoned, and my eyes followed the arrowhead formed by the hollow of her throat and her collarbones, downward to linger on her—*baseball*. Focus, Atticus! Any kind of liaison with Malina would not end happily.

"We have to find them first," she said, "which is the point of tonight's divination. Once we know where they are, we can fight back from here. Nothing so dramatic as eight simultaneous hexes, but we will pick off one here and one there until you are ready to confront them directly. I will keep you informed. And when the Bacchants get here—most likely tomorrow night—I'll let you know where they are as well."

"Then I suppose there is nothing left to discuss except whatever you have of mine that you really shouldn't."

"Ah, yes." Malina pushed herself up from the couch and put her wine bottle on the coffee table, weaving a bit on her boot heels. She gathered her hair and tied it back in a knot, talking affably to me as she led me to a bedroom currently doing service as a witch supply closet. "I do hope we'll get around to signing the nonaggression treaty soon, Mr. O'Sullivan, for despite your uncomfortable questioning when you arrived and your barbaric insistence on walking around with your sword hanging out, I feel we can live and work together peaceably going forward and even prosper, once these current troubles are behind us."

That wasn't English she was speaking: It was the language of diplomacy. "I have no objections to peace and prosperity," I allowed.

Malina's witch closet, in contrast to the décor of her living area, was painted a pale moss green and lined with cedar shelves sporting rows of glass bottles. I tried to find one with something unspeakable in it—a human brain or deer lips or otter balls—but saw nothing but herbs, oils, philtres, and a curious collection of claws from big cats. She had claws from tigers, snow leopards, lions, and black jaguars, as well as cheetahs, cougars, and bobcats. She also had beaks from several birds of prey, but otherwise her supplies were entirely plant-based.

In the center of the room was a wooden worktable bought from IKEA's kitchen department. It supported the obligatory mortar and pestle, a knife for chopping, a peeler for tubers, and an electric hot plate she had plugged in via extension cord. I was vaguely disappointed to see she had a regular saucepan resting on the hot plate rather than a black iron cauldron—and even more disappointed that there wasn't a hapless amphibian in there. A smaller copy of the large painting in the living room hung opposite the worktable; the three Zoryas watched from the walls, waiting to bestow their blessings on Malina's work.

"Who supplies your herbs?" I asked. "I could probably be of assistance if you're having trouble finding something of sufficient quality and freshness."

"We get most everything at an herbalist in Chandler," Malina said, "though I'm sure we're going to need much more bloodwort shortly if we're to deal properly with the *hexen*. Have you any available?"

Bloodwort was one of many common names for yarrow. Witches used it in some divination spells, but it could also be used in spells of both protection and attack. For my part, I employed it extensively in my apothecary business, including in several proprietary tea blends: Virus Immuni-Tea for the onset of colds and flu, Digestive Facili-Tea for various gastrointestinal ills, and a truly trippy mixture I called Enhanced Visibili-Tea. I made the latter for artists who wanted to see the world differently, because, in sufficient concentrations, yarrow could cause a temporary color shift in the eyes.

"Sure, I have pounds of the stuff, because I use it all the time. I grow it in my backyard, all organic and very potent. How much do you need?"

"Three pounds should safely see us through." Malina nodded. "Could you have someone bring it to us?"

"Certainly. I'll send a courier in the morning. You can pay him. I'll send along a list of my other herbs in stock, too, and another list of what I can grow for you provided that you give me sufficient notice."

"Good, let there be commerce between us." Malina moved over to a shelf near the painting of the Zoryas and looked at an uncorked, unlabeled bottle—also uninhabited by anything that I could see. Sitting next to it on the left, and stretching down the length of the shelf as well as two shelves above it, were jars containing locks of hair with people's names labeled on the front. All of those people were completely in Malina's power, whether they knew it yet or not. I felt a twinge of pity for them.

"It should be here," Malina said tensely. "The last person to visit this floor was the officer who informed us of Waclawa's death." She pointed to the labeled jar next to the empty one. Inside was a lock of sandy hair, and emblazoned on the label in purple ink was the name of Kyle Geffert. "Your hair should have been deposited in this empty bottle here," she said, then looked up to the air vent through which her air-conditioning was softly blowing. Presumably any hair collected from visitors in the hallway got routed through the ductwork to land in the empty bottles, but nary a red hair from my head was to be found in any of them.

"What in the name of Zorya Utrennyaya is going on?" Malina scolded the bottle as if it would answer her, and I fought to keep a smile off my face.

Ha-ha. My personal binding was stronger than her enchantment. Neener neener, Malina. You can't catch me.

CHAPTER 6

Washing a filthy Irish wolfhound is entirely unlike washing a Chihuahua. It takes three or four buckets of water just to get the wolfhound thoroughly wet, for example, while one bucket will most likely drown the Chihuahua.

I have discovered over the years that if I wish to remain fairly dry through the process, I must distract Oberon from the tickling of bubbles and soap with a really good story, or else he will shake himself mightily and spray water and foam on every wall of my bathroom. Bath time is therefore story time in my house, and Oberon enjoys getting cleaned up as a result.

What I enjoy is Oberon's obsession with the story until the next one gets told. He'd been vicariously living out the life of Genghis Khan for the past three weeks, constantly badgering me to muster the hordes on the Mongolian steppe and start a land war in Asia. Now I planned to take him in a completely different direction.

"When we were messing with Mr. Semerdjian's head earlier," I said as I began to soak him, "you asked me who the Merry Pranksters were. Well, the Merry Pranksters were a group of people who joined Ken Kesey on the magic bus in 1964 for his trip to New York from California."

<Ken Kesey had a magic bus? What could it do?>

"Its primary talent was scaring the hell out of social conservatives. It was an old school bus painted in Day-Glo colors—really bright fluorescents—and given the name of Furthur."

<So Kesey was some kind of warlock?>

"No, just a gifted writer. But I suppose his magic bus started the cultural revolution of the sixties, so that's pretty powerful magic. The Pranksters would give away acid for free to whoever wanted it in an effort to shake people out of their dreary lives of conformity. Acid was legal then."

<Wait, you never told me what acid was.>

"It's the street name for LSD."

<I thought the street name for that was Mormon.>

"No, that's LDS. LSD is a drug, and they called it acid because the full name was lysergic acid diethylamide."

<That sounds like it comes with lots of side effects.>

"Fewer than most prescriptions nowadays," I said, applying a sudsy sponge to Oberon's back. "But back to the Pranksters. They dressed in Day-Glo colors too, tie-dyes and funky hats, and all had really cool nicknames like Mountain Girl, Gretchen Fetchin, and Wavy Gravy."

<Wavy Gravy? Seriously?>

"Every word is true or I am the son of a goat." I had him now.

<Wow! That's the coolest name I have ever heard in my life! What did Wavy Gravy do?>

So I told Oberon all about Wavy Gravy and the Electric Kool-Aid Acid Tests, the origin of the Grateful Dead, the entire hippie scene, and the moral imperative to Stick It to the Man. I made sure he understood that Mr. Semerdjian was the Man and we had been sticking it to him really good so far. He came out of the bath all clean and ready to put on a tie-dye shirt with a peace sign on it.

As Oberon paraded around our living room spreading peace and gravy (Gravy is Love, he explained), my subconscious chose that moment to allow a bubble of memory to boil up to the surface: Did Mr.

Semerdjian really say he had a rocket-propelled grenade in his garage?

I didn't think those were available at gun shows, so I put it on my list of things to investigate, then hit the pillow, grateful to have survived another day.

CHAPTER 7

I made sure to make a proper breakfast in the morning, since I would be off fighting demons: a fluffy omelet stuffed with feta cheese, diced tomatoes, and spinach (sprinkled with Tabasco), complemented by toast spread with orange marmalade, and a hot mug of shade-grown Fair Trade organic coffee.

Having slept on it, I decided that the only thing to do about the Bacchants was to make somebody else get rid of them. It would cost me—perhaps dearly—but I'd live through it and so would Granuaile. I'd considered using wooden weapons, or perhaps bronze or glass ones, but, regardless of weaponry, I'd still have twelve or so insanely strong women to defeat and no defense against catching their madness.

It was time to work the phones. First I called Gunnar Magnusson, leader of the Tempe Pack and head of Magnusson and Hauk, the law firm that represented me. Werewolves wouldn't be affected by the Bacchants' magic. He received me coldly and rebuffed me in short order.

"My pack will not be getting involved in your territorial pissing match," he said. "If you have legal matters to attend to, then by all means call upon Hal or Leif. But do not think of my pack as your personal squad of supernatural mercenaries to call on every time you get into trouble."

Clearly he'd been stewing over the aftermath of our battle with Aenghus Óg and Malina's coven. Two pack members had died that night in an effort to rescue Hal and Oberon. There was no use arguing with him in such a mood, so I simply said, "I beg your pardon. May harmony find you."

It seemed I had plenty of fences to mend with my lawyers. It would be futile to call Leif; for one thing he was hiding from the sun at this time of day, and for another he'd want me to go after Thor in exchange for his help with the Bacchants.

Though I didn't want to do it, I placed a call to North Carolina, dialing a number Granuaile had given me when she returned from there last week. It was the number of Laksha Kulasekaran, an Indian witch who now went by the name of Selai Chamkanni. The name change was necessary because Laksha's spirit now inhabited the body of Selai, a Pashtun immigrant from Pakistan who had been in a coma for a year after an auto accident. Since Selai had already become an American citizen years ago and had convenient documents and bank accounts already in place—and, more importantly, no desire to awaken from her coma—Laksha slipped out of Granuaile's head and into Selai's, thereby acquiring such accoutrements as a house and a husband.

The husband was foremost in Laksha's mind when I asked how she was adjusting to her new life.

"He is disturbed that I emerged from a coma with a strange accent and a new sense of independence but so thrilled that I seem to have lost all sexual inhibitions that he's willing to overlook my disrespect."

"Men are so predictable, are they not?" I grinned into the phone.

"For the most part. You have managed to surprise me so far," she replied.

"I'd like to invite you back to Arizona for a short while."

"See? That is most surprising."

"Killing Radomila and half her coven has left something of a power vacuum in the area, and some undesirable things are rushing in to fill it. I could use your help, Selai."

"Please, when we are in private, continue to call me Laksha. What kind of undesirables are you dealing with?"

"Bacchants."

"Real Bacchants?" Her voice sharpened. "Genuine maenads from the Old World?"

"They're coming here by way of Las Vegas, but, yes, they are that kind."

"Ah, then that sword of yours will be of no use against them."

"Right," I agreed. "Could you catch a plane out here? I will pay for it."

"You will pay for much more than the plane," Laksha said. "You want me to bring karma to these Bacchants, am I correct?"

"Yes," I admitted. "My old archdruid would have said the only good Bacchant is a dead Bacchant."

"But by doing so I will increase my bad karma, and I have a dire karmic debt as it is. You will owe me a great service in return."

"I can pay you a significant sum of money."

"I do not speak of money. I will require a service of you, as you are requiring a service of me."

"What kind of service?"

"The sort that you can perform and I cannot. I will call you from the airport when I arrive and explain then. It will probably be late in the afternoon or the evening by the time I get there."

"That's fine. I will look forward to seeing you, Laksha."

I tried to think of what service a scary body-snatching witch might require of me, but after a few seconds I dismissed it as idle specula-tion when I had other things to do. I called my apprentice to give her instructions for the morning.

"Atticus? Are you all right?" she asked when I called her. "You kind of worried me last night."

"Sorry about that," I said, blushing in embarrassment and glad she could not see. "I was demented after fending off a demon attack. I'm going out to kill another one—a big one—with Coyote, but I should be back after lunch. Couple things I need you to do. Got a pen?"

Granuaile snagged something to write with and took down Malina's name and address for the yarrow delivery. "Don't go yourself; make sure it's a courier." I didn't want my apprentice unwittingly delivering her hair into one of Malina's glass jars. "Then have Perry show you where we keep the applications—I need to hire some more help. Thumb through those, make some calls, and line up a few interviews for later this afternoon. If they're still unemployed, they should be available."

"You seriously need more help? It's been dead in here."

"I'm going to be gone more often. That dead patch of land out by Tony Cabin needs my attention. It won't come back for centuries without my help." Aenghus Óg had killed many square miles of the earth by opening his portal to hell, and while he would be paying for it by spending eternity burning there, the land was still barren and cried out for aid.

"Oh, yeah, absolutely. Won't you need a car for that, though?"

"Nope. You get to drive me, so you'll be gone more often too."

"Okay, now it makes sense."

"That's what senseis do. While I'm gone and it's dead in there, work on your Latin, using that software I bought you."

After ringing off with Granuaile, it was time to rummage around in my garage. It held all sorts of things instead of a car—shuriken, sai, a couple of shields, fishing tackle, and plenty of gardening tools. It was also where I stored my bow, a modern compound number with ridiculous pull on it. I couldn't draw it without magically boosting my strength; I figured it should give the demon something to howl about. I also found a quiver full of carbon steel arrows and set them next to my bow near the front door.

With an hour to kill before Coyote was due to arrive, I jogged up Roosevelt Street with Oberon to visit the widow MacDonagh and pay some attention to her lawn.

It was only nine in the morning, but she was already out on her porch sipping a glass of Tullamore Dew on the rocks and reading a hard-boiled mystery novel. Her weathered face split into a wide smile when she saw Oberon and me trotting up her driveway.

"Ah, me dear lad Atticus!" she cried, setting down her novel but not her glass. "Yer a fine bloom o' spring on a cloudy fall day, an' that's no lie."

I chuckled at her poetic greeting. "Good mornin', Mrs. Mac-Donagh. You could lift a lonely man's heart from fifty leagues away."

"Tish! I'll have to be bakin' ye some brownies for that spot o' blarney there. 'Tis yerself that's good for the heart. Come here and give us a hug."

She rose from her rocking chair, glass in hand, and opened her arms to me. She was wearing a white cotton dress printed with a blue floral pattern, and a navy shawl was draped about her shoulders; it was finally getting chilly in Tempe, and it looked as if a cold rain would soon fall to renew the desert. She patted my back as we embraced briefly and she said, "I can't imagine such a handsome lad as yerself bein' lonely fer any reason, but it's God's truth that I'm that happy to see ye whenever ye stop by—Oh, hello, Oberon! That's a colorful bit o' clothing yer wearing." She scratched behind his ears, and Oberon's tail thumped against her porch rails. "Ah, yer a good hound, aren't ye?"

<Tell her I'm a Peace Dawg, but I think her cats are closely allied with the Man. I'm going to stick it to them.>

"Can I get ye somethin' cold to drink, Atticus? A finger o' the Irish, perhaps?"

"Oh, no, thank you. I must be off soon enough to fight some hellspawn, and I can't be impaired in the slightest." The widow had abruptly learned that I was a Druid shortly after she learned that werewolves weren't just the stuff of legend. When most people are confronted with a paradigm shift like that, their clutch burns out and they need a new mental transmission. The widow, however, had hardly lost any speed, taking it all in stride and even mothering me a bit when I showed her my missing ear. She'd given me a tube of smelly ointment from Walgreens, unaware that I could make much better for myself from scratch.

"Ah, fighting more demons, are ye? Well, won't Father Howard be pleased to hear that?" She chuckled. She moved back to her rocking chair and invited me to take a seat next to her.

"Father Howard?" I frowned. "You've told your priest I'm a Druid?"

"Tish, I'm still not that daft, me boy. And even if I were, it's not like he'd be believin' me. To him I'm no more'n that saucy Katie Mac-Donagh what comes to Mass mellow ev'ry Sunday; he won't be payin' me no never mind regardless o' what I say."

<Going to church drunk—I mean mellow—that's pretty groovy. If the magic bus came through here now, I bet she'd hop on.>

"You think Father Howard discounts you, or takes you for granted?"

"Oh, g'wan with ye now! Of course he doesn't!"

"Okay, sorry, but I had to ask."

The widow's face fell and she stared out at her lawn. "Well, now, maybe he does a bit." She turned quickly and shook a finger at me. "But only a bit, mind!"

"How so?"

"Ah. Well, y'know I'm the oldest parishioner what goes there. He's quite the youngster himself, and he's there to minister to the college lot. Here I am a widow whose soul isn't in any danger from temptation, so why worry about me then? I'm a settled issue fer him. Now, I know it's probably just me vanity talkin', but I suppose it'd be nice not to feel taken for granted."

"Of course. You deserve to feel appreciated."

"Especially since I might be helping to keep the universe ticking, right? Wasn't that the gist of what y'were trying to tell me before ye ran over there," she waved toward the Superstition Mountains, "and got yer ear chewed off?"

"Sorry." I shook my head, trying to clear it of her coarse phrasing. "I don't quite follow you. Remind me of what I said."

"Ye said all the gods are alive. All the monsters too."

"Oh, right. They're all alive, except for the ones that are dead."

<I think you should submit that statement to win the Nobel Obvious Prize,> Oberon said.

"And the impression I got was they're alive because we believe in them, right?"

"Um. With lots of fine print, right."

"So in a sense it's we with faith who create gods, not the gods who create us. And, if that's the case, then it's we who created the universe."

"I think that might be taking a big step into the windowless room of solipsism. But I see your point, Mrs. MacDonagh. A person like you with such powerful faith should not be ignored. Why, faithful people around the world have made miracles happen."

"Really? How do they do that?"

"You've heard of people having visions of the Virgin Mary?"

"Sure, all the time."

"Those are created by faith. You could probably make one happen."

"All by meself?"

I nodded. "Absolutely. Mrs. MacDonagh, when you think of Mary, what does she look like to you? Could you visualize her clearly for me, describe her to me?"

"Why, sure I can. 'Twouldn't be a very good Catholic if I couldn't, now would I?"

"If Mary were to appear on this earth now, what do you think she'd look like?"

The widow seemed pleased to be asked. "Ah, she'd have the patience of eternity in her eyes, she would, and the beatitudes in her smile. I suppose she'd be dressed sensibly for the modern world—to blend in, y'know, something cotton and navy blue."

"Why navy blue?"

"I don't know, it's just what I associate with her. She's not the flamboyant turquoise type, is she now?"

"All right, go on. What sort of shoes?"

"The sensible kind. But classy, y'know, not cheap tennis shoes made by a poor wee girl in a sweatshop."

"Would she wear one of those habits, the elaborate headgear you always see in churches?"

"I should think not. It's hardly the fashion anymore. A simple white headband keepin' her hair out of her eyes would be the thing."

"And if she came here, to Tempe, what do you think she would want to do?"

"A saintly woman like that? She'd probably be down on Apache Boulevard, ministering to the homeless and the methamphetamine addicts—what do they call 'em, that slang term?"

"Tweekers."

"Right. She'd be helpin' the tweekers, she would, down on Apache Boulevard."

<Ever notice how Apache Boulevard is a lot like Mos Eisley? "You will never find a more wretched hive of scum and villainy.">

When Oberon says things like that, it takes all my will not to dive into a *Star Wars* nerdfest; I resolutely ignored him, because I had to get the widow in the proper frame of mind. "That's lovely, Mrs. Mac-Donagh. Sure she would work a powerful lot of good on Apache Boulevard. Why, if she were down there, she could help me slay this demon from hell by blessing my weapons."

"That's right, she could. Wouldn't that be divine?"

Oberon and I examined her expression and found a tiny smile on the widow's face, pleasant yet inscrutable. <Does she realize she made a pun?> Oberon asked.

I don't know. I can't tell.

<Dude. She's pranking us right now. She's totally On the Bus.>

"Mrs. MacDonagh, I want you to concentrate, or rather meditate on this—no, I want you to *pray* that this happens today, right now, putting all your faith into the power of Mary's miraculous healing and the good work she would do ministering to the addicts on Apache Boulevard. Picture her in your mind as clearly as you can."

"And ye think if I do that, then Mary will come down from heaven and walk the boulevard, freein' people from addiction and tellin' them to go and sin no more?"

"It's entirely possible. Depends on how she's feeling today."

"Well, o' course she's feelin' dandy!" the widow scolded me. "She's the mother o' God, for the love o' Pete!"

"Yes, but Mary has free will, does she not? You would not imagine her as beholden to your prayers. She can decide for herself whether she would like to be made manifest in the image you offer—whether she should intercede or not. Aren't all prayers based on this assumption?"

"Well, I suppose they are. But it's so strange to think of it like that. It's all backward."

"It's only a slight modification of causality. Faith is the bedrock of it all. It doesn't work without your faith. No religion does. As a pagan who subscribes to a completely different pantheon, I could never induce Mary to come here."

"But Atticus, how can my one wee prayer—"

"Faith, Mrs. MacDonagh! Faith! If you want a scientific explanation, I cannot give you one. Science cannot close the fist of reason around the miracle of consciousness any more than I can turn my sword into a light saber."

<Now, that would be wicked cool! You could dress in one of those brown robes and trade insipid lines of dialogue with your padawan, Granuaile.>

Not now, Oberon.

<Admit it. You're vaguely disappointed with her calling you Sensei. Secretly you want her to call you Master.>

Gods Below, go inside and chase the cats already! "Begging your pardon," I said to the widow, "would you mind if Oberon went inside for a bit?"

"Eh? No, me boy, not at all. Good exercise for me pussies. They're good, dog-fearing cats."

Oberon chuffed. <I like it when they hiss at me and it brings up a hairball.>

Don't break anything in there.

<Anything that breaks is always the cats' fault.>

I let him in the front door and immediately heard his joyous barks and the terrified howling of the widow's cats. The widow and I chuck-led over it together as I sat back down and she took a sip from her glass.

"So do you think you could pray over that for me?" I asked when the commotion inside died down a bit.

"The Virgin Mary on Apache Boulevard? Sure I can, if it'll make yer heart glad."

"It would," I said. "Don't forget to mention she could help me slay a demon escaped from hell. Pray hard, if there is such a thing, and focus on what she would look like and when she'd do it, which is dur-ing the next couple of hours. And while you're at it, I'll give your grass a trim."

"Attaboy," she said, and smiled beatifically at me as I rose from my chair and trotted down the porch in search of her push lawn mower. I found it in the garage and hauled it out for a bit of brisk exercise as the widow shut her eyes and began to rock softly in her chair.

I didn't know if this would work, but I had hope. Mary tended to make a lot more visits than the rest of the Christian saints and angels, and in the dozen or so times I'd run across her, it was always a result of some prayer for intercession someone had made on behalf of a group of people.

If it didn't work, then I wouldn't sweat it; I'd just take the arrows into a Catholic church and ask a priest to bless them. Anyone's strong Christian faith would be effective against the demon, but Mary's per-sonal blessing would be quite a coup if I could count it.

After finishing the lawn, I returned the mower to its place in the widow's garage and joined her on the porch. Her eyes opened after a moment and there were tears welling up in them.

"Ah, Atticus, I do hope she heard me and comes on down like ye say. I know she's been lookin' after me Sean, God rest him," she crossed herself at the mention of her deceased husband, "but I don't think he'd mind if she popped out for a bit to help some souls down here goin' through a dark patch right now. 'Twould be a mighty bless-ing, an' that's no lie. But whether she comes or no, it does me heart good to think she might and that there's hope fer those benighted people who might find God in the kindness of her smile. Thank ye fer suggestin' the prayer to me."

I took the widow's small, spotted hand and gave it a brief squeeze. We sat together on the porch and watched the storm clouds boil in from the east until it was time for me to meet Coyote.

"Off ye go, then," the widow said when I made my farewell and told Oberon it was time to leave the cats alone. "Tell Mary I love her if ye see her. Oh, and Atticus me boy?"

"Yes, Mrs. MacDonagh?"

"Maybe ye should wear a helmet this time," she teased me, "in case the demon wants to nibble on yer nose or something."

CHAPTER 8

Coyote was only five minutes late.

The tires of a Ford Escape hybrid squealed as he rounded the corner. He braked sharply in front of my house, marking the pavement and sending up the smell of burned rubber. He got out of the cab and laughed. "This here is one hot ride, Mr. Druid, yessiree!" He slapped the hood a couple of times to punctuate his enthusiasm.

"You really think so? I'd think something sportier would be more fun to drive than that."

"I meant hot as in 'freshly stolen.' Stealin' cars is almost as fun as stealin' horses used to be a couple centuries ago. You ready?"

"Yep." I held my bow, and the quiver of arrows was strapped to my back. Oberon was all set up inside with *One Flew Over the Cuckoo's Nest* on DVD. I'd promised to get him the audiobook version later so that he could appreciate the trip from inside Chief Bromden's head. "Did you remember to bring a bow?"

"Sure did. An' I got me a squirt gun filled with holy water for laughs."

"All right, then. Mind if I drive?"

Coyote laughed. "Sure, Mr. Druid. This is your rodeo. I can't wait to see where you're gonna find us some holy arrows."

"Arrows are right here," I said, jerking a thumb over my shoulder at my quiver. "They're just not holy yet."

Coyote laughed again. "You're just gonna dip 'em in holy water, aren'tcha?"

"Maybe." I grinned to hide my irritation. "Maybe not. Wait and see."

Apache Boulevard wasn't nearly as bad as Mos Eisley. After the light rail was built, developers began to reinvest in the area and tried to gentrify it. But there were still stretches of low-rent trailer parks and cheap stucco boxes that passed for shelter, unpaved driveways, and yards full of soiled mattresses and rusted car parts—visual cues in America that signify poverty and discord and a spiritual waste-land.

At a few minutes after ten in the morning, all the meth addicts were asleep and there was very little for Mary to do. The people walking around Apache Boulevard at that time all had someplace to go; they all had a shred of hope in their lives. Nevertheless, there was a small knot of people crowded around her when I saw a navy-blue dress and white headband between Martin Lane and River Drive. There were even a few stray dogs and some alley cats rubbing up against her legs, as if they were gentle domestics.

To double-check whether I was looking at a true manifestation of Mary, I activated a charm on my necklace that I call "faerie specs." It's a spell that shows me what's going on in the magical and supernatural spectrum—if there's anything more to look at than the normal collection of proteins, minerals, and water.

"Aggh!" I squeezed my eyes and turned off the specs immediately, jerking the wheel of the Ford a bit.

"What's wrong, Mr. Druid?" Coyote asked.

I blinked and saw spots. "That's definitely the Virgin. Bright white light." I turned the Ford into the first driveway I saw and put it in park. It was the entrance to a decrepit trailer park, covered in gravel and broken glass. Nothing grew there but misery and despair, the people living there cut off from nature and walking the world unbound from it.

Coyote and I got out, and I retrieved my quiver of arrows from the cargo area. As we approached, Mary was blessing a large Latino man dressed like a tough guy—an O.G. veterano, perhaps. He wore a blue bandanna and dark sunglasses, even though it was completely overcast, and his gray flannel shirt was buttoned only at the top, leaving a white T-shirt to show underneath. Tears were streaming out from underneath the sunglasses.

"Your pardon, ma'am, but I wonder if you would mind blessing these arrows for us," I said. "We're off to fight a demon."

She smiled and chuckled fondly as she addressed me. "Child," she said—she always called me that, even though I was older than she was—"I came here with no other purpose in mind."

"The widow MacDonagh wanted me to tell you she loves you," I said.

"Ah, Katie." The Virgin's smile became even brighter. "She prays to me daily, you know. And recently she's been asking to keep you safe. So you must remain safe, Mr. O'Sullivan, and return my love to her. She has a beautiful soul."

"Yes, she does."

"Let us see these arrows of yours."

Being careful with the fletching, I slowly drew the arrows out of the quiver together and then handed the quiver to Coyote. I presented them to the Virgin across both my arms, so that the heads were pointed north, to her right.

She closed her eyes, laid her hands gently on the heads, and spoke a few lines from the Benediction in the Latin Mass: "*O salutaris Hostia quae coeli pandis ostium. Bella premunt hostilia; da robur, fer auxilium.*" The form of her blessing was rather unexpected. I was hoping for an original composition, but upon reflection I supposed it was an appropriate sentiment: *Our foes press on from every side; thine aid supply, thine strength bestow.* She held on to the arrows for about ten seconds after she finished speaking. I'm sure if I had dared to use my faerie specs, I'd have seen some really interesting magic being woven around them—a split second before the light of the Virgin burned out my eyeballs.

When she finished, she opened her eyes and released the slightest bit of tension that had built up in her shoulders. She smiled benignly upon me and then widened it to include Coyote.

"The last of the Druids and one of the First Peoples are off to fight a fallen angel from the Fifth Circle."

I'd been smiling back at Mary until I processed the end of her sentence. At that point I didn't know if I'd ever smile again. "A fallen angel? One of the original host?"

Mary nodded. "Yes. It is twisted and blackened now, the light of heaven snuffed out long ago."

"Hoo-ee, Mr. Druid. Sounds like powerful medicine to me," Coyote said. He wasn't kidding. Fallen angels weren't ordinary demons. I wasn't sure Cold Fire would even work against such a being, since they were condemned to spend eternity in hell rather than spawned there.

"And the Fifth Circle," I said, "if I remember my Dante, is where the wrathful and the sullen are punished."

"That's correct, my child," Mary affirmed.

"Gods Below, how did Aenghus Óg manage to summon something that powerful?"

Mary beamed patiently at me, ignoring my invocation of a different pantheon. "I do not think he summoned it so much as provided an avenue for its escape. Still, the binding placed on it as a condition of its egress is still in effect, and that is the only thing keeping it in this area."

"Meaning that it won't leave the East Valley until I'm dead," I said.

"Whoa, it sucks to be you, Mr. Druid." Coyote chuckled and clapped me a couple of times on the shoulder. "Here, gimme those arrows." He took them from my arms and placed them back in the quiver. "I'll be waitin' in the hot vehicle. This white lady's a bit too shiny for me."

"You have an interesting assortment of friends," Mary observed as Coyote's boots crunched away on the gravel. "A Native Amercian deity, a pack of lycanthropes, a vampire, and a coven of Zorya worshippers."

"I wouldn't call them all my friends," I said. "More like acquaintances. Mrs. MacDonagh and my dog, Oberon, are my friends."

"Give the others time," Mary said kindly. "My work here is finished. Yours is just beginning, I fear. You will most likely need to pierce Basasael more than once before he is undone."

"Basasael?"

"That is his name. He was mighty before he fell with Lucifer."

"Christ," I whispered without thinking.

"My son is confident of your victory," Mary said.

"No kidding? Tell Jesus I said hi, and we should have a beer next time he's in the neighborhood."

"I will relay your greetings. Now go, child. You have my blessing upon you."

"Peace be with you," I said, and as I turned to resume my journey with Coyote, I added under my breath, "and asskicking be with me."

CHAPTER 9

"I gotta admit, Mr. Druid, I didn't think we'd be seein' anythin' like that. You kinda surprised me. How'd you know that shiny white lady'd be there?"

Coyote was dressed the same way as I had seen him the night before, except now he was wearing dark sunglasses. His expressions tended to run to either amused or inscrutable, and right now he was showing me the latter. Perhaps he mistrusted me. I shrugged my shoulders as I steered the SUV south to U.S. 60. "I just had faith, I guess."

"Pfffft. You don' have any more faith'n I do for the Christian folks."

I felt myself slipping automatically back into the rhythms of Coyote's speech. "Yeah, but I had faith in a Cath'lick friend o' mine. She did the prayin' for me."

"Well then, why didn' she just pray for Jesus to come down and smite the demon or somethin'? We coulda slept in."

"'Cause Jesus don' like to come down very much. People keep thinkin' of him bein' nailed to a cross or wearin' a crown of thorns, or else he's got huge bloody holes in his hands an' feet, an' that's just gotta be damn uncomfortable. Plus the people in these parts tend to think he was a white guy with straight brown hair, but he was dark-skinned. Shucks, I bet you know what that's like, when people think o' you like one o' them stylized sandpaintings or a fetish animal. You don't wanna go prancin' around lookin' like that, do ya?"

"Hell, no." Coyote grinned. "I tried appearin' as one o' those sand-paintings once. My body was so stretched out I completely lost track o' where my ass was."

We shared a laugh over that as we turned east onto U.S. 60 and the clouds that had been threatening to dump on us all morning finally let loose. Big fat drops splattered noisily on our vehicle, and it re-minded me of those drumrolls you hear before a circus acrobat does something remarkably dangerous without a net. I had difficulty fig-uring out how to turn on the windshield wipers, and Coyote snig-gered at me until I got them on.

"So how many fallen angels you killed afore this, Mr. Druid?"

"This'll be my first, I reckon."

"Shee-it." Coyote shook his head with a rueful grin. "We're gonna die."

I looked sharply at him. "Are you approachin' this like a suicide trip? You figgerin' it's okay to die and leave me there without no one to watch my back, 'cause you can just come back from the dead any-way? I'll tell ya right now, Coyote, I'm plannin' on livin' a long time after this. If you ain't plannin' on survivin', tell me straight and I'll go get someone else to help me."

"Aw, cool your britches, Mr. Druid. I ain't gonna walk on up to 'im and ask 'im to eat me." Coyote threw up his hands. "All I'm sayin' is this ain't gonna be no picnic. A fallen angel's gonna be a far sight smarter than a reg'lar demon, and more'n a little stronger too."

"All right, then. You got any idea where the demon is?"

"Last I saw, he was perched on one o' their buildings overlookin' a courtyard area. It's got some grass and trees in it, so you can draw power there."

"We're gonna have to go through the school building to get there, though?"

"That's what I 'spect."

"We'll have to go camouflaged. School officials tend to get worried about people bringin' weapons onto their campuses."

Skyline High School is a monolithic building of stucco-sprayed cement block trimmed in hunter green. I parked in the no-parking drop-off zone, because I just didn't care about parking etiquette. I cast camouflage on both myself and Coyote, then got out and opened the cargo area, where I camouflaged both our bows, the quiver of arrows, and Fragarach too. It didn't make us completely invisible, especially in the rain, but it sure helped. Once inside, we'd blend into the bland institutional décor without trouble. Coyote pitched in by giving us something he called "Clever Stalking," which really meant we wouldn't make any noise when we moved. (I'm not sure why he didn't call it Silent Stalking; I suppose Coyote thought it was clever of him to think stalking should be a silent exercise.)

We glided by the reception desk without disturbing the matronly woman sitting there; she seemed to be emotionally involved with a game of solitaire on her computer. There were two full-time employees working at the attendance window (because taking attendance and getting money from the state is the most important job at public schools), but they were listening to parents lie on the phone about why their children weren't in school that day, so they weren't even looking up to see what was dripping all across the industrial carpet in the hallway. The doors to the courtyard gave a high-pitched squeak when we opened them, and the sound of pouring rain caused the attendance clerks to look up, but we slipped out without them spotting us.

Class was in session and the courtyard was deserted. We were underneath a roofed area that traveled around the perimeter, providing shelter for rare rainy days like this but usually offering shade the rest of the year. Thick ropes of runoff water slapped noisily on the concrete before coursing in swift rivulets toward drainage grates.

I turned on my faerie specs and had no trouble figuring out where Basasael was lurking. He was directly across from us, perched on the steel roof, in a Doppler-shifted cloud of wrong. The feathered wings he had eons ago were now leathery and batlike. The rest of him was still humanoid in appearance, just blackened and spiky and pulsing with evil, like a subwoofer vibrating a car's windows and blurring the view.

What made him particularly repellent at the moment was his open mouth, out of which dangled another teenage victim's leg—some poor kid who'd been on his way to the nurse's office, perhaps, or called down to see the counselor. As we watched, the fallen angel's teeth crunched down and his lower jaw slid sideways in a grotesque chewing motion.

Coyote saw it at the same time I did. "Too late to help that one, I reckon," he whispered to my right. I couldn't see him in the normal spectrum, but with my faerie specs on, he looked like a colorful collection of light streams, shifting chaotically within his form but not unpleasantly—just unpredictably. I handed him six arrows out of the quiver.

"I'll put my first arrow through his head; you go for the heart," I whispered back. "Then just keep shootin' until he fuckin' dies."

"Wow, you learn all that strategy from the U.S. Army men?"

I grunted in amusement. "No, I learned it from Attila the Hun, who lived an' died without ever knowin' you were here."

The two of us drifted apart naturally, hunters of old. We did not need to discuss strategy. When it's two against one, the two should separate so that if the target counterattacks one, his back is left open to the other. When we'd formed a triangle—Coyote and I at the base and Basasael at the top—we nocked our arrows and nodded at each other. I slid out of my sandals and stepped into the rain so that I could draw power from the earth. First I filled my bear charm back up, in case I needed to cast something on the sidewalk, then I drew enough to pull back the bow, just as Basasael was finishing off his teenaged repast. I held up five fingers to Coyote, folded in my thumb, then my index finger to indicate a countdown, then pulled the bowstring to its limit. I took quick aim and let fly in time with the countdown.

I was already grabbing another arrow as our first volley sank home. My arrow pierced the fallen angel's left eye, and Coyote's thudded solidly into the center of its chest. It screeched on several wavelengths and shuddered my bones as it toppled backward onto the roof, surprised and clutching at the shafts.

Normally, if you shoot something in the head with an arrow, it doesn't have enough motor skills left to reach up and pluck the arrow out. And shooting a critter in the heart generally robs it of the strength to stand up and roar defiantly at unsafe decibel levels. Basasael wasn't normal, for he did both of those things.

A white bubbling wound was left behind in each case, but the fallen angel threw both the arrows down into the courtyard, spread his wings, and crouched in preparation to spring at one of us. He saw us both clearly; my camouflage spell kept us hidden from human eyes but not from his.

"How many arrows we gotta use to kill this thing?" Coyote yelled.

"All Mary said was we'd have to pierce it more'n once."

"Yeah? Well maybe you shoulda pinned her down to a specific number there afore we left, dumbass!"

I agreed with Coyote wholeheartedly, as we let fly with another volley. Basasael knocked Coyote's missile aside with a blurred sweep of his left arm, but mine sank directly into his swollen gut. The force of it toppled him backward again, but this time he knew better than to stay still and let us reload. Ignoring the arrow that was turning his black skin into a white froth before bubbling away to gray, he gathered his legs underneath him and launched himself straight up into the air with a single, powerful stroke of his wings and another mighty bellow of rage I could feel in my teeth. At the apex of his ascent, he folded his wings and dove after his chosen target—me.

The eternal whine of self-pity—why me?—flashed through my brain as I aimed one last shot at the fallen angel. The answers came flooding in: I looked like nothing more than a puny human weakling; I'd shot him in the head and the gut; I was standing in the open, where he could get to me easily, while Coyote was shooting from underneath the shelter of the roof; and, because of the binding Aenghus Óg had put on him, he couldn't leave the area until he killed me. I let fly with my shot and it sailed above his right shoulder, much to my chagrin. Dropping my bow because there'd be no time for another shot, I leapt back under the roof and drew Fragarach with my right hand and another blessed arrow from my quiver with my left.

I positioned myself behind one of the roof's supporting steel posts so that Basasael would have to pick a side to attack from and reduce his speed accordingly. It turned out the post was not something he considered to be an actual obstacle. He simply bashed it aside with his right arm as his wings spread to brake his flight, and the post obligingly ripped out of its moorings and buckled a portion of the roof as if it were made of Nerf rather than steel.

"Don't you feel the least bit ill right now?" I asked. I could see the courtyard through the yawning white hole in his head. It was still boiling and hissing, eating away at his substance—as were the other two wounds—but in terms of real damage it only seemed to have pissed him off.

His feet touched down on the concrete rather than the earth, so Cold Fire was out of the question; he answered me by belching a gout of bright orange flame at my face. It looked exactly like the ball of hellfire Aenghus Óg had thrown at me. "*Hey!*" I shouted as the flame passed over me, giving me a brief sensation of heat but otherwise leaving me unharmed, thanks to my amulet's protection. "You're the bastard who made a deal with Aenghus Óg! You're the one who's been behind it all!"

I heard the squeal of the office doors opening to my right: Someone was coming out to investigate what all the ruckus was. They wouldn't be able to see me or the demon, but they'd sure see the mangled post lying in the rain and a dangerously drooping roof. They'd also be in mortal danger. It's the sort of situation that gets duelists killed: a split second of distraction, flicking the eyes away for a shadow of a moment, and suddenly it's all over. Basasael was counting on it; perhaps he saw my eyes move, perhaps he didn't, but he shook off his surprise that I didn't burn and took advantage anyway. He was still a good four feet away from me, but his right arm shot toward my chest and his fingers *extended*, then his claws did likewise, telescope fashion, aiming for my heart. He wanted to pull one of those classic demon maneuvers, ripping my still-beating heart out of my chest and then laughing at me as I watched him eat it. I dodged to my right as quickly as I could, raising my left arm to let the claws pass under, but I wasn't quick enough. I felt four rotten black spikes pierce my side, scraping against the outside of my ribs and penetrating clear through to keep me pinned to the wall.

I grunted in pain and retaliated quickly, because part of him was pinned too: I drove the tip of the blessed arrow down through the back of his corrupted hand and on through the palm. He howled and yanked his hand away, withdrawing the evil claws from my side, and in that moment of reprieve I risked a quick glance to my right.

A wide-eyed female administrator in conservative dress was talking rapidly into a handheld radio. "There's some damage to the courtyard roof and some strange animal noises, but I can't tell what's making them."

"Get back inside, lady!" I yelled. "For your own safety!" That was the best I could do for her just then. Basasael looked as if he was going to move in closer and tear my head off, so I raised Fragarach in a defensive stance and winced at the burning in my side. As the fallen angel bent his knees and hissed at me, arms spread in a wrestler's stance, preparing to spring, it occurred to me that maybe Coyote should have managed to shoot an arrow or two during the fracas.

Where was the trickster? Had he taken off and left me to face the fallen angel alone? He'd been known to do that in several stories told about him: Get the white man to agree to a course of action, then take off at the critical moment and make him look like a fool. I didn't know what more I could do to this creature by myself. Four holy arrows had obviously done some physical damage; he'd loudly announced that he felt pain from them, but he still kept coming. A morbid thought wandered into my consciousness and said hello: If Basasael ate my dumb Druid ass, would the Morrigan be able to bring me back fully functional, resurrected from—what? Angel poop?

That raised another question, at once metaphysical and profane: Do angels, fallen or otherwise, have assholes?

Coyote provided an answer in singular fashion. I heard a sickening, juicy squelching noise, and Basasael forgot all about charging me. He stood straight up on his clawed toes, feet together like a wooden nutcracker doll, his black eyes bulging and his throat ululating in a *bean sidhe* howl of agony that made me clutch my ears—or, rather, my one good ear and my one mess of pathetic cartilage niblets.

Coyote shouted *"Ha!"* once and then began to yip in amusement, scampering across the courtyard in his animal shape, taunting the fallen angel, and Basasael launched himself skyward to give chase.

While he was thus diverted, I took the opportunity to sheathe Fragarach and grab the school administrator by the collar, dragging her back to the office doors. She yelped in startlement, and I shouted at her as I tossed her inside, "Put the school in lockdown *now!* Just do it before someone else gets killed!" Every school in America had a lockdown procedure they followed to keep students safe in an emergency.

"What? Who got killed?"

"Take attendance and you'll find out. It's what you're best at, because the gods know it's not teaching them English. Damn kids don't know the difference between an adjective and an adverb!" I needed to shut up. Sometimes stress can cause me to rant.

"Who are . . . ? Why can't I see you?"

"Lockdown! Attendance! Stay inside!" I slammed the door shut for extra emphasis and hoped that would galvanize her to the proper course of action. Turning back to the courtyard, I saw that Basasael was trying to fry Coyote from the air with his great balls o' fire. Coyote was thus far a mite too fast for him, but I wasn't sure how long that would last or if Coyote would be able to withstand a direct hit of hellfire.

I scurried over to where I'd dropped my bow in the courtyard. It was still camouflaged, so I couldn't see it, and it took me a few frantic moments to stumble into it. The act of bending over to pick it up exacerbated the wounds in my side, and, duly reminded of them, I drew power to close them up and begin the tissue-mending process.

Two arrows left. Coyote had presumably dropped the remainder of his somewhere. I nocked one and tried not to laugh at the image of Basasael flying around with a feathery shaft sticking out between his cheeks. I chose my own target carefully, and the bowstring thwocked as the arrow sailed up and through the fallen angel's right wing. It tore a magnificent white hole through it and began to widen, which caused Basasael to screech and tumble ignominiously to the earth—precisely where I wanted him.

"*Dóigh!*" I shouted, pointing my right index finger at him and drawing strength from the earth as I cast Cold Fire. I immediately felt weaker, as if I were suffering from low blood sugar; my muscles were like leaden weights and sluggish to obey my commands. It wasn't as bad as the first time I'd cast it, when I completely collapsed from the effort, but it was a fact that I wouldn't be pulling that bowstring again today. I'd have to lie down and spend some time recuperating.

The school's loudspeaker crackled to life, and a stern voice of authority boomed metallically off the courtyard walls. "Teachers, please go into lockdown at this time. Once again, teachers, please go into lockdown immediately."

Apparently the repeated unholy shrieks from Basasael and random jets of flame in the courtyard had convinced the administration something was amiss, and this, on top of the commands delivered from a mysterious disembodied voice who seemed dissatisfied with the school's English instruction, compelled them to act.

Basasael began to rise slowly from the ground, the arrows clearly (and finally) bothering him now. As yet he betrayed no sign that the Cold Fire was working on him, but I had hope it would take effect in short order.

Coyote, returned to human form, had dashed back to where his bow and arrows were and called to me, "What'd ya do to him, Mr. Druid?"

"I'm not sure if I did anything," I called back. "You might wanna shoot him a couple more times."

"Oh yeah, that brilliant strategy ya learned from Attila the Hun. Almost forgot."

As Coyote nocked an arrow and began to pull the bowstring, Basasael was ripping the arrows from his hand and his belly and making horrible noises in the process. He was gingerly trying to deal with the final arrow (Mercutio's phrase about the "blind bow-boy's butt shaft" took on new meaning in this situation) when Coyote's shot took him straight in the throat, choking off all further screams. It allowed us to hear the sound of approaching police sirens.

"Yeah!" Coyote whooped and pumped his fist. "Sit down and have a tall glass of shut-the-hell-up!"

I was quickly turning loopy because, as the fallen angel was nonverbally communicating his distress with an impressive array of spastic twitches and concomitant white ejecta from his wounds, I was thinking, *It's too bad we'll never get a chance to talk over a cup of tea.* Besides the Morrigan, I rarely had conversations with beings older than I was, and I treasured them whenever they happened along.

My doubts about whether Cold Fire would work on a fallen angel were soon allayed: The bubbling mess inside Basasael's wounds began to spread all over his body, so that his legs and arms were roiling like maggots running rampant under a corpse's skin. The next second, he tried to curl inward on himself in a mockery of the fetal position, and then he exploded in a slimy mass of purulence and gore. His tarlike substance polluted the courtyard, covering grass, trees, steel, and cement alike with the remains of the partially digested teenager splattered liberally amongst the mess. The falling rain was a benediction now, for the earth had been cleansed of an ancient evil, but it would never be able to wash this away before school got out, much less before the cops got here.

"That's *right*, son!" Coyote shouted at the remains. "You don' come into *my* house an' 'spect to live!"

"By Balor's evil eye, what are we going to do about all this goo?" I said.

"What's this 'we' you talkin' about, Mr. Druid? Ain't my demon, an' it ain't my mess."

"Yeah, I know. But I can't get any ghouls out here now to clean it up. People are gonna have to deal with it and rationalize it away somehow. They can call the Ghostbusters to take a sample o' the ectoplasmic discharge or whatever. Or they'll have to bring in Mulder an' Scully, because there ain't no CSI on the planet that'll ever be able to explain this."

"I have no idea what you're talkin' about, Mr. Druid."

I didn't care to explain. I just pointed at the carnage and said, "This right here will be the birthplace of a thousand conspiracy theories about aliens an' most likely a sign of the comin' apocalypse. You watch, it'll be in the *Weekly World News*."

Coyote shrugged. "Hey, I don' care. It'll be a damn funny story whatever they come up with."

"We should get the arrows," I said. "Better not leave them lyin' around."

"Yeah, good idea," Coyote replied. I put my sandals back on before venturing out to wade amongst the hellish mess, then joined Coyote in tracking down the arrows. Police officers began to stream into the courtyard, but we kept our mouths shut, knowing that they wouldn't be able to hear us or see us, except as a flicker of movement they'd dismiss as a trick of the rain.

Once the quiver was full again, we dodged around a few police officers and administrative types to get back to the office door. I remembered one last detail before we left the scene: I had to get rid of any blood that may have dropped after Basasael stabbed me. I found a few drops near the wall, not as much as I'd feared; it had mostly been soaked up by my shirt. I grabbed a few handfuls of water from the continuing runoff and washed it away, erasing evidence for the coming forensics specialists and leaving nothing behind for witches.

The bell rang, signaling the end of class and beginning of lunchtime. Since the school was in lockdown, the kids would remain in class and simply go hungry for a while. But they'd be safe now.

Feeling pretty good about ourselves, the two of us walked back through the office building to our stolen SUV waiting in the drop-off zone. It was surrounded by police cars. Oh well.

We kept the camouflage on and walked south, thoroughly drenched and starting to get cold. "There's another high school just south o' the freeway," Coyote explained once we were a safe distance from the office, lazily gesturing down Crismon Road. "It's called Desert Ridge. Parkin' lot full o' unattended cars there to steal."

"Think I'll just call myself a taxi at that convenience store there," I replied, pointing to a friendly red-and-white logo glowing dimly through the rain. "I've caused enough grief for high school students today. These poor Skyline—what are they?" I couldn't think of their mascot, and I turned back to their marquee sign to check. It said HOME OF THE COYOTES, and I swore in Old Irish with such prolixity my father would have been proud.

Coyote was already laughing and putting distance between us. He knew I'd be annoyed at being tricked, and I was.

"Not in *your* house, eh? Did one of the Diné even die back there?" I challenged him. "You lied to me about that maiden gettin' eaten, didn't you?"

"Yep, only white people died." Coyote grinned wickedly. "But I didn't wanna let you wait aroun' until one o' my people became his breakfast, because I do have some o' my people at this school and I did wanna protect 'em."

"So you put me at tremendous risk? I wasn't really ready to confront this guy. I wanted to take him on at my place of power on my own terms."

"Now, don' be mad, Mr. Druid. I helped you take care of a big problem. You mighta not made it if it weren't for me."

"Yeah, what about that? You took your sweet time getting 'round to helpin' when he came after me."

"Well, y'know, I just couldn't resist doin' it the way I did it. You know how people are always threatenin' to shove this or that up someone's ass, but they never really do it? Well, now there's a new story gonna be told 'round the fire: 'How Coyote Shoved an Arrow Up a Fallen Angel's Ass.' Can't wait to hear myself tell it! An' don't you worry, Mr. Druid, I'll make sure to include how I got the best o' you!" He melted into his animal form and trotted off into the rain, yipping his merriment and grinning back at me over his shoulder.

CHAPTER 10

I spent most of the cab ride home muttering about thrice-cursed trickster gods, but by the end of it I was smiling in spite of myself. I wasn't the first guy who'd been tricked by Coyote, and I wouldn't be the last. I'd actually gotten off pretty lightly, walking away with nothing more than a flesh wound.

Lunch with Oberon was unusually relaxing, perhaps because I'd rid myself of a large piece of unfinished business. My hound had five Weisswurst sausages, and I had peanut butter and orange marmalade on wheat with a glass of milk. Oberon wanted to discuss what he'd seen in *One Flew Over the Cuckoo's Nest,* how Nurse Ratched was really the Man and how Wavy Gravy would have shown her a thing or two if he'd been there. He wanted to talk about where Chief Bromden went at the end, whether I thought he went back to the Columbia River or whether he might have gone out to fight against the Combine. He also, very somberly, wanted to talk about end-of-life decisions.

<If the Man ever cuts out half my brain and I'm a vegetable like McMurphy,> he said, <then I want you to do what Chief did, okay?>

I didn't know what to say. Chief had smothered McMurphy with a pillow. I unexpectedly teared up just thinking about it and scratched him behind the ears. Then that wasn't enough, so I squatted down and gave him a hug. Oberon didn't know it, but he had already outlived every Irish wolfhound that had ever walked the earth. The tragedy of his magnificent breed is their fairly short life span, only six or seven years. But I'd been giving Oberon the same blend of herbs and magic that kept me looking and feeling twenty-one instead of twenty-one hundred, a brew I jokingly called Immortali-Tea. Oberon was now fifteen and had no idea that he should have been dead years ago, not running around with the energy and strength of a three-year-old adult. *Okay, buddy,* I finally said.

Before I could descend further into maudlin sentiment, my cell phone began to play "Witchy Woman," an Eagles ringtone I'd downloaded especially for Malina's calls.

I walked out to my backyard before answering it, deciding to recharge a bit while I spoke with her. She thanked me for the shipment of bloodwort and made polite noises about its superior quality; I made polite noises back, thanking her for her business; and I thought all the while that it was good to be back to our formal relationship. Then she got down to the business I wanted to hear.

"We were able to confirm in last night's ritual that *die Töchter des dritten Hauses* are here in the East Valley, but we were sadly unable to pinpoint their precise location."

"Then you have both my congratulations and condolences. Any ideas on why you couldn't get a clearer picture?"

"Perhaps our effectiveness is reduced with only six of us left. Perhaps they have cast some sort of cloak about themselves that we are unable to penetrate. Most likely it is a little bit of both," she said. "We will try again tonight. Did you try divining their location yourself?"

"No, I haven't had the time to use my own methods," I said. "Kind of had a busy morning. I ought to have some time to try after work."

"I doubt you will have any time at all. We also performed our divination ritual to locate the Bacchants and had much more success. They are here—twelve of them, to be exact—and they plan to begin causing mischief in Scottsdale this evening. Saturnalian orgies will ensue unless you intervene."

"Is it truly important I intervene tonight?" I hadn't heard anything more from Laksha, and I might not have an effective way of doing so. "What lasting damage could one night of true bacchanalia really do to Scottsdale?"

"Mr. O'Sullivan. Bacchanalia will spread disease. It will ruin marriages and other relationships, causing untold emotional distress and greater economic damage through divorce. It encourages a lifestyle of reckless behavior and moral turpitude, and participants often become criminals in short order."

"That sounds like a weekend at the Phoenix Open."

"I am not joking. People occasionally die from their exertions, which we clearly cannot allow. And, besides that, the Bacchants will significantly increase their numbers if unchecked, and you will have a bigger problem the longer you wait."

"Well, wait a second, you said before that these Bacchants have been in Las Vegas for years."

"That is correct."

"Well then, why isn't Vegas all jacked up? Oh."

"Yes?"

"I think the question answered itself. I beg your pardon."

"Granted. They will be at a nightclub called Satyrn on Scottsdale Road. It's fairly upscale. You will need to make an effort to appear a little less scruffy."

She was baiting me, but I wasn't going to bite. "Will you say scruffy one more time for me, please?"

"Scruffy. Why?"

"I'm trying to learn your accent."

Her voice grew chilly and her accent became more pronounced. "I'm sure you have much more important things to do, as do I. Good day."

I grinned as I put away my phone. She was funny when she got herself in a snit.

Biking to work actually took some effort on my part, drained as I was from using Cold Fire. I'd have to spend the night recuperating in the backyard to recharge my depleted cells.

The widow waved to me as I trundled past.

"Did ye see Mary, then?" she called.

"Sure did!" I gave her a thumbs-up. "I'll come sit with you after work and tell you all about it."

"Ah, that'll be grand!"

The book side of Third Eye Books and Herbs doesn't need much of my personal attention anymore. With automated inventory control, the computer orders another copy for me whenever I sell something. Perry Thomas, my employee for more than two years and the cheeriest Goth kid I've ever met, could almost run the whole thing for me. He was always restocking Karen Armstrong's books, because they tended to move pretty well, along with books about Wicca and primers on Taoism or Zen Buddhism.

What Perry cannot do is run the apothecary side of things, except on the most basic level: If I point to premade sachets of certain proprietary blended teas and say, "Add hot water," he's all over it, and he happily serves my arthritic customers who come in every day for a shot of Mobili-Tea. But he cannot mix herbs on his own, cannot recognize when we're low on one herb or have too much of another, and he's simply not allowed to sell bulk herbs to anyone, because he's incapable of warning them about the herbs' dangerous properties.

He greeted me with a wave and a "'Sup, Atticus," when I jangled the bells above my door. He was restocking some books that predicted the end of the world based on what Mayan mystics said fourteen centuries ago.

Granuaile was sitting behind the apothecary counter, headphones jacked into a laptop and practicing her Latin as I had asked. Only at it for a week, she was already able to trade basic sentences with me. She didn't hear the bells tingle due to the headphones, but she saw me peripherally after a moment and flashed me a smile of about 1.21 gigawatts.

I quickly reflected that the Diamondbacks' bullpen had been remarkably shoddy last season and they had better find a solution before spring training began. Brighid be thanked, Granuaile was now fully dressed and seemed unaware that she made me dizzy at times.

A couple of ASU professors were drinking tea at one of the tables and talking politics. A small, hairy man amused me for a while with the questions he asked Perry. First he wanted to find something about the Elder Gods (he'd clearly been reading too much Lovecraft), then he wanted a book about howling dervishes, not whirling dervishes, and then wondered if we stocked anything about the mysteries of the Rosicrucians. Perry showed him what we had in each case, but nothing seemed to satisfy him, and he finally purchased only a dollar's worth of sandalwood incense. Such is life in retail.

"Three people are coming in around four o'clock for interviews," Granuaile said as I began making sachets of my most popular teas. "They all sound inordinately excited about ringing up books and boiling water."

"It's a glamorous career, no doubt about it," I replied. "Are you missing Rúla Búla already?"

"A little bit," she admitted. "Not that you're not keeping me busy"—she waved at the computer screen that was coaching her on conjugating some Latin verbs—"I just miss the people and the atmosphere."

"Me too," I said. "Think they'd let you come back and work once a week, and let me come back and spend my money there?"

Granuaile shrugged. "I can ask."

"Do, please. Oberon and I are missing the fish and chips."

The bells above the shop door chimed and two rare sights entered my shop. I think my mouth may have dropped open. A tall, lanky, elderly gentleman with a high forehead and round spectacles, dressed in black save for a white priest's collar, was followed by a shorter, younger, rounder fellow in traditional Hasidic garb. Perry greeted them with a friendly hello, and the older fellow immediately asked to see the proprietor.

"That would be me," I said. "Good afternoon, gentlemen. Is this a joke?"

"I beg your pardon?" the older fellow inquired politely, a faint smile on his narrow face. He sounded like an English butler.

"You know, a tall priest and a short rabbi walk into a pagan book-store. . . ."

"What?" He looked down at his companion, seeming to realize for the first time that he was quite a bit shorter and in fact of a different religious order than he. "Oh, gracious, I suppose it must seem amus-ing at that." He didn't seem amused, though.

"How may I help you today?" I asked.

"Ah. Yes. Well, I am Father Gregory Fletcher, and this is the Rabbi Yosef Zalman Bialik. We were hoping to speak to Atticus O'Sullivan."

"Well, hope no more." I grinned at them. "You're talkin' to him."

I laid on the college kid's informality pretty thick. These fellows didn't look right to me, and until I knew what they were after, they weren't going to see anything but the façade I presented to the gen-eral public. Their auras were perfectly human, but they churned with lust—not the carnal kind; rather, the lust for power—and that wasn't consistent with peaceful men of God. Plus, the rabbi's aura betrayed the slim white interference of a magic user.

"Oh, I beg your pardon. You seem rather young for a man of your reputation."

"I didn't know I had a reputation amongst the clergy."

"In some . . ." the priest paused, searching for the right word, then continued, ". . . small circles, we have heard of you."

"Really? What kind of circles?"

Father Gregory ignored my query and responded with another. "Well, if you'll forgive the direct question, were you involved in an unusual situation in the Superstition Mountains about three weeks ago?"

I looked blankly at him, and then at the rabbi, and told a whopper. "Nope, never been out there."

"*On ne gavarit pravdu,*" the rabbi said in Russian, speaking for the first time. *He is not telling the truth.* Father Gregory responded fluently in the same language, telling Yosef to be quiet and let him handle things. If they thought I couldn't understand Russian, I didn't want to disabuse them of the notion.

"Hey, I'm an American," I said, "and the only language I speak is English, and not too good neither. When you speak that other stuff, it makes me think you're sayin' something rude about me."

"I beg your pardon," Father Gregory said. "Were you perhaps at Skyline High School this morning?"

That question nearly triggered a flare of my nostrils. It took me to new heights of paranoia, and I struggled to maintain my mask of indifference. I knew that word of Aenghus Óg's death had gotten around, but nobody should know about the fallen angel yet except Coyote and the Virgin Mary, and I hardly thought either of them would stop to chat with these guys.

I shook my head. "I don't even know where that is. Been here all day."

"I see," Father Gregory said, clearly disappointed. Rabbi Yosef was seething silently and turning a bit red. He knew I was shoveling shit on their boots. The priest decided to change the subject. "I've heard you have quite the collection of rare books. May I see it?"

"Of course. North wall, over there," I pointed to a group of large china cabinets full of books, all locked away and lacking any recognizable organization.

The rare-book trade is another part of my business Perry can't handle, but there's so little commerce in that area that no one complains when I'm not around to handle it. The books I have are extraordinarily rare—as in there are only one to ten copies in existence, because they're handwritten grimoires and scrolls full of real, honest-to-Dagda spells and rituals for magical masters only.

I also keep many historical secrets in there—secrets that would be a bugle call for Indiana Jones and his ilk, like the supposedly lost Sotomayor manuscript. I nearly geeked out just thinking about it being there. Pedro de Sotomayor was the scribe for Don Garcia López de Cárdenas, a lieutenant of Coronado's who took eighty days to make a two-week trip to the Grand Canyon. Garcia is famous today for being the first European to see the Grand Canyon, but, according to Sotomayor, they found a gigantic hoard of Aztec gold that the Tusayans (now known as the Hopi tribe) were keeping in trust for their southern friends under assault by Cortés. Garcia and his dirty dozen took the hoard and hid it, and Sotomayor wrote it all down because they planned to come back and get it later, cutting Coronado out of the deal. None of them ever made it back to the New World, however, and Sotomayor's manuscript "didn't survive," so history only has the word of Castañeda—a guy who didn't go with Garcia and knew nothing about what really happened—that they found nothing but a geological wonder after nearly three months. The gold is still there, on the Hopi reservation, and nobody's looking for it. I like knowing secrets like that, and I admit that when I'm all alone in the shop sometimes, I rub my hands together greedily and laugh like a one-eyed, black-mustached pirate to think that I have a bona fide treasure map locked up in my cabinet.

The cabinet looked fragile, but it was a customized job: Behind the wood veneer there was steel plate, and the glass was bulletproof; it was vacuum-sealed to prevent the further decay of the paper and bindings, and the locks opened by magic only. Around the entire thing I had set my strongest protective wards, and of course there were more wards around my entire shop.

The priest and rabbi strolled over there, hands clasped behind their backs, to peruse what I had on display. They would most likely be disappointed. Writers of spell books do not emblazon the spines with easy-to-read titles. Granuaile caught my eye as I moved to follow them, and I put a finger to my lips and then mouthed at her, "Later."

Perry had already lost interest and was back to restocking the shelves.

"What sorts of books do you have here, Mr. O'Sullivan?" Father Gregory asked when I came to a stop beside him, regarding the cabinet.

"Oh, all sorts," I said.

"Can you give me an example of what I might be looking at?" the priest asked, gesturing toward a volume bound in the gray skin of cats. It was an Egyptian text written by Bast cultists, which I'd saved from Alexandria. If I waved that in front of a museum curator, he'd promptly lose control of his salivary glands.

"It's really not a section open for browsing," I replied.

"My dear boy," the priest chortled in an avuncular manner, "how do you expect to sell any of it if you won't let customers peruse your catalog?"

I shrugged. "Most of it's not for sale." I sold one purely historical work per year at auction, and that gave Third Eye a healthy balance sheet even if I lost money on the bulk of the store's business. "I look at myself as more of a caretaker."

"I see. And how did you come to take care of such a collection?"

"Inherited it from my family," I said. "If there's a certain title you're looking for, I can see if I have it, or maybe I can get it for you."

The priest looked at the rabbi and the rabbi shook his head briefly. I could see they were getting ready to make excuses and leave, but I wanted to know a little more about them. I slipped in between them and the cabinet, uncomfortably close. They took a step back and I crossed my arms in front of my chest.

"Why did you come here today, gentlemen?" I said, a challenge in my tone. I let the vapid college kid slough away just a wee bit, and they noticed.

Father Gregory looked flustered and began to stammer. The rabbi was not so easily rattled. He glared at me and said coolly in English with a telltale Russian accent, "You can hardly expect us to be candid with you when you have not been candid with us."

"You haven't earned it. You're strangers and you refuse to answer my questions."

"You answer ours with lies," the rabbi hissed. Such an affable fellow.

"Perhaps I'd tell you what you want to hear if I knew you didn't mean me any harm."

Father Gregory tried to be avuncular again. "My dear boy, we are both men of the cloth—"

"Who have wandered into a New Age bookstore asking strange

personal questions," I interrupted. "And look, you could've gotten those costumes anywhere right after Halloween."

Both of them registered shock at the suggestion they were not truly clergymen—so that was one question answered. I should be able to find them on the Internet somewhere if they were legit.

Father Gregory clasped his hands together in a prayerful attitude. "I do apologize, Mr. O'Sullivan. It appears we have started off on the wrong foot. My colleague and I represent certain interests who believe you may be able to advance their agenda."

I crinkled my brow in confusion. "Advance their agenda? Well, I have a website. I could put up a banner or something, if they're looking for publicity."

"No, no, you misunderstand—".

"Purposely misunderstand, you mean," the rabbi spat. "Come on, Gregory, this is a waste of time." He pulled at the priest's arm and stalked off toward the exit. Father Gregory shot me an apologetic look and followed the rabbi, looking defeated. I let them go, because I had research to do. They clearly knew more about me than I knew about them, and that's an extremely uncomfortable feeling for an old Druid.

"What was that all about?" Granuaile asked as I rejoined her behind the apothecary counter.

"Don't know." I shook my head. "But I'm going to find out soon."

I brooded and busied myself with preparing tea blends until it was time for interviews. The first two candidates were semi-sentient boys who stared at me with their mouths open whenever I was talking. Their eyes were dead and never lit up until I asked them if they liked video games. They'd probably have difficulty alphabetizing.

Rebecca Dane, the third candidate, was refreshing. She had a strong chin and large eyes that she had seen fit to accentuate with Betty Boop eyelashes. Her blond hair fell to her shoulders, was pulled back and clipped with silver butterflies, and her bangs stopped just above her eyebrows. Her wardrobe was a black pantsuit with a shimmery blue scarf that she let fall straight down her torso, and an impressive tinkling of silver jewelry about her neck proclaimed her to be a member of practically every known world religion. Alongside the cross I saw so often in America, there was the Star of David, Islam's crescent moon, the Zuni bear fetish, and an ankh. When I asked her about them, she fingered the ankh sheepishly and grinned.

"Oh, I tend to vacillate between belief systems," she said with a touch of Wisconsin in her voice. "Right now I'm kind of checking out the whole buffet, you know, and maybe in a little while I'll decide on what I want to put on my plate and chow down on."

I smiled reassuringly at her. "Belly up to the religion smorgasbord, eh? That's good, may harmony find you. But how do you feel about people who are looking for a specific book, maybe about a religion you disagree with?"

"Oh, I have kind of a laissez-faire attitude—you know, live and let live. Doesn't bother me if someone wants to worship the Goddess or Allah or the Flying Spaghetti Monster; they're all seeking the divine within and without."

I would have hired her based solely on her healthy attitude and self-awareness, but she proved to be something of an amateur herbalist—enough to be dangerous, to be sure, but also enough to train properly. I had visions of letting her and Perry run the store for days at a time while Granuaile and I tried to restore the land around Tony Cabin.

"You're hired," I told her, and her wide mouth split into a huge smile. "You'll start out three dollars above minimum wage, but learn the apothecary side of the business in a month and I'll double it."

She was quite excited, and that made filling out the government paperwork less of a chore. She didn't know what to think of Perry at first, but he put her at ease once he smiled and proved not to be the stone-cold Goth he looked like.

I enticed Granuaile to hang out with me for a while after work by telling her she could ask me anything she wanted about history and I'd answer to the best of my ability. I gave her full disclosure that I'd make her drive me to the airport to pick up Laksha if and when she called, and we also had the onerous chore of sipping Irish whiskey with the widow ahead of us.

"What's onerous about that?" Granuaile asked.

"Nothing at all. I was being facetious. You'll love the widow."

Granuaile had seen the widow before and vice versa, but they'd never been formally introduced. Granuaile had been sharing her skull with Laksha at the time, and the widow had been preoccupied watching werewolves landscape her front yard. The prospect of introducing them actually made me nervous—what if they didn't like each other? But I should have known I had nothing to worry about. Mrs. MacDonagh is the soul of hospitality to anyone who isn't British and doubly welcoming to redheaded freckled gals with Irish names like Granuaile. I made sure to introduce her as my employee so the widow wouldn't assume, as older citizens frequently do, that the young man and woman must be having loud, acrobatic sex every chance they got.

"Does Granuaile know all yer secrets, then, Atticus?" The widow winked as we settled down with clinking glasses of the Irish. It was a clever way of asking if she could talk freely.

"Yes, Granuaile knows how old I really am. She's going to become a Druid herself, so you can talk about whatever you like."

"She's becomin' a Druid?" The widow cast a surprised look at Granuaile. "Weren't ye raised a proper Catholic girl?"

"I'm not a proper anything, I suppose," Granuaile replied. "Majoring in philosophy kind of turns positive assertions into maybes." That was the sort of observation I had already come to admire in my apprentice. Her philosophy degree compensated somewhat for starting her training so late. Her mind had not lost any of its flexibility, and she was very quick to pick up on the difficulties she'd face in the modern world as a magic user and a pagan to boot.

We chatted pleasantly until the sun went down, when I suggested I should be getting home to Oberon. I rode my bike and Granuaile trailed behind in her blue Chevy Aveo. I let Granuaile keep Oberon happy on the front porch with a belly rub while I put in a call to Leif.

He didn't spend time on niceties like saying hello. He answered the phone with "Have you changed your mind about Thor?"

"Um . . . no," I said, and he promptly hung up on me. My disappointment must have shown on my face, because Granuaile asked me what was wrong.

"It seems my lawyer's feeling unusually bloodsucky," I replied. "Our cordial relationship may be over."

"No way to patch it up, huh?"

"Well, no, it's not like I can send him a box of chocolates. I have scruples about sending him people for dinner. And I can't possibly do what he wants me to do."

"What's that?"

"Kill a thunder god." Before Granuaile could reply, my phone started ringing in my hand. It was an unknown number.

"I'm back in town, Atticus," Laksha Kulasekaran said on the other end of the line. "Pick me up on the north side of Terminal Four."

She and I were going to hunt some Bacchants. I slung Fragarach across my back before Granuaile and I jumped back into her car, because while it would do me no good against them unsheathed, I could simply brain them with the scabbard if necessary—and I can't count how many times I've wished I had it with me when I left it at home.

CHAPTER 11

The tendency of modern American women to exclaim "Hiiiiiiiiiiii!" in soprano octaves and hug each other upon sight can be disconcerting to those unfamiliar with it. Laksha was definitely unfamiliar with it, judging by the widening of her eyes and the stiffness of her limbs when Granuaile assaulted her with effusive greetings.

At least, I assumed it was Laksha: Granuaile was hugging a young brown-skinned woman in a black salwar kameez with a gold brocade border at the neckline and sleeves. I recognized the magnificent necklace of rubies set in gold that circled her throat; it was a magical focus she claimed was demon-crafted. There was a black chiffon dupatta, also with brocade on the borders, that Laksha had wrapped around herself intricately and in which Granuaile managed to tangle her arms. I have seen more awkward hugs in my life, but few so amusing and so clearly perplexing to the person being hugged.

Granuaile finally realized that Laksha probably didn't know what the hell she was doing, and she switched from ecstasy to embarrassment at about Mach Five.

"Oh, I am so sorry," she apologized, trying and failing to return Laksha's duppatta to its former graceful sweep. "I keep forgetting you're not used to American customs yet. Women here always get excited when they haven't seen each other for a while."

"But I saw you just last week," Laksha said.

"Well, yes, but you've been so far away," Granuaile explained.

"So distance must be taken into account when deciding whether to greet someone like this?"

"Um, well, I never thought about it quite that way before, but I guess that must be true, yes," Granuaile said uncertainly.

I popped the trunk of Granuaile's car and grinned at Laksha as I picked up her bags. "Welcome back, Laksha. You look fabulous."

"Thank you, Mr. O'Sullivan." She smiled primly at me. Her lips were the color of wine in a heart-shaped face, which was framed with a cascade of glossy black hair. She had a dimple on the left side of her mouth, a diamond stud glinting on the right side of her nose, and her eyebrows were expertly tweezed or waxed or whatever the proper beauty exercise is called. Her dark eyes shone with amusement, and one didn't get the sense at all that she was used to making deals with *rakshasas* and transferring her soul from body to body. "I am rather fond of this particular form." She held up her left hand, adorned with golden bangles on the wrist, and admired it with proprietary pride. "I am thinking I would like to keep it for a while, especially since the previous owner of it yielded it to me so willingly. I have not possessed a body free of karmic debt since the one I was born in, and I confess it holds much attraction for me."

"There are no problems with it, no scars from the auto accident the young lady was in?"

Laksha gave a small shake of her head. "Nothing on the surface. She suffered some broken bones, but they are all healed. She lost her spleen. The head trauma that put her in a coma is something I can work around for now and perhaps mend with time. Of course, the muscles are atrophied and I still tire easily, but they will strengthen with a little work."

"Fascinating," I said. "Let's continue talking in the car. We'd better go before the TSA guys get impatient with us."

As Granuaile got us on the eastbound Loop 202, Laksha announced she was hungry for Mexican food.

"I know just the place," I said, and gave Granuaile directions to Los Olivos, a Scottsdale landmark since the 1950s. It was on our way to Satyrn, and it would give us a chance to talk.

Laksha was fondly anticipating a divorce from Mr. Chamkanni. "Taking off like this without his precious masculine permission will drive him to irrational behavior," she said, smiling. "He will think he's lost all control—not that he ever had any—and his friends will egg him on to put me in my place. He will make demands of me when I return. That's when I will serve him with divorce papers."

"You already have them after a week?"

"Granuaile suggested a background check on him before I took Selai's body. He's been keeping a mistress, as one might expect of a man with a wife in a coma. We have photographic proof and a divorce lawyer already on retainer. I will be keeping the house, I think," she finished smugly.

Once at Los Olivos—in a room of blue glass and gray stone, with an indoor fountain splashing in the background—we chatted amiably over chips and salsa about the myriad charms of North Carolina. Over plates of green chile burros, enchilada style, the conversation turned as serious as the food.

"All right, Mr. O'Sullivan. Tell me what you wish of me," Laksha said.

"I want the Bacchants out of town."

The witch cackled at me, making a belated attempt to cover her mouth politely. "I see. We begin with the humanitarian option. You imagine I have such powers of persuasion?"

"I hoped you would at least consider it seriously instead of laughing at it."

"Mr. Chamkanni said much the same thing in bed the first night home from the hospital!"

Granuaile nearly spat out what she was chewing and slapped the table repeatedly as she struggled to control her mirth. I steepled my fingers over my plate, elbows on the table, and waited patiently for them to wind down.

Laksha finally said with an expression reserved for small children, "Mr. O'Sullivan, you know I am not the sort of witch who changes minds. I'm the sort that ends lives. That is why I am here, yes?"

"It is."

Granuaile abruptly ceased to find our conversation amusing. "Wait." She looked at Laksha and then at me. "Are you suggesting that Laksha should kill the Bacchants somehow?"

"You know precisely how she operates," I said.

"Atticus, how can you?" asked Granuaile, scandalized. "That would be murder."

"Not to mention very bad karma," Laksha added airily. This was a fight I'd seen coming, and I wanted not only to win it but also to teach Granuaile that she could and should question me, especially on questions of morality. Just as the Tuatha Dé Danann look at the world from a Bronze Age perspective, I look at it from the Iron Age, and though it's tempered by a whole lot of modern scruples and centuries of experience, my original Celtic cultural values don't always square with American laws and mores.

"Look, they're not fully human anymore," I explained. "They're more like walking disease vectors, spreading madness amongst the hoi polloi. They have absolutely zero chance of becoming the persons they used to be, now that they're thralls to Bacchus."

"But that doesn't mean they're monsters, does it? It sounds to me like they're victims of Bacchus or his magic, and they shouldn't be punished for that."

"They may have been victims at one time, but what you have to focus on is what they are *now*, and what they are is a dozen superhuman women immune to iron weapons and fire. They can turn a dozen more women into creatures just like them tonight and ruin whatever human potential they possess. And the madness will spread exponentially if someone doesn't stop them." I thought of a modern analogy and laid it on her: "It's kind of like those zombie movies. The humans in those movies don't look at a brain-eating zombie and let him go because he's a victim."

"Okay, fine, but these aren't zombies, right? There has to be a better way to stop them than killing them," Granuaile persisted.

"Like what? Put them in prison? Can't happen. Police either get swept up in the frenzy themselves or they die trying to resist."

"Well, can't you work some of your own magic on them?" Granuaile asked.

"Yes, Mr. O'Sullivan, what about your own magic?" Laksha said with great interest.

"My magic is earth-based." I shrugged, eyeing a succulent bite of burro. "They will be in a completely artificial environment, and I doubt my ability to resist catching their madness. I would be as susceptible to it as any other human. And, besides, even if that weren't the case, I don't have a spell up my sleeve to turn a Bacchant back into a normal woman."

"Well, then, can't you talk to Bacchus or go over his head to Jupiter? You talk to the Morrigan and Flidais, why not these other gods?"

I took a bite of the burro and shook my head sadly at her as the beef, green chiles, and tortilla melted in my mouth. "Bacchus is the Roman god of the vine, and the Romans hated Druids like no one else. They and the Christians killed us all, actually, yours truly excepted, and they would have gotten me too if it weren't for the Morrigan." I put my fork down and leaned back in my chair, dabbing at my mouth with a napkin. "So I think Bacchus would roast me on a spit before he'd have three words' conference with me. And if he thought I even existed, much less got myself involved in killing his Bacchants tonight, he might decide to show up personally."

"Won't he show up anyway?" Laksha asked.

"I doubt it very much," I said. "His worshippers fluctuate like no other's. Their numbers swell like viruses until they madden someone with a large army—or, more likely, magic users protecting a territory like this one—and then they're ruthlessly snuffed. He binges on a glut of worship and then deals with the hangover, just like his worshippers have to deal with the aftereffects of their debauchery."

"So, if we are going to do this thing," Laksha said, "we must discuss payment."

"Wait." Granuaile held up her hands. "I'm still not sure why we're even discussing it. You're talking about killing people for money."

"Not for money." Laksha shook her head.

"For whatever. It's wrong."

"I thought we'd settled this," I said. "It's like killing zombies."

"But zombies are already dead and they want to eat your brains. Bacchants are living people and they just want to have drunk sex on the dance floor. That's a significant difference. Make love not war, you know?"

As Malina had done to me, I explained to her the far-reaching consequences of letting even one night of bacchanalia go unchallenged in what was now our territory. I also explained to her the Druidic belief that the soul never dies; killing the bodies would actually free their souls from Bacchus's slavery. The combination of these arguments did not fully soothe her, but she subsided and allowed for the possibility that I had chosen a reasonable course of action.

Laksha followed the reasonable argument with an unreasonable demand for payment. "Since I am performing a service for you that you cannot perform yourself, I want you to do me a service in kind," she said.

"Is this a service to be named later, or did you have something particular in mind?"

"Oh, yes, I have something very particular in mind." She smiled, circling her finger around the rim of her water glass. "I want you to bring me the golden apples of Idunn."

I laughed. "No, seriously, what do you want?"

"I'm quite serious. That is what I want."

My grin slid off my face and crashed into my burro. "How is that a service in kind? It's on a completely different scale."

"I think not. A dozen frenzied Bacchants silenced for you in exchange for a few apples—that is not so much."

"It is when the apples are in Asgard!"

"Asgard?" Granuaile gaped at me. "You know how we can go to fucking Asgard?"

"Yes, Druids can walk the planes; that's why she needs me to—hey, look, Granuaile, there's no 'we' in this scenario." I turned back to the amused Indian witch. "Laksha, this is between us only. My apprentice is not involved whatsoever in this deal, and my debts do not accrue to her under any circumstances, is that clear?"

Laksha nodded lazily. "That is understood."

"Good. Now, as I was saying, these services are not of equal value nor of equal risk. You can kill these Bacchants with little fear of reprisal from Bacchus, but I cannot steal the golden apples of Idunn without certain reprisal from every member of the Norse pantheon. It's not just Idunn who'd be after me," I said, ticking off gods on my fingers, "it's Freyja, it's Odin and his damn ravens, and it's Mr. Tall, Blond, and Lightning himself."

Laksha smiled conspiratorially and leaned forward. "You know what Baba Yaga calls Thor?"

I leaned forward. "I don't care. You're missing the point."

Granuaile leaned forward. "You've met Baba Yaga?"

"She calls him that muscle-cocked goatfucker!" Laksha slapped the table, leaned back, and laughed heartily while we stared at her bemusedly. At another time I might have found it amusing—especially since I used to pick fights with Scotsmen by calling them something similar—but not when I was trying to keep "Raid Asgard" off my honey-do list. Granuaile seemed to be having the same difficulty with the comic timing, focused as she was on the revelation that Baba Yaga was a real person familiar with Thor's intimate life.

An elderly diner from a neighboring table had been dying for an excuse to stare at the woman with rubies around her neck, and now Laksha had provided her one by laughing so loudly. She noticed the woman's stare and waggled her finger between us and explained, "We were just talking about goatfucking." The woman's eyes bulged in shock—and so did those of her dinner companions—but rather than scold Laksha for being so rude, they hastily returned to attacking their enchiladas with their dentures, eyes studiously contemplating plates of melted cheese and red sauce.

"You seem a little impatient, Mr. O'Sullivan," Laksha teased when she turned her attention back to me. "I would think one so wise and learned would have cultivated an appreciation for the many branches of a conversation."

"This is the sort of conversation where I'd like to stick to the main trunk, if you don't mind."

Laksha drummed her fingers on the table a couple of times and then grimaced in disappointment. "So be it. I will dispatch your Bacchants tonight if you give me your word you will get me the golden apples before the New Year. If we cannot agree to this, I will thank you for the meal and the visit and return to my husband, who is undoubtedly worried about his precious Selai by now."

"Why do you want the golden apples specifically?"

Laksha executed a facial shrug with a twitch of her eyebrows and a tilt of her head. "I like this body I am in. I don't want it to age; I don't want to have to change bodies every few decades."

We paused while a white-shirted man refilled our water glasses. "There are other ways to prolong life besides the golden apples," I said quietly when he had disappeared.

"Ah, yes." The witch nodded knowingly. "I have heard of these vitamins, and they may prolong life, but they will not halt the aging process."

"Don't be ridiculous. I mean truly miraculous brews."

Laksha raised an eyebrow. "Such as?"

"The ale of Goibhniu," I said. "Brewer of the Tuatha Dé Danann. His brews confer immortality."

"Ah, this is one of your gods, and you feel it will be easier to procure."

"I am owed a reward for killing Aenghus Óg." I nodded, thinking it was time Brighid followed through on her promise.

"Congratulations, but it is not an acceptable substitute. This brew of Goibhniu is almost certainly one that I must drink repeatedly to maintain my youth, which means I would be dependent on one of your gods for my continued vitality. I cannot trust myself to such an arrangement." I supposed from that comment she would not be interested in my Immortali-Tea either. It was just as well; I didn't want to brew it for her in any case.

"With the apples it is different," Laksha continued. "Once I have them, I can grow my own tree from the seeds."

I was gobsmacked. "You think you can grow a tree of Asgard here in Midgard? It can't be done. We're talking two completely different sets of soil chemistry."

"Bullshit, as you Americans say."

"He's Irish," Granuaile pointed out.

"The Irish say bullshit too," Laksha retorted, "and he's pretending to be American now anyway." She pointed a finger at me and said, "Don't try to talk me out of this with Druidic word games. The ontological nature of a mythical tree does not include details on soil chemistry. It is a magical tree, and so it will grow magically regardless of soil chemistry."

Clever witch. "It may grow magically anywhere, I grant you, but most likely only at Idunn's behest."

"That is a distinct possibility." Laksha shrugged. "But we will never know until I give it a try."

The temptation to get up and walk away nearly overwhelmed me: This wasn't my fight. It was Malina's. And if her coven couldn't hack it, then Leif could tear them apart, or Magnusson would sic his boys on them once they screwed enough of his clients. I hadn't lived for 2,100 years by volunteering to take point in every magical scrap in my neighborhood. Besides, I had an apprentice to protect and teach now. Granuaile and I could go anywhere and set up shop under a new identity, leaving these covens and other creatures to claw at one another for the privilege of drawing comfortable consulting salaries and living in glass towers. I almost did it; my leg twitched and my shoulders tensed.

But.

There was the dead land around Tony Cabin to resurrect. That was definitely my fight—a vitally important one—and no one else could fight it for me. It would take care of itself in another thousand years or so, but healing it now would erase all traces of Aenghus Óg's work in the world, and I couldn't let it lie when I'd been indirectly responsible for it happening. Its very existence nagged at me; I *felt* it through the tattoos binding me to the earth. It was like a necrotic wound on the back of one's hand that might allow the limb to function but slowly poisons the sense of health and harmony a soul needs for peace. Still, it would take me years to restore that land, which meant I'd have to stay in town and guard the proverbial castle.

It also meant I'd have to play nicely in the sandbox and pitch in when Malina needed help. She at least was willing to live peaceably with me, while *die Töchter des dritten Hauses* had forcefully demonstrated they were not.

Another thing to consider was the likelihood that I was under surveillance and could not disappear as easily as I had in the past. Father Gregory and Rabbi Yosef certainly seemed to be watching me closely or were in close contact with someone else who was. Like it or not, I had raised my profile considerably by killing Aenghus Óg, and if various beings decided they would like to test themselves against me, I'd be better off defending myself in a place where I'd had years to build up.

But why did Fortune seem to be pushing me into a street fight with Thor? Stealing the golden apples of Idunn would rouse him as surely as would sitting down on a porcupine.

"Have you been talking to my lawyer, Leif Helgarson?" I asked Laksha. "Pale, spooky bastard with blond hair and an English business suit?"

"No." She shook her head and frowned. "I thought your lawyer was the werewolf we rescued in the mountains."

"He is. I have two lawyers, but they both hate Thor. Did either of them put you up to this?"

"Most of the world hates Thor." Laksha smiled. "At least the part of the world that knows what he's really like. But, no, they have not spoken with me about this."

"Is this your way, then, of getting me to fight him? It seems like everyone wants to put us in the Thunderdome and buy front-row seats."

"No, this is my way of preserving this body so that I avoid further karmic debt."

I sighed to release some of the tension in my muscles and rubbed my eyes with my knuckles. "All right. Let's think this through. If your goal is to grow your own apple tree with the super-duper fruit of eternal youth, you don't actually need all of Idunn's apples, right? You only need one for the seeds."

"No." Laksha shook her head again and tapped the table repeatedly to emphasize her point. "I want them all, in case I get a dud."

"Well, I want to have a chance of living through this if I'm going to consider it. If I steal one apple, I might be able to get away without anyone noticing, because the mythology says she keeps her apples in a basket and it's always full. But if I steal the whole lot, every single Norse god will be after me—and after you too, I might add. Be reasonable. One apple will suffice."

"How can I be assured the apple you bring me is Idunn's?"

"Well, it'll be golden, for one thing, and after you take a bite of it you should feel pretty fucking good, if reports are to be believed."

Laksha laughed. "All right. You have proven to be as good as your word in the past. Twelve dead Bacchants tonight in exchange for one of Idunn's golden apples before New Year's Day."

We shook hands on it while Granuaile shook her head in wonder. "I've listened in on some pretty weird conversations while tending bar," she said, "but I think this is the weirdest shit I've ever heard."

CHAPTER 12

People who don't live in Scottsdale like to sneer derisively and call it "Snotsdale." People who do live there tend to call everyone else "jealous." Both groups have a point.

Scottsdale has more plastic surgeons per capita than anywhere except for Beverly Hills; some high school kids get procedures from their parents as graduation presents. Its wide residential streets of custom homes compete with one another to be featured in architectural and design magazines, and the sleek luxury autos in the garages are testosterone boosters for middle-aged men taking once-a-day Cialis to please their sleek luxury girlfriends. It's a resort town with much of its real estate occupied by golf courses and egos.

Many of the young and beautiful egos habitually crammed themselves into Satyrn, one of the city's hotter nightclubs. They would be dressed expensively, scented with something French, scrubbed and primped and teased and pushed-up and bedecked in just the right amount of bling. They were the sons and daughters of affluence, accustomed to excess and looking for more of it—in other words, excellent prey for the Bacchants.

After sending Granuaile home, Laksha and I took a taxi to a Target so that I could buy a couple of wooden baseball bats. The cashier almost cringed as she rang them up, keeping her eyes down and casting only furtive glances at me. She was probably doubting my emotional stability, since I had a sword strapped to my back and I was buying sporting goods at night. Store security belatedly realized I was carrying a weapon around their place of business, so as the cashier held out my receipt in a trembling hand, they showed up and escorted me to the exit from the register. I smiled at them and thanked them for their courtesy, so they wouldn't call the police and complicate the rest of the night.

The taxi driver decided we were a pretty odd couple and kept asking us questions. We told him we were martial arts experts in town for a convention, and he bought it. Said he was going to be a ninja once, but things didn't work out the way he planned. We had him drop us off on the far side of the parking lot, as far as possible from the entrance flanked by a velvet rope. There was no bouncer at the door—an ominous sign. A techno dance mix pulsed into the night, promising dark blue lighting and gyrating bodies inside.

"You know they ain't gonna let you inside with those things, right?" the taxi driver said as I got out and paid him.

"I think it might be anything goes in there right about now," I replied. "Thanks for the ride. Keep safe."

As he drove away and I coughed a couple of times from the exhaust, Laksha lifted an arm toward the entrance and said, "Shall we go take a look?"

"You don't need to say any special incantations or sacrifice a stray cat or something first?"

"No." She smirked at me and began to walk toward the club.

I followed her and spoke to her back. "Come on. No circles or pentagrams or candles or anything?" I knew Laksha felt confident about her ability to resist the Bacchants' magic, but I didn't know how she was protecting herself. Could her ruby necklace have all the defensive power of my amulet and more? I thought she'd need to prepare a ward of some kind, at least. For my part, there was no other defense than my amulet and a grim determination to think about baseball; otherwise, I might well fall into their frenzy.

"Sorry," she said over her shoulder.

"Wait just a second," I said as we arrived at the door. "I'm not sure I should go in. I could be vulnerable to their magic."

Laksha turned and regarded me with a curious expression. "Cannot you control your body?"

"To some extent, yes. Is that your defense against them? Controlling your body?"

"Precisely. I have utter control over this body's nervous system. In a sense I am outside of it; the input will arrive—these things called hormones and pheromones I have learned about—but I will refuse to allow the body to respond. It will not be aroused unless I wish it to be."

"That's all the Bacchants are using? Pheromones?" I had suspected this before, but I thought there must be more to it than that.

"I believe that is what they are doing, yes. Their magic targets the limbic system of the brain in a few people near them, and then these people's bodies—the expression is "share the love," I believe, with others nearby, and it spreads until everyone in an area is a slave to their sexual desires. Alcohol reduces one's resistance, weakens inhibitions, makes it all happen faster. Then they feed on the pheromones and the energy of the group, drink them in, and become impossibly strong by it."

"That makes sense." I nodded. "Different from succubi. But it means I won't have any defense at all. I'm not outside my nervous system in the way you describe."

Laksha huffed in exasperation. "Fine. At least come in for a brief look around. I will escort you out once you begin touching yourself."

"What? Hey, don't let it go that far. That's not right."

A flicker of a smile played about Laksha's lips, then it fled as she returned to the business at hand. "Leave the bats at the door. They'll recognize them as a threat."

"And not my sword?"

"It's not a threat to them. You don't want to pull them out of their ecstasy. It'll turn to rage."

Obeying with some reluctance, I followed her inside to the skull-pounding thump of techno bass beats and the multicolored strobe effect of sequenced lights on a rig high above the dance floor, which was to our left. The bar was to the right, with martini glasses hanging overhead and the premium liquors prominently displayed in front of a mirror. There were a few beers on tap, but since this was not the sort of clientele that drank anything so common, the bar did a blazing business in froufrou drinks. The floor of the bar area was a soft white laminate tile marbled with wispy ribbons of cobalt blue. A few tall white tables sans chairs were scattered around the perimeter, without a single booth or bar stool to be found. Satyrn clearly expected the joint to be standing room only every night, and so it was. Three glass chandeliers with electric fixtures soared high above the bar floor, providing a soft glow in that part of the club. Separating the bar area from the dance floor were five enormous load-bearing white columns, and the dance floor was utterly dark except for the flashes of random lights from the rig. The entire long, narrow space of the club was filled with writhing bodies in various states of undress and abandon. Even behind the bar, the bartenders were shaking and stirring each other instead of customers' drinks. Still, for all that, the bar area was more restrained than the dance floor, where most clothes had already been shed and the baby-making was unrestrained.

I felt the first twinges of desire myself and reflected that the Diamondbacks really needed base-stealing threats in their leadoff and number-two slots, because until they secured the ability to make pitchers nervous and manufacture runs, they'd be easy prey. They couldn't rely on their streaky big hitters to win enough games to matter. They had to grind it out every day . . . Speaking of grinding—no. The bullpen needed a couple of solid guys who could pitch two or three full innings of lights-out ball. They couldn't keep giving away games if the starter had a bad day.

"The lack of seating is inconvenient," Laksha complained. "I need someplace to keep this body secure."

"What? Why?"

"Do you even understand what I am going to do?"

"Not precisely. Push their souls out of their bodies somehow?"

"No, I do that only when I am taking possession. You want me to merely kill them. I will visit one's brain and shut down the hypothalamus, which regulates the heartbeat, then move to the next as she collapses, and so on. Their souls will leave naturally as a result of their deaths. It will take me less than a minute."

I frowned. "What will happen to your body while you're out doing this?"

"This body will be in a vulnerable, vegetative state until I return—which is why I need a place to sit down." A douche bag drenched in Drakkar Noir approached Laksha from behind, slipped his hands underneath her arms, and cupped her breasts. She immediately stomped down hard on his foot, lunged a step forward, and twisted to the right with her arm cocked, smashing her elbow into his temple. He went down like a sack of cornmeal. She grimaced in disgust and said, "We need to hurry. It's already getting ridiculous in here."

"Where are the Bacchants?" I asked.

"There's one over there on the edge of the dance floor." She pointed to a woman in what looked like a sheer white negligee, gyrating her backside sinuously against the hips of a young man behind her. She had a drunken smile on her face, and it appeared to me in the dim light that her teeth were unusually sharp. Everyone's auras were aboil with red carnal lust.

I lost sight of her abruptly as a wanton dark-haired beauty slid up to me and kissed me full on the mouth, her right leg twining behind my left calf and her tongue darting between my teeth. There was a team sport I was supposed to be thinking of at that point, but she tasted like cherries and something else—

She was torn from my arms with a startled yelp, and my head rocked to the right as Laksha slapped my face, hard. Oh, yes, baseball. A home run would be good. Where did that girl go?

"Let's get you out of here; you're already useless," Laksha said, forcefully turning me toward the exit and pushing me firmly in front of her. We hit fresh air before too long, having never penetrated far into the club, but when I tried to stop, Laksha said, "No, keep going. If you stay here you might be tempted to come back in."

"What about my bats?"

"Get them, quickly."

I scooped them up, and Laksha escorted me all the way to the edge of the parking lot, proclaiming that I should be safe there until she finished. And then she left me standing there uncertainly, holding two baseball bats with a sword strapped to my back and staring at the entrance to the club. I didn't think of how unbalanced that made me look to people driving by on the street until the patrol car pulled up behind me, its lights flashing so that traffic would drive around it.

"Good evening, sir," an officer called out. I nodded back to him and returned my gaze to the club, cursing my stupidity. I should have learned my lesson back at Target, but I'd been too focused on accomplishing the night's objective to worry about doing it surreptitiously. Wearing a sword was second nature to a man from the Iron Age, but to modern eyes it indicated a need for therapy.

"What are you doing there?" the officer said. I heard the patrol-car door *whump* closed. I didn't have the time or patience for this. If these guys hung around, they might wind up in trouble or seriously complicate my ability to deal with trouble if it came boiling out of the club.

"Just waiting for a friend," I said.

"With a sword and a couple of bats? You sure it's a friend you're waiting for?"

Regretting the necessity to use some of my stored power, I quietly cast camouflage on Fragarach and then responded more loudly, "What sword?"

"The sword that's—hey, what'd you do with it?"

"I don't know what you're talking about, Officer. I don't have a sword." I heard the driver's-side door *whump* as his partner got out to join him, no doubt moving to flank me to my left.

"All right, tell you what—why don't you drop the bats and show me some ID."

I cast camouflage on the bats and said, "What bats?" Of course my hands were still curled around them, but now it looked as if I was just standing there with my fists at my sides. I should have done this in the first place, and then these lads would never have gotten a call about me. But I knew they wouldn't just leave me alone now. The man with the disappearing weapons was far too curious a creature for them to ignore, and, besides, I'd made them look foolish. They'd want some payback, sure.

"Show me some ID," the cop demanded again. He was far too peremptory for my taste. Honestly, I was trying to be one of the good guys here. There were times in my past when I probably deserved to be harassed, but this wasn't one of them.

I cast camouflage on myself and asked, "Who are you talking to?" before silently stepping forward a couple of paces. That freaked their shit right out. They both put their hands to their guns and asked each other where I went. My camouflage isn't perfect invisibility, but at night it might as well be. I stepped off to the right about ten yards or so as they looked all around them and called out for me to come back. The driver suggested that they call for backup.

"Backup for what, Frank?" the first officer said. "We've got nothing here."

"Maybe he ran into the club," Frank suggested.

"You want to check it out?" I didn't like where this was going. Put a couple of guns into a bacchanalian setting and eventually those guns are going to be used.

"Yeah," Frank said, "let's go. That guy looked pretty dangerous."

I looked pretty dangerous? There was something dangerous in the club, all right, but it wasn't me. I had to do something quickly, so I decided to go the Three Stooges route, since the two cops had moved next to each other before tackling a club full of horny twenty-somethings. A Druid's ability to see the connections between all natural things and bind them together encourages mischief at times, and while I usually did this sort of thing for an immature laugh, now I would be saving their lives. I muttered a binding between two sets of skin cells so that they couldn't bear to be parted a second longer—specifically, the skin cells on the first officer's right palm and the cells on Frank's left cheek. I broke the binding as soon as it was consummated, and the effect was that the first officer gave Frank a beauty of a slap.

Frank reacted as any American might to being slapped unexpectedly in the face by his partner. "Ow! You dick, Eric! What the fuck?" Now I knew both their names. Frank lashed out and laid one on Eric before Eric could explain it had been an involuntary muscle spasm, and then it was *on*. Watching two cops have a slap fight was a pretty amusing way to pass an idle moment or two. I've rarely been so entertained while waiting for someone.

Eric had the advantage in terms of reach, but Frank was much faster. Frank was landing two or three slaps to every one of Eric's, and after a half minute of that, Eric had damn well had enough. He turned his openhanded slap into a fist, crunching it into Frank's nose. Frank yelped and staggered backward, raising his hand to his face. It came away drenched in his own blood.

"Oh, shit, I'm sorry, Frank," Eric said, holding his hands up.

"Sorry isn't going to make it better," Frank growled, and he bull-rushed his partner and wrapped him up in a textbook tackle. Eric managed to twist as he fell so that he landed on his shoulder, keeping his head from hitting the pavement. They rolled around a little bit, back and forth, neither getting the advantage over the other, but eventually Frank came up on top, rage driving him to dominate his larger opponent. He landed a couple of solid punches on Eric's face, and then they were both bleeding. Eric boxed Frank's ears and threw him off to the side but didn't pursue him. They were both dealing with more pain than they were used to, so they were content to lie there bleeding, sling various anatomical epithets at each other, and accuse their mothers of sexual adventures with farm animals. Good times.

Laksha still hadn't returned, and no one had exited the club in all this time. The music continued to thump through the walls into the night, and I wondered if I should start worrying.

The police officers hauled themselves slowly to their feet and plotted to blame their injuries on me. Their story would be that I had hit them with my baseball bats, broken both their noses, and escaped. They'd get worker's comp for fighting, and I'd get an APB for assaulting an officer. Great.

As they returned to their patrol car to radio their lies to the station, I heard what sounded like faint screams coming from the club, a high-pitched top note to the techno pulse. Laksha emerged with a wicked grin on her face, and then more people came spilling out behind her, some of them in nothing but underwear, clearly panicked and fleeing for their lives.

Laksha's grin faded as she saw the lights of the police car but didn't see me. She kept coming straight ahead to clear the press of the stampeding mob, and I hissed at her to get her attention.

"Where are you?" she asked.

"Use your other senses. I'm in camouflage."

Laksha's eyes rolled up and then she spied me standing off to her left. "Ah, excellent."

"What happened?" I gestured at the club.

"I killed twelve Bacchants, as we agreed," she said pleasantly.

"Is that why these people are panicking?"

"Partially. But mostly it's because there are three more in there and they're tearing people in half."

Since I'm an Irish lad, I'm already fairly pale, but that intelligence turned me from eggshell white to bone. Either Malina's divination had been incorrect or a few bonus Bacchants had arrived late in the game. "Well, why didn't you kill them too?" I asked.

"Because we agreed on twelve."

"I'll be sure not to fetch you any extra apples, then. Where are they?"

"I'm sure they'll be coming out after me soon enough. They'll be the ones dressed in white sheaths stained with wine and carrying staves. Bloodthirsty look in their eyes, chunks of meat in their teeth—you can't miss them."

She wasn't kidding. A particularly piercing scream drew my gaze to the entrance, where a diminutive brunette in a white nightie had seized a much taller woman by the hair and a fistful of fabric at the small of her back. As I watched, this tiny woman—who could not have weighed more than 110 pounds—heaved the larger one off her feet, spun her around like a discus thrower, and slung her in a high, shrieking arc across the parking lot, over our heads, to land ruinously on top of Frank and Eric's patrol car.

I almost wished Granuaile could have seen it; she wouldn't have thought the Bacchants were victims anymore. Laksha laughed, somehow thinking the poor woman's death was funny. We had different senses of humor, I guess.

I couldn't stay back any longer. Not only was it clear that Laksha had done all she was going to do, but now the police would be getting involved. I had to eliminate the threat before bullets started flying and ricocheting off the Bacchants' magic hides. There was no danger of being lured into their orgy now; the happy time was over and the madness had begun.

Still in camouflage, I charged the wee Bacchant as she tore after another panicked clubber. A second Bacchant emerged from the club, bloodstained and wrathful, eyes bulging as she grabbed a full-grown man and broke his back over her knee in one of those wrestling maneuvers that simply wasn't for show. Too late to save him, but not too late for the fellow the tiny Bacchant was after. As she seized him by the collar of his Dolce & Gabbana shirt, I came in low with the bat in my left hand and swept her legs out from under her so that she fell ungracefully on her backside. She made the sound a cat makes when you step on its tail, and now that I was closer I was surprised at how young she was. She had probably been pretty once, with a name like Brooke or Brittney or maybe Stacy. She might have been captain of the cheer squad and a homecoming queen, driving to school in a pink Cabriolet her daddy had bought for her. Now, however, her nails were more like claws, and her teeth were filed to points, and she had blood dribbling from her mouth—and it wasn't hers. I brought the bat in my right hand down hard on her face before she had time to leap back up. I even hit her again to make sure she was through, regretting the necessity and thinking that one never quite gets used to crushing skulls. Then I looked up to track where the other Bacchant went.

She was coming for me. She couldn't see me, but she knew something had just taken down her sister and it was still nearby. Her hair was like a frizzy halo of shag carpeting, and it was matted with blood and pieces of recent victims. She had a beaklike nose, a single eyebrow above it like a malevolent, hairy caterpillar, and the same pointed teeth that the smaller Bacchant had. Her arms looked like flabby shanks of lamb, but there was a preternatural strength inside them. I know because, when I took a swing at her with the bat in my right hand, thinking I'd clock her upside the head, she felt it coming somehow and broke it in two just by doing one of those wax-off moves from *The Karate Kid*. Now holding half a bat with some sharp splinters at the end as I followed through, I had to think quickly as she kept rushing forward, reaching for me with a clawed right hand, and bringing her left one back around. If those got hold of me, I wouldn't stay in one piece for very long. I shifted my grip on the bat handle so that my thumb was on the bottom instead of the top, and as her nails dug painfully into my left shoulder, I stabbed down with the sharpened splinters of the bat into the side of her neck where it met her collarbone. That set her back some, and she yowled as she released me to deal with it. I dissolved the camouflage on it so that she could appreciate what was causing the pain. She jerked it out as I backpedaled and shifted the bat in my left hand to my right, and though a fountain of blood spurted forth, she didn't appear to feel faint: She actually accessed a whole new level of pissed when I already thought I'd never seen anyone madder.

I stepped to my right as quietly as I could and watched her scream away what little mind she had left. Regardless of her incredible strength, that was a mortal wound, and she couldn't last much longer while losing that much blood. Bacchants aren't great healers, and she couldn't see through my camouflage, so I thought all I'd need to do now was wait a couple of minutes and make sure she didn't hurt anyone else. But the damn thing took a deep breath to scream some more and *smelled* me.

The bloody broken bat suddenly became a wooden stave thrown at my heart, as she turned and chucked it uncannily in my direction. I had to drop to the ground to avoid it, and before I could roll away, she was on me. Quickly, I thrust the second bat up crosswise toward her throat, dismissing its camouflage too, hoping she'd take hold of it rather than groping for my neck. If she got hold of my head, she could tear it clean off. She took the bait, grasping the bat at either end and trying to wrench it free from my grasp. I held on for the first spastic attempt, but just barely. Her blood was dripping steadily down on me, ruining my camouflage and supposedly sapping her strength, but I could tell she was still a couple of oxen ahead of me in the muscle department. She gathered herself for a truly mighty yank, and as she did I knew I had to end this before she could use it against me. So when she yanked a second time, I didn't even try to hold on but rather let go, which caused her to throw her hands up over her head as she unexpectedly met no resistance. That left her completely unguarded, as I intended, so I drained the last of the power stored in my bear charm and channeled it all into my left shoulder and arm. I rose in a stomach crunch and plowed my fist hard into her chin. The impact broke the first joints of my index and middle fingers, but it also snapped her neck.

That solved my immediate crisis but left me with several others. Completely drained of magical energy, I couldn't begin to heal or shut down the pain. And all the weariness of my earlier casting of Cold Fire came back to settle heavily on my frame, even as the shag-haired Bacchant settled heavily astride my hips. There were still panicked clubgoers streaming out of Satyrn, and Frank and Eric, the broken-nosed cops, were heading my way with guns drawn. To top it off, I was so drained that I couldn't maintain the camouflage spell any longer, and I became clearly visible to them. This just wasn't the right time or place to have this fight, and that's why I lost it.

Oh, were they happy to see me again. Not only was I visible, but so was my sword that had disappeared earlier, and a woman with a giant bloody wound was lying on top of me. Never mind that the sword was still in its scabbard and I was lying on top of it; never mind that a cursory forensics inspection would reveal that the wound wasn't a sword wound; in their minds I had just about decapitated the poor woman with a bad hairdo.

So it was hands up, roll over facedown away from that woman, spread your legs, take off that weapon, and then a pair of cuffs around my wrists as half-naked people continued to run away, not from me, but from whatever horror awaited inside. Once I was subdued, it gradually dawned on them that I wasn't much of a threat to the public: The public was freaking out about something else. Frank thought he should maybe take a peek inside.

"Don't do it, Frank. One of them is still in there."

"You shut up," Eric said, poking me in the ribs with his gun. Authority established, he asked, "One of what?"

"These ladies in white that have been killing people. If you have to go, use your baton, not your gun."

"Right," Frank said sarcastically. "Ladies in white killing people. Like this very dead lady in white right here. We'll be sure to follow your advice."

Frank went into the club gun first, while Eric tried to take Fragarach away from me, which was resting by my side on the asphalt. It was bound so that it couldn't be moved more than five feet away from my body, and, unlike camouflage, it wasn't a spell that depended on my current power level to be maintained. It would stay bound to me until I dispelled the binding, so Eric was about to lose a fight with an inanimate object. He was so surprised by it pulling away from him the first time that he dropped it. He tried again, and dropped it again.

"What the hell is going on? Are you doing that?" he asked.

"Doing what, Officer? I'm facedown in the parking lot with my hands cuffed behind my back. What kind of bullets do you use?"

"Shut up. Full metal jacket."

"Please tell me they're copper jackets."

"I said shut up. They're steel."

"I was afraid of that."

"Shut up."

Eric was about to pick up my sword again, but he was distracted by the sound of shots being fired in the club. Nine of them, out of those modern guns the police carry, at a Bacchant with immunity to iron. And then we heard a man screaming horribly over the techno thrum.

"Frank!" Eric cried.

"Don't go. Wait for your backup," I said.

"Shut up, damn it! That's my partner in there!"

Not anymore. His partner was already in pieces. "Well, use your baton, then! Your gun won't work!"

"Just shut up and stay there! I'll be right back."

I sighed. No, he wouldn't. There weren't any more people coming out of the building. The clubbers were all scrambling for their cars and trying to get the hell out of there, honking horns and telling everyone else to get out of their way. I struggled to my feet and staggered to the back of the parking lot, hoping I wouldn't get run over by a turbocharged Audi. Fragarach obediently trailed five feet behind me, since I couldn't pick it up.

More shots rang out from the club, but Eric didn't get as many off as Frank did before his screaming began, then ended. Sirens wailed in the night, all converging on the club, and I knew I didn't have much time to make myself scarce.

There was a thin strip of landscaping between the sidewalk and the parking lot, where a couple of palo verdes grew alongside some blue agave plants. As soon as I reached it, I drew power to dampen the throbbing pain in my fingers and start knitting the bones back together. Then I cast camouflage again and started to recharge my bear charm. The handcuffs were next. Concentrating on the molecular bonds in two of the links between the cuffs, I weakened them until I could pull the cuffs apart, grateful that they were still made of natural ores from the earth. The parking lot was quickly emptying and the sirens were getting louder. Laksha was nowhere in sight; her end of the bargain finished, she was probably on her way to the airport in a taxi.

As I slung Fragarach across my back once again, I saw the last of the Bacchants emerge from Satyrn. Her white sheath was stained almost completely red with the blood of the police officers and who knew how many other victims, and she carried her thyrsus in her right hand. I had no practical weapon to use against her except my sheathed sword, so it would have to be hand-to-hand martial arts, with one of mine already broken.

She wasn't interested in fighting, though. She walked straight toward me after taking a deep breath of the night air. I smelled another storm coming, but she apparently smelled me, and accurately enough that I might as well have not been wearing camouflage. She stopped about ten yards away as I crouched into a defensive stance.

"What are you?" she hissed. "I know you are there. I smell magic. Are you a witch? One of the Polish ones?" She was taller than the other Bacchants and built for pleasure. When she wasn't covered in gore, I'm sure she was quite fetching—as long as she didn't show her pointy teeth.

"Nope," I said. "Two more guesses."

"Are you the vampire Helgarson?" Now, *that* was an interesting guess. Besides revealing that she knew who Leif was, she must have thought him capable of something approaching invisibility and capable of caring whether some Bacchants partied in Scottsdale or not.

"Nope. I can still walk in the sunshine."

"Then you are the Druid O'Sullivan."

She could have knocked me over with a marshmallow, I was so surprised. But I couldn't let her know that.

"Pleased to meet you," I said politely, then ruined it by saying, "But not really."

"Lord Bacchus must hear of this," she muttered, and then she turned and sprinted inhumanly fast toward the club. She didn't go back in but ducked up an alley on the side of the building.

"Oh, bollocks," I breathed. There was nothing I could do. No roots to tie her up with in a parking lot. No earth to hold her fast. And I couldn't hope to match her speed, pumped up with power as she was right now and as depleted as I was.

I spat thickly on the sidewalk, delivering my self-evaluation for the evening. I'd managed to make a royal mess of the whole situation. Most of the Bacchants were dead, true, but the one who got away would bring more, and perhaps Bacchus himself, to get revenge. Two cops were dead, as were at least two civilians I'd seen outside and who knew how many more in the club. This would be major news. It might even go national.

Malina was going to be pissed, and she had every right to be. Fights in the paranormal community were not supposed to be seen by the general public. If this did go national, anyone who knew how things really worked would read between the lines and see that the East Valley was dangerously unstable.

Police cars and fire trucks screeched to a halt nearby, and one of them blocked the exit from the parking lot, corralling the last few witnesses. I wouldn't have time to conduct my own investigation inside the club; all I could do was remove my fingerprints from the bats by unbinding the oils, go home, and recuperate.

I jogged wearily south, leaving the carnage behind, and got rained on again when I reached Shea Boulevard. There was a commercial center there on the southeast corner, and I called a taxi from Oregano's Pizza Bistro to take me home.

The driver looked doubtfully at my sword and the cuffs on my wrists, but I paid him cash up front so he didn't say anything. Just to be safe in case the police questioned him later, I had him drop me off near Starbucks on Mill Avenue, then cast camouflage again and jogged the rest of the way home in the rain.

I left Fragarach on my bedroom dresser after drying it off and dissolving the bond to my body. I bound it to the dresser instead. I had a whole lot of mending to do overnight, whether it was raining or not, so I shucked off my clothes and stretched myself out in the backyard to heal properly, tattoos in touch with the earth, with a sheet of oilskin thrown over me as a makeshift shelter. I contacted the iron elemental who lurked around my shop to come eat away the cuffs on my wrists, and after the rain finally quit, my mind found rest on Lethe's shore.

CHAPTER 13

I confess to feeling a sense of entitlement at times. After living for so long—after earning my senior citizen's discount many times over—I feel I should be able to wake up in peace and enjoy a few simple pleasures. Oberon's tail thumping a greeting, for example. Sunlight in the kitchen as I make coffee. Some classical guitar playing softly as I whip up an omelet and some sausages. And when I have to wake up from spending a cold night on the wet earth, a hot shower would be lovely. If the day wants to turn to shit after that, then that's all right, but give me a few minutes' harmony at the outset so I can remember what it was like to be at peace. When my eyes blink open at the dawn, don't greet me with a giant bloody crow that's forever branded in my cultural memory as a harbinger of death.

"Caw!" it barked at me, right in my face, and I startled backward and probably made an undignified squealing noise as I rolled away frantically from that sharp beak, leaving the oilskin behind, getting cold dew and wet grass all over me.

The crow threw back its head and laughed at me. Not avian laughter, but human laughter, a throaty contralto coming out of a bloody bird's throat. "Lugh's golden stones, Druid," the crow said, "have you been lying here all this time? I left you here weeks ago, and it's like nothing's changed."

"Good morning, Morrigan," I said sourly as I heaved myself up off the ground and brushed some grass off my torso. Before it got any worse, I ameliorated my tone. "And no, I haven't been lying here all this time. It's just that yesterday was particularly taxing. If you'll give me a few moments to clean up, I'll be able to receive you properly."

"Of course. Take your time, Siodhachan," she said, calling me by my original Irish name. She flapped noisily over to my patio table, where rested a small black leather pouch closed with a drawstring of rawhide. She probably wanted me to ask her about it, but I wasn't going to start talking until I'd cleaned up. I strode right past it as if it weren't there.

<Atticus, did I hear you talking to someone?> Oberon asked sleepily from the couch as I came in through the back door.

"Yeah, that giant crow in the backyard," I replied, waving my hand at the window. "Don't mess with it—that's the Morrigan."

<Oh. I think I'll stay inside.>

"Good call."

I shook my head and sighed as I turned on the shower, waiting a minute for the water to heat up. If the Morrigan had come to warn me about another one of her auguries, I'd have a hard time containing my scorn. But perhaps she'd come to tell me where she'd been for the last three weeks. Or maybe she was ready to work on her own version of my protective amulet, and the bag contained her cold iron.

The Morrigan slid into the bathroom in her human form just as I was about to step into the shower. She was naked and beautiful, and her eyes were half lidded with desire, and I thought, ohhhh, crap.

After I killed Aenghus Óg, the Morrigan had graphically communicated that the entire episode had turned her on, and she promised to "take me" soon. People like her from the Bronze Age weren't shy about sex and never felt they had to pretend they didn't want it. As a child of the Iron Age, I was only marginally less wanton, if at all, but the Morrigan, for all her beauty, wasn't my top choice of bedmates.

She might look like a fantasy pinup now, but when in her crow form, *she ate dead people*, and that made me throw up a little bit when I thought about it. I'd been hoping she'd forgotten all about her declaration of desire, but apparently she was determined to make a conquest of me.

It's difficult to say no to the Morrigan when she really wants something. Next to impossible, really. And it's never a good idea to offend a Chooser of the Slain. The politic thing to do—the safe thing to do— would be to give her what she wanted and try to enjoy it. And once the Morrigan decided she wanted to seduce a lad, she could turn on all the wiles of a succubus without that bothersome business of being damned in the bargain. I confess to not putting up much of a fight. I think I might have said, "Hey!"

The Morrigan is not a creature to take you down slow and easy, though. Over the next few hours, I think I had one moment where I wasn't at least partially in pain. It was the first kiss—soft and tender and delicious to the point where I thought I might enjoy this after all. But then her nails were scratching me, I got slapped a few times, there was a whole lot more biting than I've ever endured, and I lost a handful of hair at one point. And if I wasn't doing what I was supposed to—like the several times when my phone rang and I wanted to answer it, thinking it was Granuaile calling to ask why I hadn't shown up for work—her eyes glowed red and she spoke like Sigourney Weaver telling Bill Murray, "There is no Dana, only Zuul." There's just no arguing with that tone of voice. In other words, I was fucking scared, and that's the way the Morrigan liked it.

In the last hour she began to speak in a tongue older than I was: I think it was Proto-Celtic, a couple of vowel shifts and aspirated consonants away from anything I recognized, and since she didn't seem to expect me to respond, I let her babble away. It sounded ritualistic, and it gradually dawned on me that we were performing sex magic of some kind, though I had no idea what she was trying to accomplish. She eventually declared herself satisfied and gave me permission to stop. We'd long since moved to the bedroom, and I collapsed, gasping, onto the sheets.

There really isn't any postcoital afterglow to speak of after that kind of sex: There's just a sense of relief that you survived without disfigurement, plus a dire need for Gatorade.

"Oww," I whispered.

"You're welcome," the Morrigan chuckled.

"For the pain?"

"No, for the ear."

"What?" I reached up my hand to where my cartilage niblets had been and pinched my fingers around something there that felt remarkably ear-shaped. "Is this real?"

"Of course it is."

"Is that what you were doing with that chanting and, uh, stuff?"

"Yes."

I was overwhelmed with gratitude. Regenerating my demon-chewed ear had proven to be far beyond my abilities, and now I felt whole again. "Morrigan, thank you so much! That was so nice of you—"

The breath whuffed out of me as the Morrigan's fist slammed down onto my stomach and pushed up on my diaphragm. "What did you just say to me?" She grabbed my jaw and yanked it to face her, so that I saw her eyes glowing red as I fought to recover my breath.

"Ca—cuh—curse your meddling," I managed to wheeze.

"That's better," she said, and released me. I guessed there would be no cuddling session.

<Um, Atticus, are you maybe finished now? I'm really hungry.>

Oh, Oberon, I'm so sorry. She wouldn't let me go.

<It's all right. Are you okay? Because it sounded like she was pulling out your short 'n' curlies in there.>

Yeah, I bet you never had a French poodle treat you like that.

I turned to the Morrigan and remembered my duties as host. "May I offer you any refreshment?" I asked. "Perhaps a meal within the compass of my limited pantry?"

"I will accept whatever you see fit to offer me," she said.

Statements like that cannot be taken at face value. It sounded like she'd be happy with a sardine sitting on a Ritz, but, in truth, if I offered her anything but the very best in my house, I'd be insulting her.

I tiptoed gingerly out of bed, bruised and bleeding and stinging where sweat had trickled into the wounds. Everything hurt because I was completely drained of power. I'd have to go back outside and draw some strength from the earth to begin healing, and I felt as if all I did anymore was spend my time fixing up my damaged body.

<Holy Cat Fight, Atticus! She scratched you up pretty good,> Oberon said when I emerged from the bedroom.

Yeah, it was a festival of pain. Let me close up these cuts and I'll start in on our very late breakfast.

Since I'd completely missed the morning routine I'd been looking forward to upon waking up, I decided I'd have it anyway, even though it was afternoon. I put on a pot of coffee and then spent a few moments in the backyard, soothing my screaming skin. Feeling marginally better, I returned inside and played the latest release from Rodrigo y Gabriela on the stereo while I cooked an enormous breakfast: three-egg omelets with cheese, diced ham, and chives, a couple of packages of maple-flavored sausage (mostly for Oberon), skillet potatoes mixed with chopped white onions and red bell peppers, and toast with butter and orange marmalade.

The Morrigan emerged from the bedroom as I was plating everything. She was freshly scrubbed and groomed and nude, and she sat down at my kitchen table without a shred of self-consciousness. I didn't have a stitch on either, and I felt pleased to have a small time where I could behave like a Celt again, without worrying about the social customs of Americans.

The Morrigan was making an extraordinary effort to be affable as I served her. I think she tried to smile politely as I gave her a cup of coffee (she took it black), but it was a dismal failure and I pretended not to notice. Oberon, for his part, was eating his sausages as quietly as he could, casting nervous glances at the Morrigan to make sure she wasn't coming after him with those fingernails.

She paid me compliments on the food and drank five cups of coffee to my one, in addition to a glass of orange juice and a taller glass of water. She also asked for a second omelet and two more slices of toast.

<Where is she putting it all?> Oberon asked as he watched her shovel it down.

I don't know. Go ahead and ask her if you like.

<No, thanks. I want to live.>

Once she finally proclaimed herself full and dispensed with another round of obligatory thanks, the niceties of custom had been observed and she could proceed to business.

"Have you wondered where I've been the past few weeks?" she asked.

"Yes, the thought had crossed my mind."

"I've been occupied with a civil war in Tír na nÓg. The battles have been glorious."

"What? Who was fighting whom?"

"Aenghus Óg's partisans decided to rise up against Brighid and myself, despite the fact that their leader had fallen and failed to follow through on his promises. After the first wave broke, a purge was necessary, and that took the majority of the time."

"Did any of the Tuatha Dé Danann fall?"

The Morrigan shook her head. "They were all lesser Fae to one degree or another. But they had some impressive weapons bequeathed to them by Aenghus Óg. Brighid's new armor got a strenuous test."

"Brighid took up arms herself?" The Tuatha Dé Danann are loath to put themselves in mortal peril when they can get someone else to die for them.

The Morrigan nodded. "Aye. And I am forced to admit she acquitted herself well. She is as fearsome a foe as she ever was."

"So it's all over now?"

The Morrigan shrugged. "The fighting is over, so it is as far as I'm concerned. I'm sure there's something political going on, but that holds no allure for me. What does hold allure for me," she narrowed her gaze and pointed at my amulet, "is that fascinating necklace of yours. We have a deal, you and I, and it is time you began to fulfill your end of it."

Our deal was simple: I'd teach her how to make her own version of my necklace, which protected me from most magic by suffusing my very aura with cold iron, and she'd never, ever take my life. It wouldn't save me from accidental injury or the effects of old age, but it sure was nice to know I couldn't end violently without the Morrigan breaking her word.

"I'm perfectly happy to do so. Did you bring any cold iron?"

"Yes. A moment," she replied, and got up to fetch the leather bag I'd seen earlier on my patio table. I cleared away the dishes and told Oberon he was the best hound a Druid could ever want.

You were extraordinarily patient this morning, and I appreciate it, I told him.

<Yeah, well, she scares the bejesus out of me, so it's not hard to sit around and cower when she's in the house.>

I understand completely. I'll try to send her away as soon as I can.

<Thanks, Atticus. I think I'll go take a nap in the bedroom, stay out of your way.>

I gave his head a couple of scratches as he padded by, and then the Morrigan returned. She loosed the drawstring on the bag and up-ended it on the table, spilling out several chunks of cold iron meteorites of varying sizes and purity. None was larger than the size of my palm.

"Which one should I use?" she asked. I sat down and picked up each one, examining them carefully.

"Well, as the wee green puppet once said, size matters not," I replied. "At least as a raw meteorite. You want the purest amulet possible without sacrificing strength. Totally pure iron is actually weaker than aluminum, so you have to alloy it with something to give you some kind of steel. These here look like they're mixed with iridium instead of nickel, so you're in good shape. You can simply melt 'em down and cast them into whatever mold you like."

"Melt them down? I beg your pardon, Druid, but doesn't the amulet need to be cold forged?"

"No, that's a myth of the mortals. The power of cold iron isn't the temperature you use in forging it. A better term would be *sky iron,* because the power is in its alien origin."

"Ah, I see," the Morrigan said. "If it has no bond to this earth, it will repel or destroy magic better than iron born of Gaia."

"Exactly," I agreed. "Now, my amulet weighs sixty grams," I said as I flicked it, "and that's after I punched a hole through it to string it on my necklace."

"Is the necklace silver or white gold?"

"Mine is silver, but you can use whatever you'd like."

"Will the amulet be more powerful if I make it weigh more than sixty grams?"

"Yes, it grants you more protection, but it also precludes you from casting your own spells. To my mind, that's a severe drawback. You have to find a weight that strikes a perfect balance between protection and magical flow, and for me it's sixty grams. I don't know if that's a universal constant; perhaps a different weight would work best for you. But I arrived at that size after much trial and error."

"I can have Goibhniu make an amulet for me," she said. He was not only a brewer of magical draughts, but also the most accomplished smith of the Tuatha Dé Danann, after Brighid herself.

"Good idea." I nodded. "Have him make as many as he can from the material you have here. At a guess, I'd think you have enough to make two at least, perhaps as many as four. I'd like to have one for my apprentice, if you don't mind."

"Not at all. I think it is good you are training Druids again. You should train more than one, Siodhachan. The world could use a strong grove."

That was suspiciously close to a compliment for the Morrigan. She had even spoken kindly. I figured it would be dangerous to point it out, however, so I said briskly, "If suitable candidates present themselves, I will consider it."

The Morrigan pivoted quickly back to business. "Let us say that I have returned from Goibhniu with a cold iron amulet weighing sixty grams and a chain of silver rope. What happens next?"

"Next you have to bind the cold iron to your aura. Unless you'd rather just use it as a talisman."

"Bah. I already know how to make those. They are only good against direct external threats, and they do nothing to your aura."

"Right. So look at my aura. Where do you see the iron?"

The Morrigan narrowed her eyes and directed her gaze slightly above my head. "It appears like filings inside the white interference of your magic. Specks of cookies in the cream."

"What? I had no idea you liked ice cream."

The Morrigan's eyes flashed red. "If you tell anyone, I'll rip off your nose."

"Okay, back to the aura, then. Those iron specks are actually tiny knots. I have bound the iron to my aura all over, so that when a spell targets me or locates me via aural signature, it runs into iron right away and fizzles out. You have to be scrupulous about making a good scatter pattern, so there aren't any holes in your coverage for a spell to get through, and be so thorough that whole-body hexes cannot distinguish you from the iron. That saved my life just two days ago."

"What happened?"

"Some German witches slapped an infernal hex on me. When it works, you simply go up in flames. But since the iron bindings in my aura are aliases that—"

"Stop. What do you mean by aliases?"

I grimaced at my own foolishness. "I apologize, Morrigan; I forgot you are unfamiliar with computer jargon. An alias is nothing more than a tiny file that points to another, larger file. It's a proxy because it only represents the real thing rather than being the thing itself. I cannot very well walk about with an actual cloud of iron filings around me, can I? But magical proxies that point to a real cold-iron amulet are easy to live with."

"Ingenious."

"Thank you. When this hex hit me, instead of my body burning, the iron proxies bound to my aura directed the entire thing to my amulet." I tapped it a couple of times for emphasis. "It heated up so quickly that it burned my skin. I would have been bacon without it, and in fact the same hex turned a local witch into cinders."

"Remarkable," she said. "This happened two days ago, you say?"

"Yes, that's right."

"I received absolutely no premonition of your impending death at that time." She shook her head slowly in fascination. "You were completely protected."

I wondered if she thought I was completely protected against the Bacchants last night. And then I wondered if she would get any premonitions about my fate at all, now that she had agreed never to take me. "Well, the burning skin was torturous. It was like watching fifth graders trying to perform Wagnerian opera."

The Morrigan waved the point away. "But you have the means to deal with that. You were never in mortal peril. And this protects you from hellfire as well."

"Yes, even that which is spewed from a fallen angel."

"How do you bind the cold iron to your aura? Doesn't the iron resist your magic?"

"That's the tricky part for sure. Once I had the idea for this, I spent a couple of decades trying to do it myself, but I couldn't because you're right, the cold iron laughs at all attempts to mess with it. You need the help of an iron elemental. You have to befriend one, basically, because it's a lot of work for them too. Like I said to you before that business with Aenghus Óg, the protective process alone took me three centuries."

The Morrigan cursed in that Proto-Celtic language of hers and her eyes reddened. "I am not a goddess of smiths! I have no talent for iron, nor for making friends!"

"Perhaps you could view it as an opportunity for personal growth rather than an obstacle. As a goddess of death, making friends wouldn't make sense, I suppose, since you must eventually take them all. But I can walk you through that process too. It's not difficult."

"Yes, it is."

"I respectfully disagree. Iron elementals like to eat faeries. I'm sure you can lay hands on a few of those."

"Easily," she agreed, nodding. "They breed like rodents in Tír na nÓg."

"Great. Now, when the iron elemental thanks you for the faeries and suggests that you were kind or nice to offer such a tasty snack, do *not* threaten it with violence in response. Instead, smile and say it's welcome. You might even share that you rather enjoy a bowl of ice cream now and then and that you imagine faeries must be something like ice cream to them."

The Morrigan's face underwent a curious exercise. Her eyebrows knitted together and her lower lip seemed dangerously close to trembling, but then she scowled and the scarlet glow of her anger flared again in her eyes. As quickly as it appeared, it faded, and uncertainty crept again into her features. She looked down at the table, her raven hair falling forward to mask her face, and she spoke to me from behind a black curtain. "I can't do this. Making friends is not in my nature. I am a stranger to kindness."

"Nonsense." I flicked my gloriously shaped right ear. "Here's living proof of your kindness. Irish generosity thrives within you, Morrigan."

"But that was sex. I can't have sex with an elemental."

Lucky for the elementals, I thought.

"That is true, but there are other ways to be kind to people, as I'm sure you're aware. I think the trouble is that you never let people be kind to you in return. Tell you what: I'll get you ready to make friends with an iron elemental. You can practice all the intricacies of friendship with me. I'd be honored to be your friend."

The Morrigan rose abruptly from her chair and scooped the iron meteorites back into the leather bag, her face hidden by her hair all the while. "I enjoyed the sex and the meal and the instruction," she said formally. "You have been a most gracious host." She tied the drawstring tightly around the pouch. "I will visit Goibhniu and return when I have the amulets."

Without another word, she bound herself to a crow's form right on my table, snatched the pouch in her talons, and then flew out my back door, which opened by itself to allow her egress.

CHAPTER 14

I spent maybe thirty seconds thinking the Morrigan had left so quickly because she was getting a bit *verklemmt* over my offer of friendship. I should have known better.

A polite knock at the door startled me and set Oberon off to barking three times before he said, <It's Brighid. She said hello to me.>

Brighid is at the door? A note of panic in my mental voice made my hound laugh, for he knew as well as I that I couldn't answer the door right now. I was still naked and only partially healed from the Morrigan's abuse—and that, I realized, was precisely what the Morrigan wanted. Nothing about the timing of these visits was accidental. Once again, I would have to play catch-up with the designs of these goddesses and try to figure out what their true motives were. A few weeks ago they had both played me beautifully to achieve their own ends, and now I could see it was starting again. I should have asked the Morrigan more questions about that civil war in Tír na nÓg, for that had something to do with Brighid's sudden appearance, sure as a frog's ass is watertight.

"Well, I know how to get some answers," I said to the door as I scrambled into my bedroom. Oberon met me there with his tail wagging.

<Answers to what?>

"To all my questions," I said, throwing on a pair of khaki cargo shorts and a green cotton T-shirt. The door thumped again, not as politely as before; there was definitely a note of impatience in the way she knocked on wood. "Now, look, she can obviously hear your thoughts, so I want you to pipe down and head out to the living room and wait. And when she comes in, I want you to stay behind her at all times."

<Why?>

"Just do it, please," I said shortly, and immediately felt sorry for my arbitrary tone. Usually I enjoy arguing with Oberon. He's great with the give-and-take. But he didn't understand the stakes here, and I couldn't explain them to him while Brighid was listening in on his side of the conversation.

<Okay.> Oberon's tail drooped as he left the room, and I deflated a bit too, but if this was going to work, Brighid could have no warning. I didn't know if I'd even go through with it, but I had to be prepared. I picked up Fragarach from my dresser and slung the scabbard across my back, then hurried to answer the front door.

Brighid smirked at me when I opened the door, and it was like one of those cheesy commercials they play during football games: An obscenely beautiful, sultry woman in next to nothing appears mysteriously; a ghost wind generated off camera blows her hair in a way that suggests wild abandon; she pouts sexily at this utterly regular schmoe with a weak chin; and he completely suspends his disbelief that she'd ever be interested in him, because he's got an ice-cold beer in his hand. The mysterious wind in this case was almost certainly generated by Brighid herself, and it wafted her scent to me, which was just as I remembered it: milk and honey and soft ripe berries. Damn.

Now, I'm not a regular schmoe, and I certainly don't have a weak chin, but I'm as susceptible to beer commercials as the next fella, even though it's just living vicariously in a pubescent male fantasy. None of those commercials came close to the real, live goddess that confronted me in my doorway.

Brighid was wearing several layers of sheer blue material, tied or bunched in such a way as to barely cover her naughty bits, yet providing a tantalizing glimpse of each through the fabric. A golden torc circled her throat, and another accentuated her left biceps, while delicate ropes of twisted metal adorned her wrists. Around her waist were several thin golden chains. Her red hair cascaded around her face in languorous waves like Jessica Rabbit's, and she had gold thread braided into it here and there. And the pouty come-hither look, achieved by pursing the lips a bit and looking at me with sleepy eyes? She had that *down*. The ladies in the beer commercials were hot, no doubt, but when a goddess wants to make an effort, no one else can even open the jar of mustard, let alone cut it.

Brighid was much more my type than the Morrigan. She didn't eat dead people in any of her forms, for one thing, and it was she who ignited the fires of creativity and passion within the hearts of all Irish. But even if I wanted to give Brighid whatever she had come for—and I wasn't sure I did—I realized that the Morrigan had done her best to ensure I couldn't.

The entire cast of the Morrigan's visit changed for me now that Brighid was standing in front of me. The two of them had never been antagonists, but neither had they been fast friends. A healthy respect and perhaps an unhealthy envy existed between them, a rivalry of equals to see who could be first among them all. What had kept each from the other's throat before was Aenghus Óg and his cabal, but now that there had been a purge in Tír na nÓg, perhaps the two of them were clawing at each other and I was either a prize to be won or a means to a different end. *The scratchy sex, the ear, the second omelet . . . it was all the Morrigan's Machiavellian machinations!*

<Atticus, you know I can hear you when you're all spazzed up, right? That was a lot of alliteration for a doubtful Druid deliberating over a deity's dubious designs.>

"Welcome, Brighid. You've left me speechless," I said over the end of Oberon's mockery. She might wonder what I was thinking.

"Atticus," she purred. I'm not kidding—she *purred* at me. Brighid can not only beat Hank Azaria at producing voices, she can do multiple voices at the same time. She can sing three-part harmony all by herself in addition to the lead. It comes in handy when she's crooning ballads as the goddess of poetry, and now I saw—or rather felt—how it could be used for other purposes. "I hope I have not come at an inconvenient time," she said in voices evocative of rose hips, caramel, and silk. It made me feel warm inside, but I shivered outwardly, like a tuning fork quivering in hot chocolate.

"Not at all. Won't you please come in?" I stepped aside and gestured for her to enter, the Bronze Age host once more.

"You are kind," she cooed as she slunk by, a shimmering vision of soft blues and pulsing gold. *Damn.*

She flicked her eyes around the edges of my living room. "Your modern home is interesting."

A very diplomatic compliment that might not actually be a compliment. "It's comfortable, at least. May I offer you any refreshment after your long journey from Tír na nÓg?"

"Ale, if you have any, would be splendid."

"Coming right up." I shot forward into the kitchen, beckoning her to follow, and grabbed a couple of Kilt Lifter ales out of the fridge, tucked back behind the craft lagers. She nodded as I handed her one, then said, "There has been much unrest in Tír na nÓg since you slew Aenghus Óg. His confederates finally revealed themselves, and I was forced to spend some small time putting them to rout. They waged a propaganda war too, if you can believe it."

I nodded. "I can believe it. What sort of nonsense did they spew?"

"Chief among their complaints was my lack of consort," Brighid snorted, "as if Bres ever did anything useful or practical in his long life. All he did was sit there and look pretty. He was a pretty man," she sighed, and then her face drew down into a tiny frown. "And a petty man."

Where Bres was concerned, I had nothing to say. I'd killed him, yet here was his widow in my kitchen, spreading a wee bit of shit on his memory and dressed for epic bed sport. I couldn't even manage a noncommittal grunt. There are no etiquette books that cover this particular situation, so I just took a long pull on my beer.

"But you are not petty, are you?"

"It would be rude of me to say yes when you put it like that."

She laughed richly at my lame joke, and I finally understood what Chris Matthews meant when he said on national television that he felt a thrill go up his leg. I could think of nothing to do except take another long drink to disguise my reaction.

"No, you are not petty. And you have a sense of humor as well. Bres had none. That is why I think you should be my new consort."

I sprayed a mouthful of beer onto the linoleum.

<Ha! If you think I'm licking that up, you're crazy,> Oberon said.

"Oh, I must have surprised you," Brighid said.

I put my thumb and index finger together with a couple centimeters of space between them. "A bit," I admitted.

"I suppose it sounds a bit unusual, but, like the Tuatha Dé Danann, you have found the secret to eternal youth. You are more powerful than Bres ever was, and you have proven yourself the equal—nay, the better—of two of our number. With my imprimatur and aegis, none will dispute your right to rule by my side, and certainly none will dispute whom I choose to take to bed."

Ignoring the dangerous end of her sentence, I focused on the first part: "Forgive me, Brighid, but it has never been my ambition to rule over anyone."

"You need not do it, then," she said, shrugging off my objection. "Bres didn't do anything either, which suited me perfectly. It's a figurehead position, but the Fae feel that it needs to be filled."

"I see. And where would I need to be to satisfactorily fill this figurehead position?"

"In Tír na nÓg, of course." She finally took a sip of the ale she had asked for.

"Can I not remain here, if there is no ruling for me to do?"

"You will have other duties," she purred in that triple voice that turned my insides to Jell-O.

"But I rather enjoy this plane. There's so much change and advancement to appreciate and an abundance of knowledge to absorb."

"You can still sample these things as you wish, making brief trips as often as you like to the mortal plane. But there are more stimulating things to experience as my consort than the latest technological toy. There will be embassies to the world's gods and wonders to behold, and you will visit all the planes on my behalf."

"And my initiate? My hound? They cannot go to Tír na nÓg."

<What? Hey, whoa, this sounds like a bad idea.>

"We can accommodate Oberon." Brighid smiled. "Your initiate would be more problematic, as a mortal who would be constantly at risk of falling prey to the more mischievous of the Fae. Tír na nÓg would not be kind to her, and I doubt she would survive long. But she has not sacrificed much. She cannot have learned any of our mysteries yet in these few weeks. Pay her for her time and have done."

"It is not so simple. I have given my word she would be trained fully."

"Bring her if you must, then. I cannot guarantee her safety."

"But you can guarantee mine and Oberon's?"

Brighid shrugged. "There is no need. You are able to take care of yourself."

<Um.>

Yeah, buddy, I know, we'll talk later. To Brighid I said, "This is a most generous offer and yet wholly unexpected. To become the consort of one's own goddess is beyond the scope of any man's ambition. I confess myself unprepared to give you an answer at this moment, for much may depend on my response, and I feel it would be irresponsible of me to provide one without giving all ramifications their due examination."

"So formal." Brighid shook her head. "I must have made it seem like a business transaction. You mistake my meaning."

She set her ale down on my kitchen table and stepped close to me. Her hand groped below my belt but pulled away, disappointed.

Brighid's face clouded. "What's the matter, Atticus? Do you not find me attractive? Am I not desirable to you?"

<Oh, great big bears! Beam him up, Scotty! Now!>

"It's not that, not that at all," I said, clearing my throat uncomfortably as I reminded Oberon that Brighid could hear him. "It's just that I'm extremely tired at the moment—exhausted, in fact—and while I can do you any other service, I simply can't do . . . that. Right now, I mean. Later would be good." I nodded, smiling. "Great, in fact."

Brighid's nose wrinkled. I heard her sniff a couple of times, and then she abruptly stepped back and tore my shirt down the front, revealing the scratches and bruises from my morning's exertions. Brighid's face flushed and her eyes bulged as she drank in the evidence of my dalliance with her rival.

"I knew it!" she shouted. "You've lain with her! You're the Morrigan's creature!" And that's all the warning I got before she unleashed the flames of her wrath against me in very literal terms. Fire whooshed out from her fingers and palms to char me toasty in my own kitchen. It didn't burn me directly, thanks to my amulet, but it did behave differently than the fallen angel's hellfire: Whereas the hellfire gave me a flash of heat before fizzling impotently, this ball o' fire got channeled directly to the cold iron on my chest, where it began to burn painfully, just like the German hex had a couple of days ago. That was a mystery I'd have to ponder later. Right then I had a friend to protect, skin to heal, and several fires to put out.

<Hey, you can't stick it to my Man!> Oberon barked.

That's why I wanted you behind her. Don't attack yet; I'm okay.

I drew Fragarach from its sheath, wincing at the heat in my palms, and pointed it at Brighid's throat. "*Freagróidh tú!*" I yelled.

"*No!* Release me *now!*" she shouted back. She struggled to move but could do nothing but twitch, held fast in the blue glow of a spell crafted by her own brethren ages ago.

"You're giving me commands? You just tried to fry me and you want me to obey you now? That's not how it works. And you're the one who said I was fit to wield this sword."

"You said you'd never wield it against me!" she blazed.

"True," I admitted, "but that was before you tried to kill me."

Her eyes shifted to find Oberon. "Release me now or—"

She stopped as I pressed Fragarach to the hollow of her throat. "Understand me, Brighid: If you ever hurt Oberon, your very long life will end directly afterward. You know I can move between the planes as I wish; there is no place you can run that I cannot follow."

"You dare threaten me, a guest in your home?"

"You tossed out all the rules when you lost your temper. So we're going to have a nice, long talk, you and I, and Fragarach will make sure you are not deceitful."

<Atticus, the cabinets are on fire behind you.>

Thanks, buddy. "Please take a moment first to put out the fires you started."

"Why shouldn't I let the whole house burn?"

"Because that would be rude when it's a simple matter for you to put them out. Please put them out so we may talk peaceably."

"Peaceably?" Brighid sneered. "With a sword at my neck?"

"Touché. But this would not be necessary had you acted with restraint. I ask you politely once more: Will you put out the fires?"

"What's next? Torture if I refuse?"

"No, I'm not the Inquisition. I will find other means to put them out if you will not." Fragarach could not compel her to act; it could only compel answers. I had a fire extinguisher in the garage, and I'd have to drag her there and back if she didn't agree.

The goddess of fire grimaced but focused on something behind me and growled in Irish, *"Múchaim."* Then she focused on me and said, "It is done."

Is it done? I asked Oberon.

<Yep, she snuffed them.>

"Of course I did," Brighid said, reminding us that she could hear Oberon.

"Thank you." I nodded, as smoke roiled near the ceiling. "Let's be seated, shall we?" I moved the sword slowly, allowing Brighid to shuffle in an undignified way to a chair at the kitchen table, then lowered it by degrees until she was able to sit down. I took a seat across from her, moving her ale out of the way.

"Excellent. Now let's review what happened here, shall we? You showed up uninvited and I welcomed you in. I offered you refreshment and you accepted. You made a proposal to me and I said I would think about it. You ripped off my shirt and then tried to kill me. Now I ask you, which part of that sequence of events breaks every law of hospitality in our culture?"

"You left out the part where you fornicated with the Morrigan."

"Not while you were here. Answer my question."

Sullenly, Brighid said, "The part where I ripped off your shirt was a minor breach of hospitality."

"We are making excellent progress," I enthused. "How about the part where you tried to kill me? Was that not also poor conduct for a guest?"

"Yes—strictly speaking. But you gave me cause!"

"No, Brighid, I did not. If I had agreed to be your consort first and then fornicated with the Morrigan in front of you with Def Leppard on the stereo, then that would have been cause to incinerate me on the spot. But I am a free man and I gave you no such cause. And beyond that, I cannot fathom why you'd react like a jilted high school girl. This wasn't done out of jealousy, was it?"

"No," Brighid said. "I was not motivated by jealousy."

"I thought not. And did you propose that I become your consort out of any true affection for me?"

"No."

"Of course not. Before we get to the real reason you asked me to be your consort, I would like to address your accusation. If I were truly 'the Morrigan's creature,' as you put it, then I could have killed you already, and indeed I should have and would have. We would not be talking right now if I were beholden to her will or if I were part of some evil plot to usurp you."

"Then what is between you?" Brighid asked.

"She regenerated my ear for me," I said, flicking the lobe. "Sex magic."

Brighid flinched. "I did not know you had lost it. No one told me."

"Yep. I lost it in the Superstition Mountains when I was killing Aenghus Óg for you. Speaking of which, did you tell Flidais to kidnap Oberon to make sure I showed up?"

The goddess sighed. "Yes."

<Grr. You know, you're not as nice as I originally thought.>

"I couldn't agree more, Oberon," I said. "Brighid, I want you to think a moment about what you have done here. I am the last man on this plane who truly worships you in the old way. I gave you full rites on Samhain just a few nights ago."

"Yes, but you gave them to the Morrigan too."

"As I should! And to Ogma. And to Manannan Mac Lir and all the rest. For they are my gods, as you are. And now to be served thus, after millennia of faith in your goodness and beauty and purity of spirit—and for what? Let's have that answer now. Why did you truly want me to be your consort?"

"I want the secret of your amulet. I can study it better in Tír na nÓg."

"Is that your sole motivation?"

"No. It would thwart the Morrigan."

"Thwart her how? That's more important to you, isn't it?"

"Yes. She wishes to be supreme in Tír na nÓg, and she is using you to make it happen."

"You are no better," I pointed out. "You wish to be supreme, and you would use me the same way. I'm disgusted with you both. And you know what really chaps my hide here?"

<Testify!>

"It's that you've come down so dramatically from your pedestal. I can't even have a proper crisis of faith and vacillate between the image of perfection and my shattered illusions, because you've left no doubt that there is nothing divine about your nature. Do you not see how you have debased yourself, or do you persist in thinking that you acted justly in trying to kill me? Wait—don't answer that yet." An inconsistency demanded resolution. "Why did you try to kill me with fire?"

Brighid shrugged. "Usually it gets the job done." This admission—

made under a spell that brooked no deceit—told me that Brighid still knew nothing about my deal with the Morrigan, or she wouldn't have even tried to kill me. Regardless, it was perplexing behavior.

"But you expressly knew that my amulet protects me from most magic," I said. "Did you forget that?"

"No. I just didn't think it would prove strong enough to stand against me."

"Ah, you thought your magic was stronger than mine."

"Yes."

"When mortals take excessive pride in their abilities, it's called hubris. I don't think there's a word for when immortals do the same." She regarded me stonily, unrepentant. "So. What will you do when I release you from Fragarach?"

She really didn't want to answer this one, and I had to wait until the spell forced her to comply. "I will tear the amulet from your neck and then set you on fire once you are unprotected."

<What? Where's the gravy?>

I sighed. She wouldn't be able to tear the amulet from me, but that didn't matter as much as her stated intentions. "Well, that puts us in a very awkward position, doesn't it? I'd rather that both of us lived and found some way to part amicably. Tell me, Brighid, why do you feel I deserve to die?"

"I still think you're the Morrigan's man. And you humiliated me."

"I'm not the Morrigan's anything. I am my own man. And any humiliation you feel is justly deserved, because you have behaved inexcusably. We've already established that it was your actions, not mine, that breached hospitality. You're behaving like a petulant child and not taking responsibility for your actions, like one of the blasted Olympians. And I would like to point out that you have not suffered publicly. No one knows what you have done. It can remain our secret, and I think that this is a breach we can mend. What say you? Are you willing to negotiate a peace, or are you resolved that I must die for imagined offenses?"

"Release me and I will negotiate with you."

I laughed at her. "I wasn't born yesterday, as the people here are fond of saying. For perhaps a short time you will negotiate. After that, you will try to kill me, correct?"

Brighid gritted her teeth, frustrated that I had seen through her "truth" so easily.

"Yes," she admitted, after trying in vain to resist answering.

"I thought as much. So, you see, I must keep you under this spell to ensure you negotiate in good faith."

"I have no such assurance from you."

"Well, I haven't tried to kill you yet when you've given me ample cause; I've never broken hospitality with you; and I've remained faithful to you for over two thousand years. I don't think you should be questioning my moral character right now. You cannot say any of those things to me. You have behaved rashly, even unwisely, Brighid, because you fear the Morrigan is out to get you, and if I had behaved with the same lack of restraint, you'd be dead and the Morrigan would already be First among the Fae. And it can still turn out that way." I leaned forward and pointed at her with my free hand. "You have wronged me, Brighid. And you owe me an apology. Much depends on your answer. What say you?"

"An apology wrung from me at the point of a sword would be worthless."

"I beg to differ. At the point of this particular sword it would have to be heartfelt, or else you wouldn't be able to say it. So this is a fundamental test of your constitution. Can you admit that you were wrong? Most deities can't; it's simply impossible for them. But you were human once, before we Irish made you gods. Take your time and think about it."

Brighid's eyes flashed with a blue flame, and I wondered if she had learned to do that just so she could compete with the Morrigan's red flashes. Maybe I should try to figure out how to make my eyes flash green so I could freak out the baristas at Starbucks. "No, you foolish mortal," I'd say as my eyes glowed, "I ordered a *nonfat* latte."

The goddess broke eye contact and focused on emptiness, pressing her lips together, her jaw muscles visibly flexing. She clenched her fists and her entire body began to smoke, with isolated flames erupting here and there on her skin. I assumed she was dealing with anger issues.

Keep quiet while she's doing this, okay? She's forgotten you're there and I don't want to remind her. Oberon nodded that he heard and understood.

At length the fires went out and she relaxed, her muscles unclenching and the tension sloughing off her shoulders. She took several deep, shuddering breaths but eventually sighed deeply, placed her hands flat on the table, and looked down at her lap.

"Siodhachan, I have breached hospitality with you in an egregious manner. Please accept my sincerest apologies for my behavior."

"Fairly spoken, Brighid. I accept your apology. But let us discuss the future now. If I release you from Fragarach's spell, will you attempt to harm me or my hound?"

"No. Nor will I ever seek vengeance for the humiliation I have suffered. However, I cannot promise we will never come into conflict over other matters."

"That's understandable, but perhaps we could avoid unpleasantness by discussing other matters now. What do you think might bring us into conflict in the future?"

"Any liaison you have with the Morrigan."

"Why? Should I not be able to liaise with whomever I wish?"

"Couple with her all you like," Brighid sneered, "though I suspect there is more pain than pleasure in the act." She jerked her chin significantly at the scratches on my torso. "What I mean is any sort of alliance that will threaten my position in Tír na nÓg."

"All right, explain to me what it is you fear. You think I might help the Morrigan usurp you?"

"Yes, that is precisely what I think."

"Well, I freely tell you that I do not want that to happen any more than you do. I'd much rather have you running things than her."

"Thank you," Brighid said warily after a pause to judge my sincerity.

"But I feel it only fair to tell you that I have sworn to teach the Morrigan, and no other, the secret of my amulet."

Brighid's eyes flared blue. "That is what I am talking about! With that as her defense, she could slay me easily!"

"Relax. You have plenty of time to make your own. The Morrigan will not be making one of these overnight. It takes centuries. And while I feel at this time that I must turn down your generous offer of becoming your consort, you are still welcome to come here and study the amulet whenever you wish."

"What did she promise you in return for teaching her about the amulet?"

"Nothing that need concern you. It has nothing to do with supplanting your position."

"Be careful, Druid. She is treacherous."

"She has been more straightforward with me than you have, Brighid. And she has taken an interest in my life for the vast majority of it. It is no wonder that she has beaten you to discovering this new Druidry of mine. You, on the other hand, have ignored me until just recently, now that I have something you want. So if you find yourself at a disadvantage, you have no one to blame except yourself."

Brighid closed her eyes and took a deep breath, determined not to lose her temper again. "Yes, this has been a day for my inadequacies to be made plain. Are you finished?"

"Just about. Will you agree to leave in peace and inform me in advance of your visits in the future?"

"Yes."

"And my promised reward for killing Aenghus Óg? Rather than becoming your consort, I would like your forgiveness for today." I released her from Fragarach and lowered the sword to the table but kept my hand on the hilt. "I look forward to your next visit and hope it will be much more congenial than this one."

"I shall not break hospitality again," Brighid said as she rose to her feet. "But neither shall you hear again an offer like you heard today. I could have been yours, Druid, but no more. Think on that the next time the Morrigan is gouging out pieces of your flesh."

She made sure I saw plenty of what I'd be missing on her way out the door. Damn, damn, damn.

<Can I talk now?>

Sure, Oberon. What's up?

<Usually I think your paranoia is really funny. But right now I'm just glad you told me where to stand so that I didn't get set on fire by She of the Violent Mood Swings.> He reared up and put both his paws on my shoulders and gave me a sloppy lick in the face. <Thanks, Atticus.>

CHAPTER 15

There were multiple missed calls on my cell phone. Some were from Granuaile, some from Malina, and a couple from Hal Hauk, my lawyer. I called my lawyer first.

"Atticus! Tell me you weren't involved in this Satyrn Massacre business," he said without preamble.

"Satyrn massacre?"

"That's what the papers are calling it. Capital M."

"Oh. Well, look, why don't you come over," I said, because anyone could be listening.

"Gods of light and darkness preserve us. Don't move, I'll be right there," he growled, and then hung up.

Granuaile was next. "Are you all right?" she asked.

"I'm afraid you'll have to define your terms."

"You're still in one piece and everything still works."

"Then yes, I'm all right."

"Good. Thought you'd like to know that priest and rabbi came in again."

"They did?" I frowned. "What did they want?"

"They asked me to open the rare-book case. I told them I couldn't."

"Right, because you can't."

"Right. They looked pretty pissed. And then they asked all these questions about you. Religious stuff, like whether you were a Christian or a Jew or a pagan, and whether you practiced your religion faithfully."

"What did you tell them?"

"I said those were questions better answered by yourself. They wanted to know when you'd be back, and I had to tell them I really didn't know."

"Well, hopefully I'll be in before the day is through. Can Perry and Rebecca run things tomorrow?"

"Sure. What do you want me to do?"

"Latin, of course, and get your job back at Rúla Búla."

"Already got it. All it took was a phone call and some groveling to Liam."

"Excellent! I want you to come over in the morning so I can see about doing something for your personal protection. I haven't done a divination recently, but I'm getting one of those hunches."

"The paranoid kind?"

"What other kind is there? Hey," I said, my voice dropping and lilting with dulcet, honey-bunny tones, "can I tell you one of the many reasons I love you?" This wasn't an abrupt flowering of love between us. It was a code phrase, one that Granuaile herself had suggested.

"Look, sensei," she'd said upon her return from North Carolina. "I don't know if things are going to get crazy again like they did with Aenghus Óg, but if they do, we need a way to communicate alibis successfully over the phone. You can't just send your lawyer over every time you need to work something out. You might not always have time. The cops might get to me before he does. I might be out of town when you need me. And that whole business was so messy, so much could have gone wrong. So we should plan ahead and Be Prepared, you know, like the Boy Scouts."

"Fuck the Boy Scouts," I'd said. "Be Prepared was my motto before there were any streets to help little old ladies across."

"Oh. Right." Granuaile had paused, and when I failed to fill the silence, she asked, "Does that mean you already have a plan, sensei?"

"No, I'm just establishing my primacy over the Boy Scouts."

Granuaile's lips quirked upward. "Duly noted. I have a plan, sensei, if you'd like to hear it."

"Of course I would. Thinking ahead like this is why you'll make a good Druid. Seriously," I added, because we were still too unfamiliar with each other for her to see through my customary curtain of wit.

"Thank you." Her cheeks had colored faintly at the praise. "Well, you have to assume these days that all your cell-phone calls are being listened to, and maybe your home and business phones too. That means you have to say what you mean in code. But if the code is too obscure or in a foreign language, they'll flag your ass for suspicious activity and put you on a no-fly list—"

"Beg your pardon," I interrupted. "Who are *they*?"

"The government. The cops. The Men in Black. Maybe even the Boy Scouts. Them."

"Ah. Please continue."

"So we need a simple code, and I was thinking that since we've already pretended that we're romantically involved in one alibi, we should stick with that concept in future situations."

"We should, eh?" The beginnings of a smile played at the corners of my mouth.

"Just pretending," she'd emphasized, her cheeks flushing more hotly. "Then we can call each other as necessary, throw out a code phrase, and then lay the alibi down."

"What's the code phrase?"

"Oh. Um. Well, it's a question in keeping with the pretense of our relationship. It's 'Can I tell you one of the many reasons I love you?' And then the other person says, 'Sure,' and then you just explain what we did last night and where and so on, putting in something cute or lovey-dovey for verisimilitude, and bam! You've slipped an alibi right past the ears of the military-industrial-authoritarian-douche-canoe complex."

I had raised my eyebrows and nodded appreciatively. "Hey, that's not bad," I told her. "It's even a turnoff to eavesdroppers when you get all sickeningly sweet with your voice. Listening to other people be ooey-gooey with each other is a guaranteed recipe for nausea. So let's call it a plan and hope we never have to use it."

Now that we had to use it, only a week after she'd brilliantly made the suggestion, Granuaile picked it up with only the slightest of pauses. "Sure you can, Atticus," she said, her voice turning syrupy. "Anytime you want to tell me why you love me, I'm all ears, baby."

"Well, you know how last night we went out to that park north of Indian Bend Road that has the lights on all night, and we hit baseballs for Oberon to chase? I just thought it was special how you picked up the baseballs all covered in drool and bite marks when I know you hate that kind of thing."

"Well, Oberon's sweet," Granuaile replied. "We were out there a long time. How many balls do you think we hit?"

I was so proud I could have popped. Such a clever mind. "We had a dozen," I replied. "And don't forget, those two bats are still in the trunk of your car."

"Oh, they are? I don't remember, are those yours or do I need to return them to someone?"

So quick. She knew precisely what to ask. When I'd first agreed to make her my apprentice, it was partially under duress, but now I could see that I was wildly fortunate. "Those are mine. The wooden ones are mine, the Wilsons. The aluminum bats were the borrowed ones; I've already returned them."

"Oh. Is that all?"

"That's it. The balls and bats are in your trunk, and you're my snookie-wookie marshmallow fudge love pie."

"Aw . . . wait. Did you just call me a Wookiee?"

I chuckled. "Caught that, did you?" I ended my conversation with her and then made my last call from my home phone. I'd saved it for last because I knew I'd be getting scolded. Lambasted. Reamed, even, in a Polish accent.

"That was poorly handled last night, Mr. O'Sullivan," Malina said immediately.

"Those kinds of opponents aren't my specialty," I replied, wary of using the word *Bacchant* on a phone, untapped or not. "And I got most of them."

"What do you mean, *most* of them?"

"There were fifteen, not twelve, as your divination foretold, so that was poorly handled, Ms. Sokolowski." Talking about divinations and spells on the phone never worried me. Anyone listening from the government would dismiss us as fruity New Age hippies.

"How many got away?" Malina asked.

"Just one."

"Ah, she will return to Las Vegas, then. But she may bring more next time."

"Well, I can't help next time. If that last one had wanted to fight, I'm not sure I could have taken her. What news of the *hexen*?"

"We have managed to bid farewell to two of them."

"From your condo?"

"Even so." She sounded a bit smug.

"You knew them previously?"

"No, these were younger members, not so well protected and not so wise about masking their true nature."

That told me that Malina didn't necessarily need hair or blood to deliver a lethal attack from afar. And she knew how to pick magic users out of a crowd. Good to know. "Well done," I said. "Does that mean you know where the rest of them are?"

"Unfortunately not. We are getting closer, however. We've narrowed it down to Gilbert. But we need more bloodwort."

"All right, I'll send over a courier with three more pounds. No one's going to be asking about the two you bid farewell to, are they?"

"You mean the way people are asking about what you did last night? No, there was nothing suspicious in their leave-taking."

"Oh. I see." Accidents happen.

"You should try subtlety sometime. But, look, they're going to know they didn't succeed in getting us their first time around, so you should prepare for more attacks, however it is that you do that."

"Attacks like the first one?"

"No, I imagine they'll try something different. It probably won't be as flashy, but the result will leave you just as dead if you're not protected."

"Okay, thanks for the warning."

A car screeched to a halt outside. <Your werewolf lawyer's here,> Oberon said. <Bet you he smells like citrus air freshener.>

I bet it's vanilla.

I quickly said farewell to Malina and opened the front door to see Hal stalking up my front steps, a scowl on his face and a newspaper in his hand. "Good afternoon, sir! My, what impeccable tailoring you have."

Hal stopped in his tracks and eyed me warily. "What the hell happened to you?" he said, taking in my shirtless and heavily bruised and scratched form. He gestured at my wounds and asked, "Is that from last night?"

"No, it's from the rough sex this morning."

"Smart ass. Sorry I asked. Hey, did you get your ear back?"

"Yep. That was definitely the best part of my day so far."

Hal sighed in relief and waved the newspaper significantly. "I'll say, you lucky bastard. Police are looking for a guy that matches your description with a missing right ear. I thought they had your number on that one."

I threw up my hands, perplexed. "How do police even know what to look for? The only two cops who saw me got killed."

"Well, some of the modern-day fops fleeing the club saw you handcuffed on the ground in custody of the now-deceased police, so naturally the living police are anxious to figure out what happened to said suspect. They have your clothes and hair color along with the missing ear to go on, and that's it. No descriptions of your face, since you were sucking asphalt."

"Any mention of my tattoos?"

"Happily not. Your tats must have been facedown because of the way they had you cuffed, so they're searching for a tatless, earless guy." Hal sniffed the air speculatively and frowned. "Is something burning?"

"My house was for a while, but not anymore."

"Oh," he said, and the fires of his curiosity were extinguished, just like that. "Well, it's kind of irritating even out here, so would you mind if we sat on the porch?"

"Not at all." I gestured to a chair and Hal handed me the newspaper as he took it. Oberon thumped his tail against the chair and pushed his head under Hal's hand.

"Hey, pooch," Hal said, obligingly giving Oberon's head a scratch.

<I win. He smells like citrus on top of wet dog.>

Did it ever occur to you that maybe he's trying to mask the wet dog smell with the citrus?

<That doesn't make any sense, Atticus. Wet dog is a perfectly acceptable way for a werewolf to smell. I think it must be the other way around.>

SATYRN MASSACRE, the newspaper screamed at me; *25 dead including two officers in nightclub nightmare.* The photo showed body bags lined up outside the club.

SCOTTSDALE: Police are still searching for suspects in the aftermath of the city's worst mass murder, which occurred last night in the Satyrn nightclub on Scottsdale Road. Witnesses were unsure exactly how the killings began, but the deaths of two Scottsdale police officers ended the carnage.

I scanned the rest of the article quickly. "Huh. They mention the broken bats, but they don't mention my sword in here," I said.

"You were whipping your sword around in front of all those witnesses?"

"No, no," I said. I explained what happened last night and the alibi I'd cooked up with Granuaile via lovey-dovey code. "I still have my receipt from Target," I pointed out, "and chances are good they'll find that security tape anyway, if they're any good at their jobs. So we'll just say Granuaile's bats are my bats, slightly scuffed and used from a night of baseball chasing with my dog."

<This means I need to chew on some baseballs, doesn't it?>

Yes, it does. But if you're nice about it, I'll put some gravy on them first.

"Prints on the bats?" Hal asked.

"Took care of it."

"So you couldn't possibly be their man from the club because you have an ear and you still have your bats intact—I see." Hal nodded. "That might confuse things quite a bit if it were to come to trial, especially since the missing-ear detail is being so widely reported. There's your reasonable doubt right there. But you're still in a heap of trouble if any of those witnesses reported seeing the sword. You've been riding around with that thing on your back the past few weeks, everyone up and down Mill Avenue has seen you wearing it, and they might have noticed you didn't have an ear either."

"So what? The sword never left its scabbard. Nobody died from sword wounds."

"They'll use the sword to place you at the scene, Atticus. Look, do you still have it around here?"

"Of course. I have *two* fancy-schmancy swords now." The other one had belonged to Aenghus Óg. His sword was named Moralltach—the Great Fury—and it had fallen to me by right of besting him in a duel.

"I suggest you hide both of them right now, and hide them well. Don't lose a minute."

"What? Why?"

"I think Tempe's going to be working with Scottsdale on this to make sure they do things right, because of how royally they screwed up in your shop," Hal said, alluding to a search warrant gone fantastically wrong that ended up with a Tempe police detective and me getting shot. "Which means they're going to roll up here with a full search warrant for your place, they'll do it all by the book, and if they find a sword, they're going to take you downtown for a long talk."

"What about bows and arrows and other martial arts stuff like sai and throwing knives and such?"

"Why, do you have any of that floating around?"

"The garage is full of it."

Hal cursed in Old Norse for a moment, then switched back to En-

glish. "Damn it, Atticus, you need to get yourself a bat cave or something for all of your shady shit."

"Why? I thought it was all legal."

"It is, but in situations like this, you don't want them to smell
smoke and figure there's been a fire. Which turns out to be literally
true in this case." He sniffed and wrinkled his nose. "What started the
fire, anyway?"

"A visiting goddess."

"Are you being serious or pulling my hair?"

"Completely serious." I didn't tell him the correct expression was
"pulling my leg," because he was doing so well otherwise. Hal was
quite a bit younger than Leif and more willing to make an effort to
use American vernacular correctly. He usually appreciated it when I
corrected him, but I didn't want to distract him now.

"Anything I should be worried about?"

"Nah, it's all Irish politics."

Hal looked at me sharply and shook a finger in my face. "That's
bloody dangerous, getting involved in that. You be careful."

I gaped at Hal. "I can't believe you just said that to me."

<Yeah, because, like, you're always careful. Fetishistically so.>

"What?" Hal protested, shrugging his shoulders and looking ag-
grieved.

"I called to ask Gunnar for help with the Bacchants yesterday and
he shut me down. No well-wishing, no pleas to be careful, nothing.
So now we're dealing with the aftermath of what happens when I try
to go it alone, and you tell me to be careful about Irish politics?"

<Can I have a treat for using "fetishistically" in a sentence?>

"Well, I know precisely where Gunnar's coming from. It's not our
job to keep the magical peace."

"Neither is it mine."

<It's really hard to pronounce. If you're not careful, you could
wind up saying, "feta shit stick-ally," and then you'd feel like a puppy
who forgot to lift his leg, you know?>

"Well, then, why did you get involved?" Hal asked.

I thought about explaining that I needed a safe place to live and work so I could restore the land around Tony Cabin, but it seemed too arcane and he might not understand why I was so eager to tackle a project that would take years to finish. I shrugged instead and said, "Irish politics."

"There you go. Bloody dangerous. Our job is to keep you out of jail when you get in trouble, not help you get into trouble in the first place. Come on." He rose from his chair and gestured inside. "I'll help you get everything stowed."

<I think Hal should get a treat too, if he keeps you out of jail,> Oberon said as we walked inside.

You don't offer werewolves treats if you want to keep all your appendages. They think it's undignified and degrading to be offered a treat.

<Well, the moon must have addled their brains when they were thinking that one through, because I don't see a downside to treats. Honestly, Atticus, it's like they have no regard for the Canine Code.>

I beg your pardon?

<The Code. Has anyone taken the time to explain to them that treats are, by definition, a savory snack of succulence, appropriate at any time and for any occasion, with the possible exception of funerals?>

No. You just made all of that up.

<Precisely! I'm such a creative hound that I deserve a treat.>

Clearly. I stopped in the kitchen to grab a handful of treats for Oberon out of the slightly scorched pantry cabinet. *After you finish these, I want you to stand sentinel on the front porch and let me know if anyone drives up, please.*

<Okay! Man, these are gravy. Werewolves don't know what they're missing.>

I collected Moralltach from the garage, a couple of other practice swords, and a roll of oilskin (the real stuff, not the synthetic fabric they call oilskin these days, because I'm a natural fiber kind of guy). Since I didn't have a bat cave, I'd have to hide everything by using magic. I got out some scissors and started cutting lengths of oilskin, then told Hal to wrap the swords in them so that every inch was covered.

"Do you have some duct tape or something to keep it all together?"

I stopped slicing through oilskin and looked up at my lawyer. "Hal? I'm a Druid. Like, for reals."

Hal flushed and muttered an apology. "Right. You can bind it yourself, can't you?"

"Yes, I can. Are you ready with that one?"

"Right. Yes."

"Hold the edges down, then," I said, and waited for Hal to do it. "*Dún,*" I said in Irish. The fibers from the edges threaded themselves into the weave of the full canvas, creating a sort of Möbius strip where the fabric had no beginning or end, save where I could see it. To Hal's eye it looked as if the edge had just disappeared and smoothed out, an unbroken piece of fabric.

Hal shook his head. "Too bad you don't celebrate Christmas. Your presents would look awesome."

We repeated the process three more times, and then I gathered all the swords and moved out to the backyard. Hal followed, his nostrils flaring at all the herbs I had growing back there. "You're not growing anything that looks remotely like marijuana, are you?"

I snorted. "Only an idiot would think so."

"Cops can be idiots sometimes."

"There's nothing precious here. They can confiscate it all if they feel they have to protect the public from my herb garden."

"Right. So where are we hiding them?" Hal was looking down at likely spots for burial, and that was the wrong direction.

"See my neighbor's palo verde tree overhanging my yard? We're going to hide them up there."

"Oooo-kay. How?" The trunk was on the other side of a very tall wooden fence, and the fence wasn't the sort I could climb easily to access the branches high above.

"You use your giant hairy werewolf muscles to throw me up into the branches and then toss me the swords. I'll bind them to the tree branches first so they won't move, then camouflage them."

"Those branches look pretty spindly. Sure they'll bear your weight?"

"Absolutely. This tree loves me. Its roots go underneath the fence, and we talk sometimes about particulates and nitrogen and the horror of borer beetles."

Hal looked at me uncertainly.

"Plus, I can temporarily strengthen the wood."

"Ah, okay, then. I'll just put my jacket over here . . ."

It was finished in less than five minutes, and Hal didn't even break a sweat chucking me up into the canopy. He usually dressed to conceal his muscular frame, because in courtrooms muscles are associated with defendants rather than lawyers. Still, he was an imposing physical presence, a "manly man" with a cleft chin and a broad smile. He wore a pair of spectacles as an affectation, for he wasn't visually impaired. He thought they made him look more gentle and intelligent to juries. "That's a pretty good spell," Hal said, squinting up at the branches where I had camouflaged the swords. "I know they're there, but I can't see them."

"They'll stay camouflaged as long as I have access to a bit of power. The bindings will stay until I release them."

"Excellent. So what do we do with the rest of your instruments of death?"

"How much time do you think we have?"

Hal shrugged. "Maybe two hours, maybe two minutes."

<Atticus, three cars are coming down the street full of guys dressed like the Man.>

Thanks, Oberon; come on into the backyard.

"More like two seconds," I told Hal. "They're out front right now."

"Guess we'll have to wing it."

"Sure." I shrugged. "It'll probably be fun."

"Put a shirt on, will you? They're looking for someone who killed a lot of people last night, and it looks like you might have done it."

"Oh, yeah." I looked down at my torso, still messed up from the Morrigan. I'd be able to heal it pretty quickly if people would leave me in peace, but that was in short supply today.

"And don't answer a single question without me right there to harass them every step of the way."

"Got it."

As we returned inside, Hal to answer the door and I to put on a shirt, I gave Oberon his instructions. *You'd better just hang out in back while we deal with this,* I told him. *Pretend you're ultra-docile. If anyone addresses you, wag your tail weakly but don't move.*

<Do I have to let the Man pet me?>

Well, you can shy away from his touch, but definitely don't bark or growl or bite anybody.

Struck by inspiration as I rifled through my shirt drawer, I picked out an old anime shirt with lots of pointy noses, large eyes, and giant swords on it. Put it on, and instant nerd!

Lots of men with suits were in my living room when I emerged from my bedroom. None of them had ever seen me before or knew what I was like, so I could play a part and get away with it.

"Dude! What the hell? Who are you guys?" I said, automatically lowering my IQ to everyone assembled.

"Atticus, these are the police," Hal said.

"Atticus O'Sullivan?" a tall sandy-haired man in a green shirt and silk tie stepped forward with his ID out. "I'm Detective Kyle Geffert with the Tempe Police. We have a warrant to search your house for any swords you may have, as well as any blunt weapons such as baseball bats."

His name rang a bell, but I couldn't remember where I'd heard it before. "Oh, cool," I said. "I hope you find my sword, because I've been looking for it."

"You lost your sword?"

"I guess so, dude." I shrugged. "I don't know where it is."

"So you admit that you own a sword?"

"Well, yeah, if I could find it. I need it for LARPing. I'm a barbarian warrior who gets plus three damage when I'm berserk." The detective blinked and looked over at Hal to see if I was pulling his leg. Hal was completely stone-faced, even nodding slightly in agreement with my story.

"How long have you been missing your sword?"

"Well, I think I lost it last night."

"Interesting. I see you have both your ears," Geffert observed.

I flicked my eyes uncertainly between him and Hal. "Um, thanks? And . . . so do you?"

"We've had reports of a man who's missing his right ear riding around Tempe with a sword."

"Really? Whoa. Guess that dude shoulda been more careful with his sword, eh?" I chuckled a few times at my own lame joke but looked down meekly when no one laughed. "Sorry. Nobody ever thinks I'm funny." Suited men were looking underneath furniture and behind picture frames to see if any swords were concealed there. One of them reported that he'd found a large assortment of edged and blunt weapons in my garage.

"Any swords?" Geffert asked.

"Not yet, just knives."

"Keep me posted." He turned back to me and asked, "Mr. O'Sullivan, would you mind telling me where you were last night?"

"You don't have to answer that," Hal interjected.

"Nah, it's okay," I told Hal, and then I said to Geffert, "I was chill-axin' with my girl and my pooch. We were hittin' baseballs in the park, and I took my sword off so I could swing away, you know? But damn if some douche didn't come by and jack it when I wasn't look-ing. I was goin' apeshit, dude, and I'm still pissed. If I ever catch who did it, he'll have to deal with my kung fu."

"I thought you said you lost your sword. Now you say someone stole it?"

"I might be remembering it wrong. I do that sometimes. I lose time when I'm in berserker mode, and I don't recall doing things."

The detective's mouth opened a bit, and he stared at me as if I were a talking slime mold. I looked down and shuffled my feet a bit. "Or maybe it was all those drugs I did when I was younger. Sometimes I black out."

Geffert nodded slowly and looked at Hal. Then his eyes abruptly narrowed and he asked, "Mr. O'Sullivan, what do you do for a living?"

"I make a lot of tea."

"That's your source of income?"

"Pretty much. I own a bookstore and tea shop." This guy had to know who I was already. Since Hal and I were suing the Tempe Police Department for shooting me last month—an unpleasant episode that was entirely Aenghus Óg's fault—there was no way they got a warrant to come in here without very carefully reviewing everything they had on me.

"Would you say your bookstore is a successful enterprise?"

I ignored him and let my eyes lose focus at a point over his right shoulder.

"Mr. O'Sullivan?"

"Huh? What, dude? I'm sorry, I didn't get that."

Geffert spoke slowly to make sure I understood. "Do you make a lot of money at your bookstore?"

"Oh. You're talking about Benjamins. Yeah, dude, I have plenty."

"Enough to pay for very expensive lawyers?"

"Well, duh," I said, pointing at Hal, "he's standing here, isn't he?"

"Why does a bookstore owner need lawyers like Magnusson and Hauk?"

"Because Tempe cops keep shooting me for no reason and searching my house for shit I don't have, and then they act all surprised when I actually have both my ears."

That made the detective clench his jaw for a moment, but to his credit, he didn't respond. He served up another question instead. "You mentioned playing baseball with your pooch. Would this be an Irish wolfhound?"

"Yes, but it's not my old one. He's still lost or run away or whatever. This is a new one. Just got him a couple weeks ago—he's all registered and got his shots and everything." I had done precisely that to sell the fiction that my old dog was really a new dog. Again, thanks to Aenghus Óg, Oberon was wanted for a crime that should have been laid at Aenghus's door. Luckily, it's far easier to get a new ID for a dog than it is for a person. Bureaucrats at Animal Control don't suspect people of getting fake IDs for their pets. They take your form and your check and give you a shiny set of tags for the collar, and that's it.

"Where is he?" Geffert asked.

"In the backyard."

"May I see him?"

"Sure, whatever, dude." I waved at the back door, and Geffert walked through it to see this new dog of mine.

The Man is coming. Remember, you're a meek little guy, turbo-tame.

<I see him. Looks like he sells trucks. I already don't trust him. But I'm going to give an Oscar-winning performance of meek.>

I peered out the kitchen window to see Geffert approaching Oberon, and my hound was as good as his word. His tail twitched hopefully on the ground, he ducked his head, and then he turned over on his back, presenting his belly and neck with his front paws hanging limply near his chest. This couldn't possibly be the man-eating animal the police were looking for in connection with a park ranger's death.

Wow, what a performance! Where did you learn to do that? Oberon usually squirmed around during his belly rubs, and he sometimes closed his mouth gently over my arm. He never stayed that still and passive, believing as he did that belly rubs should be an interactive experience.

<This is what all the tiny dogs do at the park when they see me coming.>

Geffert didn't rub Oberon's belly at all. He just squatted down to check the tags on his collar to confirm that they were recent. He stood back up and looked speculatively around the yard.

<Guess the Man is a cat person. We should play a prank on him.> Geffert started pacing around the herb garden, looking closely at the ground to see if any of it was recently disturbed.

Like what? I don't know if I can top your Oscar-winning performance.

<I'm sure you'll think of something.>

Hal stepped up next to me with an update on the search. "They're being much more polite this time, putting everything back once they move it. He hasn't mentioned removing you anywhere for questioning yet, so I don't think he will unless they find a sword."

I heard a clatter coming from the living room and went to investigate. A female detective had managed to spill my DVD collection all

over the floor. It seemed like an excellent opportunity to burnish my
character as a pathetic guy forever trapped in an adolescent fantasy
land. "Oh," I said, widening my eyes and then shifting them guiltily,
shoving my hands into my pockets, "if you find any porn in there . . .
it isn't mine." The look she gave me was three parts disgust and two
parts revulsion. "I swear." I edged away and carefully didn't smile
until I was back in the kitchen. Hal chuckled quietly.

"You are *so* full of shit," he whispered.

"Hey, the care and feeding of an alter ego is an art form," I replied
in the same low tone. "Here comes the detective. Watch him ask
about the scorch marks."

Geffert strode through the door with a frustrated frown and
seemed to notice the blackened portions of my cabinetry for the first
time. "What happened to your kitchen, Mr. O'Sullivan?"

"Oh, that." I rolled my eyes. "You know those little cooking torches
you use to set your crème brûlée on fire? Well, I was using one of
those last night on my tasty dessert and bangin' my head to some old
school hair bands, you know? And the torch was still on as I was
doing all these fist pumps and stuff and I didn't realize it."

Geffert scoffed openly. "You unknowingly caused all this damage
with a miniature acetylene torch?"

"Well, when you're rockin' out with the Crüe, it's like a religious
experience, dude. I had my eyes closed. Haven't you ever communed
with the sound gods like that before, where you can feel the shred-
ding in your bones?"

Geffert just shook his head and flipped open a notebook. He
wanted Granuaile's name and address to confirm my alibi for last
night. I told him she'd have the bats in her car but neglected to tell
him that he could find her at my shop right then. Another detective
walked up and said they hadn't found a sword anywhere yet, and the
blunt weapons in the garage were covered in dust and showed no
signs of recent use. They shuffled everything around for another
hour but found nothing that would implicate me in last night's Satyrn Massacre. I spent the time outside, watering my herbs and giving
Oberon a proper belly rub, while Hal kept a wary eye on them. I also

sank my toes into the grass and finally paid attention to the lacerations and bruises the Morrigan had given me. By the time they finally drove away, asking me politely to remain in town while they conducted their investigation, I felt good as new and fully recharged.

Hal and I popped open a couple of lagers, clinked bottlenecks, and toasted a good bamboozle. Oberon got a few extra treats for his thespian activities, and when I inspected my DVD collection, I discovered that the female detective had actually alphabetized it for me. I got to feel good for about three whole minutes, and then my cell phone rang.

"Atticus, any chance you can get over here now?" Granuaile said. "Those two guys are back, and they say they're not leaving until they speak with you."

CHAPTER 16

"Those two guys are already more annoying than the police," I said to Hal after I assured Granuaile I'd be right there.

"What two guys?"

I quickly related to him all the details I knew, which were few, and that I needed assistance in gathering intelligence on them. "Do you have a super-sneaky way of siccing a private investigator on these guys so that it can't be traced back to you? I definitely don't want any member of the Pack or friend of the Pack to get involved. I'll pay for the investigator."

"Absolutely," he said as he watched me leap onto my bike. "Mind if I drop in to take a look at them in a couple minutes, pretend to be a customer?"

"Um. Well. If you want."

"You think I shouldn't?"

"It's just that I seriously have no idea what these guys are, except strange. I don't want to put you at risk."

Hal snorted. "Whatever. I'll follow along in case you need my giant hairy muscles to throw them out." He pressed the fob on his keys to make his car alarm chirp.

"All right," I said, unwilling to argue about it. I sent a mental farewell to Oberon as I pedaled away, pumping my legs as fast as they could go. I'd be there in less than five minutes—plenty of time for me to think about what I was heading into.

For the same two men to return twice in the same day looking for me at my place of business told me that they didn't know where I lived, and that was perplexing considering how much else they seemed to know about my whereabouts. And the urgency with which they wanted to see me indicated that they'd completely exploded my dumb-college-boy façade. The rabbi had already seemed to know it when they left the first time, but somehow between then and now they must have obtained proof of my magical mojo, which meant they probably realized how rare those books in my bookcase truly were. Whatever they wanted, I was already feeling like I wanted the opposite.

It was three in the afternoon, that dead time of day, and no one was in the store besides Granuaile, Rebecca, Father Gregory, and Rabbi Yosef. It was Perry's day off.

"Mr. O'Sullivan, we have been waiting—" Father Gregory began, but I let him talk to the hand as I addressed my employees.

"Both of you scoot for the rest of the day—on full pay, of course. And, Granuaile, don't forget to stop by Target before you go home. Sporting goods, you know," I said as a reminder. We needed to follow through on the alibi right away, since Geffert was pursuing it.

"Got it, sensei." Granuaile winked at me, and she quickly gathered her things and jangled out the door, a worried-looking Rebecca close on her heels.

"What do you want?" I asked the rabbi when the door had closed. He was clearly the boss and the badass of the two; the priest was a Public Relations man.

"We want to examine your rare books," he said in his clipped Russian accent.

I shook my head. "They're not for sale."

"For research purposes," Father Gregory interjected.

"What kind of research?"

"Magic and the occult."

"I'd suggest a library for that kind of thing."

The rabbi was about to respond when his eyes shifted to the door. Hal walked in, and the rabbi's eyes bulged and his face twisted into a snarl. It seemed something malodorous was about to hit the fan, and I'd already had enough of that. I quickly confirmed that the rabbi was wearing natural fibers and crafted a binding between his jacket sleeves and his sides, so that his arms would be frozen in place. The rabbi was *fast*, though: As I was speaking the binding, he whipped a silver throwing knife out of his jacket and shouted, "Die, wolf!" in Russian. The binding took effect as he reared back his arm to throw, and the result was that he abruptly sank the knife into the carpet by his foot and Hal didn't die.

Lots of snarling and spitting ensued, but I wasn't finished. I needed to talk to these guys without weapons being thrown, so I bound the priest in the same way I did the rabbi. After that I doubled down and went to work on their legs, as they shrilly demanded that I desist. I bound the fabric of their pants from their knees to the tight weave of my store's carpet, which had the effect of dragging them abruptly to a kneeling position somewhat painfully. They let me hear all about it.

Hal was understandably upset that a complete stranger had been ready to kill him on sight, but I really didn't want him to get more involved. Gunnar was already steamed at me, and if I got Hal killed, he'd probably eat me like a Lunchable. I stepped between Hal and the two shouting, kneeling men and held up my hands. "I'm sorry, sir, but we're closed for the rest of the day. If you'd just come back tomorrow, I'm sure I'll be able to help you then." If I could make the men believe I didn't know Hal or what he was, so much the better. I nodded at Hal and tried to reassure him with my eyes that I had this. He nodded reluctantly back at me, his eyes a bit yellow, and left the shop without a word. No doubt there would be a quick investigation into these men now.

As Father Gregory and Rabbi Yosef loudly insisted that I release them or face dire consequences, I turned to them and said, "You know, I think you guys might be the worst customers ever. Not only do you badger my employees and force me to interrupt an incredibly relaxing day to come deal with you, but you try to murder another customer when he walks through the door and then complain when I prevent you from committing a capital crime. Come on, Padre," I said to Father Gregory. "What would Jesus do?"

Quivering impotently and with flecks of spittle forming on his lips, he bellowed, "He'd rain fire down upon you for consorting with minions of hell!"

"Whoa, slow down, there, Father. I think you've made several giant leaps of logic and faith and I'm not following. First, I don't know any minions of hell. Second, I don't *consort* with anyone, because I'm not fond of that word. And, third, have you ever actually talked to Jesus? Because I have, and he's not really a rain-fire-down-upon-bookstores kind of guy, just so you know. Now, who are you guys, really?"

"You have no idea who you're dealing with," the rabbi seethed.

"Well, yeah, hence the nature of my query." His beard seemed to be unusually active for a collection of facial hair. When a fully bearded man is talking, you expect a certain amount of twitching about the edges as his jaw moves around. But when the rabbi stopped talking, his personal topiary kept moving. "Hey, do you have some roaches living in your beard, or what?" The movement stopped as soon as I mentioned it. I turned on my faerie specs and it looked like a normal beard. The silver knife, though, thrust into the carpet, drew my attention. It was glowing with some extra juju but, oddly enough, only on the hilt, not the blade itself.

"Nice knife you got there, Rabbi," I said, squatting down to examine the juju a bit more closely. The red pattern it made connected ten dots in a familiar sequence, then repeated as it wrapped around the hilt. It was the Kabbalistic Tree of Life.

"You may have it if you let us go," the voice said from the vicinity of the beard.

"Wow, no shit?" I said. The rabbi didn't strike me as the negotiating type, so he must have hoped I'd just pick it up and say it was mine. The spell on the handle must do something nasty if anyone but the rabbi touched it.

"Yes, think of it as a gift."

"My mom told me to beware of hairy men bearing gifts."

Father Gregory said at his stuffy English best, "It's supposed to be Greeks bearing gifts."

I paused to regard him coolly. He was an odd fellow, considering he was clearly a British native and at least partially successful in the Catholic hierarchy yet also fluent in Russian and playing second violin to a Jewish guy who treated him like a trained show dog. Perhaps because of that, he demonstrated a desperate need to be right. Or righteous. Or both.

"My mom didn't know the Greeks existed," I told him. "She was worried about cattle raiders coming out of what is now County Tipperary."

"Cattle raiders? But that was before St. Patrick's time. How old are you?"

"Don't you know already? You pretend to know everything else about me," I replied. "Shut up for a second while I check this out."

I wondered if the magical wards in my shop could snuff this Kabbalistic enchantment without much fuss. I'd never had the opportunity to test them against this kind of magic before, because they were designed to protect the place against spells from the Fae and from hell, as well as some of the more common forms of witchcraft. I'd run into a few Kabbalists here and there over the centuries, but they'd always been amiable sorts and I'd never had cause to think of them as antagonists, until now. This enchantment was still active because, essentially, it didn't meet the definition of magic according to my existing wards. I was near certain it was naughty, especially if this would-be killer rabbi wanted me to touch it, so I directed the attention of my standing wards to the knife hilt and expanded my definition of magic to include the Kabbalistic Tree of Life. The enchantment broke under the attack of my wards, and the red tracery of the juju faded. I flipped off my faerie specs and examined the hilt in normal vision. It was smooth black onyx inlaid with two sets of gold filigree characters. At the top, near the blade, were three Hebrew letters that spelled *Netzakh,* or *victory,* the seventh Sephirot in the Kabbalah. Underneath that, at the base of the hilt, was a curious logo that looked like a stylized capital *P* with a halo.

"I'm confiscating this," I announced, plucking it out of the carpet with no ill effect, much to the rabbi's shock. "I accept no gift from you. When it comes to knives in my shop, I maintain a use-it-and-lose-it policy." I twirled it in front of the rabbi's face a couple of times to make sure he saw that his magic knife didn't hurt me, then I walked calmly behind the counter of my tea station.

"So how about it, Father, feel like making nice? If I was as evil as you seem to think I am, wouldn't I be sucking the marrow from your bones right now or something colorful like that? Why don't I brew us a cup of tea, I'll release you guys, and we'll just sit down and talk things over calmly?"

"*Ne doveryaite emu!*" the rabbi spat in Russian. *Don't trust him.* I still didn't want to give away the fact that I understood everything he said, but maybe the priest would respond to a general plea.

"Look, Father," I said, "I don't know what this guy is saying, but if he's coaching you on manners or diplomacy, I think he's shown definitively by now that he doesn't know much about either one."

"His temper may be short," the priest admitted, "but he was right to attack the wolf."

"What wolf?"

"That man who entered the store was a werewolf. You cannot pretend you didn't know this."

I wondered how they knew so quickly Hal was a werewolf, but I suspected that challenging them on the righteousness of their actions would get me closer to information about who they were. "Well, so what if he was? He was in human form and he wanted to buy a book. That's no reason to kill him."

"Werewolves must be slain on sight!"

"Says who?"

The rabbi was thrashing about in his jacket, trying to get his arms

free by pulling the whole cloth of the fabric over his head or . . . something. His hat fell off and his face was flushed, and his beard began to
move again. I could have bound the bottom of his coat to the top of
his pants and that would have stopped it, but his contortions were
mildly entertaining, and I wanted to see what he would do if he
worked himself free. I stayed behind my tea counter and made no
threatening moves.

"Werewolves are abominations of nature. Nearly every religion
acknowledges this."

"Ah, now I see. Do you guys also have a thing about vampires?"

"If by a 'thing' you mean a predisposition to kill them, then, yes,
we do."

"How do you feel about witches?"

"We do not suffer them to live!" The priest flushed again, and I
decided witches were a touchy subject with him.

"Right. You couldn't possibly have said anything else. So what
about me, then? What do you think you've been talking to?"

"You are a holy man, like us."

That was a surprising answer. "Um, didn't you just say a couple
minutes ago that Jesus was going to rain fire down upon me?"

He answered me in one of those condescending this-is-for-your-
own-good voices. "There will be a reckoning for the time you have
spent associating with infernal powers, but we recognize that you
follow the old path of the Druids."

My eyebrows shot up. They knew what I was after all. "And where
does it say that Druids associate with infernal powers? Because we
don't."

"It was Druidic magic that opened a portal to hell in the Superstition Mountains," Father Gregory asserted. "And you were there."

Bloody Aenghus Óg. "Yeah, and I killed most everything that
came out of that portal. That was my only association with those
powers, okay? I destroyed them."

"And the demon at Skyline High School?"

"That was the fallen angel Basasael. Also slain by yours truly."

The priest paled even faster than he blushed, demonstrating remarkable facility in cutaneous blood flow and its constriction. "You slew a fallen angel?" he nearly whispered.

"*On ne takoi sil'ny!*" Rabbi Yosef growled from underneath his jacket. *He is not that strong.* Well, I'm strong enough to render you impotent, I thought. He looked close to getting himself free.

"Yes, I did, Father. So, look, I'm willing to let you guys walk out the door with nothing lost but a knife and a little bit of dignity, but I don't want to see you again. You're not welcome here, and I'm never going to show you my books. I don't sell them to fanatics of any stripe. Let's just live and let live. When it comes to hell, we're on the same side, anyway. Can we agree to that?"

"I cannot speak for everyone," Gregory said, casting a meaningful glance at the rabbi squirming in front of him. "But for my part I am satisfied."

The rabbi finally got one arm free of his jacket, and the other quickly followed. He immediately began to chant in Hebrew and trace a pattern in the air with his hands. I flipped on my faerie specs to watch. As he spoke and moved his fingers, tiny points of light in various colors hovered and then connected themselves in a gossamer threadwork. I saw already that it would be a spell based on the Kabbalistic Tree of Life, so I let him proceed. As soon as he finished and tried to execute it, the shop's wards would recognize it and shut it down. The priest glanced at me nervously as his colleague chanted, wondering if I was going to do anything, but all he saw was my air of unconcern.

"Ha!" the rabbi cried when he finished. He closed his eyes and tilted his head back, fists clenched and held out at nine and three like he was driving a big rig, waiting for something to happen. Maybe he thought an angel would appear and kick my ass, or grant him strength, or give him a special brownie. After a couple of seconds of expectant heaving of the breast, he opened his eyes, turned his head, and saw me smirking at him.

"Nice try, Rabbi Yosef." I released the binding on the priest's clothes and said, "You're free to go, Father Gregory. If you ever return, I will not be so polite or forgiving. This is your only warning."

"Understood," the priest said, clambering creakily to his feet. He shook out his arms and then took a few uncertain steps toward the door. "Come on, Yosef," he said.

"Oh, the rabbi will join you outside in a few moments." I smiled. "We have something to discuss in private, if you wouldn't mind."

Father Gregory checked with the rabbi to make sure this was okay with him. The beard nodded first, and then the rest of the head followed. The priest stepped out, and the bells above the door jangled noisily in the silence.

"The father seems like a forgiving man," I said once we were alone, "but somehow I get the impression that you're the sort to carry around a grudge. Am I right, Rabbi Yosef?"

"If you have no traffic with hell or other abominations, then I will have no traffic with you," he grumbled through a jaw clenched in anger. "But I have taken your measure, Druid man. You traffic with these things all the time. You are unconcerned by werewolves. I am sure that bookcase is full of unholy works. And I would not be surprised to find you acquainted with witches and vampires. It will not be long before I am duty-bound to confront you. But it will be my job, not a grudge, that brings the hammer down."

"Ah, it's your *job* that makes you act like such an asskitten. I get it now. You think you're one of the good guys and I'm one of the bad guys. That's okay, I'm used to it. But remember that I have your number, Rabbi—it's ten—and the height of my ambition for many years has been to be left alone. Please do not disturb my peace again." I released the binding on his pant legs and gestured to the door. "You're free to leave now."

He leapt to his feet and leered at me, then took his time about brushing off his knees and picking up his coat and hat, just to demonstrate that he wasn't scared of me at all. Still, he said nothing more, and his beard remained motionless as he pushed open the shop door violently and exited into the late-afternoon sun.

I locked the door behind him and flipped the OPEN sign to say CLOSED. First I gathered three pounds of yarrow, packaged it for Malina, and called a courier to come pick it up outside and deliver it as soon as possible. Then I turned off the shop lights and retreated to the Eastern Philosophy stacks, out of sight of the windows. I sat on the ground and crossed my legs underneath me, resting my hands on my knees. There I spent a good three hours laboriously updating my personal wards to defend against Kabbalistic magic—something I never thought I'd need to worry about—and also reinforcing the quick protection I'd tied to my shop's interior wards and copying them into my exterior defenses.

There were still many unanswered questions about those two—primarily regarding their shadowy organization and how they knew anything about my activities out here—but at least I had some solid leads now. They were religious zealots out to save the world from evil as they defined it; one of them had something living on his face; and I had a very interesting knife to give to the Tempe Pack.

I strongly suspected that the rabbi would be watching my store, either to follow me home or to attempt some sort of skulduggery, so I had plans to foil him.

My shop, to all appearances, has only the single entrance. There is no back door, no fire exit, no other means of visible egress than the single glass door with a deadbolt on it. That would never satisfy a paranoid sort like me. I needed an escape route in case something big and nasty or official arrived. In a closet marked EMPLOYEES ONLY, next to the bathroom, I had a steel-rung ladder bolted into the wall that led to a trapdoor in the roof. Said trapdoor couldn't be opened from the outside, in both practical and magical terms. I was the only one who could budge it.

To give the rabbi the slip, I climbed the ladder with the silver knife between my teeth, pirate style, and crept out onto the roof, staying low in the early-evening shadows. I cast camouflage on myself and shed my clothes, regretting the necessity of leaving my cell phone behind. I tied one end of a piece of string around my key ring and the other end around the hilt of the knife. That done, I bound my form to the shape of a great horned owl and firmly gripped the string in my talons. I then cast camouflage on it, the keys, and the knife and lifted off, silently, invisibly, into the Tempe night. I didn't fly straight home but rather lit high up in the branches of a large eucalyptus tree near Mitchell Park. I spent a good quarter hour just looking around to see if anything had followed me, on both the mundane and the magical planes. How the rabbi could have possibly followed an invisible bird he didn't know to look for was beyond me, but paranoia was my standard operating procedure.

Finally satisfied, I glided home and spiraled down into my backyard, where I released the binding and returned to my human form. Oberon was very happy to see me.

<Mr. Semerdjian's back from the hospital,> he said. <We can stick it to him again when he's feeling up to it. I hope he feels better soon.>

I cooked dinner for us, then gave Hal a call from my home phone to suggest he pick up the silver knife to aid in the investigation of Father Gregory and Rabbi Yosef. I left it on the front porch for him, the blade carefully wrapped in oilskin for his protection, then immediately began to work on shielding my house from Kabbalists. Once I finished, hours later, I felt mentally drained from the exertions of the day, but I crashed gratefully on my bed and counted myself lucky that I didn't need to spend another night healing outside.

CHAPTER 17

The Morrigan tried to wake me up gently this time, but she still managed to startle me into a waking nightmare.

"Gah! Please tell me you're not horny," I begged, clutching the sheets and trying to hide behind a pillow.

"No," she replied, smirking, even though she was sitting naked on the edge of my bed, raven hair falling on alabaster skin. "I have returned with the amulets." Four black droplets of cold iron shifted with the percussive clack of rocks in the palm of her hand. "Goibhniu was quick."

"Ah, that's great." I lowered the pillow and sighed in relief. "Very good. Because I don't think I could take another day like yesterday."

The Morrigan laughed, genuinely amused, and it did not sound remotely malicious to me. "You look well, Siodhachan. You are completely recovered."

"Physically, yes. But you left me in an awkward position with Brighid, and you know you did."

The goddess of death snorted. "I saw that she redecorated your kitchen."

"She tried to kill me, Morrigan. She could have killed my hound."

"I felt no danger for you at any time." Her head shook slowly and a tiny smile stretched across her face.

"Will you ever feel that danger again, now that you've agreed not to take me?"

"Oh, yes, I know I will, because I already have. It's coming."

"It is? When?"

"Very soon. Today or tomorrow. You battle with shadowy figures."

I was bemused. "That . . . kind of sounds like a horoscope."

The Morrigan laughed again. She was in an extraordinarily good mood. "I suggest you perform your own divination. Soon. But for now I come bearing gifts. These three extra amulets are yours to dispose of as you wish. And there is a package of fresh sausage in the kitchen."

"That's very generous, Morrigan," I said, taking the three amulets from her. They were teardrop shaped, with a loop at the top to string on a necklace. "Oberon's going to love the sausage. Shall I cook breakfast for us? Are you hungry?"

"Yes, I'm rather famished. And you make such excellent omelets."

"Okay," I said, whipping off the bedspread and padding barefoot toward the kitchen. I had to go to the bathroom, but I was putting that off until I had the Morrigan settled. I didn't want a repeat of what happened the last time.

Some watchdog you are, I told Oberon, who was sitting meekly by the refrigerator.

<She scares me.>

What? I've never seen her in such a good mood. I gave him an affectionate scratch under the chin and got out the makings for coffee.

<That's what scares me. She's never even petted me, and now she's bringing me sausage? She wants to fatten me up for something terrible, I just know it.>

I don't think that's it, buddy. I think she's happy because she feels she's beaten Brighid somehow.

<Well, it's disconcerting. Wait, discombobulating. I should get a snack for that. It's discombobulating because now I don't know what to expect, except a snack.>

You must proceed on the expectation of good manners, both yours and hers. That is the essence of hospitality.

The Morrigan walked into the kitchen and took a seat at the table. "Good morning, Oberon," she said with a smile.

<Three kinds of cat shit, Atticus, she's talking to me!>

So go over there and wag your tail. She won't hurt you, I promise.

Oberon got to his feet, kept his head low, and wagged his tail slowly, half expecting to die.

"Oh, you're actually coming to see me? I'm honored," the Morrigan said. Oberon's tail wagged a bit faster. "This is quite a feather in my cap, to be acknowledged by the great Druid's hound," she added. Oberon bumped his snout under her arm, flopping her hand expertly onto the back of his neck. She immediately began to pet him with a series of massaging squeezes, chuckling softly as she did so.

<She thinks petting me is an honor,> Oberon said, his tail wagging enthusiastically now. <This is an unexpected position to take for a goddess of slaughter, but I applaud her defiance of convention.>

Breakfast was pleasant. The Morrigan asked for advice on what to do next with the amulet, and I advised her to wear it as a talisman for now and cast spells with it off and on to discover what difference there was. She had to discover a way to cast spells without any interference whatsoever from the iron. In the meantime, she should introduce herself to an iron elemental and give it a few faeries, asking nothing in return. Repeat as necessary until the elemental asked if it could do anything for her. "That might take years," I warned. "It took me three years to get to that point, and I'm a friendly guy. Never betray a moment's impatience."

"Where did you get the faeries to feed it?"

"Aenghus Óg kept sending them after me."

"Ha!" the Morrigan barked. "So in a way he was helping you all along to build the defense that enabled you to stand up to him."

When the Morrigan left, I finally relieved my grateful bladder, then discovered I was only mildly late to get on the road with Granuaile. My cell was still on top of my shop's roof, so I used the phone in the kitchen to call her to come pick me up. After that, I got my wands out of the garage to perform a long-overdue divination.

My wands are twenty sticks with Ogham script carved into one end. Each of the sticks stands for a different letter of the Ogham alphabet, and these in turn are associated with the trees of Ireland, together with a host of prophetic meanings.

I took my wands out to the backyard and cleared my mind. I focused on my friends and their safety, then, without looking, I withdrew five sticks from the bag and threw them gently into the air, letting them fall in front of me. How they fell—and how I interpreted them—would hopefully give me a glimpse of the future.

I saw willow, alder, hawthorn, blackthorn, and yew. The latter chilled me quickly; it prophesied death. Fortunately it did not definitively cross the alder or willow—which I took to mean both male and female friends—yet it threatened both, lying between them, as a stark possibility, a possible outcome. Hawthorn and blackthorn—magic guardianship and danger. My friends needed magical protection: The German *hexen* would attack again soon, perhaps at any moment.

"Out, out, thou strumpet Fortune!" I cried with all the venom of Charlton Heston.

<What's a strumpet?> Oberon asked.

"It's a Shakespearean word for *whore*."

<Cool word! It rhymes with *trumpet*. And *pump it*. Why didn't the Black Eyed Peas use it in their song? Aren't rappers always looking for cool new rhymes? They should kick it old school with the Bard.>

I snorted. "Indeed."

<Who'd you call a strumpet?>

"Fortune. It's a quote from *Hamlet*. The idea is that Fortune is fickle or unfaithful, as strumpets must be by the nature of their business. The character who says it continues, 'All you gods, in general synod take away her power;' because he doesn't like what Fortune has in store for him. Well, I'm not a god, nor am I in general synod with anyone, but perhaps I have a way to take away Fortune's power to do you harm." I had three amulets of cold iron that I could use like talismans—three people I could protect. "Come here, Oberon. Let me see your collar."

\<Aw, no, not more tags?\>

"Not this time. This is a special magical talisman to protect you from the Man."

\<Gravy! Thanks, Atticus!\>

"You're going to need to hold still for a few minutes while I activate it. We have to make sure the Man can't get past all the juju to grind you down, you know?"

\<Oh, I dig it, I totally dig it. I'll just pretend I'm one of those crazy Sphinx cats.\>

"Excellent." Protective talismans are fairly simple to construct from most objects, but they vary in strength depending on the base material and the skill of the caster. Cold iron naturally provides the strongest protection, but its magic-negating properties also make it tremendously difficult to twist to one's own purposes—unless you've been watching how iron elementals do it. Like wards, you have to be specific about what you want the talisman to protect against—you can't simply say, "Protect me against everything," because absolutes are not only impossible to empower but dangerous in practice. Cold iron is almost an absolute in itself, but I specifically crafted Oberon's talisman to watch for Fae magic, infernal hexes, several forms of old craft from Europe that the *hexen* might employ, and Kabbalistic spells. He'd be at least partially open to Obeah, Voudoun, and Wiccan craft, as well as most anything from the Indian and Asian traditions and the vast sea of shamanistic practice, but I had to put my money down somewhere.

Granuaile was knocking on the door as we finished up, and after she confirmed that she'd picked up some bats and baseballs for my Satyrn Massacre alibi, I got to repeat the practice on her.

"Aw, sensei, you shouldn't have," she said, as I presented her with the amulet. She was wearing a gold chain already, and the amulet was a bit heavy-looking once she had strung it up. She had a couple of freckles near her collarbones, and I resolutely kept my eyes up there.

"I hope it won't throw off your wardrobe too much," I said. "But you should wear this from now on. If you're not wearing it, then it's doing nothing for you. Eventually you'll bind this to your aura as I've done with mine, but until then it'll just be a talisman for you. I'm going to empower it for you now. Want to see what it looks like?"

"What do you mean?"

"I'm going to cast a binding to make the magic spectrum visible, and then bind your sight to mine so you see what I see."

"You're going to let me watch you do some cool Druid shit?"

"Yep. But you should always remember to speak of such things with reverence and awe."

She didn't miss a beat. "You mean you're going to initiate me into the sacred mysteries of Druidic craft?"

"That's much better; well done." I turned on my faerie specs, found the threads of Granuaile's awareness, and bound them to mine. She gasped when the knot was completed and her point of view wrenched outside her own head.

"Whoa!" Her arms splayed out, searching for balance. "My first out-of-body experience."

"Don't move or you'll probably fall over. Shut your own eyes."

"Okay, okay. That's better. Hey. Where's the magic? You said there'd be magic."

"Patience. I haven't started yet. But look here." I raised the back of my right hand into my sight and examined the power glowing white through the loop of my tattoo. In the visible spectrum my tattoos did nothing, but the strength of the earth shone underneath them like a backlit neon sign when I looked at the truth of things. It appeared that I had an indigo racing stripe down my right side with a pulsing white halo.

"Wow! You're lit up like Vegas! How does it glow under the tattoos? Never mind, tell me what all these threads and knots are— Wait. No. What the hell are all those knots coming out of my head? They're really intricate."

"That's a sensory hitch. You're looking at the binding of your sight to mine."

"No way! You can see spells? They just hang around in the air like Celtic artwork?"

I laughed softly. "Most Celtic works of art *are* spells, or at least they were at one time. The bonds between all living things are there for Druids to witness and manipulate as we choose. There are so many bindings that choosing what to see and focusing on it will become your most treasured skill."

"Really? I'm having no trouble focusing."

"That's because you're using my eyes," I reminded her.

"Oh yeah. Dunce cap for me. So all spells look like this?"

"No, just Druidic ones. Some spells I cannot see very well or even identify, but you can always tell that something is wrong when parts of people are cut off from the world, when their ties are smothered or altered somehow. I will show you what other spells look like as the occasion arises."

"Cool. This is so fucking cool."

"Reverence and awe?" I prodded her gently.

"I meant to say this blessed mystery fills my soul with light."

"Heh! That's excellent. All right, now I need to concentrate, and you should probably keep your exclamations to yourself while I'm doing this," I said, as I refocused on the amulet. "Don't move either."

"Okay."

I gave Granuaile the same protections I had given to Oberon. Though she kept quiet as she saw the dim green web of protection spread out across her body from the amulet, she gasped when the binding was complete and energized, since the threads flashed and shimmered briefly with white light before fading back to a soft green.

"All right, that's finished. You're protected from line-of-sight magical attacks only. If someone gets hold of your hair or blood, this won't do you a lick of good, because they can then cast a spell that attacks you from within, underneath this shell of protection."

"You mean the kind of stuff Laksha can do."

"Precisely. And the coven living on the floor above you. Now watch what happens when you remove the amulet from around your neck—can you take off that necklace using my eyes?"

"I think so. Hold on." She reached behind her neck and loosed the clasp of the chain, removing the amulet and holding it in her right hand, which she dropped to her side. The gossamer threads of my binding sloughed off, retracting like a tape measure into the amulet in her hand.

"See that?" I said. "If you don't wear it, it's useless."

"So I have to wear it all the time?"

"That would be safest, but you can remove it when you know you're secure in a warded room. Your condo counts, because I've warded it."

"So if I looked at my door through your sight, I would see the wards you've put there?"

"Yep. You can see the wards on my house here if you'd like. I can lead you outside to check them out."

"How bitchin' would that—I mean, you honor me, sensei."

I chuckled. "Put the amulet back on first, and watch yourself armor up." She did so, and it was a serendipitous bit of caution. Hands on my shoulders, she followed me out front to the edge of my lawn, commenting as she went on the network of bindings all across the porch and the grass and the mesquite tree that had helped me fight off the wheel bug demon. Then, as we were about to turn around to appreciate the wards on the house itself, I heard a sharp thumping noise behind me, as though someone had slapped their hand down onto the cushion of a couch. Granuaile grunted, and I felt her fingers clutch desperately at my shoulders before they tore away. I whirled around to see her falling backward onto the lawn. Before I could discern what had happened or even ask her if she was all right, my amulet *punched* me in the chest, knocking me backward until I was staggering into the street. I realized this had happened to me before, but it had been during World War II in the southwest of France. And between one awkward step back and the next, I had one of those singular moments of gestalt, where the synapses of several memories and the clues lying idle in my subconscious connected and delivered a single word to my frontal lobe, loaded with anger and revulsion and a bitter kernel of vengeance long denied: *them*.

A flicker of movement in my peripheral vision drew my head to the right, and I caught a glimpse of a slim woman drenched in hellish juju fleeing around the corner toward Mitchell Park. If I hadn't been using my faerie specs, I wouldn't have seen her at all; she was probably cloaked or camouflaged in the normal spectrum, and she was definitely one of *them*—and now I had a name for an old enemy that I'd longed to meet again since the early 1940s. There was not a doubt in my mind that the witches who'd attacked me and my charges during World War II were the same ones attacking me now, and they called themselves *die Töchter des dritten Hauses.*

CHAPTER 18

There was no time to waste. I released the binding on Granuaile's vision, restoring her own sight, and shouted to her as I ran down the street, "Get back in the house and stay there!" She'd be safe inside from further attacks. I lengthened my stride and sprinted, hoping I'd be able to catch up to the witch who had just tried to assassinate me and my apprentice.

As I came around the corner of 11th to Judd Street, I spied her turning right onto 10th Street. That would take her in short order to Mitchell Drive, where I imagined she would turn north and head for the park—or possibly University Drive—in a bid to escape. Yet when I arrived at Mitchell Drive, the sound of her soles clapping on the asphalt drew my gaze to the south instead. I was in time to see her disappear around the corner of 10th Place, a brief afterthought of a road with absolutely no residential frontage. It was an outlet that would take her to Roosevelt Street, where again I presumed she would turn north—and the thought turned me cold inside.

That would lead her past the widow MacDonagh's house.

Did she know the widow was my friend? The widow had no protection; she was completely vulnerable, and she was probably sitting on her porch that very instant, open to attack, if the witch had not already paid her a visit.

I used to try to protect all my friends in the early days, but gradually I realized that the very process of protecting them often painted them as targets—or pointed the way to where I was hiding. It became counterproductive to keeping my location secret, so I long ago fell out of the habit. Running after the witch now, I realized that the situation had changed and I'd failed to see it: I was no longer hiding, so my friends might as well be wearing sandwich boards that said, *Hurt me to hurt the Druid.*

I redoubled my efforts and considered drawing on my depleted store of magic to accelerate my progress, but then I caught sight of her and understood that she was hoping I'd do just that. She was purposely running in the middle of the road, which meant she knew I got my power from the earth. She was not about to run anywhere near someone's landscaping, where I could draw power and never tire; if I wanted to attack her magically, I'd have to remove myself from the earth and risk draining my power entirely.

That smelled like a trap.

My options were somewhat limited. I had enough magic left in my bear charm for a spell or two, three if I was lucky; most of it had been burned up creating Granuaile's talisman and binding her sight to mine.

I had shoes on, so I couldn't draw power without stopping to take them off. I couldn't shape-shift to a hound without getting naked first, and that would not only put me farther behind but would risk exposure in a couple of ways. Another possibility suggested itself to me as I continued pounding down the pavement after the witch, though it certainly carried the risk of revealing my true nature and I'd never tried it before. I reasoned that here on 10th Place, with no windows looking out at the street, I could manage it with minimal risk of witnesses. In my estimation, it was worth a gamble; I couldn't let the witch get away without answering her blow somehow. If she wanted to pick a fight with me, she had to know there was going to be a price to pay.

I stripped off my shirt as I ran and tossed it into the street, then triggered the charm that would bind my form to an owl while still on the run. My arms unfurled into wings, and my legs shrank up into my body, leaving my jeans and sandals to tumble after my shirt. I didn't crash and burn and no one saw me do it, including the witch, so I decided to chalk it up as a good idea.

Flapping powerfully to gain altitude, I banked northeast immediately to cut off the witch, who was now heading north on Roosevelt.

She came into view as soon as I cleared the last roof of 10th Place, churning her legs straight up the middle of the street. I climbed higher to get out of her peripheral vision. I lined myself up behind her and saw her check her six to see if I was still pursuing on foot. She didn't see me closing from above. I dove at her just before she drew even with the widow MacDonagh's property on the left. I kept my eyes on my target, so I didn't know if the widow was on her porch or not. The witch saw no shadow as I descended, and when she heard the softest flutter of my feathers as I backwinged, there was not time enough for her to duck. My talons scratched into her scalp, and I clutched them convulsively and pulled away hard to my right, even as she screamed and ducked. I came away with a bunch of her hair in my talons, more than enough for me—or Malina—to do something mischievous with.

But first I had to get away. The witch knew almost immediately what had happened: Normal owls don't attack running heads of hair for their nests. She knew it was me and what I could do with a handful (or taloned footful) of her hair. She stopped and shouted a curse at me in German, which hit me just like the last one did. My amulet slapped me hard in the chest and knocked me spinning through the air. I flapped my wings spastically, trying to regain control, but I was at low altitude already and could see that I was going to crash pretty hard—hard enough to break my delicate bird bones if I didn't do something. I hurriedly unbound myself from the owl and crashed with a whuff of breath onto the street in my human form, rolling and skidding and scraping my hide up with a beautiful case of road rash.

The witch's hair floated free from the grasp of my human feet—which cannot be said to have much of a grasp at all. She spat that curse at me again, and I lost what little breath I had remaining as the amulet punched me once more. Well, that was enough of that.

I was still rolling from the fall and kept at it, diving naked for the lawn of the nearest house. I sank my fingers into the grass and got only the tiniest trickle of power into my bear charm before I was torn away and hauled up by my own hair into the street.

Instead of resisting and trying to tear free by lunging forward, I pushed into a backward somersault. The unexpected maneuver forced her to let go, because her single right arm could not hold my entire weight propelled by my legs. I tumbled ass over teakettle and rose to my feet, squaring my shoulders and crouching defensively, to find myself facing not one but two witches in the street. Where had the second one come from?

My back was to the widow's house, and the witches guarded my approach to the lawn in front of me. They looked different now—the hellish juju was muted and I could see some of their features in the green haze of the faerie specs, so I presumed they were now visible to humans and flipped off my spell to check them out in the normal spectrum.

They looked like they wanted to be Pat Benatar. Or maybe Joan Jett. They wore form-fitting black leather pants with boots rising to mid-calf, spaghetti-strap black camisoles, and snarling, toothy expressions glowering at me underneath feathery, heavily sprayed hairdos from the eighties. The one I'd pursued was a blonde. The new one was a brunette. I was surely looking at a cosmetic façade. Like Malina and her coven, these German witches were hiding their true ages with spellcraft. Unlike Malina and her coven, I had absolutely no doubts about their malignant intentions; there was cruelty in the faint lines around their eyes, and their thin lips smiled only at other people's pain. *Die Töchter des dritten Hauses* had tried to kill me during World War II, and now they were after not only me but Granuaile too.

I heard police sirens wailing somewhere nearby and wondered if Granuaile had called them. As we scrutinized one another, looking for an opening, a weakness opened up behind me. "Atticus? Is that yer naked bum what I'm lookin' at?" the widow called from her porch.

With a word they could have killed her, that same brief curse in German that they had used against me three times now. There was nothing I could do to prevent them. They would process it in another second and see how they could hurt me. So I had to distract them.

A clump of the blond witch's hair was lying on the asphalt where it had fallen from my feet, just to my right. I dove for it, snatched it up, and strung the strands across my mouth lengthwise, as if they were a gag. Then I used the last of my magic to transform myself to a hound and bounded south down Roosevelt, back toward my house.

The witches shouted in dismay and gave chase immediately, the widow forgotten—if she'd even registered on their consciousness at all. If I reached my house, my wards would protect me utterly, and they could not allow that to happen.

I tumbled messily in the street as my amulet punched me twice in quick succession, but I scrambled to my feet and veered across to the houses on the west side, where I could weave in and out of the land-scaping and draw more power as I ran. I was careful not to swallow or do anything else to dislodge the hairs resting between my jaws.

Though I was quickly outpacing the witches, I wasn't going any-thing near full speed. I wanted them to chase me rather than pay at-tention to the widow. And I was beginning to wonder if they had anything else in their repertoire besides the single curse they'd been spitting at me. Some witches are bloody terrors if they have the time for ritual but are limited in what they can do in face-to-face combat; other witches are amazing in combat but lack the discipline or magi-cal chops to do anything complicated when you sit them down in a circle and tell them to go to't. Lots of European witches are of the former type: Give them time and the proper ingredients, and they could open some ungodly cans of whup-ass. Rarely were they pre-pared for personal fisticuffs—or for chasing a shape-shifting Druid. I was just reflecting that I still didn't know much about the abilities of

Malina's coven and that Laksha was the only witch I currently knew who was as dangerous in your face as she was with a drop of your blood, when the Germans chasing me tried something new. They attempted to remove my necklace with a spell, recognizing perhaps that it was protecting me from the full force of their death spell.

It felt like I was a steer being wrestled to the ground. My necklace choked and pulled at me in response to the witches' summons.

It wasn't going anywhere. It was bound to me and wouldn't come off without being removed with my own hands—and right now all I had were paws. But the witches were encouraged. They hadn't been able to do me any real harm, but they were consistently able to knock me off my feet in one way or another, and they were getting closer. Drawing some power from the earth of the lawn I'd slid on and bracing myself for further abuse from my necklace, I gathered my feet underneath me and leapt forward again, widening the gap. I wanted to pant but couldn't risk losing the witch's hair; it was the only reason they still pursued me.

They were cursing their fashion sense in German, one observing that their boots weren't made for running but they'd had to do an awful lot of it this morning. The other said the running wouldn't be necessary if people would just die like they were supposed to.

They were pretty shagged out by the time they fetched up to my house, but I was completely refreshed and recharged. The sirens nearby stopped, but they sounded only a few blocks away, up near University Drive and a bit to the east.

Granuaile had locked my door, as expected. I almost changed back to human form and knocked on the door, but just in time I remembered Oberon saying Mr. Semerdjian was back. I glanced over my shoulder and, sure enough, the telltale gap in the blinds told me he was watching. If I changed now, he'd report me for indecent exposure and whatever else he could dream up. Instead, I scratched at the door with my paws and called to Oberon, as the witches huffed and puffed and swore they'd snuff me for tearing out some of their hair and making the rest of it wilt.

Oberon was looking out the front window at the witches on the edge of my lawn and growling as I heard Granuaile coming to the door.

<Should I attack?>

No, we have a witness. Must behave.

<What if they don't behave?>

If they step on the lawn they'll trigger the wards, and I think they know it.

Granuaile opened the door, and I bolted to the kitchen as she closed it and locked it up.

"Atticus? What's going on?" She peered out the window. "Where did they come from?"

I unbound myself from the hound form and gagged a bit as I spat the witch's hair onto the kitchen table. The third amulet the Morrigan had given me was there, and I snatched it up as I said, "They're the ones who tried to kill us. Stay inside until I come back."

"You're leaving again? The phone's been ringing off the hook, but I haven't been answering it."

"The widow's in danger and I have to protect her. Keep ignoring the phone and stay inside," I said as I headed for the back door.

"All right, but are you okay? Your skin looks like hamburger," she said, noting where I'd had my unhappy landing on the street.

"I'll heal." The phone started to ring, true to Granuaile's word. "Don't worry, I'll be home soon."

"Okay, sensei," she said. "Nice ass," she added as I closed the door behind me. It was a comment I'd have to enjoy later. I tossed the amulet into a patch of grass, drew power, and changed form again into an owl. I hadn't shape-shifted this much in ages, and it was starting to hurt. I collected the amulet in my talons and pounded the air until I cleared my neighbor's fence, keeping below the rooftops so the witches wouldn't see me. I hoped they'd be foolish enough to test my wards or at least waste their time shouting at my house.

The hope was short-lived. I cast camouflage on myself while in the air, and when I had to cross my street to head north to the widow's house, I saw the witches already chugging back toward Roosevelt, grimly frustrated and looking for someone to take it out on.

I landed on the widow's porch, screeching to get her attention, and her eyes widened. I unbound myself and remembered to cover my goodies just in time. The widow smiled widely and cackled.

"Whoo-hoo, Atticus, have ye come to give me a show? I think I have a couple of dollars in me purse inside."

Crouching down carefully to pick up the amulet off her porch, I said, "Yes, let's get inside quickly, please." I had to get her out of sight before the witches got there.

"It's open—get yer naked bum in there." I dashed indoors, asking her to please hurry, and I darted to her bathroom and yanked a towel hanging from the shower stall to wrap around my hips.

"Aw, why'd ye put away yer twig and berries?" the widow teased when I emerged. "I thought ye were goin' t'give me somethin' to confess on Sunday."

"We need to lock up the house," I explained. "We're in danger. Witches are on their way. Do you have a necklace you can put this on?" I showed her the amulet. The widow had lived through the Troubles in Ireland. She knew by my tone that there wasn't time to ask questions.

"Yes, in me bedroom I have some gold chains," she said, her teasing smile gone.

"Grab one quickly and then meet me in the bathroom. We have to keep you out of sight of the windows until I get this on you."

"All right. But ye'll owe me an explanation," she said, walking as quickly as she could to her bedroom. I dashed around her house, which was full of lace and oak furniture with overstuffed cushions, making sure the doors were locked. I quickly bound the metal of the locks to the jambs, making them a piece of solid metal; even with an unlocking spell, the witches would be unable to budge them. Still, since the widow's house wasn't warded, the doors would slow them down for only a few moments. They would break through the windows if they wanted us badly enough, and I suspected they did.

The widow was in the bathroom, waiting for me with a gold chain. I closed the door and locked it, then explained what was happening as I strung the amulet on her chain and clasped it about her neck. The pounding on the front door began as I spoke.

"There are two German witches out there who want us both dead. They can kill you with a word without this protection. It's a talisman, and it'll punch you in the chest if they sling their spell at you, but don't take it off, because that just means it's working, okay?"

"Okay, but why do they want to kill us?"

"The short version is that one of them's having a bad hair day," I said. "I'll have to give you the long version later."

Big front windows with panes in them don't shatter all at once, like the sugar glass you see in movies. They can take an impact or two with loud *whumps*, and maybe a crack, before they completely shatter. After the first impact, the cats yowled and scattered somewhere to hide. It sounded like the witches were using the widow's patio chairs to batter away at the windows. I compartmentalized it and concentrated on activating the widow's talisman. Even when the glass shattered and I heard them cursing in German as they climbed into the living room, I kept focused on my task. I finished up just as someone rattled the locked bathroom door.

"*Sie sind hier drinnen!*" one called to the other.

"Get down into the bathtub and pull the curtain," I whispered to the widow. "I'm going to take care of this."

They began to kick at the door, which would not stand the punishment for long. Those courtesy locks on residential bathrooms are there to prevent your family members from walking in on you while you're exercising your colon; they're not designed to keep out homicidal *hexen*. If I waited for them to bust through, I'd lose the initiative and give them a shot at the widow. So I didn't wait.

Concentrating on the locking mechanism, already buckling after a couple of kicks, I began to whisper an unbinding on the metal as I waited for kick number three. After it came—quite nearly shattering the lock anyway—I completed the unbinding and let the stressed metal relax. Then I yanked the door open, the steel crumbling like a day-old muffin, catching the kicker off balance and back on her heels. It was the brunette. I rammed my fist into her surprised schnoz, and she cracked her head painfully on the wall of the hallway, her knees failing after a moment and dragging her to the floor. The blonde,

standing to my right outside the doorway, shouted *"Gewebetod!"* at
me, and my amulet promptly punched me back into the bathroom.
My towel came loose and I decided to take advantage of it, as the
blond one encouraged the other one to get up and fight. I noticed that
she didn't pursue me; she just yelled at her companion to stop fooling
around.

Pulling the towel taut between my hands, I twirled it locker-room
fashion until it was coiled tightly lengthwise.

"Nice bum," the widow said softly as I approached the doorway,
and I almost laughed. But the blond witch had the drop on me outside that door, and I had to nullify her advantage; laughing would
unwisely give her a proximity warning.

The brunette wasn't even looking at the door; she had designs on
hauling herself back into the living room, and I saw her reach up to
the other witch, out of my view, for a helping hand. The direction of
her eyes told me precisely where her partner was. Bingo.

I lunged forward, shot my right arm out, and whipped the towel
up to head height. I heard it snap satisfyingly against something, and
a sharp cry of pain followed from the blond witch immediately afterward. Douglas Adams was right: There is nothing so massively useful
in the universe as a towel.

Dropping the towel and somersaulting into the hallway, I came up
to see both witches retreating into the living room to regroup. The
blonde had a hand raised to her right eye, and the brunette looked
shell-shocked by the amount of blood streaming down her face.

"Vielleicht sollten wir ihn später erledigen," the brunette said. *Perhaps we
should finish him later.*

"Nein!" the blonde objected, moving into the kitchen. *"Er ist allein
und unbewaffnet. Wir machen es jetzt."* *He is alone and unarmed. We do this
now.*

Of course I was alone. Did she think I had a posse or something?
But it was also true that I was unarmed, and she was heading for the
butcher knives. I shouldn't have dropped my towel. I was considering
going back for it, when our collective attention was drawn to the
squealing of tires outside the house. A blue BMW Z4 convertible

switched off and Hal leapt out, his nostrils already flaring with the scent of blood in the air.

"*Er ist ein Wolf! Das ändert die Sache,*" the brunette said. *He is a wolf! That changes things.*

Damn right it does, witch.

CHAPTER 19

Dropping a werewolf into a witch fight is like dropping a tank into a snake pit. The snakes might have fangs, but the tank isn't going to feel their bites. Likewise, the witches could cast spell after spell at Hal and he'd just say, "Stop, that tickles"—right before he tore out their throats. The *hexen* understood that their odds of survival had dipped severely with Hal's arrival, and they wasted no time in beating a strategic retreat. I had to duck and dodge a couple of hastily thrown knives, so I couldn't slow them down as they scrambled for the exit. Hal tensed and flashed his canines as the witches bolted through the window and across the lawn to the street, but he made no move to pursue them; he simply kept his eyes on their retreating forms.

I started to give chase, but I remembered my profound lack of clothes just before I leapt through the window. A naked man pursuing two women down the street would probably be misinterpreted by the general public.

"Bloody curses," I ground out softly. Then my voice rose in anger. "Curses in seventy dead languages, Hal! Why didn't you stop them?"

He scowled but replied calmly, his eyes still tracking the witches. "Gunnar's orders, Atticus. You know I can't get involved in your fights."

He walked slowly toward the porch while keeping his eyes on the witches until they hopped into a Camaro and screeched away onto University Drive. Then he turned to look through the broken window and pulled up short.

"Great gods of seething darkness," he said, putting his hands on his hips, "why the hell are you naked in the widow's house?"

"What? Oh, shit."

"And you've got a new set of scratches and scrapes all over you. So help me, if you tell me it's from the rough sex again, I'll deck you right now."

"Wait, Hal, let me explain—"

"I've been calling and calling you on your cell, and now I guess I know why you didn't answer."

"No, that's not it, you don't understand—"

The widow chose that moment to emerge from the hallway—the hall that led to her bedroom—and loudly observe with a slightly flushed and smiling face, "Well, that was quite an exciting bit o' fun, wasn't it, me boy?" She gave me a smart slap on my rear and cackled.

"Aw, that is just *wrong*," Hal spat.

"Hal, please."

"Look, I don't want to kink shame—you should enjoy your thing—but what you are into is definitely not ever going to be my thing."

"Damn it, I flew here as an owl, and right after that, those witches attacked us! That's all! Mrs. MacDonagh, tell him!"

"That's what happened, all right. Why are his panties in a twist, then? Who is he, anyway?"

"He's my lawyer," I explained, and then it occurred to me that he'd seemed in an awful hurry to find me. "Why are you here, Hal?"

"Well, I had to finally call Granuaile on her cell to find out where you were, since you weren't answering either your cell or at your house. She's got your alibi, don't worry."

"Alibi for what?"

He sighed heavily and shook his head. "Tell me you've at least heard the sirens in the neighborhood."

"Yeah, why?"

"Well, all the cars those sirens belong to are currently parked a couple blocks away, in front of your shop. Your employee is dead on the sidewalk."

The widow and I both gasped. "Which one?" I asked. "I have two now, besides Granuaile."

"Some boy," Hal muttered. "I didn't get his name. A customer called 911."

"Perry?" I said. "Perry's dead?"

"Unless your other employee is also male, then it's Perry."

"Gods Below," I breathed, piecing together the recent chain of events. "The brunette must have killed him while the blonde hit me at my house. Simultaneous strike. And then she joined the blonde on Roosevelt here because that was their getaway car. . . . Manannan Mac Lir take me for a fool."

"Well, I could probably track them if you'd like; they can't be far," Hal offered. "I can't fight, but I can take you to them."

"No, no, I've got them." I waved a hand to put him at ease. "I got the blond one's hair. There's no escape for her now, and the brunette will be with her, and the rest of them besides."

"The rest of who?"

"I'll explain. Just let me go get a towel."

The widow offered to make us sandwiches, even though it was still midmorning. She offered us whiskey too, but we allowed that tea would be grand, since she clearly wanted so much to fix something for us. She busied herself in the kitchen while Hal and I sat in the living room to catch up. I knew Perry's death would hit me hard later; right then I had to focus on making sure no one else got hurt because of me.

"I need to wrap this up tonight," I said, once I'd recounted the events of the morning. "They've already killed Perry, and they tried to get Granuaile, and the widow—hell. I can't let them keep taking shots at me and all my friends. And they've done other things to me, Hal; I ran into them decades ago. They need to go down. They deserve it, believe me."

"I believe you," he said. "What do you need from me?"

"Three things," I said, ticking them off on my fingers. "First, I need the widow looked after until this is done. Do you think the Pack could keep an eye on her, since she knows about you all?"

Hal grimaced. "Gunnar won't like it, but I'll watch her myself if I have to," he said.

"That's going to be tough, because I need you for the second thing. Leif told me that the nonaggression treaty with the Sisters of the Three Auroras is ready to go. Could you do that with me now? Witness the signing?"

"Well, later this afternoon, certainly," he said. "I'm due in court at one for a hearing with another client. And you should make a statement with the police in the meantime, because you can bet they're going to want to talk to you about Perry."

"Yeah, yeah, you're right. Okay, we'll do that next. Third thing is, arrange a better alibi for me tonight than killing time alone with Granuaile. I've been leaning on her too much, I think, and when the shit comes down tonight, I want something ironclad."

Hal nodded. "All right. I'll send a couple of reliable sorts over to kill time with her at your house. They'll have a *Lord of the Rings* festival or something and testify you made the popcorn if necessary."

"Oh, damn, that's a good idea. I'd much rather do that than what I have to do."

Hal made a couple of calls and arranged for one wolf to entertain the widow for the rest of the day and another three to join Granuaile at my house later that evening.

"Okay, let's go talk to the cops," I said, with a degree of insouciance I didn't feel. I didn't want to go at all, because the stark fact of Perry's death was waiting for me there, and once I saw him I wouldn't be able to compartmentalize his absence.

Hal flicked his eyes downward and raised his eyebrows. "In a towel?"

"I have a set of clothes and my cell phone on top of the shop. Just drive me up the alley and I'll get them, no sweat."

Hal rested his face in his hands. "Dare I ask why they're up there?" he said through his fingers.

"I left them up there because I had to ditch that creepy Russian rabbi. Did you find anything out about him yet, by the way?"

"No." Hal shook his head. "Still waiting to hear. We have someone good working on it, though."

We waited until a member of Hal's pack arrived to keep the widow company—it turned out to be Greta, who'd only just survived the fight in the Superstition Mountains. She looked askance at me standing there in nothing save a towel, but she made no comment.

"Take Mrs. MacDonagh for a nice drive out of town," Hal suggested, pressing a hundred-dollar bill into Greta's hand. "Bring her back in the morning, and we'll have this window fixed up."

"Oh, can we go to Flagstaff?" The widow clapped her hands in hopeful joy. "There's a steak house up there what has singin' waiters, and a fine wee wolf lady like yerself ought to be lovin' some steak, am I right?"

Greta didn't speak but looked meaningfully at Hal. He sighed and gave her more money, then beckoned me to come along to the car.

I bid farewell to the widow and assured her I'd have everything straightened out the next day.

"Oh, I know ye will, Atticus," she said, and then a mischievous glint fired in her eyes. "Christmas isn't all that far away, ye know. Would ye be likin' a nice set of boxers this year?"

"Mrs. MacDonagh!" I said, embarrassed.

"What? Yer the sort that wears briefs, then? They make 'em in all sorts of fancy colors these days, y'know. When me Sean was alive ye got white or nothin', but sure it breaks me heart t'see ye goin' commando when ye don't have to."

"Going commando?" I exclaimed. Hal and Greta had tried at first to mask their amusement at this conversation, but now they were sniggering openly. "Where did you hear that?"

"The telly, o'course." The widow looked up at me uncertainly, then glanced at the werewolves wiping tears from their eyes as they laughed. She got a little testy then, suspecting they might be laughing at her, and she explained with some heat, "I saw it on a rerun of *Friends*, when Joey wore Chandler's clothes and did lunges while goin' commando. Did I say it wrong?"

"No, you said it fine, but—oh, bollocks." It was becoming impossible to make myself heard over the howls of the werewolves. "Enjoy your time with Greta up in Flagstaff. Come on, Hal. And, hey, I'm not paying you to laugh at me."

"Okay, okay, but you keep that thing on nice and tight," he gasped, pointing at my towel. "I don't want your naked ass sitting on my leather seats."

CHAPTER 20

Hal navigated his slick Z4 down the back alleys until he was only a building away from my shop, and he parked it in someone's private space.

"Hang out in the back and I'll toss everything down to you," I said. "The cell phone will be first, so don't drop it."

"My reflexes aren't that bad, Atticus," Hal reminded me.

"Right. Shield your eyes, then," I said, stepping out of the car and dropping my towel. "Naked Irish guy."

"Aggh! I'm snow-blind!" Hal said. I flipped him the bird and then transformed into one, lifting myself with a dozen strokes to the top of my shop, where my clothes and phone lay precisely where I'd left them. Perched on the back edge of my store, I couldn't see any of the police cars in the front, which meant they couldn't see me either.

When Hal hissed up at me that he was in position, I carefully dropped my phone, jeans, and shirt down to him, and then one sandal at a time. I saved my underwear for last, just to make a point, and Hal very pointedly did not catch them. Oh well. I'd just have to go commando.

After checking my many missed calls, I punched up Granuaile's number.

"Hey, sensei. Is the widow okay?"

"Yes, she's fine. But you've heard about Perry."

"Yeah. It's horrible. You're going to get them back, though, right?"

"Yes, tonight. But right now I have to talk to the cops."

"Okay, but before you do, can I just tell you one of the many reasons I love you?"

"Sure," I said, recognizing her code for an incoming alibi.

"While we were watching *Kill Bill: Two* so that you could try to learn the Five-Point Palm Exploding-Heart Technique, your fly was open the entire time. It was adorable."

"That's right, barbarian warriors don't hold back, baby," I said, trying and failing to impart some levity into my tone. I regretted the decision now to masquerade as a LARPer. It had been amusing at the time, but I didn't feel like playing a part while trying to deal with Perry's death.

"Thanks," I said. "Listen, I need you to stay there. Some guys are coming over tonight for a *Lord of the Rings* festival."

"Oh?"

"Yeah, it's going to be great. You'd better get steaks out of the freezer, though. Big meat-eaters, those guys are." We rang off and then I nodded to Hal. "Okay, I'm ready. Let's get this over with."

Hal and I emerged from the alley next to my shop in time to see crime-scene photographers taking pictures of Perry's body, sprawled faceup with one hand on his chest, a small pool of blood underneath his head where he'd cracked it on the cement.

I've seen a lot of dead people in my time. Looking at them gets easier when you've had as much practice as I've had. Kids still get to me, though—the innocent who never get a chance to choose whether they will take up swords or plowshares.

Perry had never been a swords kind of fella. The most violence he'd ever done was to his own earlobes, with those ridiculous silver gauges. But he'd never been a plowshares fella either; he never could remember the difference between chamomile and creosote, no matter how many times I explained that they were completely different plants.

She must have lured him outside somehow; she couldn't have thrown that killing curse, whatever it was, inside my shop. Probably had no trouble either. Perry would have looked at the black leather and stepped right out to ask how he could help.

I didn't have to pretend to be upset when Detective Geffert spotted me. I should have seen this coming. The divination had even warned me that death approached one of my male friends, but I had interpreted that as Oberon rather than Perry.

"Mr. O'Sullivan," Detective Geffert said, walking briskly over to where Hal and I were standing. I didn't make any sign that I'd heard him, because I couldn't take my eyes off Perry.

"Mr. O'Sullivan," Geffert tried again, "God knows how you must feel right now, but I need to ask you a couple of questions."

It was a surprisingly considerate approach. I'd half-expected him to be belligerent and suspicious.

"Go ahead," I said woodenly.

"Begging your pardon, Detective," Hal interrupted, "but you're with homicide, aren't you? On what basis have you decided that this is a homicide?"

"We won't be able to make that determination until we get the coroner's report," Geffert admitted, "but we're collecting evidence and taking statements just in case. Due diligence, you know." Hal nodded curtly and subsided, and the detective turned back to me. "Mr. O'Sullivan, where were you this morning before you arrived here?"

"I was at home," I said. "With my girlfriend. Watching *Kill Bill: Two*."

"Is she still there, at your house?"

"Yes."

"Did you get your home phone number changed? We've been calling there using the number in our files for some time now, and no one's answered."

"I never answer. It's always telemarketers on the other end." My voice had all the richness of expression of a cement block.

"Don't you normally work on days like this?"

"Normally, yes. But I was planning on going out to the Superstitions today, so Perry was going to open the store."

"How'd you hear about what happened here?"

"Hal dropped by." I jerked my head.

"And how'd you hear about it, Mr. Hauk—did I remember correctly?"

"Yes, that's right," Hal replied, then explained, "We have a police radio in the office. When I heard my client's address mentioned, I naturally came to investigate."

"I see." Geffert took a moment to catch up with his notes in a small handheld pad, then returned to questioning me.

"How long did the victim work for you?"

"More than two years. I'd have to look up the exact hire date if you want that."

"Was he a dependable employee?"

"The very best."

"Did he have any enemies that you know of, any trouble outside work at all?"

I shook my head. "He was a quiet dude. If he had troubles, he never showed it."

"How about at work—was there any friction with you, or another employee, maybe a regular customer?"

"He and I got along like peanut butter and jelly. Can't speak for anyone else."

"Could you name any other employees and your regulars?"

"Rebecca Dane is my other employee. Just hired her the day before yesterday. My regulars are Sophie, Arnie, Joshua, and Penelope . . . I don't know their last names. They come in first thing every morning for Mobili-Tea, rain or shine. They would have already shown up before this happened."

"What's Mobili-Tea?"

"A tea I make that helps with arthritis."

"Is there any video footage in the store?"

"Yes, I'll get the tape for you." He had to have known the answer to that already. My security-camera footage was precisely what Hal was using to sue Tempe in my wrongful shooting weeks ago.

"Any drug use that you're aware of?"

"No."

"Any other health issues that he may have exhibited or shared with you?"

"Nothing, dude."

"All right. Is there anything else you can think of, anything at all, that might have hinted that this was coming?"

Besides my divination that morning? No. A giant flock of guilt flew in and settled down upon my shoulders. "'Not a whit,'" I said softly, past a tightening throat. "'We defy augury.'"

"Beg your pardon?"

"'There is a special providence in the fall of a sparrow,'" I whispered, my vision blurring a bit, Perry's still form losing focus.

"Did you say Providence? As in Rhode Island?"

I wiped my eyes and looked at Geffert for the first time, suddenly wary. "No, I meant providence as in the guidance and protection of a higher power."

"Oh. What was the rest of that? Something about August?"

"It was a private elegy for the deceased," I said dully. "Nothing pertaining to the investigation."

He cocked his head sideways at me and said, "Your vocabulary has markedly improved, Mr. O'Sullivan."

Shit. A couple of lads from the coroner's office were bringing out a body bag, and I turned to watch them. "Gotta develop the noggin along with the nunchucks, dude," I replied in the same low monotone I'd used since I arrived. "I don't just sell books, I actually read them too."

"That makes sense," the detective said affably, but now that my mask had slipped, however briefly, I doubted he was fooled anymore. "Forgive me. One more question. Have you found your sword since we spoke last?"

"No."

The detective paused and wrote something down on his notepad that was significantly longer than "No."

"Okay, that's all for now," he said, "but I'd appreciate it if you'd answer your phone in case we need to reach you."

"Right." Geffert moved away and sent an officer over to accompany me inside and get my security tape. Even if it showed the witch coming inside to lure Perry out, it would do them no good. I locked up the shop, flipping the sign to say CLOSED. I called Rebecca Dane, informing her of the sad news and telling her to stay home for the next couple of days, then after they'd taken Perry's body away I rode my bike home, since it was still there from the previous night when I'd left on the wing.

Detective Geffert was already in front of my house, questioning Granuaile and confirming my story for that day and also checking out the bats and balls Granuaile had bought at Target—they'd never caught up with her the previous night to check out my alibi for the night of the Satyrn Massacre. Brilliant as she was with little details, she'd remembered to have Oberon chew on the balls a bit, and Geffert was fingering them with distaste while standing in front of the open trunk of her car as I pulled up. Granuaile was standing next to him and rolled her eyes at me by way of greeting. Oberon was lying down on the front porch and gave me a quick update on what he thought I needed to know.

<The Man is here again, and he still hasn't tried to pet me. He kinda smells like mildewed socks and tuna fish.>

"Ah, Mr. O'Sullivan," the detective said, tossing a baseball back into Granuaile's trunk and slamming it closed. "Long time no see." I said nothing, just nodded to him.

"You arrived at your store earlier on foot," he said, "but now you arrive here on this bike. Where did that come from?"

"My store."

"Your store. And why was it there?"

"I left it there yesterday, obviously."

"Why?"

"Because sometimes I like to walk home." And sometimes I like to fly home. Detective Geffert eyed me steadily, looking for signs of deceit, and I gave him my most placid expression in return. He broke eye contact first, shoving his hands in his pockets and finding something interesting on the tips of his shoes.

"You know, my ears are actually pretty good. I heard what you said earlier. 'There is a special providence in the fall of a sparrow,' you said."

"So?"

"So that sounded to me like something you were quoting. I called in to the station and talked to our dispatcher, who used to be an English major, and she told me that was a line from *Hamlet*." His eyes flicked back up to study my reaction.

"Right," I confirmed, keeping my expression neutral.

"So what are you hiding, Mr. O'Sullivan?"

I shrugged. "Nothing."

He shook a finger at me. "That isn't true. Yesterday when we searched your house, you walked around like you didn't have an IQ above eighty. Today you're quoting Shakespeare off the top of your head."

My patience evaporated like a dewdrop in Yuma and my anger throttled my better sense. "'Is't not enough to break into my garden, and, like a thief, to come to rob my grounds, climbing my walls in spite of me the owner, but thou wilt brave me with these saucy terms?'"

Geffert's eyebrows shot up. "What play is that from?"

"*Henry the Sixth, Part Two*," I said.

The detective frowned. "How much Shakespeare have you memorized?"

"All of it. *Dude*." I don't know why I sneered at him; it wasn't smart to taunt him like that and make busting me a personal crusade. Yet regardless of how wise it wasn't, I held his eyes recklessly with a testosterone challenge flaring away in mine, and he saw not only that but confirmed the spark of intelligence he'd glimpsed earlier. Then he knew that I'd sold him a bill of goods the day before, played him and all his cronies for fools. His jaw clenched and his shoulders tensed, which Granuaile and Oberon both noticed.

<Hey, Atticus, ixnay issingpay off the oppercay.>

"Will that be all, Detective Geffert, or was there something else?" Granuaile asked.

"That will be just about all," he said, still holding my eyes. "For now. You have arranged things very nicely, Mr. O'Sullivan. Your girl-friend even showed me the receipt that matches your visit to Target two nights ago. But she could not explain why you were missing your ear in the Target security video but you seem to have one now."

"I had it in Target too," I lied.

"The video shows you did not."

"A low-resolution video in terrible lighting. My ear is real, not pros-thetic, and ears don't grow back overnight, do they? Go ahead and see for yourself, Detective. I give you permission." I turned my head to the left a bit and gestured up at it.

His eyes shifted to my right ear, and he reached up with his left hand and tugged on it gently, more to discern whether it behaved and felt like cartilage than anything else. Frustrated, he said, "I have an autopsy to attend. Please remain available if I have further questions."

The three of us said nothing. We simply stared at him until he climbed back into his car and drove off. I spent some time rehashing recent events with Oberon and Granuaile, and it was a somber after-noon of regret and sorrow until Hal came by to pick me up. Though I never thought I'd say it in my long life, I was going to make peace with witches.

CHAPTER 21

We called ahead to make sure they knew we were coming and all enchantments would be dissolved for the duration of our visit. The entire coven was waiting for us in Malina's condo when we arrived just after four p.m.

"This is Bogumila," Malina said, gesturing to a slim brunette who regarded me steadily with one large eye; the other eye was hidden behind a dark curtain of hair that occluded half of her face, and I wondered what I'd see if I peeked behind it. She nodded curtly at me, and the candlelight Malina favored shimmered across the curtain as it rippled gently with the movement.

"You may call me Mila in public," Bogumila said. "The Americans stare if your name is too ethnic."

I nodded with a half grin, and Hal—whose full name was Hallbjörn—said, "I know exactly what you mean."

"Berta is over there in the kitchen." Malina pointed to another dark-haired woman. Berta, a festively plump personage, was snacking as she prepared a tray of hors d'oeuvres, and she gave a friendly wave at the mention of her name. Malina proceeded to introduce the other three members of her coven, all of them blondes. Kazimiera was very tall and leggy, her tan skin and bright white teeth suggesting that she'd grown up on the beaches of California rather than under the cloudy skies of eastern Europe. Klaudia was the petite, waifish sort, with a pair of sleepy eyes and a set of pouty lips, her hair cut short and layered at the neck and her bangs teased around her face in a wet, languorous fashion, giving the impression that whenever you saw her, she had just finished having sex before you walked into the room and would now like nothing more than a French cigarette. I used to carry around a cigarette case expressly for the purpose of offering them to women like her, but that social custom lost its luster when people finally realized that offering someone a cigarette was the same thing as offering them lung cancer. Still, I patted absently where my vest pocket would be if I'd been wearing a vest, as in the late Victorian era.

The last of the Polish witches, Roksana, had her thick hair pulled back so tightly from her face that it appeared to be a crash helmet, but after routing itself severely through a silver loop at the base of her skull, it exploded into an untamed curly mane. Her owlish blue eyes regarded me steadily through a pair of round spectacles. She wore a power suit with a white blouse, shoulder-padded purple coat and black pants, and the pointy-toed black boots I'd come to associate with Malina. After a quick survey, I realized they all wore the same boots—and all of them wore something purple, though in Kazimiera's case it was present only on a brooch she had fastened to her coat above her left breast.

I introduced Hal, because some of the witches had not met him yet. He produced two copies of the nonaggression treaty from his briefcase, all business, and likewise seven extremely sharp quills that we would use to sign it. The witches and I were each given a quill, and the signature pages of the treaties were settled on the black coffee table in front of Malina's couch. One by one, the witches stabbed their palms with the quill and signed each copy of the treaty in blood. Then it was my turn.

I had argued for some time against signing in blood, when a fountain pen would have done just as well in legal terms; I did not want the coven to have any of my blood, period. The coven had argued vociferously for it, and eventually I gave way. In magical terms, it was much more binding, and those terms were far more strict than the legal ones. "People break the law all the time, Mr. O'Sullivan," Malina pointed out. "People rarely break magical contracts, and those who do fail to live long afterward. Signing in blood is therefore not only for our protection, it is also for yours."

Still, now that the moment had arrived, and six bloody signatures darkened as they dried in front of me, I hesitated. Signing it would contradict centuries of what I considered "best practice" in denying witches the opportunity to snuff me. But, truly, I saw no way forward without their help, and I needed it if I ever wished to have peace enough to restore the land around Tony Cabin. The sharp sting of the quill lingered as the blood welled out of my palm, and I did nothing to dampen the pain as I signed the treaties; it was right that I should feel it.

A general sigh of relief traveled around the room as I finished, tension releasing and tightly closeted smiles bursting free.

Berta clapped and said with a grin, "We should celebrate. Who wants chocolate and schnapps?" The suggestion was generally regarded as a fantastic one, and she bustled happily about, pulling out glasses from cupboards. The other witches came forward and shook Hal's hand and mine, thanking us for our vision and willingness to cooperate; never had they felt so valued and respected; et cetera.

The hot chocolate and schnapps was served up with a plate of fresh-baked cookies that Berta had somehow produced, the hors d'ouevres forgotten in favor of dessert. Malina rolled up the coven's copy of the treaty, and Hal took mine and put it back in his briefcase so that the cookies could rest on the coffee table. Half of the coven sat themselves on the couch, and the rest of us pulled up assorted chairs so that we all sat in a sort of rough ellipse, with our chocolate and cookies in front of us and the orange and cardamom candles glowing merrily behind us around the room. It felt like one of the old European coffeehouses, except with far more purple than was advisable or permissible in Amsterdam or Paris.

I complimented Berta on the chocolate, then I said, "Tell me about *die Töchter des dritten Hauses.*"

The witches all cleared their expressions. "What would you like to know?" Malina said in neutral tones, but only with some effort. She seemed to be controlling her anger against them rather than concealing anything from me.

"Could you perhaps fill me in on the nature of their grudge against you?" I asked. "You said it began during World War Two, but I'm a little sketchy on what you were doing then. I only heard a little bit of the story when we first met."

"What did I tell you then?"

"You told me that you all met somehow in Poland during the Blitzkrieg," I replied, "and an indeterminate time after that, you wound up in America."

"That was all? Okay, we found each other in Warsaw," Malina said. "Or, rather, Radomila found us and brought us together. And once we'd formed a coven, there was much discussion of what to do. We were divining almost constantly, trying to see what would happen, what we could do, where we could go. We saw the horror that was coming and knew there was nothing we could do about it in Poland—things had progressed so far, so quickly, that our protections would be useless, and the people we needed to reach in Germany were unreachable. We may have been powerful as witches go, but even we could not turn back the Panzer divisions or stop the SS from doing whatever they pleased. We did see where we could do some good, though, so we left Warsaw a week before it fell and made our way into Bulgaria."

"Bulgaria?" I frowned. "But that was an Axis power as well."

"Yes, but on what terms? Czar Boris the Third joined the Axis to prevent German invasion of his country, but he committed no Bulgarian troops to the fighting. Hitler wanted him to invade Russia and ease some of the pressure on his eastern front, but Boris refused. He also flatly refused to send fifty thousand Bulgarian Jews to the death camps in Poland. I think we did well there for a while."

My jaw dropped as the import of her words hit home. "You're seriously taking credit for that?"

"We settled in Sofia and stayed until the assassination. We saved many lives."

I ignored her self-congratulation and asked, "Whose assassination?"

"We're still talking about Boris the Third."

"Ah, yes. Who do you think killed him? There wasn't a grassy knoll in the palace of Sofia."

Die Töchter des dritten Hauses.

I shook my head. "No, I'm sorry, I do know a little bit about his death. They exhumed the body and performed an autopsy and confirmed he died of heart failure, nothing more."

"Precisely," Roksana said in her clipped English, and glanced at Malina by way of apology for jumping in. "It wasn't a poisoning by the Germans, which is one of the conspiracy theories running around, nor was it a scheme of the Russians. It was the German *hexen* who got past our wards and killed him with a curse."

"They have a curse that causes heart failure?"

The Polish witches all nodded in synch, and the visible half of Bogumila's mouth said, "It is a spell of necrosis that they aim at the heart. It merely causes a small area of tissue to die, but if that tissue is heart tissue, the result is a fatal coronary."

"It's their favorite tool in combat," Klaudia volunteered. So that was what they'd tried to kill me with and why the amulet punched me in the chest each time. And that was how they'd killed Perry. I'd known the curse they were throwing around was deadly, obviously, but I didn't know precisely what it did to people. The medical examiners would pronounce Perry dead of an inexplicable heart attack, nothing more.

"It's practically their *only* tool," Berta snorted around a mouthful of cookie. "They can hardly do a damn thing otherwise without a demon to help them."

"Yes, but unfortunately there are far too many demons willing to help," Roksana said. "Though they always demand their price."

"Wait." I held up my hands. "Back to Boris. Why in nine hells would the *hexen* want to kill him?"

"Just like Hitler, they wanted him to invade Russia," Roksana replied.

"So are we talking about the proverbial Nazi witches from hell?"

"No, no, no." Malina shook her head. "They were around long be-fore the Nazis, and they certainly have survived where the Nazis did not. They merely took advantage of the Nazis to get what they wanted."

"So calling themselves the Daughters of the Third House has noth-ing to do with the Third Reich?"

"Not that I know of," Malina said uncertainly, and Roksana con-firmed her supposition.

"They were called that before the Nazis even existed," she said. "But we have no idea what it means. They've never sat down to chat with us about their origins."

"All right, so what did they want? Why kill Boris?"

Malina said, "They wanted what Hitler did—or, rather, Hitler wanted what they did—Russia."

"What? You're suggesting he launched that entire bloody stupid offensive due to their influence?"

"That's precisely what I'm suggesting," Malina agreed, nodding. "They sent him succubi and they gave him the proper dreams of *Lebensraum*—they'd done the same thing with Chancellor Theobald von Bethmann-Hollweg in World War One. And when the eastern front was going poorly and Boris refused to send troops in 1943—thanks to our influence—the *hexen* killed him and everybody thought Hitler had done it."

"It didn't turn out the way they'd hoped, though." Roksana smiled grimly. "They hoped the Bulgarian regents left behind would be more malleable and harder for us to control and protect, but the regents proved ridiculously foolish and weak, and instead of invading Russia, Russia invaded Bulgaria and that was that."

"Which was fine with us, really," Malina explained. "The Bulgarian Jews were safe and the *hexen*'s plots were foiled, so that was all that mattered."

"They've always wanted revenge for our role in that, however," Roksana added, "because they probably still think they could have won if Bulgaria had joined in."

"Why did they want to invade Russia so badly?"

The coven members looked at one another's faces to see who wished to answer. It was Kazimiera who finally spoke. "There is a group of witch hunters based there that plagues their kind especially. If they found us by accident, they would not hesitate to attack, but they actively hunt *die Töchter des dritten Hauses* because of their associations with demonkind. The *hexen* hoped the SS would take care of the witch hunters and eliminate a thorn in their side. Himmler was obsessed with the occult and would have found them for sure if he'd had a free hand in Russia."

Rabbi Yosef Bialik's Russian accent and shadowy organization came to mind. "I'm surprised Stalin didn't stamp them out. Any idea what these witch hunters called themselves?"

The ladies all shook their heads slowly yet in unison. It was a creepy effect. I wondered idly if they practiced such maneuvers.

"And how do you know that the *hexen* were motivated by these mysterious Russians—or, rather, by their desire to kill the Russians?"

The witches swiveled their heads in synch to Malina and so did I, waiting for the answer. Her eyes fell to her lap. "We captured the one who assassinated Boris the Third and interrogated her. Thoroughly. Radomila led it," she said, referring to their erstwhile coven leader, "but I was present. She told us much before she died. And that is another reason *die Töchter des dritten Hauses* hate us so much."

"I see. Well, they appear to have had much influence on Germany's side. They had access to the Führer himself, you say. Did they also suggest to him, via succubi or some other method, all of that master-race nonsense? Did they suggest the death camps and so on?"

"Not that we know of," Berta said, a few crumbs of her third cookie spraying from her mouth as she talked. "They just wanted to use Germany as a club to bash Russia with. They weren't Nazis; they were opportunists. Believe me, I would like to assign to them every evil of that war, but the most unspeakable atrocities were committed by humans without any infernal influence whatsoever."

"She's right," Klaudia agreed, "the Holocaust wasn't their idea. But they didn't seem to disapprove either. And they joined in when it suited them."

I frowned. "How do you mean they joined in?"

"They were specifically hunting Kabbalists for a while—"

"Kabbalists!" I exclaimed. I slapped my forehead. "So that's why he didn't die."

"Who didn't die?" the witches all said in polyphonic harmony. They were like a Greek chorus.

I sighed and collected my thoughts. "I have known since this morning that I have met these *hexen* before—or at least seen their work. They tried to kill me outside my home with the same necrotic curse they used on Boris the Third, but my wards deflected it." I purposely failed to explain that my cold iron amulet deflected it. Nothing in the nonaggression treaty required me to reveal the true nature of my defenses to them. "The last time my wards reacted in such a manner was during World War Two."

Berta stopped chewing and looked at me with widened eyes. "Really? Where were you?"

"I was in the Atlantic Pyrenees, escorting a Jewish family into Spain, where they could have taken a train all the way to Lisbon and gained passage to safety in South America."

Berta held up her hands. "Stop right there. This sounds good," she said, and hauled herself off the couch. "I'm going to make popcorn." The other witches made sounds of protest, perceiving that it was rude somehow to expect me to weave a tale worthy of movie snackage, but Berta waved off their protests. "Come on, he's a Druid; he'll love playing the bard for a while." More protests followed, but they were halfhearted, and eventually the witches turned to me with pleading looks to forgive them for being so ineffective.

In truth, it made me feel closer to the witches. One thing that's never changed in two millennia is that people love to hear war stories—at least, stories in which their side wins. The gods know that there was little enough in that war to cheer about other than the eventual victory. But the coven had lived through it, I had lived through it, and we had both fought in it, albeit in an unconventional manner. It was a bond between us, and telling this story would strengthen it and provide the foundation for shared victories to come.

Seeing that I would be required to speak at length, I mentally reorganized my tale. The real reason I didn't take a more active role in the war was that the Morrigan had forbidden it. During that period, our relationship had been a bit uncertain.

"Do you know how many battles there are for me to watch over throughout the world right now?" she'd asked me when I'd tried to enlist with the British. "I cannot be worrying about you every bloody moment and making sure you don't step on a mine or get bombed by the *Luftwaffe*. Stay out of the war, Siodhachan, and don't do anything to draw attention to yourself—specifically, attention from the Fae."

I didn't want to imply that I had any sort of relationship with the Morrigan now, though, so I told the witches a half-truth once Berta returned to the couch with bowls of popcorn and indicated that I could proceed. The witches all leaned forward in their seats, and so did Hal. He'd never heard what I'd done during the war either.

"As you know, I was hiding from Aenghus Óg at the time, as I had been for most of the common era, and I could do nothing overtly magical that would draw his attention. But neither could I simply hide in the Amazon and wait for it all to be over: My conscience would not allow it. So I became a *maquisard*, joining the French Resistance in the southwest, where I shepherded Jewish families through the wilderness to escape the Nazis.

"The people in my network knew me as the Green Man. If someone insisted on a Christian name, I called myself Claude and left it at that. The families under my care arrived in Spain faster and healthier and more reliably than those of any other smuggler. All told, I saved sixty-seven families, taking them in large groups at times. That's not on the scale of your fifty thousand saved in Bulgaria"—an accomplishment I privately doubted they could reasonably take credit for—"but it was my small contribution to peace. And you must keep in mind I was in the Gascony region, which was fairly overrun with Nazis, away from the bulk of the *maquisards*. Getting them safely out of the cities was often more trouble than taking them across the mountains.

"Only one family in my care failed to make it out of France. I picked them up outside Pau, and we were to take the Somport Pass over the Pyrenees. The father was a kind man who doted on his children, a scientist of some kind, but I couldn't tell you their names even if I wished. So much of the work was an anonymous business, for everyone's safety." I paused to take a sip of my hot chocolate, which had cooled somewhat, and Berta watched me impatiently.

"They were a fairly young couple with three children: a boy of ten, a girl of eight, and another boy of five. The boys had little suits on—their best—and the girl had a gray wool coat buttoned over a red dress. The mother was dressed in similar fashion, with a heavy coat worn over a dress. The father carried a briefcase of papers and photos, and the family had nothing more than the clothes on their backs. The father—well, there were traces of magic in his aura that I didn't take the trouble to examine, but now I see that he was a Kabbalist, and his wards were sufficient, as were mine, to deflect this necrotic spell of the *hexen—Gewebetod, ja?*"

"*Ja,*" Malina nodded. "That is the word they use."

"Six witches ambushed us in the night before we were even halfway to the Somport Pass—one witch for each member of our party, which led me to believe we'd been betrayed somehow. The mother and three children fell immediately, clutching their chests as they landed in the leaves of autumn. I fell down too, because I had felt the strike upon my wards, and I expected a grenade or a spray of machine gun fire next. I cast camouflage on myself once I hit the ground, then crawled as quietly as I could away from where I had fallen.

"Whatever noise I made was masked well. The father was the only one left standing, but he was screaming the names of his wife and children, then crouching over them and trying to revive them as I headed for cover."

"His Kabbalistic wards shielded him." Berta narrowed her eyes and nodded knowingly.

"Correct. But I did not know this at the time. I never heard him utter a spell, I'd never bothered to check his aura closely, and so while I suspected he must be special somehow—why else would we be singled out for such attention?—he could have just as easily been politically important, rather than magically. In any event, he was too carried away with his grief to respond to the attack. I do not know why his family had no protection—perhaps his abilities were a secret even from them; perhaps they would not have approved. I simply do not know.

"The question of his power, however, was quickly rendered moot. Six figures leached out of the surrounding forest, darker shapes hovering in the darkness, and they poured bullets into him out of handguns fitted with silencers. He fell dead on top of his wife, and when the figures ran out of bullets, they reloaded and shot his still corpse again and again, many times in the head and in the chest, so that the body was so unsuitable, he could not possibly recover by any kind of sorcery.

"They even stood and watched the corpse for a while, to make sure no healing began, and all that time I remained silent and unmoving, perhaps nine or ten meters away, next to a tree. There was nothing I could do for any of the family at that point. I had no defense against bullets besides the ability to heal, and these figures had already demonstrated what they would do if they suspected I could; and, beyond that, I was armed with nothing but my sword. I also had no idea who or what the assassins were, besides witches of some kind. Given the setting, I assumed they were some secret squad of Himmler's who'd been sent after this particular man.

"Eventually one of them noticed I wasn't there. '*Gab es nicht sechs von ihnen? Ich zähle nur fünf Körper,*' she said."

"*Scheisse!*" Berta cursed in German. "What did they do then?"

"Wait a moment, Atticus," Hal interjected. "I don't speak German. What was that you just said?"

"*Weren't there six of them? I count only five bodies.*"

"Oh, shit," Hal said, and grabbed a bowl of popcorn out of Bogumila's lap. Her visible eye widened comically, but otherwise she made no protest. "What happened next?" he asked, throwing a handful in his mouth.

"They chose one of the witches to stay behind and watch the dead Kabbalist for miraculous healing, while the other five spread out looking for me. They couldn't see through my camouflage, though, and they quickly passed my position and melted into the woods."

"They had no infrared abilities or a half-decent sense of smell?" Hal asked.

Klaudia shook her head and answered him. "As Berta said earlier, they are practically useless in the field without a demon riding along. Had there been one with them, they would have spotted him easily. They probably had some sort of aid for night vision but nothing to penetrate the kind of cloak he had on."

Camouflage isn't a cloaking spell—it's camouflage—but I didn't bother to correct her as I continued. "That left me alone with a single witch and an opportunity to take a little vengeance for the family before I made my escape. The man's suit jacket was made of natural fibers, so I formed a bond between his left sleeve and his side, which caused his arm to move abruptly down. As you may imagine, this movement of a supposedly *über*-dead corpse startled the witch excessively, and she shrieked and began emptying yet another clip into the poor man. Using her noise as cover, I drew my sword, dashed forward ten meters, and struck off her head."

This elicited a round of cheers from the Polish witches, and there was a general toast and more schnapps poured before I could continue.

"She fell next to the family, and I pelted down the mountain toward Pau as the other witches returned to investigate the shrieking. I was far ahead of them by the time they discovered the body and figured out what must have happened. They gave some pursuit, but they never came close. I stopped using the Somport Pass for the duration of the war, and I never saw them again or figured out why they attacked us, until just now when you gave me the information I lacked."

"So what happened when they attacked you today?" Kazimiera asked. "Did you kill another one?" Her tone was hopeful.

"No, the setting where we met was not appropriate," I replied, disappointing the entire coven. "But I did acquire a little something," I added, as I reached into my pocket and withdrew the blond witch's lock of hair, "that should enable us to find them a bit more easily."

"That's theirs?" Malina asked incredulously, eyes riveted on the hair held between my thumb and forefinger.

"It's from only one of them, but, yes," I said. "Can you figure out where they've been staying with this?"

The witches all nodded together and said, "Definitely."

CHAPTER 22

"Have you changed your mind about Thor?" Leif asked.

"Yes, yes, yes!" I said as fast as I could, but he hung up on me anyway.

That turned out to be a mistake, though: He'd been halfway to flipping his phone closed on what he assumed would be my negative answer, when he heard my thin, tinny affirmative as it snapped shut. He called me back immediately.

"I beg your pardon," he said, "but did you say that you have changed your mind?"

"Yes, I did say that," I confirmed, "but only if you're super-duper sweet to me."

"What must I do in return for your aid?" he asked warily.

"Help me kill some witches in Gilbert."

"That is all?"

"Well, there's only two of us and about twenty of them."

"That is all?"

"They're pretty mean and they might be dressed like the Go-Go's. I'm talking Aqua Net and those shirts that hang off one shoulder and everything."

"It sounds atrocious, Atticus, simply heinous to the nth degree, but I have no idea to what you are alluding."

"Then how about this? We might literally catch some hell, because they're baking demon babies in their wombs. Maybe some other surprises, who knows."

"Fine, fine. When do we do this?"

"Tonight. Right now. Call up your ghoul friends; there will be plenty to eat when we're finished."

"And when do we kill Thor?"

"I'm going on a scouting mission to Asgard before the New Year," I said, leaving out the part where I'd be stealing one of Idunn's golden apples for Laksha. "After I return—and that should be before the New Year as well—we plan our raid and put our affairs in order. You get your A-team together, whatever badasses you have in your network, and I will get the lot of you into Asgard."

"Will you give me your oath on this?" Leif asked.

"Dude, I'll even pinky-swear."

"I beg your pardon?"

"I'll give you my oath. Just come pick me up in your batmobile."

Leif hissed his displeasure into the phone. "I have never turned into a bat, no vampire ever has, and that particular myth of Mr. Stoker's is growing tiresome."

"If we live through this, Leif, I swear I'm going to make you read some damn comic books."

CHAPTER 23

Leif showed up at my house wearing a steel breastplate and a broad grin. "I have not lived this long to let a few witches stake me tonight," he said, leaning casually against his Jaguar. He was wearing one of those old-fashioned white linen shirts with enormous poufy sleeves underneath his breastplate. He didn't go full Renaissance, however, and complement this with breeches and a codpiece. Instead, he wore a black pair of Levi's and some Doc Martens with a surplus of buckles.

"You have one other vulnerability, I think," I said. "And we need to address it."

His grin disappeared. "They have sunlight in a bottle or something?"

"No, but they will probably have some hellfire available. Eight of them are carrying demon spawn. You're rather flammable, am I right?"

"Well, yes, now that you mention it."

"I have a fix for that, strictly a loan item for tonight only."

"All right." I gave him Oberon's talisman and activated it to protect him. He regarded me doubtfully and flicked the amulet hanging from his neck. "This hunk of metal will keep me from turning into ashes?"

"You'll feel the heat, but it shouldn't burn you."

He raised his brows and rolled his eyes briefly by way of a facial shrug and said, "Fine. Are we ready to go?"

"Couple more things we have to do first," I said, and wagged my head significantly at the house across the street. "You remember my inquisitive neighbor?"

"Of course."

"He let it slip the other day that he has a rocket-propelled grenade in his garage. I'd like to see if he was telling the truth and, if so, liberate it for the greater good of the East Valley."

Leif's head didn't move, but his nostrils flared. "He is in the house right now."

"Oh, aye, and he's watching us through his blinds."

"What do you propose we do?"

"You charm his ass and get him to open the garage for me. I'll brazenly walk in there and take what we need, then you tell him to forget it."

"If he has military weaponry in there, we should report him to the ATF."

I sighed in exasperation and pinched the bridge of my nose. Who would have thought a bloodsucking lawyer would actually care about the law? "Okay, but only after we take some to play with."

Mollified, Leif said, "He is looking at us now? Through his window?"

I slid my eyes sideways to confirm that the blinds were still parted. "Yes."

Without warning, Leif whipped his head around and stared across the street at the blinds. They fell closed after a couple of moments.

"Got him," Leif said. "Proceed. The garage should open in a few seconds."

We strode across the street, and the heavy door began to rumble open ponderously. It occurred to me that I'd never seen it open at all; Mr. Semerdjian drove a silver Honda CR-V and always parked it in his driveway.

The rocket-propelled grenade—one of several—was there. And

so were a crate of standard fragmentation grenades, several crates of automatic weapons, and handheld surface-to-air missiles. There were also a dozen flak jackets hanging on the wall.

"Wow," I said. "It's just like my garage, except with extra overkill."

"Clearly these weapons are not for personal defense," Leif said at the threshold. Mr. Semerdjian was under his control, but he hadn't invited Leif into his home of his own free will yet. The man was standing, somewhat slack-jawed, by the door that led into his house. "Mr. Semerdjian," Leif addressed him, "please explain why you have all this weaponry here."

"It's for the coyotes," he replied.

I looked up sharply. "What did he say? What coyotes?"

Leif repeated my question, since Semerdjian wouldn't answer anyone but him.

"Coyotes. The men who smuggle people across the Mexican border."

"Oh, *those* coyotes," I said. "Okay."

"I supply two different gangs of them," Semerdjian continued. "They always need something extra to get away from the border patrol these days."

Leif pumped him for more information about his suppliers and customers, while I loaded up. I took a flak jacket, remembering that *die Töchter des dritten Hauses* liked to use handguns, then I snagged two RPGs and stuffed five frags into my pockets. I laid the RPGs in the trunk of Leif's Jaguar and then called across to him that I was just about ready to roll.

Granuaile and Oberon were inside the house, entertaining three werewolves with the extended version of *The Fellowship of the Ring*. One of them was Dr. Snorri Jodursson, and I called to him to follow me into the backyard for a minute. He inquired after my health and thanked me for paying his huge bill so promptly, then vaulted me up into the branches of my neighbor's palo verde tree, where I unbound Fragarach and Moralltach but kept them camouflaged. That was the full extent of the aid I could expect from the Tempe Pack, under Magnusson's orders.

After depositing the weapons in the trunk of Leif's Jaguar, I was truly ready to pick a fight—or, rather, to finish one that *die Töchter des dritten Hauses* had picked with me.

"Come on, Leif," I called across the street. "Wrap it up and drop a dime on him later. Let's go pick up the nice witches now so we can go kill the naughty witches."

CHAPTER 24

The Sisters of the Three Auroras came down from their tower quickly and met us in the underground parking garage. They walked briskly in their pointy boots toward a line of slinky two-seat sports cars. Malina and Klaudia stepped lively to an Audi TT Roadster; Bogumila and Roksana made for a Mercedes SLR McLaren; and Kazimiera and Berta, something of a mismatched pair, looked as if they were going to squeeze themselves improbably into a Pontiac Solstice. Unlike the German *hexen,* they knew what decade it was and how to properly dress in black. Bogumila had actually pulled her hair back into a practical ponytail, and I was mildly disappointed that the previously hidden side of her face was perfectly pleasant, no hideous scarring or missing chunks of flesh or gaping ocular cavity with a worm wriggling around inside.

"Time is of the essence," Malina explained as their cars' security systems chirped at them. "I think we've shielded ourselves from divination, but if they somehow penetrate it and know we're unprotected now, they may have time to repeat the hex that killed Waclawa and wipe us out all at once. I'm sure they have demons ready and waiting to aid them."

"The clock is ticking, eh? How long do we have?" I wasn't worried about being found through divination; no one but the Morrigan could find me that way, thanks to my amulet. And Leif had nothing to worry about either, because it's tough to divine dead guys, and they'd have to know he was involved ahead of time before trying.

"Once they begin the ritual, perhaps as little as twenty minutes. Follow us and we'll talk on the phone."

Leif became a little bit envious as he watched the witches pull out in front of him. "Those are very nice toys. What do they do for a living?"

"Consulting."

"Really? What sort of consulting?"

"Magical, I guess, in the sense that they magically draw a salary without truly consulting anyone."

"How very clever of them. Though I suppose it is not all that different from real consultants."

"Malina made the same observation," I said as we turned left onto Rio Salado and headed for Rural Road to catch the 202 east. My cell phone began to play "Witchy Woman," and I said, "Speaking of whom, she probably wants to consult with me on our plan of attack." I flipped open my phone and cooed, "Hel-loooo," with my voice gliding up into an interrogative tone at the end.

"You're sounding remarkably cavalier about this confrontation," Malina said, her Polish accent pronounced. She was already getting herself into a snit.

"I'm simply living in the moment and enjoying it. The near future holds a kill-or-be-killed situation, so I am sucking all the marrow out of life while I can. Leif has a crush on your car, by the way."

Malina ignored all this and said, "We are traveling to Gilbert and Pecos, so we'll be heading south on the 101 right after we get on the 202. They're on the top floor of a vacant three-story building. Something's waiting for us on the bottom two floors, but we couldn't see what it is."

"So you and your sisters are going in while Leif and I wait outside?"

A cold silence greeted me for a few beats, then Malina said, "No, it's going to be the other way around." I could almost picture her grinding her teeth as she said it.

"Oh, that's too bad, because we were going to stop off at Starbucks and get a couple of lattes while you took care of this."

"That's the famous vampire Helgarson you're riding with, isn't it? Is he fond of lattes?"

"I don't know." I looked over at Leif, who was grinning—he was hearing both sides of the conversation, of course—and said, "Malina wants to know if you like lattes, and I want to know if you're famous."

"No to both," he said, as we screamed onto the 202 on-ramp.

"Sorry, Malina," I said to the phone. "He's not famous."

"Perhaps it would be better to call him infamous. It is irrelevant at this point. What is relevant is that my sisters and I are not great warriors. Were the odds even and they did not cheat with modern weapons, I would say, yes, we could walk in and win a magical battle against most opponents. But we are outnumbered more than three to one."

"How many are there?"

"Twenty-two. Some of them have firearms, but they are not great warriors either. And while they may be expecting you, Mr. O'Sullivan, they will not be expecting Mr. Helgarson to get involved. I imagine the two of you together will be quite formidable."

"She's complimenting our martial prowess, Leif," I said to him.

"I feel more manly already," he said. The short distance on the 202 was already covered and we were merging onto the southbound 101.

"What will you and your sisters be doing once we arrive?"

"We will be setting up an illusion around the perimeter of the building so that it will appear to ordinary citizens that nothing unusual is happening, even if there are gunshots and explosions and *hexen* being tossed out the windows. We will also prevent any of them from escaping, should they take it into their heads to flee your . . . expert swordplay."

Leif and I both had a good laugh at that, and I could almost see

Malina rolling her eyes as she sighed noisily into the phone, signaling that she hoped we would get the silliness out of our systems soon.

"We will also take care of the blond one when we get there," Malina added, when she felt we'd wound down sufficiently to understand her.

"Oh? Why didn't you do it already?"

"Because then they'd know you gave her hair to us. It is better they not know for sure we are working in concert until it's too late for them to plan around it."

"All right. Then we'll be responsible for twenty-one witches. Plus whatever demons they have hanging around."

"Correct. All of whom you must kill quickly. They will almost certainly begin *Die Einberufung der verzehrenden Flammen* as soon as they know we are below, counting on their defenses on the bottom floors to hold until they're finished."

"You're talking about the infernal hex that killed Waclawa. They call it, what—The Summoning of Consuming Flames?"

"Yes."

"Could they target Leif with this ritual?"

"Absolutely. The demon involved in the ceremony provides the targeting. They don't need hair or blood or anything else to find someone. It's why I'm a bit uncertain about our shielding from divination."

I looked soberly over at Leif. "That trinket I gave you won't save you from that," I said. "It's only good for hellfire attacks thrown at you using line of sight. So the bell tolls for thee, my friend, if we let it toll at all. You'll go up like a Roman candle."

"Then our best defense lies in the speed with which we dispatch them?" Leif asked.

"That's right."

"Is the Roman-candle expression accurate? What happens if they are successful?"

I relayed the question to Malina, begging her pardon for asking her details of Waclawa's death.

"I cannot help you there," she replied. "We didn't see it happen—I've never seen it happen. We see only the aftermath. In this case, we got the report from Detective Geffert."

"Geffert!" I exclaimed. "I knew I'd heard his name somewhere before! He visited you in your condo, didn't he?"

"Yes. You know him?"

"He's the one who's been pestering me recently. You have his hair in a jar, don't you?"

"Yes," Malina confirmed.

"Very interesting. That might come in handy later. But look, for now, we'll move fast once we get there. We'll put a couple of grenades through their windows and maybe take out a few if we're lucky, then we'll move in downstairs."

"Did you say grenades?"

"Yeah, we have a couple of RPGs, so we'll be starting out with a bang. Hope your illusion can contain explosions."

"Where on earth did you get RPGs?"

"Garage sale across the street," I said. We rang off so that Malina could share the news with her sisters. Leif put in a call to Antoine, the leader of the local flesh-eating ghouls, as we exited onto the Santan Freeway and headed east to Gilbert Road.

"Antoine. I have an all-you-can-eat buffet coming up real soon. Load the boys into the truck. It is a three-story building on Gilbert and Pecos. Twenty-two witches on the menu, some of them carrying demon spawn."

I didn't have the same quality hearing that Leif did to pick out the individual words, but by his tone Antoine sounded pleased.

After exiting the freeway, the building soon towered above us on the south side of Pecos, as much as any building in Gilbert could be said to tower over anything. The Phoenix metro area tended to sprawl instead of build up, and three-story buildings in these suburbs meant a fairly ritzy office address. This building had been meant to house multiple businesses, but once the recession hit, it never scored a single tenant. Architecturally, it sported large glass walls with periodic steel-reinforced columns of cement blocks; some attached wedgelike structures of painted, textured Sheetrock provided just a wee bit of rakish modernity and broke up its boxlike sterility. Streetlights revealed that it was painted largely in beige, gray, and sage green along its solid parts, while the wedges were the color of sun-dried tomatoes.

The building sat right on the edge of the street, with a large empty lot to the south. We parked there, and they surely saw us if they had anyone watching. The single entrance faced the parking lot, to the left of center. Leif and I mounted the RPGs to our shoulders and cautioned the Polish ladies to stand away from the breeches in the rear. Malina said not to worry; they were going to spread out and surround the building as best they could right now. We should just aim high so they wouldn't be in the line of fire. I chose the top left corner of the building, where a lookout was most likely to be watching us, and Leif chose a wall of glass on the third floor to the right of center. We carefully aimed through the optical sights, then pulled the triggers on the count of three. The rocket trails hissed above the witches' heads and hit at first with a dull *thunk*, followed shortly by the sound of shattered glass and the concussive shock wave. That would get their attention.

"Clock is running now. They're going to come after us with that hex for sure."

I groped for the two swords in the trunk and figured out by touch which one was Fragarach. I slung it across my back and handed Moralltach to Leif.

"Let's keep them camouflaged for a surprise. Once they're covered in blood they'll be visible, but the first couple of critters we run through will wonder where the swords came from."

Leif chuckled, slipped his arm through the strap, and said, "Oo-rah." We had about a sixty-yard dash to make it to the building, since we had parked some distance away. We both drew our swords and advanced, and I took a grenade out of my pocket too. I could feel the battle madness coming on as I ran, a cocktail of adrenaline and testosterone and a heightening of my senses. In the old days, Celts used to charge into battle naked, wearing nothing but a torc around their necks. I'd fought my share of battles like that—very recently, in fact—but I'd long since found I could run faster when my goodies weren't flapping around between my legs. Now I even wore shoes, because there was no way I'd be able to connect to the earth here anyway. The sum of my magical power was stored in my bear charm, and I hoped I'd have little occasion to draw on it. Fragarach would have to do my work for me.

When we arrived at the entrance—two very large glass doors with brushed-metal handles—we saw nothing but an empty lobby faced in dark granite and two hallways near the back, one of which presumably led to the stairwell and the other to the elevators. Leif was going to drive his fist through the glass, a dramatic announcement of our arrival, no doubt, but I asked him to wait. With a little concentration and a little expenditure of magic, I was able to unlock the door by binding the bolt to the open position. I then tore out the pin of the grenade with my teeth, opened the door silently, and tossed the grenade to the back hallway on the right-hand side, where I assumed the elevators were, along with anyone (or anything) waiting in ambush. It rebounded off the back wall and, thanks to the angle, disappeared down the hall so that we would be safe from shrapnel when it went off.

It exploded satisfactorily, but we heard no screams of dismay. We entered and shuffled forward, swords raised defensively, and I asked Leif, "You smell anyone?"

The vampire shook his head and said, "Not on this floor. Only dust."

That relaxed me somewhat, and I almost got squashed to Druid marmalade because of it. A huge column of basalt fell from above as I squared with the dust-clouded hallway, and only my peripheral vision and reflexes allowed me to roll out of the way in time. It crashed loudly onto the floor of the lobby, shattering the tile and sending aloft a small spray of ceramic shrapnel. But then the column of basalt didn't lie still, the way stone should. It *moved*, back and up, until I saw that it was attached to something much larger looming in the cloud of hallway debris—namely, the torso of a very large basalt golem, with eyes like pilot lights set deep in a boulder it used for a head.

"Another behind you!" Leif shouted, and I rolled again as a second massive arm smashed the tile where I'd been lying into ceramic tortilla chips. This one had been waiting in the opposite hallway, guarding the entrance to the stairwell. I was back up against another glass wall with a single door in it. Beyond was a large, undeveloped office space, with a bare concrete foundation, no dividing walls, open ductwork in the ceiling, and plenty of room to dodge a couple of golems.

"We need space!" I said, and I scrambled to my feet and tried the glass door that led into the interior. It was unlocked—there was nothing to steal in there. Leif dashed through it right behind me, and the basalt golems promptly smashed through the entire wall in pursuit. I felt some shards tug at the flak jacket and one cut the back of my left arm, but I ignored them for the moment as we sprinted to put some space between us and the golems. The building gave us plenty of room to run; I guessed there was about twenty thousand square feet in there.

"These stone guardians may pose a problem," Leif said wryly. They moved with all the grace and silence of a landslide, the chalky scrapes of their joints heralding the thunderous impacts of every step they took. "They don't have any juicy veins for me to tear out, swords won't cut them, and they won't stop unless we leave."

"Nonsense," I said. "Golems are nothing more than Kabbalistic enchantments—" I stopped, realizing I might literally have the magic touch where they were concerned. I could laboriously unbind the rock into its component elements, but that would take time I didn't have and energy I didn't want to waste; a simpler solution was available, thanks to Rabbi Yosef. "Hey, I want to try something," I said. "Pick one and charge it—just climb up its face or something so it isn't watching me. I'll follow up."

"How much time do you need?" Leif frowned. We were fast approaching the east end of the building, and soon we'd have to turn and face them anyway.

"I need only a second or two," I explained as the golems rumbled behind us. "Don't let it grab you or anything. If you can do the same with the other one afterward, even better."

"Okay," Leif said, "here I go." He pivoted on his right foot and leapt at the nearest golem, spitting out one of those hoarse, hissing vampire cries that signal to victims they're nothing more than a walking package of Go-Gurt. He stepped neatly on the golem's knee and leapt up to its head, ramming an elbow into its nose and actually chipping off a few pebbles, before using its half-raised arm to launch himself over the head. Leif hung by a single hand off the golem's pitted volcanic skull, until it tried to flail at him with its arms. This distracted the second golem too, which veered to take a swipe at Leif dangling off its brother's back, and that was my chance. I darted forward and rested my palm upon the thigh of the first golem, and after a moment its struggles ceased, its eyes flamed out. The Kabbalistic enchantment had been snuffed by the wards bound up in my aura, and it fell heavily backward as Leif leapt away. The second golem was still focused on Leif, and it was a simple matter to dash behind it and repeat the process, a brief touch on the rocky hamstring sufficing to end its animation and send it tumbling on top of its brother.

"Hecate's frosty tits, how did you do that?" Leif demanded. "I thought we were going to spend all our time dodging them."

"A better question is, how did the *hexen* manage to create them?" I asked. "They're not Kabbalists. In fact, they used to kill them during the war—oh. That's how. They stole the spells off their victims."

"Fill me in later," Leif said. "The clock is ticking."

"Right. Think you could toss one of the golems' heads through the ceiling and make us a hole to get to the second floor? I don't fancy walking back there," I gestured to the west end of the building, "and climbing up a booby-trapped stairwell."

"Neither do I. Let me see how much they weigh." I could match Leif's strength if I had access to the earth—we'd tested it once with an arm-wrestling match in a park—but right now he had to play the Herculean one, with my magic in short supply. He lifted the second golem's head, which must have weighed a good half ton or more, and hefted it experimentally in one hand. It appeared to strain him as much as a juggler might handle a grapefruit.

"Throw it at an angle, perhaps, then follow up with one of your grenades?" he asked.

"An excellent plan," I agreed, taking out one of the grenades, "but you'll need to throw me through the hole afterward. I don't have a lot of juice right now."

Without another word, Leif chucked the boulder up through the ceiling with a magnificent concussion and a cry of twisted steel, and it almost plowed through to the third floor as well. I was glad it didn't: The idea of the *hexen* taking potshots at us from above held little savor for me.

I tore out the pin and lobbed a grenade through the hole, in the direction of the elevator shafts and the stairwell to the west, where I figured the floor's defenses would be concentrated. In such an open area, the grenade ought to do plenty of damage.

Unfortunately, its explosion killed only a single one of the creatures waiting for us. Leif tossed me through the hole, sword drawn, and I landed somewhat ungracefully to face the charge of seven bloodied and enraged demon rams coming from the stairwell entrance. Goat-headed, curly-horned, and cloven-hoofed, they had the torso and arms of the Spartans in *300*, and no amount of Visine would ever get the red out of their eyes. They were armed with spears, but I noticed that they also had long knives hanging from their right sides. They were undisciplined; they should have charged me in a wedge. Cold Fire was out of the question, since none of us was touching the earth. They'd all have to be dispatched the old-fashioned way.

As I charged them, a quick count gave me eight—seven, plus one melting into goo by the stairwell—and it had been eight demons, by our earlier count, who had impregnated *die Töchter des dritten Hauses*.

"Come on, you horny bastards!" I cried as I slapped away the tip of the vanguard's spear and then slashed through his throat, which his bulging eyes seemed to think was unfair; he thought he'd been charging an unarmed man. I danced away to the left to force them to turn and break their momentum. The next two chuffed balls of hellfire into their left hands and threw them at me as they tried to change direction.

I lunged right through them, heedless of the flames from which my amulet protected me, and beheaded them both with one stroke. The others now realized I was armed and slowed their approach, moving more cautiously and trying to surround me as I backpedaled away from their spear tips. Leif leapt up through the hole behind them and cut down two more. The remaining two divided their attention between us. One of them threw his spear at me as he charged. I ducked under it and then he was on me, his long knife drawn, and we each grabbed the other's sword arm as he bowled me to the floor. We rolled around, each trying to gain advantage.

His breath was hot in my face—fiery, as a matter of fact—and those bulging muscles weren't an illusion. I had to draw on some power from my bear charm to keep him at bay.

"You killed my father," he snorted in a basso profundo rumble. "Prepare to die!"

"Inigo Montoya? Is that you?" For a moment I had no idea who he was talking about, then I realized he must have been referring to the large ram that escaped during the battle at Tony Cabin. "Oh, I know who you mean now," I said as we grappled. "Hey, I didn't kill him. That was Flidais, I swear. You can find her in Tír na nÓg, or I could send her a message if you like. No?"

Moralltach hacked through his spine before he could answer, and he fell lifeless on top of me.

"Oof. Thanks," I said to Leif as the vampire kicked its corpse off me; the demon had already begun to soften and dissolve into sludge. Leif had sent the other ram back to hell as well.

"Well, get up," my lawyer said impatiently. "Remember the clock."

"It might not be ticking anymore," I said. "I think these fellas were the demons necessary for the ritual. Look along the wall there." I pointed to some dimly glowing runes around the stairwell. "And check out these markings on the floor. These rams were bound here, and judging by the amount of filth, they've been here for some time."

"There could be more of them upstairs," Leif pointed out.

"You're right. Better safe than dead."

"How many grenades do you have left?"

"Three."

"Very well, we will follow the same procedure as before," Leif said, sheathing Moralltach and walking over to where the golem's head had fallen, sagging dangerously into the floor, "but do not hold anything back this time."

He was about to pitch it from where he stood, near the center of the building, but I cautioned him that perhaps we should move back to the far eastern edge and proceed from there. "I'll toss my grenades all toward the elevators and stairs, clearing out the middle of the floor, and when we go up, we make sure to clear out these back edges first so we can't get taken from behind. If they're smart, they will have stationed someone there at the corners."

"I am chill with that," the vampire said stiffly, tossing the half-ton boulder up and down like it was a tennis ball as he walked to the far edge of the building with me.

"You're trying to be cool *now*, Leif? Seriously?"

"I am the shit, home slice, straight up," he replied.

"No. I mean, don't get me wrong, this is a great effort, but you still need to use more contractions. And your tone is so formal, it's like you're complimenting the pudding at a duke's dinner party. No one's ever going to believe you're from the hood. But let's work on it later. Right now there are some witches up there in dire need of just desserts."

"Fucking H!" the vampire shouted, shaking his free left fist. He enunciated the *g* very clearly and projected his voice from his diaphragm, like a trained opera singer.

"It's fuckin' *A*, not *H*, but yeah, Leif, go ahead, let's throw down."

Leif paused and frowned. "Do you not mean we should throw up?"

"No. See, when you throw up you're vomiting, but when you

throw down you're starting a fight, as in throwing down the gaunt-
let."

"Ohhhh," he said. "I thought you were speaking literally."

"I do beg your pardon. Let's literally throw up, but figuratively
throw down."

Leif threw up. He hurled the boulder through the ceiling with so
much force that it plowed not only through the third floor but also
through the roof. I don't know where it landed. I lobbed my three
grenades after it to the left, center, and right and waited for them to
explode. Once they did—and this time we heard screams, along with
more shattering glass—Leif chucked me through the hole and I faced
the northeast corner.

A witch was standing there, as I predicted—and it was the brunette who'd killed Perry, whose nose I had broken at the widow's
house. There was no attempt to sling any spells my way; she had a
handgun pointed at me and proceeded to fire without ceremony, her
teeth bared in a feral snarl as she did her best to kill me. I dropped and
curled my legs tight, arms up to protect my head, and let my flak
jacket take the punishment, but the whip of a bullet on the left side of
my head and a sharp sting told me she'd winged me good. Hot blood
dribbled down my neck and sharp blows punished my back, and
then a slug tore through the outside of my left thigh before she had to
reload. I blocked the pain there and started to close up that wound
with some of my stored power, enduring the throbbing in my back
and the sting on the side of my head as I got to my feet. I put up a hand
to check the wound and realized with horror that she'd shot off my
left ear, and in my adrenaline rush I hadn't realized how bad the
wound was.

"The gods damn you, look what you've done!" I cried as she fum-
bled with her second clip and I charged, drawing Fragarach. "If I want
to grow this back I'll have to endure the most terrifying sex imagin-
able! Gaahhhhh!"

She was frantically trying to get her gun reloaded, but the crazed
Irish lad coming at her with a blade covered in black demon's blood
had a deleterious effect on her fine motor skills. With as little cere-

mony as she'd afforded me, I ran Fragarach through her abdomen and out her back until the point scraped against the glass wall. The gun and ammunition dropped from her hands, and a soft, keening sigh escaped her lips. I twisted the blade, and a more satisfying scream gurgled forth. I'm not the type to say, "That's for so-and-so!" as I deliver well-deserved punishment unto an enemy, but I was sorely tempted to say something in this case. Still, why bother? She knew what she'd done. She aged before my eyes as the life left her and her cosmetic façade sloughed away. I yanked Fragarach loose and beheaded her to make sure she wouldn't rise again.

Off to my right, Leif had already ascended and was engaged with someone in the southeast corner. I hoped they were still ignorant of what he was and would try slapping him with that necrotic spell. Perhaps, before he cut them down, they'd have time to realize they couldn't stop the heart of a man who was already dead.

Nothing had come after us yet from the direction of the grenade explosions, but as I turned to check, I saw there was an awful lot of dust and debris floating around right now, and there was no telling what awaited us on the other side of the cloud. Flashes of violet light drew my attention to the street below. Bogumila was busy doing magical battle with a heavily bearded man in Hasidic garb; she was the source of light, a torus of purples and lavenders whirling around her right hand, which was raised above her head and casting a bright cone of protection around her. The light illuminated the man's face—it was the Rabbi Yosef Bialik, sure enough, and he had finally tracked down a witch. Problem was, he was fighting the wrong one. His absolute definitions of black and white were causing him to take down friends as well as foes.

Much as I might have wished it, I was in no position to help Bogumila, and I couldn't get into position without clearing this floor first. I had to start my count: The brunette was one down, twenty to go. I reluctantly left the window to see if I could help Leif and clear our backs before we advanced. I'd taken only a few steps when I saw him slice a woman clean in half with Moralltach. As her torso slid greasily off her hips and the two halves crumpled to the floor, he whipped around at my approach and grinned when he saw me. "Nice ear," he said. "Would you like me to lick your wounds?"

"Shut up. How many did you get here?"

"Two," he said, gesturing to another still form, now wrinkled and gray, lying behind him.

"Okay, three down. Let's go. We need to count and make sure we get them all."

I turned on my magical sight and peered west into the dust cloud. There were figures moving on the far side near the stairwell, barely perceptible through the choking haze. A crosswind through the shattered walls of glass to the north and south was clearing some of it out, but full visibility was still a few minutes away.

"Shadowy figures," the Morrigan had said. I'd do battle with shadowy figures. Well, one of the figures wasn't human; it had a distinctly demonic aura. I realized that, where they were located, they probably would have had shelter from both the RPGs we launched and a very good chance of taking cover from the grenades I'd tossed if they heard them clatter on the floor. I crouched low, took a deep breath, and kept Fragarach in front of me as I stepped into the gunk, depending on Leif to follow.

There were broken, bloody bodies strewn about, withered arms and knobby knees twisted unnaturally; all their glamour was gone in death. I would count them later. There were ten figures ahead that I could see, grouped in a loose circle, some of them seated on the floor chanting something in low tones, and nearly all of them showing the telltale signs of hell. As soon as I processed that, it set me to sprinting: The seated ones were in the midst of a ritual and the others were guarding them, because they were close to completing it. I had no idea who their target was, but I didn't want anyone on our side to die because I exercised undue caution.

I hurriedly cast camouflage on myself, remembering that they hadn't been able to see through it during the war. After that, my thinking self practically disappeared and I became an extension of my endocrine system.

One of the standing figures—a female silhouette—had an automatic weapon of some sort and heard me coming across the rubble. She sprayed a dozen rounds or so in my general direction; I saw the muzzle flashes at the same time that the slugs knocked me back on my ass, gasping for breath and counting my lucky stars that my neighbor was an arms dealer. She saw Leif coming next and turned the gun on him, but bullets bothered him about as much as bee stings, and many of them pinged off his steel breastplate anyway. I'd let him worry about the guards; it was the seated figures in the ritual that had to die *right now*.

I got up on my knees, gripped Fragarach's hilt in both hands, raised it over my head, then threw it at the nearest skull in sight. It flew true, crunching messily through the back of the head and out the witch's mouth before the guard halted its progress through her pate. Leif decapitated the machine gunner almost simultaneously and was amputating another guardian's arm at the elbow when a small piece of hell busted loose.

Halting a demonic ritual in progress is usually disastrous for those involved, and so it was for the *hexen*. Instead of completing the hex intended for Malina or some other Sister of the Three Auroras, the two remaining witches—one of them on her back with her legs spread wide—were instantly immolated in the consuming flames they'd been trying to summon. Out of those flames rose a very large demon ram, bigger than those we'd seen on the second floor. It was laughing heartily, because we'd caught him *in flagrante delicto* and the death of the witches had unbound him, setting him free on this plane. Everyone, including Leif, stopped what they were doing to see what he would do. The ram regarded us evenly for a moment—he wasn't fooled by my camouflage—and decided he had no desire to take us on; there was so much more fun to be had elsewhere, with people who couldn't fight him. He turned his head north and lowered it as he charged, punching yet another hole in the glass wall and plunging into the street below, extending his hooves as he fell to absorb the shock in his powerful haunches.

Such an escape attempt was precisely what the Polish coven was waiting for. I scrambled to the edge to look below; Malina had stationed herself at the northwest corner, and though she had seen that Bogumila was under assault at the northeast corner, she hadn't abandoned her post, lest something like the ram get away.

She attacked it fiercely, and all the faster so that she could run to help Bogumila. She shouted something indistinct in Polish, shot her empty right hand up into the air, and seemed to pull out of it a sort of red neon whip. She cracked it expertly before slinging it around the ram's legs as it tried to disappear into the night. The ram bellowed and gasped fire as it fell onto the asphalt of Pecos Road, but Malina wasn't finished. With another exclamation in Polish, she snapped the whip handle all the way down to the ground, sending a massive sine wave along its length. When it reached the ram's legs, the wave tossed it shrieking up into the air by its feet, as if it weighed no more than a hummingbird. Malina flicked her wrist and let the whip handle go, and it spiraled up, following the ram, until it wrapped itself crushingly around the creature like a constrictor. The ram bleated desperately for a heartbeat before it exploded above the street in an impressive corona of orange and green fire.

The ram's doom fell at our eye level, three stories up, and I heard shocked gasps behind me at this demonstration of Malina's power. I laughed, looking back at the remaining German witches, and said to them in their language, "I can't believe you started shit with her when you had only one fancy trick in your bag. She can pull exploding hell-whips out of the fucking *air*." I'd always suspected Malina's coven had serious mojo up their fancy designer sleeves, but until now they'd never had the chance to show it. The rotten apples in their bunch had been faced with werewolves at Tony Cabin, and nothing they could have pulled out of the air would have helped against the Tempe Pack, unless it was silver.

The *hexen* appeared unsure of where my voice was coming from, so I spared one more fleeting glance for Bogumila and Rabbi Yosef before finishing up what we'd come to do. The rabbi's beard looked significantly larger than it had before, moving with much more animation as well, but Bogumila's purple whorl of protection seemed to be keeping her safe for the moment.

While I was worrying about someone else's ass besides my own, one of the witches snuck up on me and delivered a sucker punch to my jaw, the kind that film directors love to play in slow motion, where the face ripples around the mandibles and promises a bouquet of colorful bruises later. Clearly, my camouflage had been compromised. I lost several teeth and tasted blood in my mouth as my head hit the glass and I dropped to the floor. I was treated to a couple of vicious kicks to the abdomen before I had time to fully appreciate the pain in my skull and assess the damage done. The flak jacket probably saved me from broken ribs, because the impacts were loud enough to remind me of the sound effects in Shaw Brothers' films. My vision swam as I took a frenzied glance up at my assailant. Her face might as well have been one of those little yellow signs people used to put in their cars; hers said DEMON ON BOARD. Red glowing eyes and hot dung breath steamed visibly and promised there would be no light banter while she tried to slay me. She got another kick in while I turned off the pain in my head and ramped up my speed, a quickening of neuromuscular function I always used to keep up with Leif in our sparring sessions. It didn't leave much magic in my bear charm, but I hoped it would get me out of the spot I was in.

As she aimed another kick at my head, I set my arms underneath me and whipped my foot around to sweep her plant foot from under her. I leapt up and fought off a spell of dizziness as she collapsed, howling. I backpedaled to the west as she scrambled to her feet, and I took the few seconds I'd bought to assess the new tactical situation.

The five remaining *hexen* were still months away from squeezing a demon child through their pelvis, but apparently they were now enjoying all the perks associated with carrying a casting ram to term—abilities awakened, perhaps, by the abrupt deaths of their brethren. They had increased strength and speed, senses that could penetrate my camouflage, and a newfound talent for throwing hellfire. The other four were busy hurling angry orange balls of it at Leif, and he cringed away from them instinctively, retreating back east, unable to recall or trust in the face of so much flame that the talisman I'd given him should render him fireproof.

Fragarach was still lodged in the brain of a dead witch, and if I was allowed the time, I could have created a binding between the leather on the hilt and the skin of my palm, causing it to fly to my hand in one of those sweet Skywalker moves. My attacker, however, had no intention of affording me the opportunity. She charged at me with a cry of apeshit rage, her hands extended and her fingers transforming visibly into blackened claws. Said claws raked at my belly, and I was glad I'd stepped back instead of counting on my flak vest to stop them, because they caught the first couple of layers of it and shredded it as if it were no more substantial than crepe paper. I'd hate to see what they'd do to intestines—especially mine.

I couldn't counter weapons like that with nothing but my bare hands available. She wasn't wearing leather like many of the others; her clothes were all synthetic fibers, dead and removed from nature, so I couldn't pull or push her around with any bindings. My best option was to get out of her way and hope I could retrieve my sword.

She circled around to the center, though, cutting me off. The west end of the building loomed at my back, and a dangerous drop yawned to my left now as I pulled even with the broken glass wall through which the demon ram had plunged. The witch lunged at me, grinning evilly. She took a swipe at my head that forced me to dance back toward the window ledge, then another that I ducked under before scooting to the right, heading for the west wall. She was quick enough to shoot out a foot and catch me square on my bloodied left ear, though, and the detonation of pain sent me reeling into the corner. Through a ringing and buzzing haze, I dimly heard her cackling; apparently she had me where she wanted me—on the ground with nowhere to go.

Flames engulfed me, billowing sheets of it like hellish laundry waving in a dry wind, and I began to laugh too, as I struggled painfully to my feet in the midst of it. It was hot, no doubt, but my amulet protected me. I centered myself—quite a trick with my brains scrambled as they were—and peered through the fire at my target. She was only five feet away, her hands throwing fire and a demonic rictus painted on her face. I shuffled closer, set my left foot carefully—and winced at the bullet wound in my thigh—then I lashed out with a textbook karate kick to her gut, right where the demon grew in her center of gravity. She staggered back, snarling, and her hands quit gushing flame. She didn't go down but instead stood still for a few seconds, dumbfounded that I didn't look the least bit crispy or melty by now. I slid to my right, heading in the direction of my sword, and by the time she finally processed that, I already had a decent lead. Just as she tensed to spring after me, however, a familiar red hellwhip sailed through the open glass wall and wrapped itself around her hips. It yanked her screaming from the building, and I didn't bother to go over and watch; I knew that Malina would finish her off, and there were still four more *hexen* to worry about.

They were giving Leif all he could handle—probably more, to be fair. He'd run away from their hellfire all the way around the building, circling the great hole in the floor where he'd thrown the golem's head, and now, as I pulled Fragarach out of the witch's skull with a loud *schluck*, the *hexen* had tacked about to come at him from several angles. Hellfire blazed at Leif from four different directions, and this time he could not dodge it. His inhuman scream ran cold fingers down my spine as I lost sight of him briefly in the conflagration. He came out of it shortly afterward, and while most of him was still untouched, the poufy sleeves of his linen shirt had ignited outside the thin skin of his talisman's protection. The sleeves were now giving him trouble, as the flames licked up his arms and began to eat away at his pale, undead, and highly combustible flesh. I didn't see Moralltach in either hand; he must have dropped it somewhere. He ran north, straight toward the massive hole in the wall where a grenade had blown out the glass, and I saw what he intended.

"No," I breathed, knowing he couldn't hear me. "That's hard-packed clay." He leapt from the third floor, shrouded in spreading flame, his shriek falling with him to the street below in search of earth to smother the fire. I hoped he'd find some in the landscaping between the building and the street; the fight wasn't supposed to have driven him to such desperate measures. He'd have to dig through dry, clay-based dirt to quench those flames, and I didn't like his odds.

Neither did I like mine. I was one Druid with a possibly fractured jaw, a missing ear, a wounded thigh, and very little magic against four *hexen* jazzed on demon energies. They turned as one and hissed at me, understanding that I'd eliminated one of their sisters somehow. They looked a whole lot stronger and faster than I felt.

Well, I thought wryly as I hefted Fragarach and prepared myself for their charge, at least I'm good at swordplay.

Inchoate battle cries erupted from their throats as they sprinted at me from maybe thirty yards away. Klaudia chose that moment to burst through the stairwell door, armed with a silver dagger in her left hand and looking like she'd just had fabulous sex somehow on her way up. She raised her right arm above her head—a gesture that seemed to precede most of the spells her coven cast in combat—and said, "*Zorya Vechernyaya chroń mnie od zła.*" The immediate effect was a cone of purple light sheathing her form, much like Bogumila's, but perhaps a bit more solid looking. The charging *hexen* pulled up and redirected their attention to Klaudia, whom they recognized as one of their old enemies. Two of them let loose with hellfire that bloomed from their arms like time-lapse orchids, and Klaudia calmly ignored them as it washed up against the purple light and found no passage through. The other two kept coming with a physical attack, and those received her special attention.

Her languid manner sloughed off, and suddenly she moved with liquid grace, crouching and then pivoting on her right foot as she swept the blade of her dagger across the eyes of the leader. She crossed her left foot in front of her right, then spun on it and leapt around in a sort of Chun-Li move, delivering first a right boot, then a left to the head of the second witch. Both *hexen* were down inside of two seconds, though I doubted they were dead. Their demon spawn would heal them up in no time.

Still, I admit that I gawked; I gaped, even. Malina had told me that her coven wasn't trained for combat, yet Klaudia had just displayed stark evidence to the contrary. But then I thought she must be the exception to the rule; if the dark side of her coven had fought so well at Tony Cabin, more than two werewolves would have perished that night.

Shaking off my astonishment, I advanced to help, as the two downed *hexen* clambered to their feet and the flamethrowers were finally registering that nothing was burning inside that purple cone.

The answer to enemies who heal annoyingly fast is always, always decapitation. That is why swords will never go out of style. Fragarach sang through the neck of one of the flamethrowers, and I added a stab for Junior in the gut before the body fell. That reminded the remaining three that I was still around. Their minds and their jaws became unhinged as they bellowed hot roars of red ass-breath and charged me all at once, forgetting entirely about Klaudia. She hadn't killed any of them yet, after all, while I'd been responsible for quite a number so far.

These last three had very little of their humanity left. They were old, old witches, and they'd been selling wee parcels of their souls to hell for so long that nothing but a single forlorn box of humanity was left in what was once a full warehouse. Something else occupied their skins now, something that made their eyes burn in their heads and black claws grow from their fingers.

I gave ground before the charge, whirling the blade in front of me in a defensive pattern. One, then two of their cursed faces dropped out of my vision, due no doubt to some guerrilla effort of Klaudia's, but I still had one more to deal with—and she was faster than me.

Perhaps I'd slowed down. The pain of my injuries was building, for I'd done no real healing to any of them; I'd just continued fighting and probably exacerbated them in the process. The witch lost her left hand to Fragarach in order to get a good shot at me with her right. Her claws tore down through my flak vest at my left shoulder, ripping not only through it but also through my pectoralis muscles. I fell backward and she clung to me on the way down, trying to dig in farther with her nails, attempting to turn the claws up under my rib cage and do serious damage to my organs. Her left side, however, was unguarded and vulnerable. I shoved Fragarach sideways through her guts as she straddled me, twisting it madly to make sure the demon felt the blade. She convulsed spastically and vomited blood before her eyes finally cooled and she fell still. On top of me.

My left arm didn't want to move. I tried and it hammered me with pain. I used the last of my stored magic to shut it off; I couldn't think in a cloud of agony. I yanked Fragarach out of the witch—a messy business—then put it down long enough to shove her off me with my right hand. I sat up to see if any *hexen* were left.

There weren't. Klaudia had eviscerated the last two, killing the demon spawn first, and then she'd slashed their throats for good measure. Now that the battle was over, her purple wards were gone and her waifish charisma was back. We were the only living creatures on a floor littered with bodies, and yet she made it all cool somehow just by standing there. Even covered in blood, her expression had the sleepy, languid sensuality of an underwear model.

"Thanks for the assist," I said. "Where did you learn to fight like that?"

She shrugged. "Vietnam."

"You've *got* to be shitting me."

She grinned and her eyes sparkled mischievously. "Yeah, I am."

I shuddered as I came down off my adrenaline high and exhaustion set in. But when we heard a thin scream and the pale lavender glow outside the northeast windows abruptly winked out, we bolted for the stairs and hoped we wouldn't be too late.

CHAPTER 25

The situation outside was a giant bowl full of gloom and grim. I got around to the north side first, because Klaudia had run around to collect Berta, Roksana, and Kazimiera. I saw no sign of Leif. Bogumila lay dead on the concrete, looking old and terrified in death, and Malina was righteously pissed. My earlier suspicion of the rabbi's beard now appeared justified, for it exhibited all the qualities one might associate with a distant relative of Cthulhu, with four long, hairy tentacles squirming radially from his jaw, two on either side of his chin. The two on the left were wrapped tightly around Bogumila's throat, and now they were trying to disentangle themselves from the woman they had strangled to death. The other two were trying to reach Malina, but she was laying down some heavy-duty protection as I approached.

She chanted four lines in Polish, and since I was finally in range to hear, I recorded it eidetically for reference. As she reached the end of each line, a booming clap thundered from her palm along with the colors violet, blue, red, and white, swirling around her in sequence like exuberant streamers in a gymnast's floor exercise:

"Jej miłość mnie ochrania,
Jej odwaga czyni mnie nieustraszona,
Jej potęga dodaje mi sił,
Dzięki jej miłosierdziu żyję!"

Malina translated them for me later and explained that each line was a spell in itself, affording her "certain strengths and protections" through the benediction of the Zoryas. Her words meant: *By her love I am protected, By her courage I am made fearless, By her might I am made strong, By her mercy I am spared.*

When Malina finished, there was an impenetrable yet translucent shield around her, and she looked like she was just getting warmed up. It was far beyond the conic wards I'd seen from Bogumila and Klaudia.

Rabbi Yosef's crazy squid beard had seen enough; the tentacles quailed and would go no further. They started to retreat, rolling up quickly into the rabbi's face as he considered how to deal with a far more accomplished witch, then he startled and took a step back as he saw me coming, covered in the gore of witches and demons and my own blood, with Fragarach held ready in my hand. I didn't hesitate, didn't say hello, just raised my sword to his throat and said, "*Freagróidh tú.*" He froze up in the blue glow of the spell and started spluttering something at me in Russian. "You will not speak except to answer my questions," I said, and he promptly shut up.

"Thank you, Atticus, that will make this so much simpler," Malina said.

"No, stop," I told her, as she was gearing up to lay him out. "I need to talk to him first."

"He must pay for Bogumila's death!" Malina blazed from behind her shield.

"Yes, he must. But first he will speak plainly to me for the first time. What is the name of your organization, sir?"

He fought it, of course, but eventually he said, "The Hammers of God." Understanding clicked in my head. That stylized *P* on the hilt of his knife had been a hammer.

"Where is Father Gregory tonight?"

"He is on a plane back to Moscow."

"How many are in your organization?"

"I do not know the exact number."

"Give me your best guess. How many might show up to avenge you should you disappear tonight?"

"At least twenty Kabbalist fighters like me. That is standard when one of us disappears. But they may send more if they think the threat warrants it."

I turned to Malina with a wry grin. "It is prudent that we stopped to chat, is it not?"

"He still must pay," she insisted, as Klaudia, Kazimiera, Berta, and Roksana raced to join us and surround him.

"You want to face twenty or more of him?" I asked.

"He is lying about that."

I shook my head. "You've experienced this spell yourself, Malina. He cannot lie. Perhaps there is another way we can make him pay yet avoid a confrontation that may lead to more bloodshed on our side."

Malina clearly found this suggestion distasteful. She wanted to kill his ass right then and there. "What do you propose?"

"Take a few nice locks of his hair while I've got him here. He'll know he's in your power then. You can send him some explosive diarrhea or something like that, something painful and humiliating yet short of death, and you can also set up a dead man's enchantment so that if you die, he dies too. And then we'll explain to him, in small words, how he killed a very nice witch who was trying to help us kill all the evil witches upstairs, and he and his Hammers of God should just leave us the hell alone from now on, because we have the East Valley well under control."

Malina weighed my words. She knew that she was more than a match for the rabbi, but he'd been stronger than Bogumila. Twenty more of him against the five remaining members of her coven weren't good odds, and she understood this. She agreed, albeit with great reluctance, and dispelled the light show swirling around her. Her sisters accepted the decision without comment, but I could tell they didn't like it either.

"There, Rabbi, you see?" I said. "Heinous witches don't let asspuppets like you live. Only merciful ones who understand, like me, that you're trying to do the right thing but you're just too dim to understand what it is. So we're going to show you. Right after Malina takes some of your hair."

Malina flipped off his hat and tore a giant handful from his scalp, stuffing it into the pocket of her leather jacket. We all enjoyed his pain. Then I released the rabbi from Fragarach, bound his sleeves firmly behind him in a similar fashion to what I'd done in my shop, and we led him through the building and explained how we'd completely eliminated *die Töchter des dritten Hauses*, a coven that had hunted Kabbalists like him for centuries. While he was busy fighting Bogumila, Malina had personally taken care of a large demon ram and another *in utero*. Klaudia had eliminated two more. Leif and I had accounted for the rest between us (I confirmed that we had slain twenty-two), and the vampire disdained demonkind so much that he'd refused to sink his fangs into any of the witches.

To the rabbi's frothing accusations, I replied that, yes, I tended to enjoy the company of vampires and werewolves and witches, because all the ones I knew were extraordinarily well scrubbed and had fantastic taste in automobiles; but none of us suffered a scrap of hell to dwell in our territory unmolested, and we had, in fact, been far more effective against them than the Hammers of God had been so far. So please you, good rabbi, get the fuck out of our town and stay out.

He agreed to leave, albeit with much grumbling and resentment. I figured it was even money he'd come back with friends. We did not wish him farewell.

I found my missing teeth and felt certain I could heal them back into place with a good night's sleep on the earth. I recovered Moralltach and its scabbard near the hole in the floor. Of Leif, however, there was no sign.

Malina joined me at the spot where I'd seen him leap from the building. We looked down at the the rocky landscaping below and saw no sign of disturbance there.

"I'm so sorry about Bogumila," I said to her in low tones. "And Waclawa." I said nothing about Radomila or Emily or any of the others who'd died in the Superstitions.

"Thank you," she said, almost too quiet to hear.

"Did you chance to see what happened to Leif?" I asked.

"I saw him fall," Malina said, sniffling a bit. She wiped at the corner of her eyes and nodded. "He was right between me and Bogumila. I don't think the rabbi even noticed, though how he could miss a flaming vampire is beyond me. He ran east down Pecos; that was the last I saw of him. I remained at my station in case any more *hexen* fell down."

I looked off toward the east. Lights on the north side of the road indicated buildings, but, after a few lots down on our side of the street, there was nothing but darkness.

"East, you say? Is that undeveloped land over there?" I pointed.

"I don't know," Malina said. "We should probably check it out."

Antoine's refrigerated truck rolled into the parking lot as our small convoy of sports cars pulled out onto Pecos, steering carefully around the golem's head that Leif had thrown through the roof. Bogumila's body was bundled gently into Roksana's Mercedes. We waved and wished Antoine and his ghouls *bon appétit*. His gang would have the place cleaned up before sunrise, leaving nothing but property damage and a large pile of rocks behind for the police to wonder over.

I was riding with Malina and Klaudia in the Audi. Klaudia sat on my lap, her torso twisted around to face me and a leather-clad arm draped around my shoulder. With her other hand, she was caressing my injured jaw with a delicate tip of a fingernail. She made cooing sounds of sympathy, and I couldn't take my eyes off her lips.

"Klaudia, stop that," Malina said. "Now is not the time to tease Mr. O'Sullivan."

My head cleared immediately, and I shuddered at Klaudia's knowing smile. She had enchanted her lips like Malina did her hair.

I was glad the ride would be brief; Klaudia had discovered a loophole in our nonaggression treaty already. It was the second time an attraction charm of the Polish witches had worked on me. My amulet had eventually shut down Malina's, and I had no doubt it would have done the same to Klaudia's, but in each case it had worked long enough for them to do me harm if they had wished it.

"It's all right," Klaudia said brightly. "I think he and I understand each other." She patted my chest with the hand that had been caressing my jaw. "Don't we, Mr. O'Sullivan?"

I nodded and turned my gaze to the darkness outside. She was letting me know for future reference that she was every bit as dangerous as Malina.

A quarter mile east on Pecos, we found a charred and blackened Leif facedown on an empty expanse of gravel, next to a trench of violently churned earth. He'd obviously managed to quench the hellfire engulfing him and drag himself a short distance away, but now it appeared he'd reached the end of his strength.

"He's not dead," I said to the witches assembled around his body.

"Yes he is." Berta begged to differ.

"Well, yes, you have a point, but I mean he'll be okay. Still dead. But fine."

"What about you?" Malina asked. "Your face looks like someone took a meat tenderizer to it."

"I'll be fine too," I assured her. I was already feeling marginally better now that I had contact with the earth. "Just help me get Leif back to his car."

Parts of Leif flaked off and blew away when we moved him. One of his fingers crumbled and fell like the tightly packed ash of a hand-rolled cigar.

"Eep!" Kazimiera cried when she saw this.

"It's okay," I said. "It'll grow back. I think."

We fished Leif's keys out of his burned jeans and decided, for his own safety and mine, that he should make the return trip to Tempe in the trunk. Klaudia volunteered to run back and get his car. "Don't ever tell him we did this, though," I said as we stuffed him into the ass end of his Jaguar. "I don't think he'd take it well." Berta tittered.

I bade the witches farewell and expressed my hope they would prosper and grow strong again. It was the language of diplomacy and we all knew it, but it was the proper language in that time and place.

Dr. Snorri Jodursson was already at my house, watching *The Fellowship of the Ring* with my apprentice, so it wasn't tough to find someone to take charge of Leif's recovery. Snorri said he'd simply raid the blood bank, and he was nice enough to put my teeth back in place for me before I lay down to heal in the backyard. Said he wouldn't even charge me this time.

As I stretched out gratefully on the familiar grass of my lawn with a worried Oberon nestled against my side, I hoped the near future would bring me a small portion of peace. I was tired of these constant distractions and the alarming rate at which I seemed to be losing my ears, and if the chaos would consent to desist for a while, I would heal and mourn and focus properly on what to do next.

There was a parcel of wilderness that needed my attention, which I had neglected for far too long.

EPILOGUE

I t's rare that I take the form of a stag. Though it's the largest shape I can take, it's still a bit lower on the food chain than I would like, and rare is the occasion when one of my other forms will not serve me better. But when the job at hand was lugging fifty-pound bags of topsoil miles across rugged terrain, it was the best option I had.

Granuaile and Oberon followed along and hauled a few things of their own as we hiked out to the blighted zone around Tony Cabin. They were carrying tools, our lunch, a set of clothes for me, and a five-gallon blue agave plant. I had a harness and travois hooked up to my shoulders so that I could drag 450 pounds of rich topsoil, teeming with all sorts of bacteria and nutrients, along the ground.

When we reached the edge of the blighted zone, my heart nearly broke; we were still four miles away from Tony Cabin, and there was so much to heal. If the cabin was at the center of a perfect circle, that meant we had fifty square miles to mend. The trees were little more than standing dead wood, and the cacti were lumps of desiccated tissue stretched over dry wooden ribs. The brush was all kindling now, lifeless and essentially petrified: There were no ants, no beetles, no bacteria or fungi to break down the plants and nourish new growth in the spring. But we had to start somewhere.

I unbound myself from the stag form and put on the clothes we'd brought along. Using the shovels Granuaile had carried, we dug up a few dead plants just off the trail and resolved to compost them. Then we excavated a small trench that led from living land into the drained area, much deeper than it was wide, and filled it with all the soil we'd hauled in. We spread the dead soil we'd dug up across the living, so that leaves and bugs and grasses and so on would fall or crawl upon it and gradually reinvigorate it.

We planted the agave in the trench and had to satisfy ourselves with pouring a couple of bottles of water on it to help it make the transition and take root.

<So is that it?> Oberon asked, sniffing at the plant. <It looks kind of lonely, sitting there alive all by itself when everything else is dead. All that work and you hardly made a difference.>

"This is just the beginning, Oberon," I said aloud so that Granuaile could hear. "It's an important first step."

<Should I pee on it to make it feel at home?>

"Maybe next time. That might be too much of a shock right now."

<Can't you do some cool Druid stuff and heal the land magically?>

"Eventually I can get the earth's attention and help it along, but there's nothing for it to work with right now. Life is its medium, and there's no life in that area, not even bacteria. We need to keep bringing in the raw material."

<Well, I think you should get some heavy equipment and a couple hundred dump trucks.>

I laughed. "How would I get heavy equipment here? There are no roads to this place. You know what the trail is like. It's too rough. And most of this land is wilderness—completely untamed bush."

Oberon looked down the trail toward Tony Cabin, still some four miles distant, then considered the lone agave near his feet. <This is going to take a long time, isn't it?>

"Yeah, it's a big job, but I won't feel well again until it's finished. When I stand here and call to the earth, nothing answers."

<Oh.> Oberon looked up at me. <I know that has to make you sad.

But call to me instead, Atticus. I'll always answer. Your fly has been open all this time, by the way, and Granuaile hasn't said a thing.>

Thanks, buddy, I said silently as I tried to surreptitiously zip up my jeans.

<See? I got your back *and* your front. I deserve a treat.>

ACKNOWLEDGMENTS

I know not how it goes with other writers, but for me, five months to finish a novel is akin to Maximum Warp, and it would not have been possible without my primary readers: Alan O'Bryan, Andrea Taylor, and Tawnya Graham-Schoolitz took time out of their busy lives to read each chapter as it was produced and give me valuable feedback. Allen Rouser, Mike Ruggiero, and Nick Steinkemper also read the work as early fans and gave me their thumbs-up.

Katarzyna and Leszek Rosinski were invaluable as translators for the Polish and Russian passages, and Andrea Hümer helped me out with the German. Any mistakes are mine, of course, and the accuracies are theirs.

Detective Dana Packer of the Lincoln, Rhode Island Police Department helped by discussing what police procedures would be like in a case like Perry's. If the fictional Detective Geffert strays in any way from what he should have done, it's because I didn't hear Detective Packer correctly.

Evan Goldfried is my agent extraordinaire at JGLM, and I'm always appreciative of his tireless efforts on my behalf.

My editor at Del Rey, Tricia Narwani, is undeniably the hoopiest frood in North America—but that's not all! She's also brilliant and helpful and I trust her judgment utterly. Her assistant editor, Mike Braff, deserves a proper spangelhelm for enduring the many slings and arrows of my outrageous pranks, and I am thankful for his help as well.

My wife and child were extremely supportive during the process, and words cannot express the depths of my gratitude for their love, encouragement, and curiosity about what Atticus and Oberon would do next.

The three-story building described in this book's climactic battle is actually located on a street in Gilbert called Germann, rather than Pecos. I changed the name of the street because the locals inexplicably pronounce it like the word *germane*, which bears no phonetic relationship to the spelling, and I also did not wish to suggest, even by implication, that the German witches had chosen it as a forward base because of its seemingly close ties to their nationality. A decade later in 2021, the building is very much occupied, but it did spend many months unfinished and unoccupied at the time I wrote the book, just as described.

You can follow me on Twitter and Instagram with the username @kevinhearne, and I have a spiffy website at kevinhearne.com with all kinds of goodies on it. Hope to see you somewhere on the Internet.

A WEE NOTE FROM THE AUTHOR

Grimoire of the Lamb is a novella set before the events of Hounded. Atticus's hideout in Arizona hasn't been discovered by Aenghus Óg yet, but that time approaches. I wrote it because I wanted to give a bit of an origin story to all the Druids, not just Atticus, and there are few magic systems we know about that are older than those of ancient Egypt. I was also fascinated by some work by climatologists and paleontologists that suggested that thousands of years ago, the Sahara Desert used to be a lush green area pocked by lakes and so on, and while they have theories as to why it changed, they don't know for sure.

At one point, Atticus refers to his raid on the Library of Alexandria prior to the time of Emperor Aurelian, carried out at the behest of Ogma, and reveals the ill-gotten gains of that particular heist. Those who wish to read the full account of that heist will find it in Besieged, a collection of Iron Druid novellas and stories.

GRIMOIRE OF THE LAMB

People today think ancient Egypt was ineffably cool. I blame this misconception on hieroglyphics and (to a lesser extent) on the Bangles.

The truth is that the ancient Egyptian elites regarded most people as chattel for the ruling class and practiced some of the blackest magic history has ever seen—or, rather, *hasn't* seen, because they were deadly serious about keeping their secrets. But they wrote such happy tomes as *The Book of the Dead* and illustrated joyful kids' books like *Little Scarab Shat Blood* and *Anubis Eats the Hearts of the Disobedient*. I'm not kidding; I saw them before the Library of Alexandria was ruined by Emperor Aurelian.

I saw plenty at Alexandria in its heyday. In fact, I saw quite a few things I never should have seen, which is why I now avoid the country when I can. My logic, if it could be called that, suggests that if I never think about the country again, the old deities of Egypt will forget that I once snaffled their sex rituals and necromantic tomes. Calls from Cairo, therefore, automatically excite more than their fair share of suspicion. When I picked up the phone in my shop and the voice in my ear identified himself as "Nkosi Elkhashab from Egypt," I toyed briefly with the idea of hanging up before he could even state his business.

The problem was this: Long ago—in what I suppose I must now call my "youth," even though I was already a couple of hundred years old at the time—I raided an extremely restricted section at Alexandria. It was at the behest of Ogma, one of the Tuatha Dé Danann, so to please that particular god I wound up vexing several others in the Egyptian pantheon. Not so much that they would take the trouble to hunt me down, but neither am I precisely welcome in their territory anymore. Bast, in particular, has several bones to pick with me, aside from the fact that I'm not a cat person. I have a book of hers—or, rather, a book that belonged to her cult—that contains some fairly lurid descriptions of her "mysteries." It is physical evidence of the old saying that there is more than one way to skin a cat: The parchment itself is made of catskin—a fine quality bordering on vellum—and the cover is a thicker, tanned catskin leather to protect the contents from minor water damage. I'd thwarted a couple of attempts by her agents to steal it back or assassinate me, but I could also say the same for most of my Egyptian collection. Almost all of it had been cursed or enchanted in some fashion and had given me more trouble than it was worth. I held on to it now just to be stubborn, to say "Neener neener!" to all those ancient mages and gods who thought they could scare a Druid into giving away his hard-earned (if ill-gotten) library. I tended to hoard magical tomes the way dragons hoarded treasure—and protected them with the same ferocity.

Mr. Elkhashab, however, wanted what amounted to a cookbook. "If you are the rare-book dealer Atticus O'Sullivan . . . ?"

"I am."

"Then I am told you have a collection of extremely rare works from Egypt," he said, his voice rich with the lilt of an Arabic accent. I could easily speak Arabic with him, but it was better for now to let him assume I was an American and, therefore, statistically speaking, limited to English and two years of another language in high school.

"Are you from the Ministry of Antiquities?" I asked. These days, admitting you had old stuff from Egypt would earn you a visit from men with mirrored sunglasses.

"No, Mr. O'Sullivan." He chuckled in surprise. "My relationship with them is rather strained. In any case, I doubt they even know of the existence of the particular work I'm looking for. Nor are they likely to care, since it has nothing to do with the pharaohs. It's simply a book written in Coptic, either first or perhaps second century, and it contains a collection of recipes for cooking lamb. Might you have anything remotely resembling such a book?"

I did indeed. Privately I called it the *Grimoire of the Lamb*, because it was otherwise untitled. It had somehow been shelved incongruously amongst some darker works at Alexandria—including Bast's catskin collection of sexercises, which I now called *Nice Kitty!* This was the first time anyone had ever asked about the grimoire, however. The number of people who could speak Coptic today, including myself, was probably only a few hundred. I'd kept the book as a curiosity, but this man's inquiry raised a whole new line of questioning.

"I might," I said, and fished for more information. "Can you give me any more clues about what this might look like?"

"I have never seen it or read any descriptions of its physical appearance. But it was thought to have been in the Library of Alexandria at one time."

Affecting my best clueless-American tone, I said, "Didn't that burn down?"

"Yes, but the book I seek was removed prior to that."

"It's pretty old, then. Papyrus or parchment?"

"Parchment of unusual quality." He'd nailed it. What was his source?

"It's probably severely degraded by now; might be unreadable. Would that be a deal-breaker for you?"

"No, not at all, sir," he said.

I walked out from behind the tea station to the rare-book case on the north wall of my shop; the sale of something like this could ensure a profit for the year and maybe the next one as well, recession or no. Not that I couldn't afford to take a loss. The sale of rare books and antiquities was just one of many get-rich-slow schemes I'd come up with throughout my very long life. The slow part was living until pop culture aged long enough to take on the luster of dignity and the physical product deteriorated to the point where it could whisper of a halcyon epoch before the buyer's time.

My rare books were heavily secured for both the mundane and the magical world. I didn't need to unlock the bindings and disable the wards just to check on the grimoire—I could look through the bulletproof glass. It was still there, sitting amongst my Egyptian goodies.

"All right, I have it. Thirteen recipes for lamb."

"Excellent!" The excitement in his voice carried across the Atlantic very well. "How much? I can wire you the money immediately."

"No, you'll need to purchase it in person."

A pause on the other end of the line. "Can you not ship internationally?"

"I can, but I won't. This is a magical text. I don't trust them to the mail."

"Magical? It is an ancient cookbook."

I couldn't believe he was trying to play dumb now. I had that market cornered. "Mr. Elkhashab. Where did you hear of this book and where did you hear that I might have it?"

"Your store is world famous for antiquities," he said, not answering either question. "I'm simply contacting as many rare-book dealers as I can." I gave up trying to be patient. Normal customers don't look for ancient Coptic texts that should have been burned long ago.

"Please do not insult my intelligence. Earlier you said you had heard that I might have it. So you were either lying then or you are lying now. I do not need to sell this book, Mr. Elkhashab. I am quite content to keep it, because I think we both know it is the only copy in existence. If you wish to purchase it, you will need to make a trip to the United States and negotiate with me in person. I will not deal with representatives, lawyers, or even familiars."

He didn't splutter or feign ignorance of familiars. He merely said in a stiff voice, "It will take me some time to get there."

"I'll be here," I said, and then added, "Most likely," since I didn't know what kind of time he was talking about.

"Then I will see you soon," he said, and hung up. I promptly forgot about him and prepared a blend of Creativi-Tea, since I had some fantasy role-players coming in for their weekly dungeon crawl, and the DM always wanted a little something extra to keep him on top of his players. It was similar to Mental Acui-Tea, which was my most popular blend around midterms and finals. During those weeks, students from Arizona State would file into Third Eye Books and Herbs and buy plenty of sachets to get them through the week—their rationale being that one week of real studying would make up for a semester spent staring at the bottom of a red plastic kegger cup instead of their books. Word of my "sick tea"—where *sick* had somehow been transmogrified into a positive adjective rather than an indicator of disease—had spread throughout the Greek societies after it helped one frat member pass his finals. This testimonial, along with some others, had given my shop the nickname of "Sick Hippie's" amongst the wasted dude crowd, as in, "Bro, I need to pass or I'll be cut off from my trust fundage. Let's go get some tea at Sick Hippie's."

For the record: I am not a hippie. But I guess in today's world a knowledge of herbs and a counterculture vibe was enough to earn me the label.

I happily lost myself in the daily needs of the shop and thought nothing more of the Egyptian, until he walked in a week later.

When he crossed my threshold, I knew immediately, because the wards on my shop warned me that a magic user had entered my personal space. That's about all they did, though; I hadn't set up anything to shut down Egyptian magic systems—the odds of having to deal with that in Arizona were pretty slim.

He was a middle-aged man with a lengthy but well-groomed beard; it was forked and fell below his sternum. He had wrapped the "tines" of the fork in strips of leather, allowing a puff of hair to explode out the ends. An unabashed unibrow protected deep-set eyes, which flicked about nervously. His hair was hidden underneath a rounded white brimless hat halfway between a skull cap and a fez, the sort commonly seen in North Africa. His kaftan and pants were similarly white, though the kaftan was embroidered with gold thread around the neck and the buttons in the center, and also around the edges of his sleeves. It was a look, in other words, that suggested he was a devout Muslim. I suspected that was a convenient disguise for him, though, or he wouldn't be tripping my alarms as a magic user.

After a quick scan of the shop, during which he determined that I was the only employee currently working, he looked disappointed and approached me at the tea station. "Pardon me," he said in his accented English. "But I am looking for Mr. O'Sullivan."

"That's me." A twitch of the unibrow indicated his surprise. I look like I'm twenty-one and far too young to be an expert on anything, much less rare books. But he recovered quickly.

"Excellent! I am Nkosi Elkhashab. We spoke on the phone about the Coptic book full of lamb recipes."

"Ah, yes, I remember," I said. "I assume you wish to see it."

"Yes. If it is indeed the book I seek, I hope we can come to some profitable agreement." He was all smiles and charm.

"I'll be happy to show it to you," I said, "but after lunch." His face fell. "The book is not currently on-site," I lied, "but in a secure location. If you come back this afternoon, I will have it ready. Enjoy Tempe, in the meantime. Mill Avenue has many diverting places to shop and eat."

The unibrow dipped in the middle, signaling his displeasure, but it smoothed out as he realized that anger would do him no good under the circumstances.

He nodded curtly and said, "Until this afternoon, then."

I nodded back. "See you." I watched him leave and then picked up the phone to call one of my attorneys, Hal Hauk. As a lawyer, he had his hands in more than a few kinds of pies. As a werewolf, he had his paws in some additional pies made with supernatural ingredients. Some of them were shady. Seedy, even.

"Hey, Hal. It's Atticus. Need everything you can dig up on a character calling himself Nkosi Elkhashab out of Egypt. . . . As soon as possible. . . . Yep."

Hal would hire a private investigator and they'd do what they could from this end, then they'd hire someone in Cairo to find out more. In the meantime, I had my own methods of finding out the truth, and that's why I needed some time before I sat the grimoire down in front of this guy. He couldn't be simply a gourmet out to find a gastronomic miracle using ancient grains. Modern recipes for lamb have come a long way. Look at what those guys on the cooking shows can do with mint jellies and mango chutneys.

I closed up the shop a few minutes before noon and hopped on my bicycle for the short ride home to the Mitchell Park neighborhood. I waved at the widow MacDonagh as I passed; she was cradling a glass of Tullamore Dew and serenely perusing the pages of a gory British crime novel. She was a sweet lady from the old country for whom I occasionally did some yard work, and who always enjoyed harassing me.

"Ye should wear a helmet or some knee pads, ye know," she called from the porch. "It's dangerous to be that sexy 'round here, heh heh."

At home, a couple of barks came from indoors: my Irish wolfhound announced that he was guarding the place before he realized it was me. Through the special binding I'd created between us years ago, I heard his thoughts in my head: <Atticus, is that you?>

Yep. Home for a quick bite and to pick up something. Think you can handle some tuna salad for lunch? I opened the front door and he was there, tail wagging. I gave him some love behind the ears and chucked him under the chin.

<Maybe if you subtract the salad! It will make my breath smell like ambrosia to cats. Or even like catnip to cats.>

Sorry, Oberon, they're not going to get stoned on your tuna breath.

<I suppose that would skew things unfairly to the dogs if that were true, wouldn't it? Well, can we chase the tuna with a slice of turkey or something?>

Sure. I opened three cans of tuna—two for Oberon and one for me—and mixed up a quick salad with some celery, chives, chopped grapes, and mayo. I slapped this mixture between fresh bread with some romaine lettuce and called it lunch. I took it with me into the garage, where I had a large iron trunk bound shut in several ways. Only one of them was a traditional, mundane padlock. It took me about ten minutes to unbind everything, but once the lid was free to lift up on its hinges, I extracted a scabbard with a very special sword inside.

It was Fragarach—absolutely no relation to *Fraggle Rock*—an ancient Fae sword that I had come by about as honestly as I'd come by the *Grimoire of the Lamb*. Since there were a couple of Irish gods who'd dearly like to have it back, I tended to shield it in iron from divination and not play with it too much. For this occasion, it was worth the risk of revealing my hiding place. Fragarach's name in Irish means the *Answerer*, due to an enchantment on it that forces targeted dastardly types to answer questions truthfully. It would help me solve a mystery that had perplexed me for centuries.

I had the grimoire waiting on the counter for Mr. Elkhashab when he returned to the store. While the light of avarice blazed in his eyes as he flipped greedily through the pages "for appraisal," I brought out Fragrach from under the counter and spoke the words that would ensnare him.

"*Freagroidh tu,*" I said, and the Egyptian wizard was abruptly caught in a hazy blue aura that would not let him move or speak untruths in answer to my questions.

"What is your name?" I asked.

"Nkosi Elkhashab." So he hadn't been lying about that.

"What is your quest?"

"To find the lost book of Amun."

I would ask him more about that in a moment, but I couldn't resist completing the Monty Python line first: "*What . . . is your favorite color?*"

"Red."

Excellent. Back to serious interrogation. "Why do you wish to find this lost book?"

"The thirteen spells will restore Egypt to its rightful place as supreme among the world."

So it wasn't an ordinary cookbook after all. "You told me they were lamb recipes before. What are they really?"

"They are recipes to alter fate. Six recipes alter your destiny in different ways; seven alter the destinies of your enemies."

"Let me guess. The thirteenth recipe slays your enemy."

"Correct."

Well, I no longer had to wonder why this book was in the restricted section. "Why do all the recipes involve lamb?"

"None of them involve lamb."

That slowed me down. "Lamb is listed as the first ingredient in every recipe."

"No. The lamb is supposed to be sacrificed to Amun before you begin the recipe."

Gods below! Blood sacrifice to kill your enemies or make yourself rich or whatever definitely classified the grimoire as a book from the dark side. And this guy couldn't wait to get his hands on it.

"Where did you hear about this book?" I asked him.

"I used to work in the Ministry of Antiquities. We discovered some records at the Alexandria site some years ago, and I came across a reference to the work there. It made clear that the book had been removed before Aurelian. Its existence was confirmed in other work I recently discovered."

"How did you find out about the sacrificing of the lambs and everything?"

"It is described in the writings of Nebwenenef, Egypt's greatest sorcerer. He is the author of this grimoire."

I blinked, then swallowed. In the origin story of Druids that every archdruid taught his apprentices, Nebwenenef was the name of the sorcerer who'd killed the Saharan elemental five thousand years ago. But the grimoire was a first- or second-century work. How did he write it if he'd already been dead for three thousand years? "Where did you find these writings?"

"Underneath my home."

"It was buried?"

"Yes."

"Who else has seen these writings?"

"No one."

That was a small blessing, at least. "Do you know who I am?" I asked. This was a rather important question and not intended as a threat to him in any way. If he knew too much, I'd have to leave the area.

"You are Atticus O'Sullivan, rare-book dealer."

"That's all you know about me?"

"You clearly have some magical talent. I am not sure how much or of what kind."

Maybe not all was lost, then.

"How did you discover I might have a copy of this book?"

"I summoned an imp of the Fourth Circle of Hell. He told me."

Well, that would do it. And it also meant I was probably still safe here; the imp would have already traveled back to hell without telling anybody else where or who I was, or this guy wouldn't be standing in front of me now. "So you dabble in all sorts of black magic, not simply the Egyptian sort?"

"Yes."

"And the imp told you what about me, exactly?"

"He said you possessed the lost book of Amun and thought it was a cookbook. He said your magic was probably earth-based."

Clever imp, leaving out the fact that I was a Druid. "What else did the imp say?"

"He said you have excellent defenses but cast few offensive spells, if any."

That was true enough. When I wished to give offense, I usually gave it with the blade of Fragarach.

"Hypothetical question. If we were in a galaxy far, far away, would you try to become a Sith lord?"

"I do not know what that is."

"Sith lords can shoot lightning out of their hands, and they cackle maniacally as their enemies turn crispy before their eyes."

Elkhashab smiled. "That sounds very good. Yes."

I'd heard more than enough. I neatly snatched the grimoire from his fingers and placed a protective hand over it, then dispelled Fragarach's binding and lowered it.

"I'm very sorry for the inconvenience, Mr. Elkhashab, but this grimoire is not for sale."

His eyes blinked rapidly. "Not for sale? But you told me to come here to negotiate."

"Negotiation does not guarantee that you will be able to purchase the goods."

I began to pull the grimoire closer to me, and that's when everything went pear-shaped. Without a single telltale warning in his facial expression, Elkhashab's left arm snaked forward and he *punched* me. Not hard enough to break my nose or anything—it was more of a jab than a determined attempt to destroy my face—but it was enough to make me rock backward and take my hand off the grimoire. That was all he wanted. He grabbed the book and bolted for the door, figuring that if he couldn't buy it, he'd simply steal it.

He plainly did not know much about my magic. Before he was out the door, I began to construct a binding between the leather of the cover and the wool carpet I kept as a doormat. Since both were of natural materials, once I energized the binding the book would fly out of his hands and I'd be laughing at him.

It didn't work out that way.

I energized the binding and the book tried to escape, but he held on with one hand and made a gesture with the other like flicking water from his fingers, and the binding *broke*.

I was so shocked that he was halfway across Ash Avenue before I could think to try again. But now he had the grimoire held close to his chest, and my line of sight was ruined. I watched him scramble into a rental car across the street and thought a different binding would serve me well. Though pure synthetics shut me down, nature is present in even some of our most refined products: I bound the rubber of his tires to the bitumen in the asphalt concrete as I strode forward to reclaim my property. South of University Drive, Ash Avenue doesn't have a lot of traffic, so I didn't need to worry much about getting plowed into the pavement.

He started the car and shoved it into gear. When it didn't move, he rolled down the window and looked at the front tire. I activated my faerie specs—a charm that allows me to see in the magical spectrum—to see what he would do. I wanted to know how he destroyed my bindings.

His aura was strange. Next to his skin, he was limned in white, like any magic user, but beyond that it was muddy, as if somebody's kid had decided to mix all the finger paints together to see what magical hue would result. Tiny flashes and hints of color winked here and there, but mostly it was monkey-shit brown.

Elkhashab flicked his fingers at the front tire with the same motion he'd used before, and I saw what appeared to be a spout of water gush forth and blanket my bindings. It was odd, undisciplined magic; bindings have definite structure and appear as Celtic knotwork, and even the magic of other systems, like Wicca or Vodoun, have an orderly look to them as they execute, a latticework that may not look like knotwork but clearly represent an architecture of thought and purpose. His magic looked like a particularly splody ejaculation.

He tried to accelerate, but the back tire held him fast. The bindings on the front tire had already melted—or perhaps dissolved—away. He flicked his fingers toward the rear, the bizarre miniature flood gushed forth in my magical sight, and my binding ceased to exist.

Elkhashab stomped on the gas and squealed away with the *Grimoire of the Lamb*. I let him go because I was fighting ignorance as much as the man himself. His magic was a little frightening. The tattoos that bound me to the earth and allowed me to draw on its power were bindings as well. Could he toss some of his magic spooge at me and unbind me from the earth? I needed to find out, but not by trial and error. The error could well be fatal. Instead, I'd see what Hal had turned up and shift myself to Egypt before Elkhashab could fly out there. When he got home, eager to sacrifice a lamb and start some evil shit, he'd find me waiting for him.

He'd also be extremely paranoid. If I were Elkhashab, there would be no way I'd ever believe that someone like me would simply let him go. And he'd be right.

I called Hal on my cell phone. "Hal, have you got anything on that Egyptian character yet?"

"You haven't even given me two hours, Atticus," Hal growled.

"He just stole one of my rare books. One of the really evil ones."

"Not one of those summoning ones where you can call up something to eat Utah for breakfast?"

"No, it's the kind where you can kill anyone you want. Ideal for political assassinations."

"Shit. He swiped it from under your nose?"

"He's a serious magic user. He's got something that can dissolve my bindings. I need to go after him in Egypt, and I need some help tracking him down."

"You want me to contact a pack there?"

"Is there a pack in Cairo?"

"Sure is. Guy named Yusuf is the leader."

"That would be wonderful. I only need their tracking services. You know I'm good for whatever they charge. And please email to me whatever info you dig up and I'll check it when I get to Egypt."

"What are you going to do when you find him?"

"He wasted his chance at mercy when he stole the book. And he told me what he's going to do with it." He'd also told me who had written it, and that made the grimoire itself something I should have burned long ago. "So I think I'll be applying Druidic law."

"Going to kill him, eh?"

"Old school."

About five thousand years ago, the Sahara Desert was a lot more lush than it is today. It was still a desert, but more like the Sonoran Desert—plenty of plants and animals around, instead of miles of sand dunes and a few weak clumps of sharply bladed grass. It wasn't all that bad a place, until the sorcerer Nebwenenef bound the Saharan elemental and tried to take its power for his own. He died trying to contain it, and the elemental died as well, its magic spreading up the

Nile river valley, lying around for other wizards and Egyptian gods to feast on. The desert became an überdesert, and Gaia decided that sort of thing should never happen again. That's why she created Druids.

The primary responsibility of Druids is to protect the earth's elementals from any sort of magical attack. Mundane attacks—like stopping industries from polluting the environment—are not really our business, but people tend to think that's the sort of thing Druids would be worried about. I do worry about it, of course, but those attacks happen on such a vast scale, with every smokestack and exhaust pipe, that there's very little I can do—and those sorts of threats to the earth didn't exist when Druids were first conceived.

Guys like Elkhashab, who desire power over men, sometimes try to harness the power of the earth to do it, however, and in those rare cases there's quite a lot I can do. Elkhashab's counter to my bindings indicated that he had a trump card for the earth's magic, and as such I was quite literally bound to destroy him. Plus, you know, anyone following in the footsteps of Nebwenenef demanded all my attention. And less important in the grand scheme of things, but which I tended to remember: he'd also punched me.

I wouldn't underestimate him again; this might go quickly, or it might not. If the latter were to be the case, I needed to make arrangements.

The current girlfriend was first: Since I couldn't tell her that she was dating a man who was thirty times as old as her grandfather and who sometimes had to deal with shady warlocks, a text message that I had a family emergency and I'd be gone for a week would have to suffice. We traded texts for a bit; she offered condolences, wondered if she could help, hoped it would work out for the best, and that was that.

Oberon was a little harder to convince.

<I want to go with you! I'm supposed to protect you and wag my tail in an encouraging manner when you are afflicted with self-doubt!> he said.

It's going to be extremely dangerous, Oberon.

<All the more reason I should go! My teeth are sharper than yours, and once I take something down to the ground, it doesn't get up.>

How many cats do you think you could handle at once, Oberon?

<What does that have to do with the price of beef in Boise?>

There's a cat goddess there named Bast. She doesn't like me at all and has forbidden me to return to Egypt.

<So? You've been to Egypt anyway, haven't you?>

Yes, but only in the deserts, where there were no cats. This time I'll be going to Cairo, where there will be plenty of them.

<Well, can't you do something to make her purr?>

I don't think so. A lightbulb turned on in my skull. *Well, now that you mention it, maybe.*

<Then it's settled! You'll do that thing and I'm coming along.>

I could probably use someone to watch my back.

<I'm useful like that!>

The store was much easier to take care of. I didn't have any employees yet who could run things in my absence, so I simply closed up the shop with a sign outside promising to return in a few days. Before I did so, I removed *Nice Kitty!* from the rare-book case. Perhaps a peace offering would make searching for Elkhashab a bit easier.

According to my driver's license, I had recently turned twenty-seven, two whole years past the point American rental car companies considered me responsible enough to rent one of their vehicles. Age restrictions of all kinds tend to amuse me. I secured a compact car and squeezed Oberon into the backseat with a giant rawhide bone to keep him busy. I took Highway 87—the Beeline, the locals called it—north to Payson, and then 260 east toward Christopher Creek, up on the forested Mogollon Rim. There I could park the car in a campground and shift planes, using a tether I had created to Tír na nÓg.

Once I chose a spot at the Tonto–Horton Creek campground, Oberon bounded out of the car and barked at the surrounding ponderosa pines.

<Count yourselves lucky, squirrels! I know you're out there! If I

didn't have pressing business on the other side of the world right now, you'd never see the sun set!>

They can't understand you, Oberon.

<Oh, I think they understand well enough from my barking.>

They are indeed lucky. Let's go.

I had Fragarach slung across my back in a scabbard and Bast's pre-historic porn instructions in a leather satchel; I had wrapped and bound the book three times in oilskin to protect it. There were also two daggers in the satchel, because I thought there was a chance of some quick and close fighting. I put one hand on Oberon and another on a tethered tree; Oberon put a paw on the tree as well, and then I pulled us along the tether to a similar tree in Tír na nÓg, far from the Fae Court and those who would like to find me. Not wishing to linger and risk the chance of being spotted, I redirected my focus and searched for a suitable place to shift into Egypt. I had created tethers there long ago in case I ever needed to visit on just such duty as this, and though I tried to maintain them along with the occasional help of Fae rangers under the direction of Brighid, First among the Fae, many were missing now, no doubt destroyed by an ever-expanding city. The best I could do was a date ranch north of Cairo. I'd made the gamble that the trees on the ranch would stick around awhile, and it had paid off.

Cairo was nine hours ahead of Arizona time, so we arrived there at three in the morning. It was harvesting season for the dates, but it would be hours before the workers came along to discover us. I cast night vision on us both and we stole out of the grove undetected.

<It's fun to sneak around. It's like we're ghosts! Or shadows!>

And you look marvelous.

<We are handsome phantoms, aren't we?> Oberon said.

Yeah! You know, that would be a great band name.

<And we're on a world tour! Where are we now?>

North of Cairo. We need to find an Internet café so I can see what Hal has dug up on this guy. I didn't have a cellphone since I disliked the idea of carrying around a tracking device. It's also difficult to ex-plain how a phone could ping on a tower in Arizona one minute and in Cairo the next. *Keep an eye out for cats, but, whatever you do, don't bark at them.*

<Can I growl?>

No. We don't want to draw attention to ourselves. Just give me a heads-up if you see them coming.

We managed to hitch a ride into town in the back of a flatbed truck, but the early hour frustrated me. Until people woke up and cafés opened, there was little I could do. Still, we were hours ahead of Nkosi Elkhashab, who might still be waiting to board a plane back in the United States. Even if he was already airborne on a charter flight, we still had hours before he could possibly touch down.

We hadn't specified to the truck driver where we'd like to be dropped off, and in hindsight that was a huge mistake. He stopped near an open-air market, saying he had to pick up a load of bread from a local bakery and drive it back north, and we thanked him for his courtesy.

That's when a quizzical meow ruined everything.

<Cat alert!>

Thanks, I heard. I saw too. It was a gray tomcat with white socks, peering out from the darkness of an alley.

I asked the driver before he ducked into the bakery which way to the Nile. He pointed east and said, "A few kilometers that way."

Let's go, Oberon. Stay by my side. Do not attack or even give a dirty look to a cat here. I ran south toward a major street that ran east–west. Oberon easily kept pace with me.

<Are we really running from a cat?>

He and every other cat in the city, yes.

<What if they attack?>

Then you may kill if you have to.

<Seriously?>

Seriously. But once they begin attacking, they won't stop. We want to avoid that as long as we can. There are thousands of cats in Cairo and only two of us.

<Oh. How much is a thousand again?>

Oberon was great about picking up new words from me and improving his speech all the time, but he had difficulty holding on to concepts of time, and any number larger than twenty was simply "a lot" to him.

It's more than you've ever seen in one place before.

<Well, there was that one time you showed me what a pet store was like. There were a lot of cats in there.>

Right. So think of how many cats would be in twenty pet stores.

<Whoa. That's a huge mess of cats.>

But now double or even triple that, and you've got a thousand.

<No way! That's not fair!>

Exactly. That's why you don't want this fight to get started. It won't be fair.

We turned left and headed east toward the Nile. For the first half kilometer or so, we were in the clear—at least as far as cats were concerned. In the crepuscular light of an approaching dawn, I could see that the air wasn't very clear. There was plenty of smog and a thin cloud of dust blown in from the desert, and I smelled more rotting garbage than I would have liked. Since the muezzin hadn't sounded yet for morning prayers, traffic was still extremely light—and that was a blessing, because there didn't seem to be any discernible laws that drivers followed. I was nursing a faint spark of hope that we might have gone unobserved when Oberon jinxed it by remarking that we appeared to be running away from nothing.

<Maybe you're overreacting, Atticus. It was only one meow from one cat, after all. If those toy terriers at the dog park ever find out that I did this, I'll never hear the end of it. They're terrible bullies, you know. You wouldn't think it, but they get all up in my nose because they know their humans will protect them.>

Before I could reply, a low, querulous "Rrrrrow!" chased our heels, and a black cat darted out from an alley to pursue us.

I slowed temporarily to kick off my sandals and then sped back up, chest heaving now. I had a limited supply of magic left in my bear charm and no guarantee of running across a place where I could recharge; this stretch of Cairo was well paved, so I was cut off from the earth. The riverbed of the Nile was my best shot, but I wanted to be ready in case an opportunity presented itself and to conserve my magic while I could.

<Okay, now I feel really stupid. Before I was just running with my human in the dark, but now I'm running away from a mangy alley cat. In public. You think maybe someone is following this on a military satellite camera? The night-vision ones where everybody's green? What are the odds that this could go worldwide on YouTube?>

There's more at stake here than your canine reputation, Oberon. This is just the beginning. You notice the cat hasn't closed the distance? It's not trying to catch us yet.

Oberon checked his six and fell back a few paces in the process but quickly resumed his place at my side. <All right, I'll admit that *is* weird. You're pretty fast for a human, but catching you should be easy. What's it waiting for?>

Friends.

We were passing through a residential area now, with apartment buildings on either side and cats coming out of the windows and emerging from the alleys. Flashes of white and gray and orange in my peripheral vision told me cats were flooding out of their homes along this street and coming from blocks away to join in the hunt. Those that emerged ahead of us didn't get in our way but rather waited for us to pass and then joined the growing herd of felines that followed us at a distance of six meters or so. Bast was behaving exactly as I predicted: She'd take me down with overwhelming numbers, sacrificing as many of her people as needed to finish me off.

Our procession started to cause trouble at intersections—at least, in those where there was any traffic to speak of. Oberon and I weren't slowing down for anything, and the cats weren't slowing down either. If there was too much cross traffic to risk stepping into the street, I turned south and ran until there was an opening, then darted across with Oberon and took the next left to continue east toward the river.

One of these zigzag moves resulted in a few of our pursuers getting run over. There was lots of yelling and leaning on car horns, not to mention plenty of blood and fur, but the cats were unfazed. The survivors kept coming after us, swarming around and between the cars, never varying their pace, and more joined them all the time.

<Well, there are enough of them behind us now that running makes sense, so that's good.>

They all want to kill us, Oberon! How is that good?

<I'm trying to accentuate the positive here.>

A breath of damp, dirty air invaded my lungs, and I smiled in relief; the moisture indicated we were approaching the Nile, though it was still an uncomfortable distance away.

It was creepy being chased by that many cats. Their feet made no noise, but I knew they were there, because a good number of the house cats had little bells around their necks, and those become damn menacing when there are more than two on your heels.

I smirked and shouted at the city of Cairo, "'Never send to know for whom the bell tolls; it tolls for thee.'"

<Hey, isn't that Metallica?>

Very close! John Donne. People get them confused all the time. We're drawing near, Oberon. I can smell the river. How's your breath holding up? Can you sprint with me?

<I thought you were already sprinting.>

I'm going to use some magic to increase my speed, see if we can leave the kitties behind. I can use it on you too if you need it.

<Give me just a little to see, and if it's too easy, then I'll tell you to keep it. I'm not going full speed yet.>

I withdrew the daggers from my satchel as I ran, and once I had them gripped in either hand, I spoke the binding that would let me use the stored magic of the earth as my own energy, allowing me to run even faster without tiring—as long as the juice held out. I hoped it would last until the river. I created a similar binding for Oberon.

A startled collective yowl rose up from the herd of cats behind us as Oberon and I suddenly pulled away. They spent some time trying to catch up, and when they discovered they couldn't, the character of the pursuit changed. The cats that were converging on us from the sides and ahead of us—those that were actually coming from the river—didn't let us pass anymore. Or, rather, they didn't let *me* pass. Oberon wasn't the target. That didn't stop him from snapping at the odd cat that veered within range of his jaws.

For my part, I only needed to keep them off my face and neck. There isn't much else a single cat can do to bring down a human quickly, and they knew it. The knives scythed the space in front of me when they jumped, feline screams rent the early-morning air as they fell to the sides, and I kept running. I tried not to do any permanent damage; I was making quick slashes, never stabbing, and hoping that Bast would feel properly guilty about this later and help those that were injured.

Deflect and maintain speed, I told Oberon as he fell behind to shake 'n' snap a cat's neck. *Killing isn't necessary, and it takes too long. We don't want the horde behind us to catch up.*

<Great big bears, Atticus, I think you're right! I just got a good look, and I don't think that many cats should be allowed!>

How many are back there?

Oberon whined. <Atticus, I don't know! My brain hurts. I think my mind has officially been boggled.>

A tabby latched on to my left shoulder, and I spun around to launch him off me. He left deep gouges in my skin as the centrifugal force threw him into a wall, but those would heal. I couldn't slow down. The spin gave me a brief glance of our pursuit, and I could see what had boggled Oberon's mind. There were far more cats back there than anyone could handle. I fought the nascent scream of panic growing in my belly.

We still had a quarter of a kilometer to go, and the cats weren't thinning out. If anything, they were getting worse. I ducked a Siamese that screeched in dismay as it sailed over my head, then struck out with my right to knock down a portly Persian as I rolled my left shoulder back to let a Peterbald ping off my arm with nary a single claw's scratch. The cats that tried to attack my legs were either kicked away or tossed aside as I churned ahead; my momentum was too great to be stopped by a ten-pound cat.

There were more ahead of me, bounding in my direction. Perhaps more than I could plow through. Oberon was providing some protection on my right side, and I was glad he'd talked me into bringing him along. I might have already gone down if it weren't for him.

"Bast!" I shouted in Coptic. I didn't know how to speak the truly ancient Egyptian language, but I felt reasonably sure she would understand the form of it commonly spoken until the seventeenth century. "I know you can hear me!" She'd identified my presence on the basis of one cat's pair of eyes, so she'd have to be deaf if she couldn't hear me through the ears of however many hundreds she had following me now.

"We don't have to do this! No more of your people have to get hurt! I can return what was stolen! Let's stop and talk!"

The cats didn't stop coming, and I didn't stop running or cutting them down as necessary. Oberon didn't stop batting them away or snatching them out of the air and tossing them aside. That was all okay. The overture of diplomacy had been made. Bast was far too proud to answer right away.

It was a mess of gore and screams for a while, my knives flashing in the wan light of a gray cloudless dawn. Lights began to flick on in the buildings we passed, slumbering citizens awakened by cries of rage and death and offering up Arabic WTFs in the still, dry air of their apartments. And then the Nile beckoned, black waters lying still without sufficient sun to light the ripples of the current, the stench of oil and untold shit rising from its surface instead of the fresh breath of life it used to be in ancient days.

The juice ran out fifty meters from the riverbank and I slowed, lungs heaving and informing me in no uncertain terms that they hated me to dickfinity.

<Hey! Where did all the love go?> Oberon asked.

Keep going! We have to make it to the river!

<I feel like I have all the turbo capacity of a dachshund right now.>

We can't stop or we're dead.

We had built up something of a lead on the horde, but they were closing fast and yowling victoriously now that they could see we had slowed. There were no more cats in front of us. They had all engaged us earlier, and now they were either pursuing us from behind or licking their wounds.

The tiny little bells grew louder. They were almost upon us and my body wanted nothing so much as a sensible jog, but I kept pushing. Thirty meters. Twenty.

There was a railing ahead that marked a ramp down to some private docks, where a few small pleasure craft were anchored. The docks were fairly long, so there were some shallows, which was good for me. The cats would be on me before I could get there, however, and that was bad.

The bells from hell were right behind me now. I switched the dagger in my left hand to my right, awkwardly holding on to both in one hand, and then slapped my left hand onto the back of my neck and held it there. I wasn't swatting mosquitoes; I was trying to stay alive. Not two seconds after I did so, the cats began to jump onto my back and claw at my legs. The scabbard of Fragarach, strapped across my back, gave them some extra purchase on my torso. They made angry kitty noises and tore through my shirt, trailing blood underneath their claws, but they couldn't sit on my shoulders and bite through to my spine with my hand protecting the back of my neck. They tried to chew through anyway, biting and scratching everything they could, while I twisted and stumbled forward in an effort to make the water. Oberon briefly interposed himself and gave me a wee bit of space to turn the corner on the ramp. I dove and rolled, being careful with the knives, but not being careful at all about delivering some punishment to the cats hanging on me. They fell off under the impact, breath knocked out of them. Oberon's bulk as a rear guard prevented any more from jumping on me while I was down, and I got up, a bloody, exhausted mess, and staggered toward the docks.

Come on, buddy, I said, a dagger in each hand again. *Into the river we go.*

<Right behind you.>

I couldn't get a full breath. I was too slow. Three more cats jumped on my back and more ran under my feet as I tumbled into the Nile. The water stung and cooled my cuts at the same time. The cats clung tightly and tore more of my flesh away—entering the water hadn't deterred them at all. More were jumping in; I heard and felt the splashes. I didn't know where Oberon was.

And then my foot touched the silt of the riverbed, the tattoo on the sole automatically renewing my connection to the earth. The energy of the Nile welcomed me, and I welcomed it as it rushed to replenish my spent energy and provide even more for healing or whatever else I needed.

I exploded to the surface, and the turbulence of it—combined no doubt with the current—tore away the few cats that had followed me in. Where I was standing, the water was just beneath my rib cage. Oberon paddled nearby. Cats were leaping into the river after me, falling short, and then discovering that they couldn't swim for shit— that is, they may have been able to keep their heads above water, but they weren't going to give me much of a fight. I was protected by the hull of a boat on my left, but there was a dock to my right. A few of the smarter cats scampered down it and leapt at me from there, but now that I could face them and not have to worry about overwhelming numbers from every direction, I could bat them away into the Nile and let them deal with the problem of swimming.

Go back a bit to where you can stand with your head out of the water, I said to Oberon. *As cats go by, dunk 'em.*

<I can stand as it is,> Oberon said, and proved it. His head and neck were safely above the water. <What about your back?>

Don't worry, I've got this now. The few that were trying to swim my way were having a tough time fighting against the current. Those that made it to me couldn't leap or get any leverage whatsoever, and a brief scratch or bonk on the head sent them floating downriver. The ones jumping off the dock at my face were slapped out of the air, and once they hit the water they didn't trouble me again.

Cats filled the dock and the shore, and the noise was getting ridiculous. Despite the hour, people would soon come to investigate and take pictures with their cell phones. I didn't want that.

"Bast!" I called over the din, speaking in Coptic. "I can return the book of your mysteries! I can give it back to you right now! It's in excellent condition! We don't need to do this! Please don't make me harm any more of your people! Let's talk!"

The cats all stopped moving at once, save for the ones already in the river. They simply sat wherever they were and stared at me. There wasn't a noise except for a few splashes and the sound of Oberon panting.

Oberon, don't do anything more. Let the cats go for now.

<Okay.>

A low female voice rose from the docks. I didn't see any cat move its mouth, but it came from one of them.

"Hrrr. Show me the book."

My leather satchel was under the surface of the river, and I pulled it out now, putting the daggers inside.

"The book has been in the water?" the voice cried. "It's useless!"

"No, no!" I said. "It's protected. It's in a waterproof wrapper. I will show you." Pulling out the oilskin parcel with *Nice Kitty!* inside, I unbound the oilskin and stuffed it back into my satchel. I held Bast's book of mysteries carefully by my fingertips, trying to demonstrate my great respect for it. I still didn't know which cat was Bast—or if she was simply speaking through one of them—so I spoke to the cats on the dock in general.

"Unlike so many other old treasures, this book has resisted the ravages of time," I said. "I have kept it sealed away from the air. Every word is still readable. Think of it, Bast! Given to the right people, this book could revive interest in you like nothing else! You would receive prayers again, grow powerful. Your influence could spread beyond Egypt, and you could enjoy the worship of millions!" This was unlikely and wishful thinking, but I knew it was thinking she would very much want to believe. As if to emphasize my point, the muezzin began to buzz throughout Cairo, calling all Muslims to prayer. Bast knew what that meant: Another god was getting the worship that used to be hers. I kept selling.

"These other gods have their holy books translated into every tongue, and now humans bow to them around the world. You could do the same with this. How many of the other Egyptian gods could manage this? None. In truth, Bast, I have done you a great service by preserving it so well."

"Hrrr. Give it to me."

"I beg your pardon?"

From the back rank of the cats, a slight shift of shadowy movement attracted my eye. It grew taller; it was a shorthaired black cat with yellow eyes and a small gold hoop earring high up on its left ear. It continued to grow and change until I was looking at a woman with a cat's head. The woman had clothes on where the cat didn't, and I thought that sort of trick could revolutionize fashion. She had one of those giant golden necklaces draped over her shoulders, like one sees in the art of the pyramids, but she didn't have a headdress. From underneath the gold necklace fell a white linen dress, belted below her breasts with a rich blue sash. Her arms, while bare of clothing, were covered in soft black fur and the occasional golden circlet; she had human fingers but very feline claws instead of fingernails on the ends of them. The muezzin finally stopped blaring and we could speak without shouting.

"Hrrr. You will give it to me now, human."

"Call me Atticus. I'd like something in return."

Bast's eyes widened at my presumption. "Ridiculous! You stole it! Return it now and take your punishment!"

"No, that's not how we're doing this. Remember, I'm doing you a favor by returning it. You thought I was dead and your book lost forever until I showed up today."

The yellow eyes now narrowed to mere slits. "You are not a normal human."

I dipped my head in thanks. "It's kind of you to say so."

"Why are you in Egypt?"

"In one of life's great ironies, someone has stolen a book from me. I have come to steal it back." And prevent him from harming the earth, I didn't say.

Bast's cat face lost its suspicion and seemed amused. "Hrr! Hrr! Hrr! Was it an Egyptian book stolen by an Egyptian?"

"Yes."

"Then there is no crime. It is justice! Do you know who stole it?"

"A man named Nkosi Elkhashab."

Bast blinked. "You mean the crocodile priest?"

Crocodile priest? That would make him a follower of Sobek, the god of the Nile. Suddenly the nature of his magic was clear. Water softened and carved away the earth on a regular basis. No wonder my bindings had dissolved. No wonder his aura was muddy brown.

"Yes, that's the guy. Do you know where he is?"

"Is this information what you wish in return for my book?" Bast said.

"No." I shook my head. "I want your permission to travel Egypt freely and your word not to reveal my presence here in any way to any other being."

"Hrrr." This time when Bast smiled, it looked predatory. "That is acceptable to me. I walk away with my book, and you walk away to be destroyed by Sobek's chosen." She held out a gray hand, palm up, to receive the book.

"Let me hear you swear it first, please," I said.

Bast hissed a little with impatience. "In return for the book in your hand, you may freely wander Egypt and not be bothered by any of my people. I will not reveal your presence here to anyone—"

I raised an eyebrow and cocked my head to signal she'd messed up. She knew it.

"—Very well, or to any god or animal. Now, give."

Happily, I waded forward and gave her *Nice Kitty!* Bast would hand it to some human scholar with woeful personal security and I would steal it back and destroy all records they made. The world really didn't need a reborn cat sex cult.

Bast flipped briefly through the book to make sure it didn't contain cartoons or something. She purred in pleasure for a moment and then remembered I was watching.

She hissed in earnest this time, then said, "May Sobek devour you."

"Oh, that's nice. Well, may harmony find you, Bast, and I am sorry for any pain I've caused your people."

She ignored me and walked away in the manner for which cats are renowned. She and the book faded into the gray light of dawn, and the horde of cats began to disperse in her wake.

<Yeah!> Oberon said as Bast faded from view. <One hound versus thousands of cats, and the hound wins!>

What about the Druid?

<Quiet, Atticus. I'm having a moment here. Basking in my own glory.>

When you're finished, let's go find a place that will let us drip dry on their floor.

My shirt was shredded and my cuts hadn't fully closed up yet. I refilled my bear charm with all the magic it could hold and then activated my healing. The ugliness would fade over time. My priority now had to be getting some local cash, a set of dry clothes, a temporary cell phone, and then some food and an Internet connection.

People began to appear on the streets after morning prayers, and I asked them for directions to the nearest bazaar. A few blocks' walk to the north, the flash of a credit card, and some spirited haggling provided me with almost everything I needed. I got directions from there to an Internet café—such places were more ubiquitous then, in the years before the iPhone.

Once I got Oberon settled with some sausage and carefully camouflaged under my table, I logged in to my email and found a nice dossier on Nkosi Elkhashab waiting for me from Hal's private investigators.

Hal had highlighted something for me: Elkhashab had been dirt poor until he'd joined the Ministry of Antiquities after college. He showed no signs of abnormal behavior until about a year into the job, when he suddenly began to buy real estate far above his income bracket and then lots of expensive goodies with which to line the walls. There was no indication he had another job, so the question on everyone's mind—Egypt's as well, for he'd been investigated—was, where did he get the money?

Elkhashab's story was that he had been selling his "art" to wealthy collectors abroad. His art consisted of some uninspired splatter paintings—the efforts of a person who looked at Jackson Pollock's work and said to himself, "I could do that." But the Ministry of Antiquities suspected, and I had no doubt they were correct, that the purchase price included rare Egyptian treasures, and Elkhashab was smuggling those abroad via different channels to his wealthy "art collectors." He was titling his pictures along the lines of "Small Bust of Sobek, Twelfth Dynasty," so that the ministry would know precisely what he was slipping past their guard. They never caught him, but they did fire him on general principles.

Twenty years later—he was now in his mid-forties—he still made a living via his art. Some of it was probably legitimate; he was commanding such high prices for his work that rich people thought there must be some value to it—if nothing else, it served as a convenient vehicle to launder their illicit money when they sold it to their friends. But the ministry felt that the smuggling continued. They theorized that he had found a tomb somewhere in the region of Al Fayyum, near what the Greeks called Crocodilopolis, and he was selling off its treasures piece by piece. He was under electronic surveillance around the clock.

Most disturbing to me was the fact that Elkhashab had two residences, not one. There was one in Cairo and another in Al Fayyum, about eighty miles southwest. I could hardly lie in wait at both places, so I'd have to call that number at the bottom of Hal's email and take an educated guess that the dirty deeds would most likely be done in Al Fayyum.

"Greetings from an old wolf in America," I said in response to a gruff greeting.

"Who's this?"

"A friend of Hal Hauk's in Arizona."

The tone of Cairo's alpha changed abruptly. "Oh, sure, I know Hal," Yusuf said.

"He told me you and your boys may be able to help me out."

"Help with what?"

"Watch an address in Cairo for me for twenty-four hours and report all comings and goings."

"You don't need my boys for that kind of work."

"The resident is a sorcerer and may try to slip by unseen."

"I stand corrected. You absolutely need us."

The incredible usefulness of werewolves—and also the reason why you don't want to get on their bad side—is that they're immune to almost all magic. Think you're invisible? Nope, not to a werewolf's eyes. Think you have an impenetrable magic ward protecting all your goodies? You don't if a werewolf walks across it. Like the honey badger, the werewolf takes what it wants. Sure, you can pick a fight with a werewolf if you have some silver, but you'd better have enough for the whole pack. And if other packs get word that you go around killing werewolves . . . well. Let's just say that nobody tries to mess with werewolves anymore.

I made arrangements with Yusuf and gave him my number in case Elkhashab showed up. He'd send the bill to Hal and everyone would be happy.

In America—before the widespread use of GPS devices—if you wished to go somewhere you'd never been before, you hired a taxi. If you were brave, you asked your father-in-law. In Egypt, you waved some money around in the bazaar, and plenty of people would happily volunteer to take you where you wished to go. We got picked up by a family of three, who were delighted to spend some time driving us around, especially since I paid for all their gas and then some.

I am not ashamed to say that, spread out in the back of an old pickup, Oberon and I napped on the way down.

Al Fayyum—spelled many different ways and sporting many different names through the centuries—is most likely the oldest city in Egypt. Herodotus described a labyrinth of surpassing magnificence there, better even than all the other wonders of Egypt, and evidence of his tale remains, but it's a bloody wreck because some ancient Roman choad ordered the place quarried. Still, despite this defilement and many others, Al Fayyum has yielded its fair share of archaeological finds. The Ministry of Antiquities had good reason to suspect Elkhashab of finding something in the area: Chances were if you dug deep enough, you'd find something no matter what.

There's an inland salt lake there called Lake Moeris, or Birket Qarūn, and it was on the eastern edge of this lake that the old cult of Sobek flourished. In Crocodilopolis, they used to keep a real crocodile swathed in bling and fed on a diet of soft pink fleshy things. It was the lap of reptilian luxury back in the day. The new lap was on Elkhashab's property, if Bast's word could be believed. More of an estate than a house, ringed by a wall made of river mud and gated, it was east of the old site of Crocodilopolis and north of the ancient labyrinths.

Al Fayyum was not nearly so paved as Cairo, so I had little trouble accessing my magic there. Oberon and I took a leisurely stroll around Elkhashab's estate, making no effort to conceal ourselves. I was looking at the walls in the magical spectrum to see what kind of wards Elkhashab had put around it. Bizarrely, he didn't have any, except on his gate. That told me he had to have something frightful waiting on the other side of the walls that couldn't be seen from the gate.

I did a pogo leap up to take a peek at the top of the wall. No wards there either. So I leapt up again, slapped my hands on the top, and pulled myself up for a good look, not caring who saw me do it.

He had something frightful waiting behind the walls, all right. It was a damn *moat*. A deep and wide one. And it was filled with hungry crocodiles. I had to admit that was pretty badass.

A few of the creatures spotted me and shifted, hoping to get a nice bite if I cooperated and leapt down to provide them breakfast. I toyed with the idea of calming their tiny reptilian brains and swimming right by, but it was too great a risk. There could be a big monster hiding under the black water that I wouldn't catch, and then he'd certainly catch me.

Elkhashab had laid out his estate like a lion or tiger exhibit at a zoo. Inside the walls, the earth rose sort of like the mound of a volcano, so that the inside of the wall was much taller than the outside and impossible to jump over. By filling that with water and reptiles, he'd also made it impossible to jump over to safety from the outside. His house therefore rested on an island accessible only by the narrow strip of land leading from his gate.

I knew that couldn't be the only entrance, though. A sneaky bastard like Elkhashab had to have some other escape route, especially since he was smuggling artifacts out of the country. He probably had a Scooby-Doo bookcase inside that revealed spiral stairs, and if you followed them down, you'd be in some creepy catacombs and eventually find a ladder that led to a trapdoor hidden in a warehouse or someplace else innocuous.

The chances of finding his secret passage inside were much greater than finding his exit point, but I had to get in there without tripping his wards. He had to come home to happy, undisturbed wards on his gate if I was going to ambush him properly.

I took one last look around and then allowed myself to slip down off the wall, disappointing the residents of the moat.

"All right. I've seen enough. To the casbah!"

Oberon trotted beside me, tail wagging. <I hope we're going to rock it. Whatever you saw over that wall reminded you that you should buy me some snacks, right?>

"Um. Right. And we need to find a place for you to hang out for the day. It's going to be impossible for you to come inside."

<Nothing's impossible!>

"Can you swing paw over paw on a rope without falling into a moat full of crocodiles?"

<Dang it! Is there really a moat full of crocodiles?>

"Yes, there is. We'll hide you well. I don't want anyone to think you're up for grabs."

I bought some food and water for Oberon and a few bones for him to gnaw on, and then we found a nice roof—there were plenty of the flat kind in Al Fayyum—where he could lounge unseen and undisturbed. After wishing him an excellent nap, I returned to the bazaar to purchase a good length of rope, a small anchor, and a single length of steel rebar. These would allow me to negotiate the moat.

Back on top of Elkhashab's wall—this time with camouflage cast on myself—I set the steel rebar about halfway into the hardened mud, with a little magical encouragement. After tying one end of the

rope to the rebar and the other to the anchor, I created a binding between the steel of the anchor and the wall of Elkhashab's back patio;
his house was constructed of the same adobe material. Once I energized the binding, the anchor flew to the house and stuck there without me having to throw it.

I had rather a lot of slack to take up—I'd overestimated the
distance—and had to retie the rope on my end to make it taut.

All this activity had drawn the attention of Elkhashab's crocodiles.
Even though I was in camouflage, once I began to swing over their
heads they threw off their customary torpor and became quite excited, scrambling over one another and trying to position themselves
underneath me. They smelled what they couldn't see. Hissing, snapping fights broke out. I have never felt so potentially tasty.

Once I had passed over the moat and it became clear that I wouldn't
fall into their waiting mouths, most of them gave up, but a few pursued me onto land, cleverly deducing that I'd have to drop down at
some point. I slowed and found the small, hungry threads of their
conscious minds and told them I wasn't breakfast. Really. Go away.
Back to the moat, there's a good croc. They obeyed sluggishly, but
they obeyed, one at a time, and I was able to make a soft landing next
to the crocodile priest's patio and dissolve my camouflage.

A quick glance at said patio in the magical spectrum revealed
that—besides being expensively furnished—it was warded. So were
all the windows. I didn't intend to use any of them, anyway. I snuck
around counterclockwise, to the side of the house where there was a
thin strip of glass block high up in place of a full window. My guess
was that this was a bathroom. Chances of plumbing being right on
the wall beneath the blocks were slim. The chances that Elkhashab
had warded his bathroom were even slimmer.

This adobe made of river mud was precisely the sort of thing I appreciated in construction materials. Though it took longer than I
may have wished, it was not difficult to unbind it and watch a me-
shaped hole appear in the wall. I still had to cut through some insula-
tion with a dagger and then kick through some thin drywall inside,

but it was easier than trying to dismantle an accomplished magician's wards.

The first of many shocks in Elkhashab's house came in a whiff of cinnamon apples. He had one of those plug-in air fresheners glowing softly next to the sink. Neat patterned towels, fluffy and folded, waited to complete hand-washing rituals. Not what I expected from a crocodile priest. Apart from that, the room looked unused—far too clean for an evil warlock's daily use. I concluded with satisfaction that this was a guest bathroom and Elkhashab wouldn't check it when he came home.

I stepped back outside for a moment to top off my bear charm. Fully charged, I crept back in with my faerie specs on, looking for more wards, and worrying a bit about mundane security as well.

I closed the bathroom door behind me, hoping he wouldn't notice in his hurry to play with the grimoire. Outside, there was a short hallway leading to what I presumed were bedroom doors. Elkhashab didn't strike me as the sort to share the same side of the house with guests, so I ignored these and moved on. There was a spacious living area with a giant TV and shelves lined with priceless figurines of this god or that goddess. On the opposite side of that, I found a foyer leading to the front door; I searched for a security system but found none. I could see wards around the front door instead.

An arched passage led to a kitchen, but there was likely little of interest in there. Another arch seemed to do nothing but give a view of a magnificent statue of Sobek set in a lighted niche, but once I got closer I saw that another hallway beckoned. These might lead to Elkhashab's private rooms. I checked the door and doorjamb of the first one before opening it. No juju. No hairs across the threshold. And unlocked.

It was a study. A writing desk sat facing the wall shared with the hallway and door; the other three walls were lined with bookshelves. Centered between them was a comfy chair with a table and reading lamp next to it.

I clapped my hands together and rubbed them. Scooby-Doo's legacy had to be here. Pull the right book and one of those bookcases would move aside. Or . . . I pranced over to the reading light and pulled the dangling chain. It turned on!

But nothing else happened.

Damn.

I began to systematically pull on every book he had on his shelves. Some of them were interesting, some were genuine grimoires I might enjoy snagging later, but most were dreck. None revealed a secret passage. I moved aside the comfy chair. I lifted the rug to look for trapdoors. Nothing. The writing desk, a long shot due to its placement, was similarly uncooperative. I sighed heavily and admitted that I could have been wrong.

There were other rooms to check. The whole house, if necessary.

I exited the study and closed the door behind me. I turned right to the next door and examined it as I had the first one. This door had nothing in the way of magical traps, but it did have the old hair-across-the-doorjamb trick. I opened the door and then bound the hair back into place as I closed it. Feel secure, Mr. Elkhashab. Nobody opened this door.

The room was an art studio. Canvases of ugly splatter paintings rested against the walls, five or six deep. An easel near the window had plastic sheeting spread underneath it with liberal staining. Despite this precaution, the floor of the studio—cheap linoleum tiles—had been anointed with droplets of various colors. A low countertop with cabinets underneath held his art supplies—lots of paint tubes and a container of paintbrushes, along with turpentine. A sink waited nearby to wash away the excess. On impulse, I tried the faucet. It sadly provided naught but hot and cold running water.

The canvases hid no secret doors behind them, and I was starting to get seriously frustrated. I'd been searching for an hour and had nothing to show for it. I moved the easel. I picked up the ceramic pot full of paintbrushes. I pulled up the edges of the plastic sheeting. I got a whole lot of nada.

Desperate, I began picking up the mess of paint tubes scattered about the counter, one by one, feeling intensely stupid as I placed them back exactly as I'd found them. Something clicked after I picked up the tube of phthalo blue. My eyes darted around the room, looking for canvases falling away. Nope. Behind me, the easel rested serenely, except for the ungodly mix of colors scattered about the legs.

On the other side of the countertop, however, a neat little square of darkness beckoned. There was a set of stone steps leading down to something that was no doubt very naughty.

I circled and took a few steps down, looking for a way to close the door. Elkhashab would never leave it open when he wanted to perform his dirty deeds. There was a rather large button labeled CLOSE in Arabic script, but it had an odd white glow around it, so I hesitated. A few more steps down and I lost all light from the studio, but there was a dim glow from some light source farther down, whether a tunnel or a room I could not tell. I cast night vision and scanned the area carefully with my improved sight. I spied a smaller, unlabeled, and nonglowing button at the base of the stairs and pushed that instead. The door mechanism slid shut and a set of dingy old incandescent bulbs winked on, illuminating what turned out to be a tunnel after all and making my night vision unnecessary. I dispelled it and proceeded cautiously down the passage, which had smooth walls of the same adobe material used in the rest of the house.

I really was walking *down* the tunnel; there was a fairly steep grade, almost to the point where I wished there had been a staircase instead. Clearly this delved underneath Elkhashab's moat and continued on from there. After a few hundred meters it dropped again, even steeper, and soon the wished-for steps appeared to ease the descent. Once the tunnel leveled out, a brief three or four meters led me to a stunning room that Elkhashab had very little to do with constructing. He'd put up the lights, of course, and his presence was smeared over the chamber like a greasy film, but there was no doubt that this room was at least twice as old as I was. Far beneath the well-documented and preserved ruins of Crocodilopolis, a grand hall stretched before me, supported by massive pillars of stone. Sarcophagi stared at me with four-thousand-year-old eyes, not with the heads of humans or Anubis but with Sobeks, unlike any ever seen before. They didn't rest prone but leaned upright against the wall. It was an archaeologist's dream. Or a dark wizard's. I had never seen a Sobek sarcophagus before, but in this room there were at least twenty, each seven feet tall. I wondered if the mummies still remained inside and if they were well preserved. I paused to take a closer look at one that seemed to be in particularly good shape.

On top of the crocodile head was the tall yellow headdress and red disk signifying Amun-Ra. Instead of the customary crook and flail held by the pharaohs, this carved figure held a *was* scepter in the right hand, signifying power, and the ankh in the left, held by the loop and with the base pointing up to the figure's right shoulder. The human body was carved from limestone with tiles of colored stones inlaid, mosaic fashion, to provide color. Some of these were gilded, and jewels still gleamed around the neck. The crocodile head was polished basalt and skillfully carved. The teeth were limestone but had been painted white at one time. Much of that paint had deteriorated, but a few discolored flecks hinted at what it must have looked like when new. The scepter and ankh were not carved of stone but appeared to be gilded bronze.

I wasn't an expert on Egyptian artifacts by any means, but these sarcophagi couldn't be older than the Middle Kingdom period—and I wouldn't be surprised if they were from the time of the New Kingdom, judging by the craftsmanship on display. Normally the limbs and feet on sarcophagi were mere suggestions, painted on or highlighted with the slightest of bas-relief sculpting, but these were fully sculpted.

Miraculous that it hadn't been plundered—not only by Elkhashab but by centuries of grave robbers. Yet there was no other treasure in the room, so if it was a traditional burial chamber, then quite a bit of stuff was missing. But why take everything else and leave these untouched? Most curious.

I was about to reach out and touch the ankh when I heard the swirl of water and an animal grunt from the next chamber down, traveling and echoing the way sound will when water and stone are involved. I froze.

There was much more than Elkhashab's handiwork to fear here.

Aside from whatever made that noise, untold ancient hoodoo could be waiting to descend upon my head—perhaps from this very sarcophagus. Though my cold iron aura would most likely protect me, prudence dictated that I shouldn't touch it without checking it in the magical spectrum first, and I let my hand drop. These weren't going anywhere; I could come back to examine them later. I had much more reconnaissance to conduct.

I crept down the hall in front of the line of sarcophagi, my eyes toward the center of the room. Elkhashab's string of bulbs, spaced at odd intervals, created puddles of yellow like streetlamps, allowing the edges of the room to languish in shadow. Past the first set of pillars, I saw some familiar markings on the floor: a circle enclosing another circle, and inside that not a pentagram but a mixture of lines, Hebrew characters, and mystical symbols straight out of *The Greater Key of Solomon*. The White Knife and the Black Knife were there, the Sickle, the Sword, and all the rest too. Elkhashab was definitely more than a crocodile priest. He dabbled extensively in the dark end of the magic pool, like Nebwenenef before him.

A supporting wall forced me to move toward the center. A doorway there led to another room, decorated with bas-relief doodads heralding Sobek's spiffiness. At least, I inferred as much from the gaping maw of a crocodile sculpted at the top.

The next room was poorly lit. A single light made a half-assed effort at fighting the darkness from the edges. The scent of water and fetid rot twitched at my nostrils; something had died in there. Maybe many somethings. The pervasive miasma was enough to make me draw Fragarach from its sheath.

Two steps into the room, I heard the water gurgling again. Cursing the weak effort of the token bulb, I recast night vision to better see what I was missing. The chamber was of a similar size to the one I had just left, except that in the center of the room there was no floor with mystical symbols scrawled across it; rather, a black pool with ripples betrayed recent movement. Pillars rose out of it to support the ceiling.

There was no great mystery about what awaited me in the gloom.

Elkhashab, that pantweasel, had left me with one or more crocodiles to deal with. A faint electric hum drew my attention over my left shoulder.

A large old-fashioned freezer lurked there, a thick cable snaking from underneath it to the room I'd just vacated. He must have run the electricity behind all the sarcophagi. I opened the lid and saw that it was full of steaks and roasts. Oberon would have approved. I took a few out and threw them to the edge of the pool, then tossed a final one into the pool itself. Something responded in the dark, and I slid along the wall counterclockwise, holding my sword point in front of me. Anything that wanted to eat me had to eat my blade first. Once I'd started to move along the longer wall, a splash sounded from the space I'd vacated, followed by serious macking noises. I saw gold glinting in the dim light, and then an enormous pocked back stretched sinuously into the water: It was the largest crocodile I had ever seen, festooned with enough metal to make reestablishing the gold standard plausible. I hurried to the next supporting wall and another doorway. There was nothing that I could see to keep the crocodile from entering the next room, but perhaps it didn't want to leave its comfy mini-swamp with easy-to-hunt rump roasts.

The subsequent chamber was fairly well lit, like the first one, allowing me to dispel night vision, but its contents were entirely different. Instead of sarcophagi along the walls, there were boxes—the wooden kind you used to see a lot of before the planet started to run low on trees and people figured it might be better to use recycled cardboard instead. They were probably full of the treasures missing from the burial chamber. I left them alone, figuring it was best to leave it all conveniently packaged for the Ministry of Antiquities. I was much more interested in the creeptastic vibe coming from the far side of the room.

Elkhashab had repurposed an ancient stone worktable, perhaps originally intended as an embalming station, by turning it into a makeshift altar. It was stained with fluids that were supposed to stay on the inside of bodies, and there were a couple of smallish skulls on either end. Around the altar itself he'd drawn a couple of large circles, symbols of invocation and protection written along the circumference and ritual materials placed carefully inside. Adjacent to these were other circles—the summoning kind. Circles of binding with pentagrams. A telltale whiff of sulfur confirmed that he'd successfully summoned physical demons here, not just the spirits suggested by the first room's circles. He had the seals of calling, binding, coercion, submission, and banishment painted perfectly between the points of the stars. Almost too perfectly.

I scanned the altar again with a new suspicion. The two skulls were facing at exactly the same angle. He had some bowls full of ritual ingredients—salt and salamander tails, that kind of thing—and those bowls were precisely equidistant from one another. The candles were brand new and of the same kind. The ritual knife was placed perpendicular to the edge.

I thought back to the guest bathroom with the air freshener and the primly folded towels. The order of the library. Even the studio, meant to look sloppy and spontaneous, had been carefully arranged that way. This guy was obsessed with neatness and order.

It made sense. The precision required to be a practicing magician was no joke.

I decided to mess with him. A fingernail's scratch across the seals of coercion, submission, and banishment would drive him crazy. He'd spend hours repainting just to make sure everything was perfect. That is, if I didn't kill him first.

Golden figurines of Sobek, Amun, and Amun-Ra stood impassively on the altar, their dead painted eyes calmly awaiting tribute and sacrifice. I smirked; Elkhashab appeared to be hedging his bets on which form of Amun would get all the love. Amun had been a headliner in the early Egyptian dynasties, but he had to share top billing with Ra later on, and Sobek was considered in some tales to be a manifestation of the combined god Amun-Ra. Elkhashab must be harboring doubts about which was to receive sacrifices from the *Grimoire of the Lamb*.

This room was the last one. Nestled in the corner behind the altar, off to my left, a spiral staircase twisted up into the ceiling. If it led all the way up to the surface, that was how he smuggled stuff out of here. He would never leave his house with contraband when he was under surveillance; he would choose to emerge elsewhere.

It also explained why he never went for the big score with a sarcophagus; never mind that it would invite too many inconvenient questions, there was no way he'd get one up through that wee well. I doubted he could get one up through the steep tunnel that led to his studio either. I wondered why he hadn't installed a rudimentary lift instead. Too conspicuous?

The staircase bore investigation. It was probably my best way out, after all. But the altar needed a closer look first. I circled it and discovered a small table nestled against the far side, almost like a hallway desk, yet lower in height so that it was invisible while looking at the altar from the direction I'd entered. Stacked on it were two sheaves of paper—no, parchment. Incredibly old stuff too, mostly illegible, the ink having faded and flaked away after centuries. In the magical spectrum, the writings were quite clear, however; they glowed with ancient hoodoo. I'd bet five biscuits that these were the writings of which Elkhashab had spoken—the writings of Nebwenenef.

My immediate impulse was to destroy them, but I decided against it, figuring that Elkhashab would notice right away and know that someone had been there. Like everything else around the altar, the sheaves were placed and organized with attention to detail, and I didn't want to give myself away yet. I'd definitely come back and take care of them before I left, however.

I turned my attention to the staircase. It was a sturdy metal one; it didn't creak or shiver as I ascended, and I gave silent kudos to whoever had installed it. My stomach, however, began to rebel as I got closer to the ceiling. Something smelled foul up there—but it was a different stench from the one in the chamber of the crocodile god.

Once I got my head in the space between the ceiling and the floor, I paused. The smell was definitely coming from the room above, but I couldn't see very much. Silently, I withdrew a dagger from my satchel and poked it up through the hole to see if it set off any kind of trap. I wiggled it around. I swirled it all around the edges. Nothing.

I did a quick peekaboo, feeling silly, but whatever—I didn't want to end more than two thousand years of existence as a victim to one of Elkhashab's booby traps. No reaction, and I didn't see much of anything. It was fair-to-middling Stygian darkness in there.

Casting night vision, I took a longer peek and did a complete survey, three-sixty. There was a break in the railing of the staircase so that one could enter or exit on this floor. It appeared to be a single chamber, smaller than the ones downstairs. There was a lone sarcophagus here, but a more conventional type rather than one of Sobek. It was situated conventionally as well, resting prone instead of leaning upright against the wall. Three large cages filled the rest of the room, and it was from them that the stink emanated. Behind me, there was just the bare stone wall, and the staircase continued to wind above into farther unknown levels. I put my dagger away.

I climbed and left the stairs to check out the cages. The first one held a small skeleton without a skull. The next held a rotting corpse, also headless, dressed in tatters of once-white linen that had been chewed on by rats. Or maybe by those flesh-eating scarab beetles from *The Mummy*, which still gave me nightmares. I couldn't tell if the body was male or female, but it was young. I remembered the two skulls resting on the altar; I'd thought them there for gravitas or a sense of theatre, but the bastard had actually sacrificed kids. Sure, demons would let themselves be bound for one of those.

Another still form lay in the third cage. The legs faced the door and the rise of shoulders concealed the head—if there was one. The reek was awful; there was a bucket filled to the brim with waste in one corner. Strangely, it gave me hope.

"Hey, kid," I whispered. Then I realized I didn't need to whisper and I should probably speak in Arabic. "Wake up!" I called. No reaction. My throat tightened, but I shouted it again. The child didn't move.

Concentrating on the lock, I bound the metal tumblers to the unlocked position, swung open the door, and entered the cage. The boy—for it was a boy, about ten years old or so—still had a head. He was alive but unconscious, and the pulse I felt at his neck was weak.

He was probably dehydrated and starved. Elkhashab had just left him in here while he went off to America to steal an ancient grimoire.

I couldn't let him stay here any longer. He needed medical attention now. As I had done before with Oberon, I created a binding so that this boy could use the magic stored in my bear charm for energy. Once the binding was complete, his eyes popped open and he scrambled away from me until he was at the back of the cage, his hands raised defensively as he begged in Arabic not to be killed.

"*Salaam,*" I said in the same language. The poor kid had every reason to be terrified. "I've come to take you out of here. Let's get away from that man." I backed out of the cage and left the door open, speaking to him from freedom. "Come on." Belatedly, I remembered that he probably couldn't see anything. He might be thinking that *I* was Elkhashab. I cast night vision on him and spoke again. "Let's go. Up the stairs. Let's get you home. Your parents are worried."

I hoped he wouldn't take too long to decide. The energy in my charm wouldn't last forever and was already getting low.

The boy's eyes grew wide. "You don't work for him?"

I snorted and shook my head. "No. I prefer life over death. If anyone dies today, it will be him, not you. Come on."

"Who are you?"

What a great straight line. A few different superhero names rushed through my head, *Whiskey Man* being my favorite for its rather dubious heroism, but he might not have ever heard of whiskey here. "Call me Atticus," I said. "What's your name?"

"Hamal."

"Are you from Al Fayyum, Hamal?" He nodded. "Good. Home is upstairs. Let's go." I held out my hand to him and he moved at last. He rose to his feet and shot toward me, leaping into my arms and wrapping his legs around my waist like a much smaller child. He held me tightly around the neck.

"Okay, that'll work too," I said, and carried him up the staircase. It rose past another darkened floor, a chamber full of more wooden boxes, then another, and then a period of traveling through solid rock. We arrived finally in a small room, clearly modern, and just as clearly a changing room. Several different outfits hung on hooks, to allow Elkhashab to emerge into the world looking completely different from however he'd entered his house. A small bank of TV monitors showed four different views of some barren desert, no doubt the area around our exit point. No one was currently pictured. I dispelled our night vision.

There were no giant red buttons here to tempt people; Elkhashab was confident that no one would find this place by accident. A simple switch on the wall next to the staircase opened a sliding trapdoor that turned out to be a piece of a fake boulder. Said boulder was hidden inside a thicket of thorns, which made our emergence a tad painful, but also completely hidden from view.

I wondered who had built all this cloak-and-dagger shit for Elkhashab. I wondered if they were still alive or if they had turned into dinner for the crocodile god below.

Once out of the boulder, I waited for the trapdoor to slide closed automatically, but it didn't. That meant that there must be a switch around somewhere to close it. After a bit of searching—made more difficult by Hamal's refusal to let go of me—I found a small painted button at the base of the same boulder. That closed the door.

Following some footprints, I took the path of least resistance out of the thicket. We were on a rocky outcropping in the desert north of the lake. The center of Al Fayyum was a few miles away to the south.

"There, you see?" I said to Hamal. "Sunlight. You're safe now." The boy said nothing, but he began to cry. No tears, though—that was a bad sign. He needed fluids desperately, and the lake wouldn't provide any. It used to be freshwater, in ancient times, but today it's a saltwater lake, cut off from the flow of the Nile.

With earth under my feet again, I replenished my bear charm and drew more to run quickly. I had no idea where to find a hospital.

I hugged the lakeshore and headed south until I hit the suburbs of Al Fayyum and found a bazaar. People were looking at me curiously—what was that white man with the sword doing carrying that filthy boy?

It was a good time to gamble on basic human decency. I began to call for help in Arabic. "This boy needs water! I found him in the desert!" I was surrounded in no time by four or five locals. Outside Al Fayyum's oasis, the desert was harsh and unforgiving, and the people knew it well.

I broke the binding that fed magical energy to Hamal, and his grip about my neck slackened enough that I could lay him down and kneel by his side. Somebody had a canteen of water and put it up to Hamal's lips.

"Not too much. He really needs medical attention. I'm a stranger here. Is there a hospital nearby?" I wanted to keep things moving along before people started asking me questions like "What were you doing in the desert?"

An argument broke out regarding the wisest course of action—calling an ambulance, or grabbing a doctor one person knew a block away, or carrying him all the way to the hospital ourselves because, you know, who knew when the ambulance would get there? For just a moment nobody was looking at me, so I cast camouflage and backed away.

They noticed me disappearing, but they couldn't figure out where I'd gone to. I stayed still and heard them quickly dismiss me, because the kid was what mattered. Exactly. Satisfied that Hamal would be taken care of and returned to his family, I hoofed it back to the ruins and gingerly crept into the thicket, where I pushed the button on the bottom of the proper boulder. The smooth mechanism slid aside and I began my second descent into darkness, fully recharged, lips pressed tight in a grim line. It was far past time for the crocodile priest to get his.

Unfortunately, he couldn't get his until he showed up. I checked my cell phone on the way down: no messages from Yusuf in Cairo.

I parked myself next to the stairs on the floor where I'd found Hamal and settled down to wait. Elkhashab would be coming, I felt sure, to try out the *Grimoire of the Lamb* as soon as possible. And he'd do it at the altar with the Amun idols, not anywhere else, and when he did, I'd take a pound of flesh for Hamal and those other poor kids.

If Elkhashab didn't come back soon, the authorities might swarm down here and take care of everything, because Hamal would eventually start talking. I'd rather inform the authorities myself, though, after the grimoire was safely back in my hands.

It occurred to me to wonder why archaeologists had never found these chambers. They were buried deep, no doubt, and there wasn't a convenient pyramid above ground shouting, "Here's where all the plunder is!" but they had all kinds of little electromagnetic radar scanner doodads these days to search for chambers like these. My guesses were that Elkhashab had spoofed their findings with his ritual practice or greased some palms—or else the real Sobek was exercising himself to keep his treasures hidden. Considering how eager Bast was to have her book returned to her, I didn't think it unreasonable to expect Sobek to be just as protective of his legacy.

During the archaeological orgy at the beginning of the twentieth century, the Egyptian gods reveled in the attention they were getting around the world. But I knew that not everything had been found, and I'm sure the joy of the gods ebbed away when they saw that the new attention they received did not translate into new worshippers. They were still keeping plenty of secrets. This place was one of Sobek's.

The more time I had to think, the more I began to respect Elkhashab's cleverness. He clearly had the talent and the stomach to do what was necessary to deal with demonkind, but he must have realized that continuing to kidnap and kill kids was simply unsustainable to do all he wanted to do. But if he could accomplish basically the same sorts of things by dispatching lambs instead of children, well, he could continue that *ad infinitum*. Nobody cared if you slaughtered lambs. They expected you to slaughter them when they sold them to you.

A splash and a terrified bleat let me know that Elkhashab had finally arrived, lamb in tow. He'd feed his giant croc and then enter the room directly below. I drew Fragarach as silently as I could to get ready and crouched near the staircase.

The bleating continued and grew louder, and Elkhashab's quiet cursing could be heard underneath it.

"I'm going to tranquilize the next one and have done with it," he muttered. "Can hardly wait to sacrifice you. There. Stay there."

More bleating, then a soft plop as Elkhashab dropped something—perhaps the grimoire?—on the altar. "There, Nebwenenef. I have brought it, you see?" he said, his voice full of victory. There was rustling from what sounded like several plastic bags being set down and dull impacts from the contents inside hitting stone. A sharp metallic ring announced a knife being yanked from its sheath.

"But, first, I have older business to conduct. Hamal!" He crooned the name, lengthening the last syllable. I nearly snarled aloud. Most serial murderers don't want to know the names of their victims. It's easier to sleep at night if you have killed only victims instead of people with names and families. Elkhashab was a different kind.

I hadn't planned on him coming up here—I imagined sneaking down while he was busy doing something else—but if he wanted to stick his head up through that hole, so be it. It would be a cleaner and quicker death for him than I'd anticipated.

Silently shifting so that I'd be behind his head when he came up the stairs, I cocked my sword hand back. His boots made a dull, hollow sound on the stairs. His white cap rose out of the hole like a giant marshmallow, then the back of his neck, and I swung—but he must have heard or sensed something, because he ducked back down and Fragarach whiffed, clanging loudly against the staircase's main support.

"Shit! Who's there?" Elkhashab cried.

I cursed silently and moved away from the stairwell. Only an idiot stays where the enemy can locate him.

"Is that you, Hamal? How did you escape?" The sorcerer thought about it and then realized that didn't make much sense. A ten-year-old boy wouldn't hang around to ambush him when he had an escape route handy. Elkhashab's conscious mind slowly caught up with what his subconscious had absorbed.

"No. That was a sword. It's you. The American wizard." He switched to English. "I know you're there, O'Sullivan. I don't know how you found this place, but you're going to die here."

He didn't say anything else, and I was faintly disappointed. I'd been hoping for a longer monologue. Perhaps he was waiting for me to respond? Fat chance of that. I wasn't going to sneeze or fart or do anything else to give away my position, least of all stick my head down the hole. Nor was he going to give me another free strike. It was something of an impasse.

He was listening hard. I heard nothing but the occasional bleat of the lamb. Elkhashab grew weary of that after a while and began to move. He struck a couple of matches to light some candles on his altar. A bowl or two got picked up and put down again. He muttered unintelligibly; either it was just very low volume or it was a language I didn't understand.

A sharp intake of breath—a hiss of pain. What the fuck was he doing? The mumbling resumed, but it quickly rose in volume until it was distinguishable as a chant in an absurdly old language, one with lots of gutturals and fricatives.

Gods below! He was summoning a demon, using his own blood so he could send it up here to off me. If he was occupied doing that, then he couldn't be watching the stairwell to take a potshot at me; he had to concentrate on the ritual. I decided to risk a peek.

Padding forward to the well, I stretched out prone on the floor, then held on to the edge with my right hand as I dropped my head and left shoulder down into the stairwell far enough to steal a quick look.

The light coming up from the lower chamber was a yellow-orange, but as I descended it turned red, and a sound like someone slamming a refrigerator door really hard *foomp*ed and rattled the staircase.

"Yes!" Elkhashab cried, and the light turned yellow-orange again. My eyes dropped below the ceiling to catch the crocodile priest in the midst of an ecstatic fist pump. He faced a demon in his circle of summoning, ignoring the choking brimstone fumes that filled the chamber. I could tell he was winding himself up for a cackle of glee before he told the spawn to eat me, but then a deep-fried gravel voice answered in much the same tone of victory, and Elkhashab's face went slack as he realized something had gone horribly wrong.

"No!" His tone had changed to the raw falsetto of pants-crapping panic. He was discovering that he could not cow his personal demon into submission with a broken seal, or coerce it to do his bidding with the seal of coercion broken as well, or indeed even banish it now. The scratch of my fingernail and his hurry to kill me had slain him. All he could do anymore was scream as the demon's claws opened up his belly and his guts slithered out. He screamed for a long time. The demon made sloppy chewing noises as he ate Elkhashab alive.

Justice.

I pulled myself up as silently as I could, but the demon had to know I was there. A demon's ability to sense prey was unmatched. He'd come for me next, but if I tried to escape up the stairwell, he'd come for me sooner and I'd be in a poor position to defend myself. As it was, I had a couple of advantages most mortals did not: I had a cold iron amulet bound to my aura, which protected me from most magic, and my sword cut through any armor. Demons didn't wear chain and plate or any other kind of traditional armor, but some of them had magical armor that made them immune to conventional weapons. Fragarach wasn't conventional.

I backed away from the staircase, because I had a feeling the demon was faster than me, even if I juiced myself up. I went ahead and did that, of course. If I made him come all the way up and locate me before he could charge, I'd have enough time to take my own shot. He might, in his hubris, even let me take a free swing at him.

Elkhashab finally died, and the demon seemed to lose interest. No fear and pain there anymore. The lamb, I realized, hadn't bleated in a while. I didn't know if it was dead or if it was hoping the demon wouldn't notice it. I hadn't seen it when I played peekaboo, but neither had I looked for it.

The demon was free to do as he wished. The one who had summoned him was dead; all bindings were off. The lamb, if it was still around, wasn't much of a soul. The demon came after me instead.

He made no noise on the steps with anything that could be called feet; there was simply a sort of deep drumroll and he was there—glowing orange like banked embers around the edges, a mouth and a distended stomach and two pairs of huge arms to shove food down the maw. He didn't have any legs at all; his black body was rounded like a balloon. He moved on his knuckles, and his mouth sneered at me.

"*Khaja gorl mahka . . .*" the demon began. The voice sounded like a grumpy Tom Waits mixed with an acetylene torch. I didn't let him finish. I didn't understand him anyway. I lunged much faster than he expected and lopped off his front left arm at the elbow.

The creature was shocked but utterly savage in reply; he roared and swung at me with his right, able to stay balanced on the back two arms, and my attempt to block cost me a broken left wrist. Both of us staggered back, wounded and wary now. I decided that attacking was my best strategy; the demon was probably unused to playing defense, and I had to make the most of my few advantages, especially since I was operating on a limited supply of magic.

I brought the sword around high on his left, precisely where it would be most difficult for the demon to block. He rotated to his side to avoid the blow and countered with a swing from his back right arm. I'd anticipated this and pivoted away, much as he had. Those back arms didn't have huge claws, I noticed. Those were used primarily for movement.

He was faster than me but crippled and unused to fighting against swords. All the demon had seen so far was two slashes. He might have concluded that this was all I could do. I feinted another hack at his left side and then twisted my wrist, sweeping the sword down and across my body to meet the right cross I knew would be coming. As Fragarach arced up, it caught the demon's wrist from underneath and severed the clawed hand. This move left my right side exposed, however.

The demon lost his shit. Down to just the two back arms and seeing an opening, he launched off his back right, and his left fist hammered my ribs. They cracked and I went down, wondering what happened to all the air in the world.

I didn't know how I was ever going to get up. My left wrist wouldn't support me. My ribs wouldn't let me roll to my right. I couldn't breathe. I supposed it was okay, though. This seemed the type of demon to bring the fight to you—especially if you were vulnerable.

He had not landed gracefully, but the creature was shifting for a charge. I lifted Fragarach's blade to make sure it couldn't be trapped against the floor, then folded up my legs to reduce the target. That was about all I could manage without any air. I gasped for some and kept an eye on the demon.

He let loose with a thunderous roar scented with all the joys of ass and pestilence. The faint whiff I got made me grateful that I couldn't inhale a lungful of it. The beast's teeth were mismatched ebony punji sticks, showcases of rot and an example to all who refuse to floss.

One massively knuckled hand swung forward, planted itself, and then seemed to buckle at the elbow. It stopped and swayed. The loss of blood—ichor, rather—from two severed limbs was taking its toll.

The creature spat, *"Barg rah!"* That was a "Fuck it!" if I ever heard one. His back arms churned and his damn black teeth were sunk into the side of my calf before I could move. I grunted and swung Fragarach at the top of his head, shearing off a slice like a cantaloupe. The blow rocked him back, and the teeth popped out of my leg before he fell over and dissolved into a sulfurous puddle of goo. The corporeal form of demons never lasts long once they're unbound.

I expelled a sigh of relief and relaxed for a moment—or at least as much as I could, considering my injuries. But the stench of the room and my pressing need to get in touch with the earth drove me to action. Despite being fully charged when I came back down, I had burned a lot of juice to boost my speed, and I didn't have enough left to do any serious healing. I compromised by shutting off the pain so I'd be able to move and concentrate. My calf, while probably infected with something nasty from the demon's teeth, was still capable of functioning. Getting up was a bit of a chore, with cracked ribs and a broken wrist, but the legs weren't in terrible shape, and I could go back downstairs and retrieve the grimoire—or, better yet, destroy it along with the writings of Nebwenenef.

Figuring I was all alone, I kind of clomped down the metal stairs when I should have kept quiet. It prevented me from hearing the noise in the next room until I reached the stone floor. I froze at the bottom of the stairwell and heard the chalky grind and thud of stone scraping against stone. The jaundiced light of yellow bulbs revealed a disturbing shadow moving on the floor. It grew as it approached the door to the chamber I thought of as the crocodile lounge. Being careful to make no sound this time, I minced behind the altar. Elkhashab's torn and partially eaten remains littered the front, I noticed, along with his plastic grocery bags. The grimoire lay open between the candles he had lit before his death. A tiny noise of fear drew my eyes to the wall on my left, back near the door. The lamb was still alive and cowering near the boxes of untold treasures. The shadow took on a solid presence at the doorway, and I crouched down out of sight as it entered with heavy, grinding footsteps.

Whatever it was scared the bejesus out of the lamb, for it screamed and quite probably shat where it stood. I risked a peek around the corner of the altar, figuring that whatever had entered the room would be focused on the lamb.

It was one of the Sobek sarcophagi—or, rather, the front of it—the lid now ambulatory, a lurching stone-and-metal horror with its backside missing and much of the paint worn away, but possessing a full complement of limestone teeth in a maw of basalt that it was now able to open. The legs functioned like articulated action figures, with stiff movements allowed by cracks in the stone around the knees and hips. The gilded bronze scepter of power that looked so fascinating when it was art turned abruptly sickening when it was wielded on living flesh. That's what the unholy thing did—it crushed the lamb's spine with the scepter in its right hand, then tossed away the ankh in its left, and picked up the body.

I had a lot to process and little time to do it.

First, how had this thing come to life? Was it, in fact, living, or was it undead? That was an important distinction for me, since Druidry forbade me to harm living things through binding or unbinding. On the one hand, its stone body and the fact that it had torn itself free of a sarcophagus suggested something undead or animated along the lines of a golem, but on the other—what if it was a manifestation of Sobek?

That was possible but unlikely to my mind. Back in Cairo, Bast had manifested first as a cat and then took a semi-human form, so it would have made more sense for Sobek to take over the living crocodile in the next room than to animate the sculptured lid of a sarcophagus.

Said sculpture didn't pause to provide me with an explanation. It placed the head of the lamb between its black jaws and tore it off with limestone teeth, then spat it out hurriedly and lifted the carcass above its head, letting the blood drain from the body into its mouth.

It didn't swallow because it didn't possess a throat, just a closed-off surface like a hand puppet—but the blood didn't spill out the sides either. Instead, it was absorbed into the stone. I silently triggered my magical sight, which drained my magic down to dangerous lows, but it revealed to me that this thing wasn't Sobek—it didn't have the blinding white aura of a god. Instead of being suffused all over with the white power of magic, the sculpture had its power centered at the back of the mouth, where the blood was pooling and disappearing. In other words, it was ordinary rock and metal animated by an extraordinary spirit. I would ponder later whose spirit it might be and why and how it had animated that sarcophagus at that particular time. A better question to ponder right then was how I was going to prevent it from tearing off my head too and gulping my blood like an energy drink.

Running away sounded attractive. The sheer size of the thing—seven feet tall and the width of a bookcase—would make navigating the spiral staircase difficult. But I didn't want to leave behind the grimoire—nor did I wish this thing to grow any more powerful than it already was. How to defeat it?

Fragarach wouldn't do me any good. It was great against armor but not so good against rock. Few martial arts were great against rock, now that I thought of it. Probably because one so rarely sees possessed sarcophagi.

Perhaps I could unbind its feet—which were only half feet anyway—and it would fall down and go boom. It was worth a shot, especially since I'd have nothing left afterward but some dregs to keep my injuries from distracting me.

I banished my magical sight mentally by using my charm, but there was no way to perform the unbinding silently. I whispered the words, of course, but even that sound echoed in the stone chamber and alerted the thing that it wasn't alone. It stopped drinking blood, cocked its head, then turned my way. It spotted me peeking from behind the altar as I finished the unbinding and energized it.

The lamb dropped from its grasp, forgotten, and its mouth opened wide. I think it would have bellowed or hissed if it had any vocal cords, and I kind of wished it did, since its silence was creepy. It whipped its left hand down to point at the floor near its ankles. Nothing happened—visually, at least. I could imagine very well what had happened in the magical spectrum, for that gesture was familiar to me, thanks to Elkhashab. My earth magic had just been canceled out by Sobek's water magic, a small flood drowning my bindings, and now I had nothing of significance left.

Hiding was pointless. Pushing up off my right hand, my left still useless, I rose from behind the altar and drew Fragarach. It would do me little good against the stone but would provide some defense against its weapon, which had a flared crest at one end and two forked tines at the other. I circled around the altar to my right, which would force the thing to pivot on its uncertain feet to face me.

It knew what it was doing with that scepter. Displaying a dexterity wholly alien to most rocks and much more fluid than the movement of the legs, it twirled the *was* in front of it and then lashed out as I approached. I deflected the first blow, then another, and its skill was such that I found myself fencing with it for a brief time. Its mouth remained open, silently promising to end me. But its weapon was inherently slower, and I was able to slap away a blow and use the opening to deliver a straight kick to its abdomen. Lacking heels on which to stagger backward, it toppled over. As it fell, however, it whipped the scepter around and hooked my plant leg—my left—with the crested end and sent me tumbling on my ass. When I collided with the ground, something crumpled further inside; now my ribs were not just cracked but broken and, in all likelihood, scraping my spleen. The fresh bloom of pain prevented me from rolling out of the way or moving much at all. It gave the Sobek creature the chance to sit up and swing at me again with the scepter, the crested end aimed at my face. Having no other choice, I threw up my left forearm to block, and it did so but scored another break in the process. It wasn't useless after all. Just painful. Wincing as I moved, I rolled out of range before another blow could rain down, using my right arm for support.

We were both slow to get up but for different reasons. I had broken bones, and it was a ridiculously top-heavy monstrosity trying to stand without any heels. It managed to get halfway up, lost its balance, and crashed to the ground again.

As I regained my footing and my magic ran out completely, letting me feel all the agony of my broken arm and ribs, I realized that keeping this thing on the floor might be all I could reasonably hope for. I didn't have a jackhammer handy. Magically we were at an impasse as well: Even if I had any magic left, the sculpture had already demonstrated that it could dissolve my bindings, and anything it threw at me would be deflected by my cold iron aura. It didn't know that yet, though. It gestured at me with its left hand—and snapped its jaws shut when nothing happened. My amulet kind of wiggled on my chest, but that was it.

"Ha! Suck it, Sobek. Or whoever you are. Kind of stupid to take an earth form if you're a water sorcerer, don't you think?"

I doubted it understood English, but I knew it could hear me, because it had reacted to my whisper before. It was also clearly able to see. So despite the lack of anything akin to normal eyes or ears, the spirit possessing that form had some basic senses. A bit slow on the uptake, though. It kept flicking its hand at me and expecting something to happen.

"Why *now*?" I asked it, thinking aloud. "You had centuries of time and presumably several years in the recent past during which you could have stumbled through these chambers. What changed?"

It gave up on trying to hex me and attempted to stand again, a noisy, scraping business that made the hairs on the back of my neck try to flee. A well-placed kick kept it seated, and I danced out of the way of a scepter strike. The strain of dodging aggravated my calf, however, where the demon had bitten me. My pain kept developing layers and flavors; this one burned with a dull fire.

"I came through here hours ago and you didn't budge. But after Elkhashab—" That was it. Elkhashab had brought the *Grimoire of the Lamb* and an actual lamb in here, right past that thing, which mattered because the first item on its to-do list when it became mobile was to eat the lamb. And the sacrifice of a lamb was required before performing anything in the grimoire. Instructions on how to use the grimoire were in the writings of Nebwenenef, and Elkhashab had even spoken his name.

"Nebwenenef?" I said, and the stone image of Sobek stopped trying to get up and jerked its head toward me in recognition.

Oh, *shit*. The legend of his death had been greatly exaggerated. Somehow he'd found a way back to the semi-living. The grimoire must have been his ticket back to power—that and those writings on the table behind the altar. The writings that had glowed in the magical spectrum when I looked at them.

A fact few people realize until they experience it is how crippling pain can be. I wanted to dash around the altar, scoop up that sheaf of parchment, and destroy it. My upper body and my calf informed me that there would be no more dashing. I limped there, anyway, as quickly as I could, during which time Nebwenenef laboriously clambered to his feet. I sheathed Fragarach behind my back and, as I passed, picked up one of the candles Elkhashab had lit. Once behind the altar, I set the candle on the small table next to the ancient pieces of script, picked them up by one edge, and held them over the flame.

Nebwenenef had my measure now. If he could keep me at a distance, I wouldn't be able to knock him down, and I didn't have my sword out to deflect him anyway. He began twirling the scepter around, building velocity, and I stole a glance down at the parchment, which should be merrily ablaze.

It wasn't—because water mages tend to protect themselves from fire, and at this point I had very little doubt that these writings were, in some sense, a piece of Nebwenenef. The water mage had bound himself to the liquid of the ink. If I kept at it, eventually the fire would win, but that could be minutes or even hours away—time I didn't have.

The scepter crashed down across the altar and smashed the top of the candle, but I wasn't there. I'd backed up, out of range, keeping the altar between Nebwenenef and me. I took a step to the right and he took one to his left, a juicy noise from Elkhashab's remains squelching underfoot.

Since my left hand wasn't gripping anything soon, I used my teeth to hold the parchment and tried to tear it, but it might as well have been steel plate. The sheaf had been warded with all the protections Nebwenenef could muster. Well, it was time to truly lay my hands on the work and stop messing about with the edges. Or, better yet, to put my useless arm to good use again.

I kept an eye on Nebwenenef and draped the sheaf over my left forearm, so that the flat of the first page rested against my skin. Whatever magical secrets it held should dissipate in a few seconds after my cold iron aura had a chance to work on it. It took only a second for Nebwenenef to know something was wrong, however. He shuddered, losing his motor functions for a moment, and nearly slipped in the slime of Elkhashab's guts. He knew he couldn't let me stand there and continue, so he circled around to my right, toward the staircase. I moved to keep myself opposite and allowed the first page to slip from underneath my thumb and fall to the floor. I rested the second page on my left arm and kept my feet moving. Nebwenenef shuddered again, and the fluidity of his arm movements noticeably decreased. My own mobility was jeopardized as I nearly lost my footing in Elkhashab parts. Nebwenenef took advantage and thrust at me across the altar with the forked end of his scepter. I saw it coming but had nothing to block it with, and my own fluidity of movement was gone thanks to the broken ribs. My attempt to sidestep was too slow, and he pierced me in the left breast, though shallowly. The tines weren't barbed, so they slid out when I backed away, out of his reach, careful not to slip in the slime. I dropped the second page and laid the third one across my arm, continuing to walk backward from the altar and leaving bloody footprints on the stone. Nebwenenef raised his scepter, as if he would hurl it at me like a spear, but he was rocked—so to speak—by a third series of fits, and the scepter dropped from his grasp. He kept from falling over only by bracing himself against the altar. When I moved on to the fourth page, he collapsed altogether, out of my sight. There were two more pages to go, and I made sure to give them a dose of cold iron too. I held on to the last page when I was finished and returned to the altar to try an experiment. Hearing nothing from behind the altar and stepping carefully around the mess, I held the last page of parchment over the sole remaining candle and was gratified to see it light up quickly this time. Good riddance, Nebwenenef. He'd lived and supposedly died long before the pharaohs but had somehow arranged this little scheme, his spirit still bound with the elemental magic he'd stolen and then spread throughout the Nile Valley.

He obviously wasn't one for talking, but I wished I could have asked him how he did it. I guessed that he had never really died so much as dissipated. Here, near Crocodilopolis, he'd slowly collected a shadow of himself and engineered a method by which he could return to power, influencing this priest or possessing that sorcerer to write down what he needed to reconstitute himself in a physical form, binding a piece of himself to ink and parchment, and then, gulled by visions of power and thinking it was all for Amun, someone like Elkhashab would assemble what Nebwenenef needed to bring himself back. I'd have to reexamine my other Egyptian grimoires to see if any of them could be used in a similar fashion, and likewise go through Elkhashab's writings to make sure he hadn't been influenced to write down anything in modern Arabic. I wondered, not for the first time, what else might have been destroyed at the Library of Alexandria. That fire might have inadvertently delayed Nebwenenef's return by many centuries.

I put the parchment on the altar to burn out and then picked up the *Grimoire of the Lamb* and set it alight as well. I would make sure to torch the other parchment pages I'd dropped, but picking those up could wait until after I had a chance to heal. I'd give them a read and see if they listed other books besides the "lost book of Amun" that would grant an enterprising sorcerer power for the low, low price of a blood sacrifice. Stepping around to the stairwell, I saw the Sobek sculpture sprawled awkwardly, facedown, in a manner that would be extremely difficult to explain to scientists. No one would believe that someone had carved the stone that way, and yet there it was, inanimate rock. I placed my foot on the back of the head, not as a gesture of victory but to make doubly sure that Nebwenenef was thoroughly exorcised from the stone. The glimpse I'd seen of his power had been centered at the back of the throat or head, and it cost me nothing to apply a little bit more cold iron there.

Climbing the stairs was a slow exercise in hurt and lightheadedness. I thanked the gods below that Sobek hadn't chosen to manifest like Bast had. Two sorcerers with the ability to use his magic had given me more than enough trouble.

Night had fallen by the time I tumbled out of the boulder and reconnected with the earth with a sigh of relief.

Oberon? Can you hear me?

<Atticus? Where are you?> His voice was small and uncertain.

A bit far away, I guess. Kind of messed up and need to heal. Will you be okay there until the morning?

<Can't I come to where you are?>

I'm worried someone will catch you if you run through the streets by yourself.

<You think they can catch an Irish wolfhound on the run?>

Maybe you're right. Can you remember how to get to Elkhashab's place?

<Sure.>

Okay. Run to the back of his place and I'll give you directions from there.

While I began to heal in earnest, I gave Yusuf a call in Cairo and told him to bring some of the boys down to Al Fayyum. They could go down into Elkhashab's hell with me and dismantle that Sobek sarcophagus lid and loot it by way of compensating the pack. I'd unbind that anchor from the back of his house and try to cover up evidence of my break-in. I'd also hug every single one of those sarcophagi to dispel any trace of magic about them. I didn't want there to be the slightest chance of Nebwenenef surviving this time. After I took whatever additional grimoires Elkhashab had hiding in his library, we'd dial up some real authorities and let them find one hell of a crime scene and an archaeological bonanza. Hopefully before Hamal woke in the hospital and told them where everything was.

"Hopping in the car now," Yusuf said. "See you soon."

Since Bast would be eager to enlist the help of a human to spread the word about her old mysteries, I'd try to snatch *Nice Kitty!* before I shifted back to Arizona, but if it didn't work out, I now thought it would be an acceptable loss for ridding the world of Elkhashab and Nebwenenef for good. Defeating such was my raison d'être, after all, the sole reason Gaia had gifted me with my powers. Though as the last of the Druids I am sometimes afflicted with survivor's guilt, that day I felt that I had justified my continued existence. I'd taken out the sorcerer who'd taken out an elemental five thousand years ago. I deserved a beer.

Oberon found my hiding place about a half hour later and sneezed.

<Auggh! Atticus, what have you been rolling in? We need to run you through a car wash!>

Sorry, buddy.

<I know I'm supposed to lick your face affectionately at this point, but perhaps I can do that much, much later.>

Completely understandable. I want to get cleaned up as well. How's your brain? Have you unboggled it yet?

<I think so. I took several naps on that rooftop to think it over, and I've come up with a visual metaphor that makes sense to me. You know those videos of summer music festivals that always show huge crowds of high people to make the band members feel super-famous?

It was like that, except the cats weren't drunk and stoned and wearing jorts. They were pissed.>

So you and I would be members of the band in this visual metaphor?

<Heck yes. I want to be a lead guitarist like Slash, because he shreds like no one else. In fact, now that I think about it, I want a huge top hat pulled down over my eyes. And one of those fake cigarettes made of bacon-flavored candy.>

Sounds like I need to get you some opposable thumbs and guitar lessons. All right. Then who would I be in this band?

<I don't know, Gwen Stefani? You have the abs to pull it off.>

I laughed, and my ribs reminded me they weren't healed yet. *You advise me well.*

<How long are we going to stay here, Atticus?>

As briefly as possible. I'm more than a little creeped out, and I almost didn't make it out of there. But in plain terms it will probably be a couple of days. I have things to do.

<Well, can we play around in the forest where we left the car before we go home to Tempe? If I don't give the squirrels a courtesy chase, they'll feel insulted.>

Okay. But you should be thankful the Egyptians didn't have a squirrel god.

<Auggh! Thanks for the mental image, Atticus! I'm going to have nightmares now!>

That'll make us even. I'm going to have nightmares too. Plenty of variations of being eaten by cats, crocodiles, and demons.

And Hamal would no doubt have his share of night terrors. He'd be haunted for the rest of his life by his experience in Elkhashab's crypt. I'd try to check on him before I left Egypt and see if there was anything more I could do. Perhaps Yusuf could make sure that he got the attention and care he needed if I set up a small trust through Hal.

I spent a couple of days healing what was broken and binding some new trees to Tír na nÓg in the cites along the Nile, since I'd been granted at least a temporary reprieve from Bast. Elkhashab had made it clear that I might have cause to return here in a hurry, since there was still so much wild magic about and old gods waiting to reawaken to power. I was still hiding from old gods myself, and I hoped my sparing use of magic hadn't been noticed.

When I got back to Arizona, I'd take some time to reexamine my old books. I'd given casual titles like *Grimoire of the Lamb* to some of the untitled work, but one or more of them might turn out to be just as dangerous if they fell into the hands of someone like Elkhashab. It would be better for everyone, I thought, if the old gods stayed buried, and old secrets remained secret.

READ ON FOR A PREVIEW OF THE NEXT THRILLING

ADVENTURE IN THE IRON DRUID CHRONICLES

HAMMERED

By Kevin Hearne

Available now!

According to popular imagination, squirrels are supposed to be adorable. As they scurry about on this tree branch or that trunk, people point at them and say, "Awww, how *cuuuuute!*" with their voices turning sugary and spiraling up into falsetto ecstasy. But I'm here to tell you that they're cute only so long as they're small enough to step on. Once you're facing a giant bloody squirrel the size of a cement truck, they lose the majority of their charm.

I wasn't especially surprised to be staring up at a set of choppers as tall as my fridge, twitching whiskers like bullwhips, and tractor-tire eyes staring me down like volcanic bubbles of India ink: I was simply horrified at being proven so spectacularly right.

My apprentice, Granuaile, had argued I was imagining the impossible before I left her back in Arizona. "No, Atticus," she'd said, "all the literature says the only way you can get into Asgard is the Bifrost Bridge. The *Eddas*, the skaldic poems, everything agrees that Bifrost is it."

"Of course that's what the literature *says*," I replied, "but that's just the propaganda of the gods. The *Eddas* also tell you the truth of the matter if you read carefully. Ratatosk is the key to the back door of Asgard."

Granuaile gazed at me, bemused, unsure that she'd heard me correctly. "The squirrel that lives on the World Tree?" she asked.

"Precisely. He manically scrambles back and forth between the eagle in the canopy and the great wyrm at the roots, ferrying messages of slander and vitriol between them, yadda yadda yadda. Now ask yourself how it is that he manages to do that."

Granuaile took a moment to think it through. "Well, according to what the literature *says*, there are two roots of Yggdrasil that drop below Asgard: One rests in the Well of Mimir in Jötunheim, and one falls to the Spring of Hvergelmir in Niflheim, beneath which the wyrm Nidhogg lies. So I assume he's got himself a little squirrelly hole in there somewhere that he uses." She shook her head, dismissing the point. "But you won't be able to use that."

"I'll bet you dinner I can. A nice homemade dinner, with wine and candles and fancy modern things like Caesar salad."

"Salad isn't modern."

"It is on my personal time scale. Caesar salad was invented in 1924."

Granuaile's eyes bugged. "How do you *know* these things?" She waved off the question as soon as she asked it. "No, you're not going to distract me this time. You're on; I bet you dinner. Now prove it or start cooking."

"The proof will have to come when I climb Yggdrasil's root, *but*," I said, raising a finger to forestall her objection, "I'll dazzle you now with what I think so that I'll seem fantastically prescient later. The way I figure it, Ratatosk has to be an utter badass. Consider: Eagles normally eat squirrels, and malevolent wyrms named Nidhogg are generally expected to eat anything—yet neither of them ever tries to take a bite of Ratatosk. They just talk to him, never give him any guff at all, but ask him nicely if he'd be so kind as to tell their enemy far, far away such-and-such. And they say, 'Hey, Ratatosk, you don't have to hurry. Take your time. Please.'"

"Okay, so you're saying he's a burly squirrel."

"No, I'm saying he's turbo-burly. Paul Bunyan proportions, because his size is proportionate to the World Tree. He's bigger than you and I put together, big enough that Nidhogg thinks of him as an equal instead of as a snack. The only reason we've never heard of anyone climbing Yggdrasil's roots to get to Asgard is because you'd have to be nuts to try it."

"Right," she said with a smirk. "And Ratatosk eats nuts."

"That's right." I bobbed my head once with a sardonic grin of my own.

"Well then," Granuaile wondered aloud, "exactly where are the roots of Yggdrasil, anyway? I assume they're somewhere in Scandinavia, but you'd think they would have shown up on satellite by now."

"The roots of Yggdrasil are on an entirely different plane, and that's really why no one has tried to climb them. But they're tethered to the earth, just like Tír na nÓg is, or the Elysian Fields, or Tartarus, or what have you. And, coincidentally, a certain Druid you know is also tethered to the earth, through his tattoos," I said, holding up my inked right arm.

Granuaile's mouth opened in astonishment as the import of my words sank in, quick to follow the implication to its logical conclusion. "So you're saying you can go anywhere."

"Uh-huh," I confirmed. "But it's not something I brag about"—I pointed a finger at her—"nor should you, once you're bound the same way. Plenty of gods are already worried about me because of what happened to Aenghus Óg and Bres. But since I killed them on this plane, and since Aenghus Óg started it, they don't figure I've turned into a deicidal maniac. In their minds, I'm highly skilled in self-defense but not a mortal threat to them, as long as they don't pick a fight. And they still believe that merely because they've never seen a Druid in their territory before, they never will. But if the gods knew I could get to anyone, anywhere, my perceived threat level would go through the roof."

"Can't the gods go anywhere?"

"Uh-uh," I said, shaking my head. "Most gods can go only two places: their own domain and earth. That's why you'll never see Kali in Olympus, or Ishtar in Abhassara. I haven't visited even a quarter of the places I could go. Never been to any of the heavens, unless you want to count Sudassa, one of the Rūpa-loka in Buddhist tradition. It's an absolutely beautiful place, but the beings there live for millions of years and are miles tall and not even visible in the normal spectrum—I had to use magical sight to see them. Ultimately, it wound up being a bit boring because their complete absence of desire meant nobody wanted to talk to me. They are on a different plane mentally as well as physically.

"Mag Mell is truly gorgeous; you've gotta go there. And you've gotta go to Middle Earth to see the Shire."

"Shut up!" She punched me in the arm. "You haven't been to Middle Earth!"

"Sure, why not? It's not a plane built by faith like the others, but by massive collective imagination. It's bound to our world like all the other planes. Elrond is still in Rivendell, because that's where people think of him being, not the Gray Havens—and I'm telling you right now he looks nothing like Hugo Weaving. I also went to Hades once so I could ask Odysseus what the sirens had to say, and that was a mindblower. Can't tell you what they said, though."

"You're going to tell me I'm too young again, aren't you?"

"No. You simply have to hear it for yourself to properly appreciate it. It involves hasenpfeffer and sea serpents and the end of the world."

Granuaile narrowed her eyes at me and said, "Fine, don't tell me. So what's your plan for Asgard?"

"Well, first I have to choose a root to climb, but that's easy: I'd rather avoid Ratatosk, so I'm going up the one from Jötunheim. Not only does Ratatosk rarely travel it, but it's a far shorter climb from there than from Niflheim. Now, since you seem to have been reading up on this, tell me what direction I must go to find where the Well of Mimir would be bound to this plane."

"East," Granuaile said immediately. "Jötunheim is always to the east."

"That's right. To the east of Scandinavia. The Well of Mimir is tethered to a sub-arctic lake some distance from the small Russian town of Nadym. That's where I'm going."

"I'm not up-to-date on my small Russian towns. Where exactly is Nadym?"

"It's in western Siberia."

"All right, you go to this particular lake, then what?"

"There will be a tree root drinking from the lake. It will not be an ash tree, more of a stunted evergreen, because it's essentially tundra up there. Once I find this root, I touch it, bind myself to it, pull my center along the tether, and then I'm hugging the root of Yggdrasil on the Norse plane, and the lake will be the Well of Mimir."

Granuaile's eyes shone. "I can't wait until I can do this. And from there you just climb it, right? Because the root of the World Tree has to be huge."

"Yes, that's the plan."

"So how far from the trunk of Yggdrasil is it to Idunn's place?"

I shrugged. "Never been there before, so I'm going to have to wing it. I've never found any maps of it; you'd think someone would have made an atlas of the planes by now, but noooo."

Granuaile frowned. "Do you even know where Idunn is?"

"Nope," I said, a rueful smile on my face.

"It's going to be tough to steal an apple for Laksha, then." Yes, the prospect was daunting, but a deal was a deal: I had promised to steal a golden apple from Asgard in return for twelve dead Bacchants in Scottsdale. Laksha Kulasekaran, the Indian witch, had held up her end of the bargain, and now it was my turn. There was a chance I'd be able to pull off the theft without consequences, but there was no chance that I could renege on the deal and not face repercussions from Laksha.

"It'll be an adventure, for sure," I told Granuaile.

An adventure in squirrels, apparently. As I faced the stark reality of being so stunningly correct, gaping slack-jawed at the colossal size of the rodent above me on the trunk of the World Tree, an old candy bar jingle softly escaped my lips: "'Sometimes you feel like a nut,'" I crooned, "'sometimes you don't.'"

I'd really hoped Ratatosk would be on the other root, or even hibernating by this time. It was November 25, Thanksgiving back in America, and Ratatosk looked like he'd already eaten Rhode Island's share of turkeys. He was properly stuffed and ready to sleep until spring. But now that he'd seen me, even if he didn't bite off my head with those choppers, he'd go tell somebody there was a man climbing up the root from Midgard, and then all of Asgard would know I was coming. It wouldn't be much of a stealth mission after that.

I had been climbing Yggdrasil without tiring, binding knees, boots, and jacket to the bark all along the way and drawing power from it through my hands, because it was the World Tree, after all, and synonymous with the earth once I'd shifted planes. While I was doing fine and not in any danger of falling off, I could not hope to match Ratatosk's speed or agility. I moved like a glacier in comparison, and Asgard was still miles away up the root.

He chattered angrily at me, and his breath blew my hair back, filling my nostrils with the scent of stale nuts. I've smelled far worse, but it wasn't exactly fragrant either. There's a reason Bath & Body Works doesn't have a line of products called Huge Fucking Squirrel.

I triggered a charm on my necklace that I call faerie specs, which allows me to view what's happening in the magical spectrum and see how things are bound together. It also makes creating my own bindings a bit easier, since I can see in real time the knots I'm tying with my spells.

Ratatosk, I saw, was very firmly bound to Yggdrasil. In many ways he was a branch of the tree, an extension of its identity, which I was dismayed to discover. Hurting the squirrel would hurt the tree, and I didn't want to do that, but I didn't see what choice I had—unless I could get him to pinky-swear he wouldn't tell anyone I was on my way to steal one of Idunn's golden apples.

I focused my attention on the threads that represented his consciousness and gently bound them to mine until communication was possible. I could still speak Old Norse, which was widely understood throughout Europe until the end of the thirteenth century, and I was betting Ratatosk could speak it too, since he was a creation of Old Norse minds.

I greet you, Ratatosk, I sent through the binding I'd made. He flinched at the words in his head and whirled around, the brush of his tail whipping my face as he scrambled up the root a few quick strides before whirling around again, regarding me warily. Maybe I should have moved my mouth along with the words.

<Who in Hel's frosty realm are you?> came the reply, the squirrel's massive whiskers all twitching in agitation. <Why are you on the root of the World Tree?>

Since I was coming up the root from the middle plane, there were only three places I could possibly be coming from. I wasn't a frost giant from Jötunheim, and he'd never believe I was an ordinary mortal climbing the root, so I had to tell a stretcher and hope he bought it. *I am an envoy sent from Nidavellir, realm of the dwarfs,* I explained. *I am not flesh and blood but rather a new construct. Thus my flame-red hair and the putrid stench that surrounds me.* I had no idea what I smelled like to him, but since I was decked out in new leathers, with their concomitant tanning odors, I figured I smelled like a few dead cows, at least, and it was best from a personal safety perspective to frame my scent and person in terms of something inedible. The Norse dwarfs were famous for making magical constructs that walked around looking like normal critters, but often these creatures had special abilities. They'd made a boar once for the god Freyr, one that could walk on water and ride the wind, and it had a golden mane around its head that shone brightly in the night. They called it Gullinbursti, which meant "Golden Bristles." Go figure.

My name is Eldhár, crafted by Fikinskjaldi son of Yngvi son of Fjalar, I told him. The three dwarf names were mined straight from the *Poetic Edda.* Tolkien found the names of all his "dwarves" in the same source, in addition to Gandalf's, so I saw no reason why I couldn't appropriate a few of them for my own use. Eldhár, the name I'd given for myself, meant nothing more than "Fire Hair"; I figured since I was pretending to be a construct, it would be consistent with names like Gullinbursti. *I am on my way to Valhalla at the Dwarf King's request to speak to Odin Allfather, One-Eyed Wanderer, Gray Runecrafter, Sleipnir Rider, and Gungnir Wielder. It is a matter of great importance regarding danger to the Norns.*

<The Norns!> Ratatosk was so alarmed by this that he actually became still for a half second. <The Three who live by the Well of Urd?>

The same. Will you aid me in my journey and thus speed this most vital embassy, so that the World Tree may be spared any neglect? The Norns were responsible for watering the tree from the well, a sort of constant battle against rot and age.

<Gladly will I take you to Asgard!> Ratatosk said. He switched directions again and shimmied backward, courteously extending his back leg to me and carefully holding his bushy tail out of the way. <Can you climb upon my back?>

It took me longer than I might have wished, but eventually I clambered up his back, bound myself tightly to his red fur, and pronounced myself ready to ride.

<We go,> Ratatosk said simply, and we shot up the trunk with a violent gait so awkward that I think I might have bruised my spleen.

Still, I could not complain. Ratatosk was even more than I had imagined: In addition to being extraordinarily large and speedy, he was perfectly gullible and willing to help strangers, so long as they spoke Old Norse. Perhaps I wouldn't have to kill him after all.

PHOTO: © KIMBERLY HEARNE

KEVIN HEARNE is into nature photography, heavy metal, and beard maintenance. He likes to plan road trips and sometimes even takes them. He is the *New York Times* bestselling author of The Iron Druid Chronicles, the Ink & Sigil series, and the Seven Kennings series, and is co-author of The Tales of Pell with Delilah S. Dawson.

kevinhearne.com
Twitter: @KevinHearne
Instagram: @kevinhearne

ABOUT THE TYPE

This book was set in Albertina, a typeface created by Dutch calligrapher and designer Chris Brand (1921–98). Brand's original drawings, based on calligraphic principles, were modified considerably to conform to the technological limitations of typesetting in the early 1960s. The development of digital technology later allowed Frank E. Blokland (b. 1959) of the Dutch Type Library to restore the typeface to its creator's original intentions.

EXPLORE THE WORLDS OF DEL REY BOOKS

READ EXCERPTS
from hot new titles.

STAY UP-TO-DATE
on your favorite authors.

FIND OUT about exclusive
giveaways and sweepstakes.

CONNECT WITH US ONLINE!
📷 ⓕ 🐦 @DelReyBooks

DelReyBooks.com